Reginald Hill

Reginald Hill is a native of Cumbria and a former resident of Yorkshire, the setting for his outstanding crime novels, featuring Dalziel and Pascoe, 'the best detective duo on the scene bar none' (*Daily Telegraph*). His writing career began with the publication of *A Clubbable Woman* (1970), which introduced Chief Superintendent Andy Dalziel and DS Peter Pascoe. Their subsequent appearances have confirmed Hill's position as 'the best living male crime writer in the English-speaking world' (*Independent*) and won numerous awards, including the Crime Writers' Association Cartier Diamond Dagger for his lifetime contribution to the genre.

The Dalziel and Pascoe novels have been turned into a hugely successful BBC television series, starring Warren Clarke and Colin Buchanan.

REGINALD HILL

DEADHEADS

HARPER

Harper
An imprint of HarperCollins*Publishers*
77–85 Fulham Palace Road,
Hammersmith, London W6 8JB

This paperback edition 2009

1 3 5 7 9 8 6 4 2

Previously published in paperback in Great Britain by
Grafton in 1987 and reprinted six times

First published in Great Britain by
HarperCollins*Publishers* 1983

www.harpercollins.co.uk

ISBN-13: 978 0 00 731308 2

Set in Meridien by Palimpsest Book Production Ltd

Printed and bound in Great Britain by

Mixed Sources

FSC is a non-profit international organisation established to promote
the responsible management of the world's forests. Products carrying
the FSC label are independently certified to assure consumers that
they come from forests that are managed to meet the social, economic
and ecological needs of present and future generations.

Find out more about HarperCollins and the environment at
www.harpercollins.co.uk/green

'There is a splendid kind of indolence, where a man, having taken an aversion to the wearisomeness of a business which properly belongs to him, neglects not, however, to employ his thoughts, when they are vacant from what they ought more chiefly to be about, in other matters not entirely unprofitable to life, the exercise of which he finds he can follow with more abundant ease and satisfaction.'

DEFOE: *The Life and Adventures of Mr Duncan Campbell*

'I shall never be friends again with roses.'

SWINBURNE: *The Triumph of Time*

PART ONE

Or, quick effluvia darting through the brain,
Die of a rose in aromatic pain.

POPE: Essay on Man

1
MISCHIEF

(Hybrid tea, coral and salmon, sweetly scented, excellent in the garden, susceptible to black spot.)

Mrs Florence Aldermann was distressed by the evidence of neglect all around her. Old Caldicott and his gangling son, Dick, had been surly ever since she had made it clear last autumn that far from being willing to admit the latter's insolent, nose-picking fifteen-year-old to the payroll, she was contemplating charging his elders for the barrowloads of fruit he had stolen from the orchard. *Scrumping*, old Caldicott had said. *Theft*, she had replied, and as she knew from her connections with the Bench that young Brent Caldicott had made several appearances in juvenile court already, she was not to be disputed with.

After that the youth had disappeared, but his father and grandfather had clearly been nursing a grievance ever since. Her recent indisposition had given them their chance.

There would have to be words. More than words. If she could find somebody to take their place, heads would roll. The thought fathered the deed.

Angrily seizing a *Mme Louis Laperrière* in her gloved hand, grasping it firmly to prevent unsightly spillage, she picked her spot, applied the razor-edged knife expertly, and with a single smooth slice removed the sadly drooping head which she dropped into a plastic bucket.

Only then did she become aware that she was being watched.

Behind the mazy frame of sweet peas which divided the main rose-garden from the long lawn running down to the orchard (and which, she noted angrily, had been allowed to form seed-pods that, unremoved, would pre-empt flower growth) lurked a slight figure completely still.

'Patrick!' called Mrs Aldermann sharply. 'Come here!'

Slowly the boy emerged.

Aged about eleven, small still for his age, he had large brown eyes in a pale oval face which was almost oriental in its lack of expression. Mrs Aldermann regarded him with distaste. It wasn't just that he belonged to the same ghastly sub-species as Brent Caldicott, though that would have been enough. But in addition she could never look upon Patrick without thinking of his origins, and then the anger came welling up. It took little to uncap her vast pool of wrath, and in particular any display of human weakness brought it fountaining forth.

She had been angry eleven years earlier when her niece, Penelope, had announced that she was pregnant. She had been angrier when the feckless girl had refused to name the father, and angriest of all when she had calmly announced her intention of bringing up the child single-handed. Even Penelope's feckless mother, Florence Aldermann's younger sister, had had the wit to get a wedding ring from the object of her particular folly, George Highsmith, carpet salesman, though neither this nor the fact that they were both dead prevented Mrs Aldermann from still feeling angry with them. No, death was no barrier to anger; indeed it could be a cause of it. She still felt furious at her own husband's display of weakness in dying of a coronary thrombosis, with so much still to do, so much still to expiate, in these very gardens two years before.

And finally her anger had turned upon herself when she collapsed in Knightsbridge on a pre-Christmas shopping expedition six months earlier. To be taken ill was deplorable; to have suffered a heart-attack, which she'd come to regard as a typically masculine form of weakness, was unforgivable.

Fortunately (she saw this now, though at the time she'd tended to blame her, as if 'weakness' were an infectious condition) she'd been with Penelope at the time, good-natured, unflappable

Penny who had not taken the least offence (indeed, why should she?) when told after her Uncle Eddie's death that the charitable allowance he'd been making her for so many years would have to stop, times and taxes being so hard, and who had seemed quite satisfied with the substitution of tea at Harrod's on her Aunt Flo's bi-annual London visits.

A few weeks later the 'sixties dawned. Could Mrs Aldermann have foreseen flower-power, pop-art, swinging London and all the age's other lunar and lunatic achievements, she would have greeted it with vast indignation. As it was, the best she could manage in her state of ignorance and intensive care was vast indifference. Shortly afterwards she recovered enough to transfer to a luxurious private clinic. Her first real emotion and almost her second heart-attack occurred when she was well enough to enquire how much it was costing her. As soon as possible thereafter she declared herself fit enough to return to Rosemont, her Yorkshire home, to convalesce. Clearly unable to look after herself properly, she, with her doctor's help, persuaded her easy-going untied-down niece to accompany her, a large saving on a professional nurse. And during the weeks that followed, Mrs Aldermann had come to value Penelope for more than purely economic considerations. She was what all self-regarding, moderately wealthy ladies of the middle class long for: a treasure. Hard-working, easy-going, entertaining of speech and unresentful of indignity, she fell short only in the department of subservient gratitude. And, of course, of Patrick.

But even with these deficiencies admitted, Mrs Aldermann as she recovered had begun to toy with the idea of offering Penny a permanent place at Rosemont which was far too large for one old woman living by herself. There would be no question of salary, of course – they were after all blood relations – but a small allowance would be in order, and there would be the large inducement of a change of will substantially in Penny's favour.

The proposal had been made. To her amazement and irritation, instead of jumping gratefully at the chance, the feckless girl had looked dubious and talked rather nostalgically of London. What had London to compare with this pleasant old house of Rosemont with its fine gardens, beautiful views, and all of Yorkshire's loveliest towns within easy striking distance? She had once seen the kind of place her niece lived in, a dingy two-roomed basement flat in a district where the bus queue looked like an audition for the *Black and White Minstrel Show*. Why should she need time to think about so incredibly generous an offer which had even included the not altogether unselfish undertaking to place Patrick at a modest though decent private boarding-school?

So now the sight of the boy spying on her added its weight to her already great burden of anger and she opened her mouth to utter a peremptory dismissal.

But before she could speak, he said, 'Uncle Eddie used to do that.'

Taken by surprise – this was after all to the best of her recollection the first time the boy, in any of his visits, had ever actually initiated an exchange with her – she replied almost as if he were a real person.

'Yes, he did,' she said. 'And Caldicott might have done it. But he didn't. So now I have to do it.'

Her intonation placed old Caldicott and her dead husband in the same category of duty-neglecters. She sliced off another sweet-smelling but over-blown *Mme Louis Laperrière* with emphatic deftness.

'*Why* do you do it?' demanded Patrick.

His tone was a trifle brusque but she graciously put this down to the awkwardness of a tyro.

'Because,' she lectured, 'once the flowers have bloomed and begun to die, they inhibit – that is to say, they *stop* – other young flowers from developing and blooming. Also the petals fall and make the bush and the flower-beds look very untidy. So we cut off the blooms. It's called deadheading.'

'Deadheading,' he echoed.

'Yes,' she said, beginning to enjoy the pedagogic mood. 'Because you cut off the deadheads, you see.'

'So the young flowers can grow?' he said, frowning.

'That's right.'

This was the first time she had ever seen the boy really interested in anything. His expression was almost animated as he watched her work. She felt quite pleased with herself, like a scientist making an unexpected breakthrough. Not that she had ever felt it as a loss that she and the boy did not communicate. On the contrary, it suited her very well. But this particular form of intercourse which underlined her own superiority was far from unpleasant. She almost forgot to be angry, though the evidence of old Caldicott's indolence was there in her plastic bucket to keep her wrath nicely warm. As though touched by her thought, the boy held up the bucket to catch the falling blooms.

She regarded him with the beginnings of approval. It occurred to her that she might by chance have stumbled on the key to his soul. Surprised by such a fanciful metaphor, she hesitated for a moment. But then her unexpected fantasy, like a bird released from the narrow cage in which it has been all its life confined, went soaring. Suppose that in Patrick's urban bed-sit-conditioned body there lurked a natural gardener, longing to be called forth? This would make him in the instant a valuable – and costless – labourer! Then, as he grew richer in experience and knowledge, he could take over more and more responsibility for the real work of planning and propagation. In a few short years, perhaps, old Caldicott's surly reign could be brought to a satisfying abrupt end, and with it the assumed succession of the gangling Dick and the unspeakable Brent.

For the first time in her life, she bestowed the full glow of her smile on the small boy and said in a tone of unprecedented warmth, 'Would you like to try, Patrick? Here, let me show you. You take hold of the deadhead firmly so that you don't let any petals fall and at the same time you have a good grip on the stem. Then look down the stem till you see a leaf, preferably with five leaflets and pointing out from the centre of the bush. There's one, you see? And look, just where the leaf joins the stem you can see a tiny bud. That's the bud we want to encourage to grow. So about a quarter-inch above it, we cut the stem at an angle, with one clean slice of the knife. *So*. There. You see? No raggedness to encourage disease. A clean cut. Some people use secateurs but I think that no matter how good they are, there's always the risk of some crushing. I prefer a knife. The very finest steel – never stint on your tools, Patrick – and with the keenest edge. Here now, would you like to try? Take the knife, but be careful. It's very sharp indeed. It was your Great-uncle Eddie's. He planted most of these roses all by himself, did you know that? And he never used anything but this knife for pruning and deadheading. Here, take the handle and see what you can do.'

She handed the boy the pruning knife. He took it gingerly and examined it with a pleasing reverence.

'Now let's see you remove this deadhead,' she commanded. 'Remember what I've told you. Grasp the flower firmly. Patrick! Grasp the flower. Patrick! Are you listening, boy?'

He raised his big brown eyes from the shining blade which he had been examining with fascinated care. The animation had fled from his face and it had become the old, indifferent, watchful mask once more. But not quite the same. There was something new there. Slowly he raised the knife so that the rays of the sun struck full on the burnished steel. He ignored the dead rose she was holding towards him and now she let go of it so that it flapped back into the bush with a force that sent its fading petals fluttering to the ground.

'Patrick,' she said taking a step back. '*Patrick*!'

There was a sting on her bare forearm as the thorns of the richly scented bush dug into the flesh. And then further up, along the upper arm and in the armpit, there was a series of sharper, more violent stings which had nothing to do with the barbs of mere roses.

Mrs Aldermann shrieked once, sent a skinny parchment-skinned hand to her shrunken breast and fell backwards into the rose-bed. Petals showered down on her from the shaken bushes.

Patrick watched, expressionless, till all was still.

Then he let the knife fall beside the old woman and set off running up to the house, shouting for his mother.

PART TWO

The rose saith in the dewy morn:
I am most fair;
Yet all my loveliness is born
Upon a thorn.

CHRISTINA ROSSETTI:
Consider the Lilies of the Field

1
DANDY DICK

(Floribunda. Clear pink, erect carriage, almost an H.T.)

Richard Elgood was a small dapper man with tiny feet to which his highly polished, fine leather shoes clung like dancing pumps.

Indeed, despite his sixty years, he advanced across the room with a dancer's grace and lightness, and Peter Pascoe wondered if he should shake the outstretched hand or pirouette beneath it.

He shook the hand and smiled.

'Sit down, Mr Elgood. How can I help you?'

Elgood did not return the smile, though he had a round cheerful face which Pascoe could imagine being very attractive when lit up with good humour. Clearly whatever had brought him here was no smiling matter.

'I'm not sure how to begin, Inspector, though begin I must, else there's not much point in coming here.'

His voice had the ragtime rhythms of industrial South Yorkshire, Pascoe noticed, rather than the oracular resonances of the rural north. He settled back in his chair, put his fingers together in the Dürer position, and nodded encouragingly.

Elgood ran his fingers down his silk tie as if to check the gold pin were still in position, and then appeared to count the mother-of-pearl buttons on the brocaded waistcoat beneath his soberly expensive business suit.

The buttons confirmed, he flirted with his fly for a moment, then said, 'What I'm going to say is likely libellous, so I'll not admit to saying it outside this room.'

'My word against yours, you mean,' said Pascoe amiably.

He didn't feel particularly amiable. He'd spent much of the previous night in the midst of a rhododendron bush waiting for a gang of house-breakers who hadn't kept their date. There'd been three break-ins recently at large houses in the area, all empty while the owners were on holiday, and all protected by alarm systems which had been circumvented by means not yet apparent to the CID. So a 'hot' tip on Sunday that Monday night was marked down for this particular house had had to be followed up. Pascoe had crawled out of his bush at dawn, returned to the station where, feeling too weary to write his report immediately, he had caught a couple of hours sleep on a camp bed. A pint of coffee in the canteen had then given him strength to complete his report and he'd just been on the point of heading home for a real sleep when Detective-Superintendent Andrew Dalziel had dropped this refugee from a Warner Brothers musical into his lap.

'Please, Mr Elgood,' he said. 'You can be frank with me, I assure you.'

Elgood took a deep breath.

'There's this fellow,' he said. 'In our company. I think he's killing people.'

Pascoe rested his nose on the steeple of his fingers. He would have liked to rest his head on the desk.

'Killing people,' he echoed wearily.

'Dead!' emphasized Elgood, as if piqued at the lack of response.

Pascoe sighed, took out his pen and poised it above a sheet of paper.

'Could you be just a touch more specific?' he wondered.

'I can,' said Elgood. 'I will.'

The affirmation seemed to release the tension in him for suddenly he relaxed, smiled with great charm, displaying two large gold fillings, and produced a matching cigarette case with legerdemainic ease.

'Smoke?' he said.

'I don't,' said Pascoe virtuously. 'But go ahead.'

Elgood fitted his cigarette into an ebony holder with a single gold band. A gold lighter shaped like a lighthouse appeared from nowhere, twinkled briefly and vanished. He drew on his cigarette twice before ejecting it into an ashtray.

'Mr Dalziel spoke very highly of you when I rang,' said Elgood. 'Either you're very good or you owe him money.'

Again he smiled and Pascoe felt the charm again.

He returned the smile and said, 'Mr Dalziel's a very perceptive man. He apologizes again for not being able to see you himself.'

'Aye, well, I won't hide that I'd rather be talking to him. I've known him a long time, you see.'

'He'd probably be available tomorrow,' said Pascoe hopefully.

'No, I'm here now, and I might as well speak while it's fresh in my mind. If Andy Dalziel says you're all right to talk to, then that's good enough for me.'

'And Mr Dalziel told me that anything you had to say was bound to be worth listening to,' said Pascoe, hoping to achieve brevity if he couldn't manage postponement.

What Dalziel had actually said was, 'I haven't got time to waste on Dandy Dick this morning, but he's bent on seeing someone pretty quick, so I've landed him with you. Look after him, will you? I owe him a favour.'

'I see,' said Pascoe. 'And you repay favours by not letting people see you?'

Dalziel's eyes glittered malevolently in his bastioned face like a pair of medieval defenders wondering where to pour the boiling oil, and Pascoe hastily added, 'What precisely does this chap Elgood want to talk to us about?'

'Christ knows,' said Dalziel, 'and you're going to find out. Take him serious, lad. Even if he goes round the houses, as he can sometimes, and you start getting bored, or if you're tempted to have a superior little laugh at his fancy waistcoats and gold knick-knacks, take him serious. He came up from nowt, he's sharp, he's influential, he's not short of a bob or two, and he's a devil with the ladies! I've bulled you up to him, so don't let me down by showing your ignorance.'

At that moment Dalziel had been summoned to the urgent meeting with the ACC which was his excuse for not seeing Elgood.

'Here, I'll need some background,' Pascoe had protested in panic. 'Who is he, anyway? What's he do?'

But Dalziel had only smiled from the doorway, showing yellow teeth like a reef through sea-mist, 'You'll have seen his name, lad,' he said. 'I'll guarantee that.'

Then he'd gone. Pascoe was still none the wiser, so now he put on a serious, no-nonsense expression.

'Can we get down to details, Mr Elgood? This man we're talking about, he works for your company, you say? Now, your work . . . what does that involve precisely?'

'My work?' said Elgood. 'I'll tell you about my work. I went into the army at eighteen, right at the start of the war. I could've stayed out easy

19

enough, I was down the pit at the time, coal-face, and that was protected. But I thought, bugger it, I can spend the rest of my life hacking coal. So I took the king's shilling and went off to look at the world through a rifle sight. Well, among all the bad times, I managed a few good times, and I wasn't ready to go back down the pit when I came out. I'd put a bit of cash together one way and another, and I had a mate who was thinking the same way as me. We put our heads together to try to work out what'd be best to do. There was a shortage of everything in them years, so there was no shortage of opportunity, if you follow me. In the end, we settled on something to do with the building trade. Reconstruction, modernization, no matter how you looked at it, that was a trade that had to flourish.'

'So you went into building,' said Pascoe, with a sense of achievement.

'Did I buggery!' protested Elgood. 'Do you know nowt about me? Me and my mate thought about it, I admit. But then we stumbled on this little business just about closed down during the war. They made pot-ware. Mainly them old jug-and-basin sets, you'll likely have seen 'em in the antique shops. Jesus, the price they ask! It makes me weep sometimes to think . . .'

'Elgood-ware!' exclaimed Pascoe triumphantly. 'On the lavatory bowls. I've seen it!'

'I've no doubt you have if you've been around these parts long enough to pee,' said Elgood smugly.

'Though them with the name on's becoming col-lectors' pieces too. Lavs, washbasins, baths, sinks, we did the lot. It was hard to keep up with demand. Too many regulations, too little material, that was the trouble, but once you got the stuff, you stuffed the rules, I tell you. We expanded like mad. Then the technology began to change. It was all plastic and fibreglass and new composition stuff and we needed to refit throughout to keep up. There was no shortage of finance, we were a go-ahead business with a first-class record and reputation, but once the word gets out you're after money, the big boys start moving in. To cut a long story short, we got taken over. We could have gone it alone, I was all for it myself, but my partner wanted out, and I.C.E. made a hell of a generous offer, with me guaranteed to stay in charge. Of course, the name disappeared from the company paper, but so what? I can take you to a hundred places round here where you can still see it. Some people write their names on water, Mr Pascoe. I wrote mine *under* it, mainly, and it's still there when the water runs away!'

Pascoe smiled. Despite Elgood's prolixity and his own weariness, he was beginning to like the man.

'And the company's name. Was it I.C.E. you said?' he asked.

'Industrial Ceramics of Europe, that means,' said Elgood. 'The UK domestic division's my concern. Brand name Perfecta.'

'Of course,' said Pascoe. 'I've driven past the works. And it's there that these er-killings are taking place?'

'I never said that. But *he's* there. Some of the time.'

'He?'

'Him as does the killings.'

Pascoe sighed.

'Mr Elgood, I know you're concerned about confidentiality. And I can understand you're worried about making a serious allegation against a colleague. But I've got to have *some* details. Can we start with a name? *His* name. The one who's doing the killings.'

Elgood hesitated, then seemed to make up his mind.

Leaning forward, he whispered, 'It's Aldermann. Patrick Aldermann.'

2
BLESSINGS

(Hybrid tea. Profusely bloomed, richly scented, strongly resistant to disease and weather.)

Patrick Aldermann stood in his rose-garden, savoured the rich bouquet of morning air and counted his *Blessings*.

There were more than a dozen of them. It was one of his favourite HTs, but there were many close rivals: *Doris Tysterman*, so elegantly shaped, glowing in rich tangerine; *Wendy Cussons*, wine-red and making the air drunk with perfume; *Piccadilly*, its gold and scarlet bi-colouring dazzling the gaze till it was glad to alight on the clear rich yellow of *King's Ransom*.

In fact it was foolish to talk of favourites either of variety or type. The dog-roses threading through the high hedge which ran round his orchard filled him with almost as much delight as the dawn-red blooms of the huge *Eos* bush towering over the lesser shrubs which surrounded it. It was beginning to be past its best now as June advanced, but the gardens of Rosemont were geared to bring on new growth and colour at every season so there was little time for regret.

He strolled across a broad square of lawn which was the only part of the extensive garden which fell short of excellence. Here his son David, eleven now and in his first year at boarding-school, played football in winter and cricket in summer. Here his daughter Diana, bursting with a six-year-old's energy, loved to splash in the paddling pool, burrow in the sand-pit and soar on the tall swing. There would be a time when these childish pleasures would be left behind and the lawn could be carefully brought back to an uncluttered velvet perfection. Something lost, something gained. Nature, properly viewed, ruled by her own laws of compensation. She was the great artist, though permitting man sometimes to be her artisan.

Now in his early thirties, Patrick Aldermann presented to the world a face unscarred by either the excoriant lavas of ambition or the slow leprosies of indulgence. It was a gentle, almost childish face, given colour from without by wind and weather rather than from within. His characteristic expression was a blank touched with just a hint of secret amusement. His deep brown eyes in repose were alert and watchful, but when his interest was aroused, they opened wide to project a beguiling degree of innocence, frankness and vulnerability.

They opened wide now as his daughter appeared on the terrace outside the french windows and shouted shrilly over the fifty yards that separated them, 'Daddy! Mummy says we're ready to go now or else I'll be late and Miss Dillinger will be unpleased with me.'

Aldermann smiled. Miss Dillinger was Diana's teacher at St Helena's, a small private primary school which made much use in its advertising of the word *exclusive*. Miss Dillinger's expression of displeasure, *I am unpleased*, had passed into local monied middle-class lore.

'Tell Mummy I just want a word with Mr Caldicott, then we'll be on our way.'

He'd seen the Caldicotts' old green van bumping along the drive round the side of the house and coming to a halt beside the brick built garden store. His great-aunt, Florence, would have been not unpleased to learn that old Caldicott had been carried off some few years after herself by septicaemia brought on by first ignoring, then home-treating, a nasty scratch received during his gardening duties. But gangling Dick had taken over the business and, in partnership with the delinquent Brent, had dignified it with the title 'Landscape Gardeners', and Patrick Aldermann now paid more for the firm's services two days a week than Aunt Flo had paid old Caldicott full time for a month. They did have greater overheads, of course, including a pair of occasional assistants, a tall youth in his mid-twenties who answered to Art and a miniature

Caldicott, in his mid-teens and almost dwarfish of stature, who generally refused to answer to Pete. Aldermann's wife, Daphne, able on occasion to turn a nice phrase, referred to them as Art *longa* and Peter *brevis*.

The gardeners had already got down to their essential preparations for work by the time Aldermann joined them. Art was heading up to the house to beg a kettle of water and cajole whatever was spare in the way of biscuits or cake out of Daphne or Diana; Brent was leaning against the van smoking a butt end; the dwarf Peter had vanished; and Dick, now a grizzled fifty-five-year-old, was studying which of the two keys he held would open the huge padlock which he opened every Tuesday and Wednesday of the year from March to November.

'Mr Caldicott,' said Aldermann. 'A quick word. Someone went into my greenhouse yesterday and they left the inner door ajar. It's essential that both doors are closed and that there's never more than one open at a time.'

'But there was only one left open, you said,' replied Caldicott with a note of triumph.

'Yes, but the other would have to be opened to get out, or, indeed, when I went in, so then they'd both be open, wouldn't they?' said Aldermann patiently. 'In any case, there's no need that I see for anyone to enter the greenhouse.'

Art returned from the house bearing water and a biscuit tin.

'Mrs Aldermann says, will you be long?' he said cheerfully.

Aldermann nodded an acknowledgment and made for the house. Behind him, Caldicott tried the wrong key.

Aldermann's daughter and his wife were already sitting in the dusty green Cortina. Normally Daphne Aldermann drove her daughter to school in her own VW Polo, but two days earlier it had been scratched by vandals in a car park and had had to be taken in for a respray

'Sorry,' said Aldermann, sliding into the driving seat. 'I wanted a word with Caldicott.'

'And I wanted to get to school in time to have a word with Miss Dillinger,' said Daphne with a frown, but only a slight one. She was used to coming second to horticulture.

'The postman's been,' she said. 'There were some letters for you. I've put them in the glove compartment in case you have a quiet moment during the day.'

'I'll see if I can find one,' he murmured and set the car in motion.

Daphne Aldermann gazed unseeingly over the extensive gardens of Rosemont as the Cortina moved down the gravelled drive. She was a good-looking woman in that rather toothy English middle-class way which lasts while firm young flesh and rangily athletic movement divert the eye from the basic equininity of the total bone structure. Four years younger than her husband, she still had some way to go. She had married young, announcing her engagement on her eighteenth birthday to the mild perturbation of her widowed father, a Church of England Archdeacon with fading episcopal ambitions. A wise man, he had not exerted his authority to break the engagement but merely applied his influence to stretching it out as long as possible in the hope that it would either prove equal to the strain, or snap. Instead, death had snapped at him, and his objections and presumably his ambitions had been laid to rest with him in the grave.

After a short but distressingly intense period of mourning, Daphne had embraced the comforts and supports of marriage. Her elderly relatives had not approved the haste. There had been talk and reproving glances and even some accusatory hints, though with that magnanimity for which upper-middle-class High Anglicans are justly renowned, a comfortable majority agreed that Daphne's contribution to her father's untimely death had been one of manslaughter by distraction rather than murder by design.

Happily Daphne, even in the guilt of grief, was clear-headed enough to feel conscientiously disconnected from the slab of rotten masonry which, falling from the tower of the sadly neglected early Perpendicular parish church he was inspecting with a view to launching a restoration appeal, had dispatched the Archdeacon. Now, twelve years and two children later, she too was aware she had many blessings to count, but close communion with her husband was not one of them. He wore around him an unyielding carapace of courtesy against which her anxieties beat in vain. Perhaps 'carapace' was the wrong image. It was more like an invisible but impenetrable time-capsule that he inhabited, which hovered in, but did not belong to, simple mortal linear chronology. He treated the future as if it were as certain as the past. It was odd that in the end such certainties should have driven her to the edge of panic. And over.

The leaky byways which formed their winding route from Rosemont were awash with morning sunshine, but clouds were waiting above the main trunk road and by the time they entered the stately outer suburb in which St Helena's stood, the sky was black. Aldermann regarded it with the complacency of one whose application of systemic insecticide the previous evening would already have been absorbed into the capillaries of his roses.

Daphne said, 'Oh bother.'

'I can easily wait and drive you into the town centre,' offered Aldermann, thinking she was referring to the weather.

'Thanks, but don't worry. I rather fancy the walk and I'm sure it'll only be a shower. No, it was that lot I was oh-bothering about.'

Aldermann had already observed 'that lot' with some slight curiosity as he slowed down outside the large Victorian villa which had been converted into St Helena's School. The 'lot' consisted of four women each carrying a hand-painted placard which read variously: WHAT DO YOU THINK YOU'RE PAYING FOR? WHAT PRICE EQUALITY? PRIVATE SCHOOLS = PUBLIC SCANDALS and, at more length, ST HELENA FOUND THE TRUE CROSS, THE REST OF US ARE BEARING IT. Two of the women were carrying small children in papoose baskets.

Aldermann drove slowly along a row of child-delivering Volvos till he found a kerbside space.

'Isn't it illegal?' wondered Aldermann as he parked. 'Obstruction, perhaps?'

'Evidently not. They don't get in the way and they only speak if someone addresses them first. But it could upset the children.'

Aldermann looked at his daughter. She did not seem upset. Indeed she looked very impatient to be out of the car. She also looked very pretty in her blue skirt, blue blazer with cream piping, cream blouse, and little straw boater with the cream and blue ribbon.

'As long as they don't try to talk to them,' he said. 'Goodbye, dear.'

He kissed his wife and daughter and watched as they walked along the pavement together. As forecast, none of the picketing group made any movement more menacing than a slight uplifting of their placards. At the school gate, Daphne and Diana turned and waved.

Aldermann waved back and drove away, thinking that he was indeed a well-blessed man. Even the rain which was now beginning to fall quite heavily was exactly what the garden needed after nearly a fortnight of dry weather. He switched the windscreen-wipers on.

Daphne Aldermann coming out of St Helena's fifteen minutes later did not feel quite so philosophical about the rain. Her talk with Miss Dillinger, albeit brief, had isolated her from potential lift-givers just long enough for the kerbside crowd of cars to have almost entirely disappeared.

Turning up the collar of her light cotton jacket, she put her head down into the rising wind and, hugging the shelter of the pavement trees, headed townwards. There was a car still parked about fifty yards ahead, a green Mini some five or six years old. A woman was leaning over the front seat putting a baby of about nine months into a baby seat at the rear. The woman was long-limbed, athletically slender, with short black hair and positive, clear-cut features which just stopped this side of wilfulness. There was something familiar about her and Daphne smiled hopefully as she completed her task and straightened up at her approach.

The woman regarded her with clear grey eyes and a half smile as the rain came lashing down.

'You look as though you'd like a lift,' she said.

'Thanks awfully. That's really most kind of you,' said Daphne, making round to the passenger door with no further ado. But as she stooped to get in, her eye caught something on the rear seat under the baby. Upside down, the words *St Helena* jumped out at her. It was a protest placard.

'It's all right,' said the woman behind the wheel. 'No proselytizing. Just a lift. But it's up to you.'

She started the engine. The wind wrapped damp fingers around Daphne's trailing leg.

She pulled it in and shut the car door.

'What a lovely little boy,' she said brightly, nodding at the blue-clad baby who nodded back as the car accelerated over a bumpy patch of road.

'No,' said the driver.

'No?'

'Little, I'll grant you. But not lovely. And not a boy. My daughter, Rose.'

'Oh, I'm sorry.'

'Don't be. It's a nice test of anti-stereotyping.'

'Really? Well, I still think she's lovely.'

The woman rolled her grey eyes briefly, but Daphne caught the contumely. It was not a safe way in which to treat an Archdeacon's daughter.

'And you,' she resumed with increased brightness. 'Are you Rose's mother? Or her father?'

The woman looked at her in surprise, then threw back her head and laughed so fervently that the car did a little chicanery on the straight road, and Rose, stimulated by either the movement or the laughter, suddenly chortled merrily.

'Mother,' said the woman. 'I'm Ellie. Ellie Pascoe.'

'Daphne Aldermann,' said Daphne. 'How d'you do?'

'How d'you do,' said Ellie gravely. 'You know, I

came out so quick this morning that I didn't have time for any breakfast. Do you fancy a coffee and a bacon buttie?'

'Why not?' said Daphne, determined to meet boldness with boldness.

'Why not, indeed?' said Ellie, and laughed again.

3

YESTERDAY

*(Floribunda. Multitudinous tiny lilac-pink flowers
with an olde-worlde fairy-tale air.)*

'So Dandy Dick's finally gone doolally,' repeated Detective Chief Superintendent Andrew Dalziel, apparently much taken by the assonance and alliteration.

'I didn't say that,' protested Pascoe.

'Look, lad,' said Dalziel, 'you spent the best part of yesterday morning with the man. Have them gold fillings finally rotted his brain or not? It wouldn't surprise a lot of folk. There's always been something not quite right about Elgood. Not marrying, and all those fancy waistcoats.'

'Queer, you mean?' said Pascoe

Dalziel looked at him in disgust.

'Don't be daft,' he said. 'He's tupped more typists in his in-tray than you've had hot dinners. There's many won't use a lav with his name on it for fear it makes a grab at them. No, he's just a bit eccentric, that's all. Nothing you'd look twice at in one of them walking adenoids from Eton; but from a miner's lad out of Barnsley, you expect plain dressing, plain speaking, and likely a plain wife and six plain kids.'

'He must be a great disappointment to all his friends,' agreed Pascoe. 'But he didn't strike me as at all unbalanced yesterday. I think he was genuinely reluctant to be making the accusation. He got it out very quick in general terms to start with, almost as though he wanted to commit himself. After that, it took a bit more time, but mainly because, once there was no going back, he relaxed and reverted to what by your account is his more normal mode of speaking.'

'Oh aye, he goes round the houses like a milkman's horse, Dick,' said Dalziel.

Pascoe smiled. His stomach suddenly rumbled and he recalled that he had missed his breakfast that morning. Ellie had been in a hurry, and when he discovered the cause and hinted a doubt whether a picket line was the right place for a nine-month-old-baby, what little time there might have been for the preparation of toast and coffee had been consumed in a heated discussion. Very heated, though not quite at flaming row temperature. Rain beat at the window of Dalziel's office. He hoped that Ellie wasn't still striding round somewhere with a banner above and little Rosie behind, dripping in her papoose basket. His stomach rumbled again.

'You should get up early enough to eat a cooked breakfast,' commented Dalziel. 'You're like something out of Belsen. Me, I was built up on eggs and rashers.'

He beat his stomach complacently and belched. Diets had failed to make any inroads on his waist and recently he had taken to citing his stoutness as evidence of health rather than the cause for concern his doctor believed.

'I should hope to learn from your example, sir. Now, about Elgood, what do you want me to do?'

It was a blunt question, arising from Pascoe's determination not to be left with the responsibility for examining or ignoring Dandy Dick's allegations.

'Let's have an action replay of what you've got so far,' said Dalziel, leaning back and closing his eyes.

Pascoe risked a long-suffering sigh and said in a rapid and expressionless voice, 'The two alleged victims are Brian Bulmer, Perfecta's financial director, and Timothy Eagles, the Chief Accountant. Bulmer died in a car accident after the office Christmas party. No other vehicles involved, icy road, and his bloodstream showed up at nearly two hundred over the limit. Eagles had a heart attack in a washroom next to his office. The cleaner found him dead.'

'What's Dick say Aldermann's got to do with this?' interrupted Dalziel.

'I was getting to that. Aldermann was drinking with Bulmer at the party, or rather plying him with drink, according to Elgood. And he shared the washroom with Eagles.'

'Post mortem reports?'

'In Bulmer's case, death from multiple injuries, and the alcohol level noted. In Eagles's case, no post mortem. There was a previous history and his doctor was content to issue the certificate. No chance of back-tracking. They're both ash now.'

'Just as well, mebbe,' said Dalziel, yawning, 'Motive?'

Pascoe said, 'Ambition. Or rather, money.'

'Make up your mind!'

'Well, he doesn't reckon Aldermann's interested enough in his work to be ambitious, but he thinks he needs more money. Getting on the Board would shove his income up considerably.'

'But he must have known that he'd be competing against his immediate boss, this fellow, Eagles,' said Dalziel. 'Why not knock Eagles off first?'

'Elgood had worked all that out. His theory is that what Aldermann was after initially was just Eagles's job. He saw his chance to get Bulmer out of the way which would probably mean Eagles's elevation, leaving a gap for Aldermann to fill. It wasn't till after Bulmer's death, when certain anti-Elgood elements on the Board started talking about nominating Aldermann merely in order to annoy and embarrass the Chairman, that he got the scent of a bigger prey.'

'Bloody hell,' said Dalziel, opening his eyes and sitting upright. 'And Dick really believes this?'

'That's why he was here. Though I think the more he talked it through – which was a great deal *more*, I've cut it down by at least ninety-nine per cent – the dafter it sounded to him. But he stuck to his guns.'

'Oh, he'd do that all right, would Dick,' grunted Dalziel. 'But there must've been something brought it on in the first place.'

'Two things,' said Pascoe. 'Evidently he had some kind of row with Aldermann last Friday. He made it clear to Aldermann that even though Eagles was dead, he was still going to block his elevation to the Board. He had to go out to a meeting then, leaving Aldermann in his office. Later he returned and worked well into the evening, long enough to need his desklamp on. It's one of those Anglepoise things. He pressed the switch and got hit by an electric shock which knocked him out of his chair. He recovered pretty quickly – he's very fit for his age, he says, does a lot of swimming – and he put it down to a bad connection. But yesterday morning something else happened. He went to get his car out of the garage. It's got one of those up-and-over doors. It seemed to be a bit stiff so he gave it a big heave and next thing, it came crashing down on top of him. Fortunately he's a pretty nifty mover. He dropped flat and the door crashed on to the boot of his car. I've seen the dent it made and he can count himself lucky.

So he crawled out a bit shaken and that's when he rang you and started shouting murder.'

'You've examined the garage door, I take it?' said Dalziel.

'Yes. It weighs a ton, but it just looked like the decrepitude of age to me. Still, the tech boys are taking a really close look at it, and I had someone collect the lamp from Elgood's office too. At a glance, nothing shows. Just wires working loose and shorting. But I've told them to double check everything, seeing as he's such a good friend of yours, sir.'

Dalziel ignored the gibe, looked towards his closed door and bellowed. *'Tea! Two!'*

The door rattled and even the disregarded telephone shifted uneasily on its rest and let out a plaintive ping.

'Coffee for me,' said Pascoe without hope.

'Tea,' said Dalziel. 'Caffeine clogs the blood. That's why all them Frog painters' ears fell off, and God knows what else besides. Did Dick say he'd had another encounter with Aldermann on Monday? I mean, had he expressed surprise to see him still alive or anything?'

'No. In fact, Mr Elgood seems to have kept out of the office on Monday. He went down to some cottage he owns on the coast. Presumably that's how he keeps so fit swimming.'

'Aye, that's the least strenuous form of exercise that goes on down there, I gather,' chortled Dalziel. 'It's stuck on the edge of a cliff that's being eaten away by the sea. They say that every time Dick takes a new fancy woman down there, another bit gets shaken off.'

'Too much caffeine, perhaps,' said Pascoe. 'Anyway, Aldermann wouldn't need to see him to know he was still alive, would he? He'd have heard in the office if anything had happened.'

'So you think there's something in it, do you, Peter?' asked Dalziel.

'I didn't say that,' said Pascoe emphatically. 'It all sounds very far-fetched to me.'

There was a perfunctory knock at the door, which opened immediately to admit a tin tray bearing two mugs and borne by a man distinguished by the elegant cut of his sober grey suit and the extreme ugliness of his asymmetrical features.

'Either we're overmanned or undermanned, Sergeant Wield,' said Dalziel sarcastically. 'Where's that young tea-wallah?'

'Police-Cadet Singh is receiving instructions on traffic duties at the market roundabout, sir,' said Wield.

Cadet Shaheed Singh was the city's first Asian police recruit, who had brought out all that was colonial in Dalziel. The boy came from a Kenyan Asian family and had been born and bred in Yorkshire, but neither bits of information affected Dalziel's comments, which were at best geographically inaccurate, at worst criminally racist.

'Well, it'll make a change from rickshaws for the

lad,' he said, taking the larger of the two mugs and sipping noisily.

'Tea,' he diagnosed. 'The cup that cheers.'

Pascoe took his mug and drank. It was coffee. He smiled his thanks at Sergeant Wield, winning a suspicious glance from Dalziel.

'What's Dick got against Aldermann, anyway?' asked the Superintendent. 'Why doesn't he want him on the Board?'

'Two reasons,' said Pascoe. 'First is, because it's become a test of his authority as chairman. Aldermann's appointment would be a serious defeat for him. Second, because he honestly doesn't think Aldermann's up to it. He reckons he cruises along, with only a token interest in the firm and his job.'

'Is that right? Might be worth taking a look at this paragon,' said Dalziel. 'I could likely find him a slot in CID.'

Pascoe ignored this and said, 'We can hardly just go barging in to his house, sir, and say we're checking an allegation that he's committed a couple of murders.'

Dalziel looked surprised, as if he could see no real objection to this way of proceeding. Sergeant Wield coughed and handed Pascoe a list of names and addresses.

'That trouble in the multi-storey on Monday, sir,' he offered as explanation. Dalziel looked exasperated. The 'trouble' referred to had been the vandalization of some parked cars by scratching their paintwork with a sharp metal instrument. It was not the kind of thing a sergeant was expected to interrupt his CID chief's conference with.

Pascoe had more confidence in Wield. He examined the list. One of the names was underlined in red.

Mrs Daphne Aldermann. Rosemont House, nr. Garfield. VW Polo, metallic green, scratchings on bonnet.

He looked interrogatively at Wield, who said, 'It's his wife, sir, I checked.'

Pascoe showed the list to Dalziel who said, 'So what?'

Pascoe said, 'It's an excuse to call, sir. Take a look at this Aldermann without him knowing.'

Dalziel continued to look doubtful. Wield tactfully withdrew.

'Still,' continued Dalziel, 'if it's your considered opinion that we should nose around a bit more, Peter . . .'

'I didn't necessarily mean . . .'

'Sharp lad, that Wield,' continued Dalziel. 'Him and that darkie would make a grand pair on night patrol. The villains wouldn't stand a chance. They'd not see one of 'em and one look at t'other would frighten the buggers to death! What else did he say when you discussed Dandy Dick with him?'

Suspecting a reproach, Pascoe said, 'I trust his discretion as well as his judgement, sir. It'll go no further. What he said was he'd rarely heard such feeble reasons for suspicion as those given by Elgood. Then he went off and came back an hour later to say that from what he'd been able to

42

learn about Elgood, for him to come to us on such weak grounds he must either in your own phrase have gone doolally, or else there was something he hadn't told us.'

Dalziel thought about this for a moment and then inclined his head in what Pascoe hoped might be the beginning of a nod but turned out to be only the beginning of a right-handed scratch down his spinal column, then across the left shoulder-blade.

Muffled, and apparently emerging from the stubble of greying hair which was all that Pascoe could see of the huge head, came Dalziel's voice.

'It's your case, Peter. Keep me in touch, that's all I ask. Just keep me in touch.'

'Yes, sir,' said Pascoe rising. 'I will.'

When he left he took his mug with him, not doubting else that Dalziel would soon have been examining the grounds with all the keenness of a sadistic fortune-teller in search of disaster.

4
CAFÉ

*(Floribunda. Unusual blend of coffee and cream in
the opened bloom, useful in floral arrangements,
sweet aroma.)*

Ellie Pascoe dunked a gobbet of bread roll in her
coffee, tested the temperature and then applied
the soggy wad to her baby's lips which sucked at
it greedily.

Daphne Aldermann regarded the proceeding
with some alarm.

'Isn't she rather young?' she ventured.

'Ignore all else but not this teaching,' said Ellie,
'that life is reached by over-reaching.'

'What's it mean?' wondered Daphne.

'Christ knows,' said Ellie. 'But don't worry. The
coffee in this place is mostly milk, sugar and chic-
ory. But the bacon butties are divine, don't you
agree?'

This place had turned out to be a café, or
more definitely, THE MARKET CAFF, a title printed

in fading letters along a sagging lintel above a steamed-up window mistily overlooking the open-air market. Stall-holders drifted in and out, each, so far as Daphne could make out, on some personal timetable which meant that every combination of food, from breakfast fry-ups through tea-time cake-and-scones to cocoa-and-sandwich suppers, was in demand.

Ellie and Rose were obviously known here and it struck Daphne that Ellie greeted the many expressions of delight in the baby with none of that instant put-downery her own enthusiasm had provoked. She doubted if the balance of sincerity and conventionality here was much different from her own, so the solution could only lie in the source, but she had not plucked up courage to make this observation to this rather formidable woman when Ellie, whose grey eyes had been observing her with some amusement, said, 'You're quite right. Working-class crap is much more tolerable than middle-class crap because they've not had the chance to know better. On the other hand, my husband says thinking like that is itself a form of condescension and therefore divisive.'

'He sounds a clever man. I wonder. Does he earn half as much as most of these workers who've not had the chance to know better?'

Ellie smiled. This blonde, horsey, country-set woman might turn out to be worth a smoking.

'Probably not. But money's not the really important thing in our class matrix, is it? And it's certainly not brains, and it's only incidentally birth. It's education, not in the strict sense, but in a kind of masonic way. It's learning all those little signals which say to other people *look here, recognize me, I'm a member of the club*. You start learning them in a very small way at places like St Helena's, which is why I'm agin them. Also I can't smoke and wave a banner at the same time and I'm trying to cut down on smoking. Have one.'

She offered Daphne a filter-tip which she took. They lit up. Ellie dragged deep on hers and said, 'First of the day.' Daphne took a quick, short puff, coughed violently and gasped, 'First of the year.'

'Why'd you take it then?' said Ellie.

'It's hardly the most offensive thing I've taken from you this morning,' said Daphne.

Ellie said, 'You're a sharp lady, lady.'

The door opened and Daphne who was facing it saw two policemen enter, removing capes dripping from the still pelting rain. One was an older man in the traditional tall helmet; the other wore the flat cap of a cadet beneath which a good-looking young Indian face peered out at the momentarily silenced customers, whose chatter instantly resumed when it became clear all that the newcomers were after was a cup of tea.

'If I'm sharp, then it's a sharpness I picked up at places like St Helena's,' said Daphne.

'And boarding-school?'

'I was a day-girl. It was only in Harrogate, but yes, it was a boarding-school.'

'Well, to quote my husband again, that's one thing you've got to give the English single-sex boarding-school. It teaches you to hold your own.'

The two policemen were coming up behind Ellie in search of a table. The elderly constable glanced down and to Daphne's surprise his stern hello-hello-hello face broke into a smile.

'Hello, Mrs Pascoe,' he said. 'How are you?'

Ellie looked up.

'Well, hello, Mr Wedderburn,' she said. 'I'm fine.'

'Haven't seen you in here for a long time,' continued the constable. 'How's the kiddy?'

Ellie's eyes flickered towards her companion to see if she'd caught the implication of the policeman's remark. She had.

'Oh, she's blooming. Blooming this, blooming that.'

'Isn't she good,' said Wedderburn, impressed by the baby's sang-froid.

'In crowds and company and public places, yes,' said Ellie. 'She saves up her bad side for private performance only. She'll make a good cop. Who's your friend?'

'This is Police Cadet Shaheed Singh,' said Wedderburn gravely. 'He's just been learning that hell is the rush-hour on market days. Singh, this is Mrs Pascoe, Detective-Inspector Pascoe's wife.'

The cadet smiled. He looked like one of those elegant handsome young princes who at one time always seemed to be playing cricket for England.

'Nice to meet you, missus,' he said in a broad Yorkshire accent which made Wedderburn's sound like Eton and the Guards.

'You too, Mr Singh,' said Ellie. 'Won't you join us?'

Singh was clearly willing but Wedderburn said, 'No, thanks, Mrs Pascoe. We'll sit over here. There's one or two of the finer points of traffic control I need to discuss with the lad here and you'd likely find it a bit boring. Nice to see you.'

They moved away.

'Well!' said Daphne. 'So I'm in with the *fuzz*.'

The word sounded alien on her tongue, perhaps because her upper-class accent squeezed it almost into *fozz*.

'And,' she continued, pursuing her advantage, 'far from being your daily port of call, this elegant establishment is merely a stage-setting to soften up your victims!'

'Not quite,' grinned Ellie. 'But, OK, I did choose it specially this morning.'

'To turn me into a Trot? Or, with your police connections, are you really an *agent provocateur*?'

'What's your husband do?' asked Ellie.

'He's an accountant with Perfecta, you know, the bathroom people.'

Ellie looked momentarily surprised, then said, 'And how's your long division?'

'Terrible,' admitted Daphne. 'But I don't see . . . ah!'

'We may be one flesh, but the minds have

an independent existence, or should have. We are not our husbands, nor even our husbands' keepers.'

'I agree, to an extent,' said Daphne. 'But it's not quite as simple as that, is it? I mean, if for instance, I told you my husband had committed a crime, wouldn't you feel it necessary to tell your husband?'

Ellie considered this.

Finally she said, 'I don't know about *necessary*. Suppose I told you my husband was investigating your husband, would *you* feel it necessary to tell *him*?'

Now Daphne considered, but before she could answer she was interrupted by a large, handsome, middle-aged woman, rather garishly dressed and with an ornate rose-tinted hair-do, like a mosque at sunset, who was coming from the counter with a coffee in one hand and a wedge of chocolate gateau in the other.

'Hello!' she cried. 'It's Daphne Aldermann, isn't it? Not often we see you in here. I always meant to keep in touch, dear, but it's all so hectic, one mad round after another, time just flies, just flies. And so must I. What a lovely baby. Coming, darlings, coming.'

This last was in response to a chorus of *Mandy*! from a distant table where three men were sitting. The woman made a valedictory gesture with her gateau and went to join them.

'So you're not so out of your depth here as I

49

thought,' said Ellie. 'I'll have to look for some-where *really* low. You should have asked your friend to sit down. She sounded interesting.'

'You think so? Well, for a start, she's hardly a friend. And in any case, there's no way you'll get Mandy Burke to join two women and a child when there's anything in trousers imminent. *Just flies* is the perfect motto for her.'

'Miaow!' said Ellie, grinning broadly. 'Mandy Burke? I've a feeling I've seen her around.'

'She runs a stall in the old covered market. Cane and mats and curios, that sort of thing. It's a little goldmine, I believe,' said Daphne. '*Mandy's Knick-Knacks* it's called. That's where you've probably seen her, unless your husband wines, dines and dances you at the best night spots a lot.'

'And what makes you think he doesn't?' wondered Ellie. 'But you're right. I know the stall. And in which of her milieux did *you* meet her?'

'Neither. Her husband used to work with mine, or the other way round really. He died about four or five years ago. I don't think I've run into her more than a couple of times since. Widowhood seems to become her. I should imagine women like her are a bit of an embarrassment to the feminist movement. So confident, so secure, so able, but absolutely anchored in a masculine world.'

She spoke challengingly and Ellie was again sur-prised at the vein of aggression she was finding in this superficially stereotyped bourgeois housewife. But before she could reply, Rose suddenly let out an enormous burp, then smiled complacently at her admiring audience.

The two women laughed and Ellie said, 'Let's have another coffee.'

'All right,' said Daphne. 'No, I'll get them. Don't worry, I won't embarrass you by pushing to the front of the queue.'

She rose and made her way to the counter where Ellie was both amused and irritated to see four horny-handed sons of toil step back and wave this long, elegantly dressed, fair-haired lady to receive service before them.

5

PERFECTA

(Bush. Vigorous growth, red-flushed blooms, heavy and susceptible to being snapped off in strong winds, otherwise long-lasting, some black spot.)

Patrick Aldermann sat at his desk in the office which still bore the name of Timothy Eagles on the door. It did not bother him. It took a great deal to bother him as the staff of Perfecta Ltd had long ago come to realize.

One of the junior sales executives had been moved by drink and seasonal bonhomie to philosophize on the subject to Dick Elgood at the office Christmas party the previous year.

'It isn't so much,' he slurred ginnily into Elgood's face, 'that things run smoothly around Pat Aldermann, it's more than no matter how many cock-ups have been cocked-up, he just keeps on running smoothly around things, you follow me?'

Elgood had used his nimbleness of foot to evade the man and headed for the bar, where he spotted the object of the analysis in close conversation with Brian Bulmer, the firm's financial director, and a hawk-faced young man called Eric Quayle, an industrial chemist by training and a captain of industry by inclination, who was also on the Board and generally regarded as tomorrow's man. *My bloody heir presumptuous*, Elgood called him, adding, *but the bugger's going to turn grey waiting*.

Quayle saw Elgood and turned away from the other two. Bulmer was doing all the talking, Elgood noticed, and he guessed that most of the Scotch from the bottle between them had gone down his throat. As Quayle approached, Elgood grabbed two glasses from the bar and a half of Scotch.

'Enjoying yourself, Eric?' he asked as he moved away, but did not stay for an answer. Besides having little desire for a bout of horn-locking with Quayle, he was also ten minutes late for a rendezvous in his private office with the new invoice clerk, who was so well-bosomed that she had to stand sideways to see into a filing cabinet.

An hour later, he had just scaled this Alpine lady for the second time when the phone started ringing, rousing him from post-coital lethargy with the news that Brian Bulmer within minutes of leaving the party had skidded into the seasonal road-death statistics.

The death had cast a light pall over Christmas which as usual he spent alone in his seaside cottage, braving the North Sea's icy waters for his traditional pre-luncheon swim. Experience had long ago taught him that shared Christmases bred sentimental notions which could lead to an unhappy New Year, so now it was his one celibate season and as he lay in his double bed, listening to the hungry tide gnawing at the cliff face, he had plenty of time to think about Bulmer's death. He mourned the man's passing but his main thought was about his successor. Timothy Eagles, the Chief Accountant, was the obvious man. Competent, predictable and loyal. He wanted such men about him and whatever *he* wanted, the Board would ultimately agree to. The memory of Bulmer and Quayle with the quiet watchful figure of Aldermann between them hardly stirred, not even when Quayle had tentatively wondered whether or not a younger man, like, say, Eagles's assistant, Patrick Aldermann, might not be a more revitalizing addition to the Board. Quayle was just flexing his muscles. It meant nothing.

Then Eagles had died, collapsing in the washroom at the end of the corridor he shared with Aldermann.

Immediately it became clear that Quayle meant business and that he was not without support. The battle was about Aldermann's candidacy for the Board, but the war was about Elgood's chairmanship. Aldermann's suitability didn't worry Quayle and his supporters in the least. He was merely their instrument to probe, irritate and display Elgood's vulnerability. The more blood they drew, the more support they would get.

He had started to use every weapon at his disposal and he had collected a formidable armoury. He had not even omitted the direct appeal to Aldermann himself. To win him to withdraw from the fray voluntarily was too great a coup not to be attempted. But things had gone wrong. Aldermann had hardly seemed to consider the matter worth bothering about. His detachment, his self-possession, the hint of secret amusement in his eyes, had got under Elgood's guard. What had been intended as a subtle operation became a bludgeoning attack.

'But it all seems so simple to me, Dick,' Aldermann had said finally. 'If I don't get on, I don't get on. Honestly, it won't bother me, don't worry about it for a moment. And if I do get on, the extra money will certainly come in very useful.'

It was then, vastly irritated that this conversation should have been mistaken as an expression of concern over Aldermann's feelings, that Elgood had moved from bluntness to brutality, made it quite clear what his own feelings about the issue were and ended by half-shouting, 'And if you get on to the Board of Perfecta, lad, it'll be over my dead body!'

The little smile, the nod of farewell (or agreement?) and Aldermann had left, keen as always (Elgood guessed) to get back to his precious bloody roses, apparently quite unmarked by an interview whose memory continued to shoot little electric arrows of rage into Elgood's chest for hours after.

Well, that had been last Friday and a very great deal had happened since then. For a time it had seemed as if things were getting out of control, rising to the climax of his visit to the police. That had been an error, but cathartic, and in the twenty-four hours since he had spoken to Pascoe, he had returned to something like full control and true perspectives. The real issue was his own control of the business at all levels. Currently there was an incipient crisis caused by proposals aimed at meeting the falling level of demand for Perfecta products in the present period of recession. To deal with this with minimum fuss would confirm his standing both with the waverers on the Board and with I.C.E. head office.

He pressed a button on his intercom. A moment later his secretary came into the office. She was a woman of nearly forty, rather square of feature with short cropped dark brown hair beginning to be flecked with grey. She kept herself to herself and the office buzz was that she was lesbian. Her name was Bridget Dominic, but no one called her anything but Miss Dominic, including Elgood, who had chosen her deliberately some years earlier, having learned the hard way that a mix of sex and secretaries leads to deadly dole.

'Miss Dominic,' he said. 'Would you pop along to Personnel and check when Mr Aldermann's taking time off this summer. Discreetly. And put an outside line through as you go.'

The woman nodded and left. She would be

discreet, Elgood was sure. And discreet enough too to give him a good ten minutes in which to make his phone call. But for once she'd have been mistaken about its content.

He dialled a London number. As it rang, he examined the course of action he was contemplating and found nothing wrong with it. The phone was lifted at the other end.

'Mr Easey?' said Elgood. 'Mr Raymond Easey? My name is Richard Elgood.'

At the same time on the floor below, Patrick Aldermann was opening the mail he had brought from home. A bank statement and the contents of several buff envelopes were put aside after the lightest glance, but one letter caught and held his attention.

He picked up his telephone and dialled. As with Elgood above, it was a London number. The conversation lasted several minutes. When it was finished he replaced the receiver and buzzed his secretary.

When she came in he was removing the wrapper from a packet. It seemed to contain some kind of book. Her eye took in the office mail which she had carefully opened and sorted. The piles stood untouched.

'Mrs Jones,' he said, 'I'll be away on Friday at the end of next week. Could you make a note of that? No, come to think of it, better make it Thursday and Friday.'

He had begun to peruse the printed sheets of the loosely bound volume, making quick little marks with a red pen.

Mrs Jones, not yet thirty but already maternal, said, 'You do remember you're taking the following Monday, Tuesday and Wednesday off, don't you? Something about your little boy's school.'

'Of course. So I am.'

He smiled at her and she basked in his smile which she admitted freely to her intimates made parts of her she didn't care to name feel tremulous.

'I dare say they can get by without me here for another couple of days, wouldn't you say, Mrs Jones?' he said. 'I dare say they can just about manage that.'

6
RIPPLES

(Floribunda. Free-flowering, lilac-mauve blooms, rippled petals, abundant foliage, susceptible to mildew in the fall.)

When Aldermann got home that evening, he found Daphne's Polo occupying her side of the double garage. He examined the bright new paintwork on the bonnet and then went into the house.

Diana came running to meet him and he swung her on to his shoulders.

'Mummy's outside,' she told him.

'It's the only place to be,' said Aldermann seriously.

The rain had stopped earlier and the clouds had continued eastward, leaving in their wake a perfect June evening. He went through the french doors of the lounge on to the balustraded terrace where Daphne was relaxing on a garden lounger.

'Hello,' he said. 'They seem to have done a good job on the car.'

'They should do for the money. And they make

you pay on the spot nowadays. No cash, no car. It's very uncivilized.'

He frowned slightly, lifted Diana to the ground and said, 'The rain's brought off one or two petals, I see.'

'Well, let them lie for a while,' Daphne said firmly. 'I'll get us a drink and you can unwind from your hard day at the office.'

She went into the house and he removed his jacket, draped it over the back of a wrought-iron garden chair and sat down. Distantly the front doorbell sounded. A couple of minutes later, Daphne returned bearing a martini'd tray and accompanied by two men, or rather a man and a boy. The boy was in uniform, the man in a dark suit. Other claims to distinction were the boy's Indian beauty and the man's Caucasian ugliness.

'Darling,' said Daphne setting the tray down on the iron table which matched the chairs, 'these gentlemen are from the police.'

Aldermann rose courteously.

'How can I help you?' he asked.

'Actually, it's me they want to see,' said Daphne. 'It's about the car being vandalized. We needn't disturb you, darling. Would you like to come back into the house, Sergeant? You did say *sergeant*?'

'That's right, ma'am. Detective-Sergeant Wield. And this is Police Cadet Singh,' replied Wield without much enthusiasm.

Singh flashed them a white-toothed smile. Daphne had already recognized him as the boy she had seen in the market café but he had shown no sign of recognizing her. Perhaps whites all look alike to Asians, she thought.

Wield who didn't want to be separated from Aldermann after so short an encounter was about to spin his prepared line of perhaps your husband might be able to corroborate one or two points when the man saved him the trouble by saying, 'You won't disturb me, darling. And I'd be interested to hear what the police are doing, and to help if possible.'

'Very kind, sir,' said Wield, pulling a garden chair towards him and posing his buttocks over it while he looked enquiringly at Daphne.

She let out a small sigh and sat down.

Wield followed suit. Singh remained standing till Wield nodded significantly at him, when he sat a little distance from the other three and emulated the sergeant by producing a notebook.

'I hadn't realized this would be a CID matter,' said Aldermann. 'Would you like a drink?'

'Thank you, no, sir,' said Wield. 'To tell the truth, sir, CID wouldn't normally be involved with a bit of one-off car bashing, but this is threatening to become an epidemic. Also we like an experienced officer to show our cadets the ropes in all departments of police work.'

Patrick Aldermann smiled faintly and Wield wondered if he were explaining too much. He put on his most serious dedicated look which could usually make children weep and strong men avert their gaze, but Aldermann's cool brown eyes never flickered and the smile remained.

Wield returned his attention to the wife and said ponderously, 'Now, ma'am. Your car is a VW Polo, registration AWG 830T. On Monday of this week you parked it in the Station Street multi-storey car park. This was at what time?'

'Oh, nine-fifteen, something like that. I dropped my daughter off at her school and then just drove straight into town to do some shopping.'

'In fact, you did a whole day's shopping, is that right, ma'am? You didn't come back to your car till after three o'clock.'

'That's right,' laughed Daphne. 'I got rather carried away.'

'One of those expensive days the ladies give us from time to time, eh, sir?' responded Wield, smiling at Aldermann. The invitation to a shared domestic laugh came from Wield's lips like a popsong from the Delphic oracle. It was an incongruity which went far deeper than his unprepossessing exterior. Sergeant Wield was, and, having never received the hypothesized conditioning treatment of a good public school education, presumed he always had been, unrepentantly homosexual. He guarded the secret from all but those few whose relationship with him depended on a knowledge of it, not because he felt guilt or shame but because he felt (a) that his business was his business, and doubted (b) that the mid-Yorkshire force was yet ready for a fairy fuzz. Occasionally he made believe that next time Dalziel growled bad-temperedly *Right, Sergeant, what have you got for me?* he would jump on his knee and offer him a kiss, but the golden rays of such sunny fancies never touched the pits and promontories of his no-man's-land of a face.

Aldermann affected to take the remark seriously, saying, 'If it were one of those days, Sergeant, I haven't seen the results yet.'

'Window-shopping mainly, was it?' laughed Wield. 'No harm done then. Except to your car. When you got back you found it had been badly scratched?'

He glanced at his notebook which he held close to his face in the palm of his hand to conceal the fact that it was his diary and almost empty.

'And you immediately reported this to the police,' he continued, as a statement not a question, but Daphne replied carefully. 'The police were already there. Someone else had found their car damaged and reported it.'

'Yes, of course,' agreed Wield glancing at the diary again. 'Now, when you parked the car that morning, did you see anything odd? Anyone hanging about for instance.'

'No, no one,' she said.

Aldermann said, 'It's hardly likely that these vandals would already have been lurking at nine-fifteen A.M., is it, Sergeant?'

His tone was one of polite enquiry.

Wield looked once more at his diary which

contained nothing more helpful than the information that the following Sunday was the 2nd after Trinity, 3rd after Pentecost and Father's Day. He said, 'We're not yet sure of the time the damage was actually done, sir.'

'But surely there have to be limits?' pursued Aldermann. 'Between the latest time of parking of a subsequently damaged car and the earliest time of complaint, for instance. Unless this lunatic was picking them off one by one throughout the day.'

'Well, that's always a possibility, sir,' said Wield as if the suggestion had been seriously intended. 'Were there many other cars about when you parked, ma'am?'

'Hardly any,' said Daphne promptly.

'No? Of course, you were parked on the roof, weren't you? The first couple of floors fill up pretty quick with business people, I suppose. But there must still have been a lot of room on the next four floors at nine-fifteen.'

'I always park on the roof,' said Daphne promptly. 'I'm not very fond of enclosed spaces, nor am I a particularly good reverser. So, open air and no other cars to hit, that's my ideal.'

'*No* other cars?' said Wield. 'You were the first on the roof park?'

'I might have been,' she said. 'I can't remember. Does it matter?'

No, thought Wield. It didn't matter in the least. His little plan of getting a close look at Aldermann at home without rousing any suspicions was not working very well. At the very least he must be arousing the suspicion that he was a half-wit. Even Police Cadet Singh had stopped writing every word that was said in his book and was making faces at the little girl.

'Won't keep you much longer,' he said. 'Tell me, Mrs Aldermann, is there anyone you can think of who might have wanted to do you a bad turn?'

'By damaging my car, you mean?' said Daphne in surprise. 'But it wasn't just *my* car, was it?'

'I know that,' said Wield. 'But according to our officers on the spot, the scratchings on your car might have been words.'

'Words?' said Aldermann. 'You mean a message.'

'Not exactly, sir. The second possible word was *cow*. This would suggest the vandal knew you were a woman, madam.'

'Well, I did leave an old hat I carry around in case it rains on the rear sill,' said Daphne. 'So it wouldn't need a detective to work out it was a woman's car, would it?'

'What,' said Aldermann pleasantly, 'was the *first* possible word, Sergeant?'

'Hard to say, sir,' said Wield uncomfortably, thinking that Dalziel, for instance, would not have found the four letters in the least hard to say.

'If it were aimed specifically at my wife, then why did the vandal damage other cars? And didn't you say there'd been an epidemic of this recently?'

This was too sharp for comfort and all Wield

could manage in reply was the stock, 'We have to cover every possibility, sir.'

'Well, I certainly don't know anyone who'd do this kind of thing,' said Daphne firmly.

'I see,' said Wield. 'And you, sir? Is there anyone you can think of who might have a grudge against you? In your work perhaps?'

Aldermann shook his head slowly as much in disbelief as negation.

'I'm an accountant. I work for Perfecta Ltd. I can think of no one there, or indeed in any department of my life, who might bear a grudge sufficiently strong to make him vandalize my wife's car and then set about several more to cover up his deed.'

The man's tone was still perfectly polite but it was approaching the politeness of farewell. It was saying that unless this idiot policeman could produce some reason even slightly above the moronic for continuing this interview, it ought decently to draw to a close.

Wield could only agree, even though it meant he was going back to Pascoe empty-handed. He had heard nothing and seen nothing worth commenting on.

Suddenly the little girl who had been sitting all this while playing a game with Police Cadet Singh which involved peeping at him through her fingers and shaking with internalized giggles whenever he caught her eye and grimaced in reply, said, 'Mummy, can I play on the swing?'

'Of course, dear,' said Daphne. 'Shall I come

and give you a push, if the sergeant is finished, of course.'

'No, I want *him* to push me,' said Diana, pointing at Singh.

'I don't think . . .' began the woman but Singh rose with his brilliant smile and said, 'I don't mind. All right, Sarge? Up you come, love.'

He swung the girl up on to his shoulder and set off down the garden.

'He sounds like a native. Of Yorkshire I mean,' said Daphne.

'You pick it up quite fast after seventeen years,' said Wield gravely.

'But he can't be more than . . . oh, I see, you mean he *is* a native?'

Wield who knew the old rule which said *Don't be cheeky to the customers unless they're nicked, or you're Dalziel*, said, 'He's a nice lad. Lovely roses, you've got, sir.'

Aldermann's face lit up with a smile which equalled Singh's.

'Yes, it's promising to be a good year. They've made an excellent recovery after that awful winter. Are you a rose man, Sergeant?'

'From afar,' said Wield. 'I live in a flat. The best I can manage is a couple of houseplants and they're likely to die from neglect.'

'Have you thought of a window-box and some of the miniatures?' asked Aldermann. 'They can do astonishingly well, so long as the box is well drained and preferably south-facing.'

'Is that right?' said Wield, alert to the change from watchful reserve to lively enthusiasm, though it was so marked that he didn't need to be very alert. 'What varieties would you recommend?'

'That's hard,' said Aldermann. 'I can point out growing characteristics, but as for looks, every man's his own arbiter. "Varieties" in roses means just that. Their variety is infinite; at least it appears so. Every year brings new advances. That's the fascination of being a hybridist. You're never really certain what you're going to get. You select your stock according to the best horticultural principles, you do all the work, everything goes according to plan, but not until you see that first bloom do you really know what you've achieved. It brings a whole new range of excitement and uncertainty into our experience!'

'I get plenty of that in my job already,' laughed Wield.

'Do you?' Aldermann sounded mildly surprised. 'I suppose policing *is* rather unique. But on the whole, isn't most of life, outside the rose-garden, I mean, surprisingly unsurprising?'

'My husband is an enthusiast and also an evangelist, Sergeant,' interrupted Daphne with a slightly strained laugh. 'I really must see to the dinner, darling. And it's time that Diana was coming in, I think. Would you see to her?'

This was dismissal, polite but clear, and Wield stood up to take his leave.

Aldermann however came to his aid.

'Diana sounds happy enough,' he said, glancing down the garden where they could see and hear the little girl squealing in delight as Singh pushed the swing higher and higher. 'And I must show the sergeant some of the miniatures he's interested in. I've got a few in a raised bed down here.'

He set off down the steps which led from the terrace into the garden. Daphne Aldermann said, 'Goodbye then, Sergeant,' and held out her hand. Wield shook it, wondering where this well-bred lady drew the line. Would she shake hands when saying goodbye to a uniformed constable, for instance? And was he right in sensing an enthusiasm to be rid of him that would have made her shake hands with a leprous cannibal?

He followed Aldermann down the garden along a narrow path between two clumps of exuberantly colourful rhododendrons to a long windowless outhouse in rustic brick. As if the shrubbery were not screen enough, the building was almost covered by a huge climbing rose which seemed to support the walls rather than vice versa. It was laden with large, ruffled, soft pink blossoms which exhaled a rich perfume.

'You like my *Madame Grégoire*?' said Aldermann as he fitted a key in the door. 'You're seeing her at her best. Another month and she'll be down to a handful of blooms.'

He opened the door and went inside, snapping on a light switch.

'It's very nice,' said Wield, following, though to

tell the truth he was finding all this colour and scented air a little cloying. His thoughts somehow drifted to his mother, a generously rounded woman who had been much given to gaudy blouses and musky perfumes and empty sentimentalities.

The outhouse was full of the instruments of gardening, all in neat array. Aldermann took a pair of gardening gloves and a pruning knife from a high shelf and removed what looked like a newspaper boy's bag from a hook, completing the impression by draping it round his neck. Wield's eye meanwhile was taken by a large wall-cabinet with a solid front held shut by a solid-looking padlock.

'Good security, sir,' he said approvingly.

'What? Oh yes. It's for the children's sake, of course,' said Aldermann. 'I doubt if it would do more than slightly delay real burglars, Sergeant, but modern gardening uses modern substances and I've got enough stuff in there in the way of herbicides and pesticides to kill an army!'

He led the way out, carefully locking up behind him. When they reached the rose-garden, the function of his neck-bag became apparent. From time to time he paused to slice off a wasting bloom and drop it into the bag.

'Sorry about this,' he said, 'but it's the only way to keep control.'

'You surely don't take care of everything yourself?' said Wield, who was still pondering the easy reference to the lethal contents of the locked cabinet.

'Hardly,' laughed Aldermann, looking round at the huge expanse of gardens. 'In my great-uncle's day – he actually created the garden, by the way – there was a full-time gardener. Times, and costs, have changed, of course. The old gardener's son started a gardening contracting business and they come out here one or two days a week during the growing season to keep things under control. I do as much as I can and almost everything to do with the roses.'

'Even that must be almost a full-time job,' said Wield.

'It occupies the centre of my life, yes,' agreed Aldermann. 'But there's plenty of room round the edges for earning a living. Not that I don't sometimes dream of being able to give all my attention here. What harm does it do a man, I wonder, when the harsh facts of existence hinder him from growing steadily into the fullness of his own nature?'

The brown eyes turned on Wield, not watchful now but vulnerably wide and full of frank, guileless innocence, yet arousing in the sergeant the uneasy feeling that Aldermann had somehow penetrated to the very heart of his own double existence.

'You may be right, sir,' he said. 'That's a fine-looking instrument.'

He nodded at the pruning knife and felt angry

with himself for the deliberate cutting off of this potentially productive shoot of personal philosophy. It was a small act of cowardice, almost certainly unnecessary, but none the better had it been necessary. Defence too can be habit-forming. It is aroused by threat. It can be activated when no threat is intended. And it sometimes continues when there's nothing left to defend. For almost a year now, since a long-established relationship had died on him, he had led a life of hermit-like celibacy. There were no roses at the centre of his existence, just a dark, destructive hiding place in which there was no longer even anything hiding.

Aldermann smiled as if he understood every thought in the sergeant's mind and said, 'Yes, I prefer it to secateurs. It belonged to my great-uncle, though curiously I was shown how to use it by my great-aunt who was strongly concerned for the good appearance of the gardens. So was my great-uncle, of course, but his motivation was not to impress others, but to express love. Removing the dying blooms is a sad but necessary task. Naturally a lover of the plants will want to use the quickest and kindest instrument available.'

He held the knife up as he spoke, in a gesture close to a chivalric salute, and the sunlight caught its curved and silvery blade.

'Now, let me see; the miniatures! Of course, that's what you want to see, isn't it? Over here. I don't have very many but you may get some ideas for your box. This *Baby Masquerade* is very pretty. The flowers change colour as they develop which would be interesting in a window. I prefer it as a miniature, myself. At full size, it's a little too garish for my taste.'

'I like the look of these,' said Wield, finding the man's enthusiasm infectious. 'What are they?'

'You have a good old-fashioned taste, I see,' said Aldermann approvingly. 'Those are dwarf polyanthas. That *Baby Faurax* is terribly pretty, don't you think?'

Wield looked down at the clusters of tiny lavender and violet pompoms and nodded. They certainly appealed to him much more than the full-sized heavy-headed bushes. They brought into his mind a cottage garden with a stream running through it and a low-roofed building in glowing Cotswold stone.

He realized he was recalling a holiday cottage where he and his lost lover had spent a joyous fortnight many years before.

'Diana! Come in now, dear!'

Mrs Aldermann's voice pushed the memory from his mind. She was standing on the terrace. From the swing came a token protest, but Police Cadet Singh swept the little girl up on to his shoulders and bore her laughing and chattering towards the house.

'I'd best be off, sir,' said Wield. 'Good of you to spare the time.'

'Shared not spared, I think,' said Aldermann. 'Goodbye now.'

He accompanied Wield and Singh round the side of the house, then diverted to a screened compost heap where he deposited the deadheads and stood looking down at them in quiet contemplation. Wield, glancing back, was reminded of a priest standing alone by a flower-strewn grave after all the mourners had gone. 'A priest' wasn't a bad image. Aldermann's enthusiasm had something of the inaccessibility of the truly religious mind. The sergeant surprised himself by feeling a sudden surge of envy. For what? Not these huge gardens and that over-large house, certainly. And definitely not his wife, nor his ox, nor his ass, nor his servants, if he had any besides the jobbing gardeners and probably the occasional char. Perhaps, then, for knowing where his centre lay and daring to act upon that knowledge?

Singh had been reluctant to break in on the rapt sergeant, but now he said, 'Was it all right me playing with the kiddie, Sarge? I thought it'd give you a bit more chance to suss out her mam.'

Wield regarded the boy in momentary puzzlement, then recalled to mind that of course he had no notion that their visit to Rosemont had anything but the business of Mrs Aldermann's car behind it. So his move with the little girl had been pretty clever. But the sergeant did not articulate his approval. Instead he said coldly, 'Enjoy yourself in the sand-pit, did you? We'll have to see if we can get you posted to permanent school-crossing duty.'

Singh glanced sideways and smiled, ready to share the joke, but the sight of that savage, rough-hewn profile made it hard to believe in Wield's humorous intent. He felt a strong need for the man's approval and tried again by saying, 'That Mrs Aldermann, when I was on traffic duty yesterday morning I saw her down the Market Caff. And you know who she was with? Mr Pascoe's wife!'

Wield unlocked the car door and slid in behind the wheel.

'Traffic duty from the Market Caff?' he said. 'I hope you're learning good policing as quick as you're learning bad habits. Get in if you don't want to walk back.'

Police Cadet Singh hurried round the car and they drove back to the station in a far from companionable silence.

7

COPPER DELIGHT

(Floribunda. Fairly vigorous, coppery gold blooms in clusters of three to five, little fading but needs protection from black spot, sweet-scented.)

Peter Pascoe dandled his daughter, marking the rhythm by chanting in a music-hall Scots accent. *'De'il and Dalziel begin with ane letter! The de'ils nae guid and Dalziel's nae better!'*

The little girl was much taken by this verse and gurgled happily, but Ellie, coming into the lounge unheard, said, 'What's the fat slob been doing now?'

'That is no way to talk of your daughter,' said Pascoe sternly.

'Funny. Not that she doesn't get called worse than that sometimes. But to get back to Dalziel.'

'Oh, it's nothing worse than usual. He's just still niggling about this Elgood-Aldermann thing. But I can't get out of him what he expects me to *do*. Wield went round there last night . . .'

'To the Aldermanns'?'

'Yes. But don't fret yourself. It was ostensibly about your buddy's car.'

'And what did he find?' asked Ellie, a trifle aggressively. She had mixed feelings about police subterfuge, sometimes seeing it as a threat to the body social, sometimes taking a kind of perverse delight in it which worried her.

'Nothing, nothing,' said Pascoe hastily, not about to reveal that when Wield had mentioned the locked cabinet, he had picked up the phone and had a long talk with the police pathologist who had reeled off a huge list of potentially lethal chemicals used in garden care, ending by saying, 'But give me the flesh, and I'll give you the substance, Inspector. Have you got flesh for me?'

'Sorry,' said Pascoe, feeling like a war-time butcher. 'No flesh. But just off your cuff, is there anything which might leave a man with a known heart condition looking as if he'd had a heart-attack? Or anything that might make a driver with a skinful of booze almost certain to crash?'

'Well,' said the pathologist doubtfully, 'there's sodium fluoroacetate. Used for killing rats and devilish difficult to get hold of. Lots of symptoms – nausea, mental collapse, epileptiform convulsions – but if no one saw the symptoms, it might pass for a heart-attack if there was a history and no post mortem. As for the other, once a man's system is invaded by alcohol, it wouldn't take much to cause confusion. One of the chlorinated hydrocarbons, like chlordane; or an organic phosphate, like parathion; but without flesh . . .'

That had been that. The reason why there was no flesh was that both Bulmer and Eagles had been cremated. Not that there would really have been a very good case made of exhumation. The lab reports on the garage door and the Anglepoise lamp had revealed no clear evidence of tampering.

'So there's nothing to support Elgood's allegations?' said Ellie.

'No, and I'll tell him so,' said Pascoe firmly. 'I'm going to see him tomorrow. I reckon he probably just got a touch of the sun, lying around at that cottage of his. He'll probably be happy to back off now he's had a couple of nights to sleep on it. I think this child is wet.'

'It's that rhyme about Dalziel,' said Ellie. 'Dump her on a newspaper and I'll fetch a nappy.'

On her return, Ellie said thoughtfully. 'You're probably right of course, about Elgood, I mean. But Perfecta doesn't seem all that healthy a place to work, does it?'

'Two deaths, one drunk, one heart? About par for the average business firm. I should have thought.'

'There was someone else a few years back. I met his widow when I was with Daphne, that's how I know. Burke was the name. He used to work with Aldermann.'

'Burke?' said Pascoe. 'That rings a faint bell.'

'Does it? Before that mighty computer mind goes to work, I think your daughter would like her nappy changed.'

'It's your turn,' said Pascoe, rising from the floor. 'I just want to make a phone call.'

He returned a couple of minutes later and Ellie said casually, 'By the way, you'll let me know if you change your mind again, won't you?'

'About what?'

'About whether you're seriously investigating Patrick Aldermann.'

'Because of seeing his wife, you mean?'

'I suppose I mean that.'

'Yes, of course I'd tell you.'

'So that I'd stop seeing her?'

Pascoe grinned and said, 'I see tiger-traps. No, so that you'd know. Nothing more.'

'So you don't mind me seeing her again?'

'I mind your asking,' said Pascoe. 'Or rather, I'm suspicious of it, as I'm suspicious of anything that smacks of wifely dutifulness. What's it mean?'

Ellie rose from the happily re-nappied baby and went to open the cupboard of an old oak dresser from which she took a bottle of Scotch and two glasses.

'Tit for tat, I suppose,' she said. 'It struck me that not so long ago I might not even have known that Daphne was the wife of a man you were interested in. You've been a lot more forthcoming about your work since I stopped mine.'

Ellie had been, in fact still officially was, a lecturer in the social science department of the local Liberal Arts College. The period of her maternity leave was now expired but as there had not been much for her to do at this fag-end of the academic year, by mutual agreement she had merely made a token return by undertaking some examination marking. Ironically, her resumption of 'work' was in reality likely to be quickly followed by a resumption of being out of work, as the following year the college's pleasant country site was to be sold off and the staff lumped with the staff of the local town-based College of Technology in an Institute of Higher Education. Most of the courses Ellie was interested in teaching would disappear, and as it was rumoured that the local authority were offering trading stamps to staff willing to become voluntarily redundant, Ellie was contemplating perpetual retirement with whatever compensation she was entitled to, so that she could settle to finishing her second novel (the first having remained obstinately unpublished).

'So I've gone gabby?' said Pascoe. 'I'll have to watch that.'

Ellie set his whisky down beside him and sipped her own.

'Faced,' she continued, 'with a choice between regarding this new garrulity as a rather tardy recognition of my strong intellect, rational judgment and complete trustworthiness, and taking it as a condescending, sexist attempt to give the little woman a sop for having to vegetate at home all day, rooted by the brat, I decided to give you the benefit of the doubt.'

'You hear that, Rose?' said Pascoe, picking up the baby and holding her face up to his. 'My life has not been in vain. I may not have much, but I have the benefit of the doubt.'

'Renegotiable on a weekly basis,' added Ellie. 'This week I've taken into account that Andy Dalziel is obviously being an even bigger pain in the arse than usual.'

'Not bigger,' corrected Pascoe. 'Different. I get worried about him sometimes. At his best he's been a great cop. But times are a-changing.'

'And he's not changing with them? Well, when the dinosaurs had to go, they had to go. And there in the wings ready to take over is *Homo erectus*!'

'You flatter yourself,' grinned Pascoe.

'But you are ready to take over, aren't you, Peter?' said Ellie thoughtfully. 'I don't mean Andy's job specifically, but you do feel the dinosaurs have been hanging on just a bit too long, don't you?'

'Do I? Mebbe so. But I also worry about them. I mean, I sometimes even suspect Fat Andy's got some powers of self-awareness, and deep down grasps what's going on. Perhaps this is why he's seemed a bit uncertain lately. Then other times I'm certain he's just making sure *I* look the idiot in all this daft Aldermann business. With a bit of luck, it'll all blow over before he gets back.'

'He's going away? Andy?'

'Oh yes. I forgot to tell you. Obviously the ACC thinks Andy's got to bend to the modern world too. He summoned him yesterday to say that circumstances were preventing him from attending the conference at the Yard next week, so he wanted Andy to be our representative.'

'Not this conference on community policing in mixed societies? The one the Yanks are coming to?'

'Not to mention Frogs, Krauts and Dagoes, as Dalziel puts it,' said Pascoe.

'God help us all. Dalziel will have them going home to train in the use of tactical nuclear weapons!'

The baby, annoyed at not being central to the conversation, gave a sudden struggle in Pascoe's arms.

'Come here, darling,' said Ellie taking her. 'Time for you to be nodding off, I think. How about a drop of Scotch to see you through the night?'

As she went up the stairs the telephone rang.

Pascoe said, 'I'll get it.'

He picked up the receiver, spoke briefly, listened rather longer and was back in the lounge by the time Ellie returned.

'Anything important?' she asked, retrieving her whisky.

'Probably not. Just sheer curiosity on my part. Though on the other hand it is rather odd.'

'Do I get three guesses?' enquired Ellie after a moment.

'Sorry,' said Pascoe. 'I was just thinking deep thoughts, that's all. No, it was your mentioning that chap Burke. I knew it rang a bell. I rang the station and asked them to check if they could. It didn't take long. Someone there was actually on the case.'

'Case?'

'Well, not a case, exactly. But there was an inquest. This chap Burke fell off a decorator's ladder outside his house and broke his neck. Verdict, accidental death. No suspicious circumstances.'

'So?'

'Well, as you said, it's a bit odd, coming on top of what Elgood's been saying. Particularly as it seems that Mr Burke was assistant to Mr Eagles, the Chief Accountant.'

'And Aldermann got *that* job?'

'That's right,' said Pascoe. 'Of course, it doesn't mean anything.'

'No, it probably doesn't,' said Ellie. 'Elgood didn't even mention it, did he?'

'No. That's true. I'll mention it to him though,' said Pascoe. 'By the way, as a matter of interest, when are you seeing this Aldermann woman again.'

'Daphne? We're having coffee together tomorrow. Why?'

'Nothing. What was your impression, by the way.'

'I told you. I liked her. Lively and bright, blinkered of course, but far from stupid. Why do you ask?'

'It's just that Wield described her as a very pleasant, ordinary, upper-middle-class wife, almost a stereotype. She didn't sound your cup of tea, that's all.'

'Wield said that? Well, I suppose the presence of the fuzz is always inhibiting. Did he tell you how sexy she was?'

'Sexy?' said Pascoe, surprised. 'No, there wasn't the slightest suggestion . . . in fact, he seemed to think she was rather plain and homely. You thought her sexy?'

'Oh yes. Not in a moist-mouth-look-at-me-shaking-my-great-tits way, but definitely sexy. Of course, Wield might well not notice.'

'Why not?'

But Ellie only smiled and rose to pour some more whisky into her glass.

8
BLUE MOON

(Hybrid tea. Richly-scented, lilac-blue blossoms,
perhaps an acquired taste.)

When Pascoe arrived at the *Perfecta* plant early
the following afternoon, he found it as silent as
a Welsh Sunday.

He hung around a small foyer for a few minutes, coughing loudly as he pretended to examine
a small display of lavatorial artefacts, many of
them with the Elgoodware insignium. Finally an
early-middle-aged woman in a severe black and
white outfit arrived and said in a matching voice,
'Mr Pascoe? I'm Bridget Dominic, Mr Elgood's
secretary. Would you follow me, please?'

Pascoe obeyed, feeling like a hen-pecked husband as he lengthened his stride to keep up with
the swift-walking woman, a picture reinforced by
the large plastic carrier bag he was carrying. After
Dalziel's hints of Dandy Dick's sultanic habits, he
found Miss Dominic a bit of a disappointment.

Perhaps advancing age had brought Elgood into the realm of erotic discipline. Miss Dominic wasn't a bad name for a good whipper.

They went up several flights of stairs (didn't they have lifts?) and arrived at a door with Elgood's name writ large on the frosted glass. This opened on to what was clearly Miss Dominic's own office. Pascoe was surprised at its dinginess. He'd have expected Dandy Dick to put on a bit more of a display. Or perhaps it was simply a delayer, like a landscape gardener's tortuous and narrow path before the trees open wide for the surprise view.

Miss Dominic knocked. The door was flung open. The view was a surprise.

Elgood, looking most undandified, stood there jacketless, with his waistcoat undone, his tie awry, his hair ruffled, and an amber-liquored glass in his hand.

For one moment Pascoe thought they must have caught him – how had Dalziel put it? – tupping a typist in his intray.

'Come in, come in,' said Elgood irritably. 'Thank you, Miss Dominic.'

The secretary retreated. Elgood closed the door behind her and said, 'Have a chair. Have a drink. And don't say "not on duty". It's Lucozade. I like to keep my energy up. Sit down. Sit down.'

Pascoe sat down. The room was bigger and pleasanter than the outer office, but still no state apartment. Nice carpet; pretty curtains framing a pleasant view once the eye travelled beyond the industrialized foreground and the suburbanized middle-distance to the rich blue-green of the pastoral horizon; walls papered a bit like an Indian restaurant and hung with some rather gaudy still-lifes and a big photograph of a fiftyish-suited group formally arranged outside a works gate over which arched in letters of wrought iron the name *Elgood*.

Elgood poured Pascoe a Lucozade and sat himself behind an old-fashioned, very sturdy desk. There was a sheet of newspaper opened on it and on the paper a half-eaten pork pie.

'Lunch,' said Elgood, following his gaze. 'You've eaten? Lucky man. You've come at a bloody inconvenient time, I tell you. I may have to chuck you out a bit rapid. On the other hand, I may be able to sit and rabbit on with you all day. You never can tell.'

'About what?' enquired Pascoe.

'About workers' meetings. We're having to make cutbacks like everyone else. I had the shop stewards in on Wednesday to tell 'em how the Board sees things. They've spent two days deliberating and this lunch-hour they called a full-scale meeting in the works canteen. It's still going on. So that's it, plant and offices idle till they get through yakking.'

'Your office staff are involved as well?' said Pascoe, surprised.

'Most of 'em. I don't have two worlds here, Mr Pascoe, never have done. Same works, same perks, that's always been my motto, though there's a lot outside that don't like it. But I've always got on well with the men who work for me. That's why I've hung on here so long.'

Pascoe, though he had the feeling that this apparent forthrightness was just another version of Dandy Dick's circumlocution which was aimed for some reason at skirting the topic of Aldermann, was interested enough to ask, 'But I thought that would be part of the deal, when I.C.E. took you over.'

Elgood laughed.

'Oh aye, it was part of the deal. But a company bent on a take-over's a bit like a lad desperate to have it away – he'll promise owt till the deal's done, but once his wick's dipped, it takes more than a happy memory to make him keep his word. But whenever anyone's wanted shut of me, there's been enough wise heads at I.C.E. to know that peace at Perfecta means money in their pockets, so I've stayed. The lads here know me, I know them. That's why I'm here now. Instant availability, that's what I offer them. While they're down there talking, they know I'm up here waiting. But let's get you out of the way, shall we? I'm beginning to think I've been a bit headstrong, to tell you the truth. I should've thought on before coming round to see you. The last thing I need at the moment is you lot poking around and stirring things up.'

'What specific bit of poking did you have in mind?' asked Pascoe politely.

'Nothing specific,' said Elgood in irritation. 'But coming round here like this. And I bet you've been asking questions. You haven't been asking Aldermann questions, have you? I hope to God you had enough sense not to do that!'

'No, I haven't asked Mr Aldermann any questions,' said Pascoe. 'Though I did in fact send someone round to his house, but it was on another matter entirely, please believe me. But I must say he reported nothing suspicious.'

Pascoe half expected an angry outburst at this revelation of his oblique approach to Aldermann but Elgood merely responded with heavy sarcasm, 'What did he expect, bloodstains on the carpet?'

Pascoe ignored this and proceeded, 'I've also looked carefully at such reports as exist on the deaths of your Mr Eagles and Mr Bulmer. There doesn't appear to be an untoward circumstance in either case.'

'No?' Elgood sounded almost relieved. 'Well, I was mebbe a bit upset the other day. You can get things out of proportion, can't you? I've had a lot on my mind recently.'

Perversely, Elgood's apparent desire to drop the matter provoked Pascoe into pressing on. He dumped the plastic bag on the desk.

'I've got your lamp here, sir. Our technical staff checked it out. A worn connection caused the trouble.'

'Bloody lousy workmanship, as usual,' grumbled Elgood.

'It could have been worn deliberately,' said Pascoe. 'By rubbing it against the edge of a desk, for instance.'

'Was there any sign of that?'

'No,' admitted Pascoe. 'But no positive evidence it *didn't* happen either. Similarly with your garage door. The spring had gone and the whole counter-weight system was therefore out of operation. Wear and tear, metal fatigue, or . . .'

'Or what, Inspector?' said Elgood irritably. 'Is there owt or is there nowt?'

Pascoe shrugged and said enigmatically. 'Nowt. Either way.'

Elgood rose and wandered across the room, glancing at his watch. He came to a halt in front of the photograph of the group at the works gate.

'So I've made a bit of a charley of myself,' he said. 'Well, it happens to everyone, I suppose.'

'Not very often to you, I shouldn't have thought,' said Pascoe.

'Not often,' agreed Elgood. 'Once in a blue moon, though, a man's entitled to act a bit daft. Well, I've had my turn, and I hope it'll see me out. Thanks for calling, Inspector.'

He turned to face Pascoe, but the Inspector did not take his cue to depart.

'There was one other thing,' he said. 'Something which seemed to have a better chance of fitting in with your notion that Mr Aldermann was shoving people out of his way rather recklessly. You had a Mr Burke working here once, didn't you?'

'Chris Burke? Aye. What about him?'

Elgood's face was thrust forward attentively, bright eyes alert.

'If I understand it right, Aldermann came here in the first instance on a part-time basis?'

'Yes, that's right.'

'And would never have joined the staff full time if a vacancy hadn't occurred, the vacancy being caused by the death of Mr Burke who was assistant to Mr Eagles, your Chief Accountant?'

'So?'

'So,' said Pascoe. 'Here's another death that helped advance Mr Aldermann.'

'Don't be bloody daft! That was four years ago!' said Elgood.

'There's no time-limit on criminal inclination,' Pascoe pontificated. 'And the circumstances of Mr Burke's death look far more suspicious than either Mr Eagles's or Mr Bulmer's.'

'What circumstances?'

'I understand he fell off a ladder and broke his neck.'

'And that's suspicious? Christ, you do scrape around, you lot, don't you? Look, Inspector, I'm sorry you've been bothered. I just got a daft bee in my bonnet, that's all. I'm sorry. It'll have given Andy Dalziel a good laugh, any road, so it hasn't been an entire waste. Now I really am a bit busy, so if you don't mind . . .'

Pascoe rose. He'd got what he'd hoped for, the withdrawing of the complaint if complaint there'd been, but he wasn't as happy as he'd expected. He went to shake Elgood's proffered hand. Over the small man's shoulder, the faces in the photo grinned derisively at him. Even without the legend inscribed at the bottom, it was easy to pick out Dandy Dick. Dapper, spruce, smiling broadly he stood at the group's centre, exuding confidence.

Then another name in the legend caught Pascoe's eye.

'I see there's someone called Aldermann,' he said. 'Any connection?'

He worked out which it was. A slightly built man with a black moustache and a rather melancholy expression (even though smiling) who reminded Pascoe of Neville Chamberlain.

'With our Patrick, you mean?' said Elgood. 'Yes, that's Eddie Aldermann. He'd be, let me see, his great-uncle. A good lad was Eddie. I got into a bit of a tangle in them early days and someone put me on to Eddie and he got it sorted and after that he managed all my finance. He was a genius with figures. Could have been a millionaire, I reckon. Would have been if his missus had her way.'

'Oh. How was that?'

Elgood's desire to be rid of him seemed to have weakened now he was into the past. The only period of history which really fascinates most people, Pascoe had often remarked, is that commencing with their own childhood and ending about ten years ago.

'Flo Aldermann was a pushy woman. Eddie

would have been happy enough working for a steady wage and getting home in plenty of time to look after his patch of garden, but Flo wanted more than that. And she was right, in a way. He had the talent, he made the money. A man should use his talents. The trouble was, he had more than one talent. The other was with gardens, roses in particular. And Flo over-reached herself when she pushed him into buying that house of theirs, Rosemont. It was too big for 'em and had been badly neglected, but she wanted it, so Eddie spent thousands doing it up. But the gardens needed doing up too, and that's where Flo got caught. Eddie wasn't an obstinate man except when it came to his gardening. Now instead of a quarter-acre he had four or five. He dug his heels in, and his spade too, likely. This came first from now on. Well, they were very comfortable, very comfortable indeed, but it was the gardens at Rosemont as robbed Flo of her million, I reckon.'

'And Patrick inherited the estate? They had no children of their own?'

'No. Flo wasn't the mothering kind. It was her niece, Penny Highsmith, that inherited. Nice lass, Penny. Bonny lass.'

Elgood's eyes gleamed with a connoisseur's enthusiasm.

'And Patrick inherited when she died?' said Pascoe.

'No,' said Elgood in exasperation. 'Penny's

Patrick's mother. She's still living down in London somewhere.'

Now Pascoe was really puzzled.

'You say she was Mrs Aldermann's niece. And her name's Highsmith? And she's still alive? But Patrick owns Rosemont and he's called Aldermann?'

'Oh aye, it does sound a bit odd, I reckon. She split up the estate when he came of age, so I gather. She missed London and the bright lights, he wanted to stay up here, I suppose. So he got the house and she went off with the rest and set herself up down south.'

'And the name?'

'He changed it, by deed poll, soon as he came of age. He thought the sun shone out of Eddie's arsehole, so it seems. Wanted to follow his example in every way. It came of not having a father of his own, I expect. Well, he managed it so far as Rosemont goes, from what I've seen. He's got a real touch with the roses, I'll give him that. But he doesn't come within a light-year of being the accountant old Eddie was.'

'Yet you took him on at Perfecta?'

Now they were back on the old track again, Elgood immediately began to show signs of his old impatience to end the interview.

'Why not? It was a gesture for old times' sake. He needed a job. I saw no harm in pushing a bit of work his way. There's room for a bit of sentiment in business, Mr Pascoe.'

'You mean he was out of work? An accountant?' said Pascoe who placed accountants with doctors, undertakers and whores in the class of the perpetually employed.

'He was with some firm in Harrogate for a bit, but he fell out with them and left. There was some talk of a bit of bother, but Yorkshire's a grand place for smoke with not much fire, so there was likely nothing in it. He'd been working private for a couple of years when I took him on. I reckon he'd been living on capital, myself, and doing most of his work in those bloody gardens of his!'

'But you kept him on? Promoted him in fact?'

Elgood shook his head angrily and said, 'Not really. In fact he was just on the point of getting the push. We had to start cutting back because of the recession. We're still at it, which is why I'm hanging around here waiting for this bloody meeting to finish. We got shot of all our part-timers for a start, from the factory through to the executive level. Aldermann was finished. Then Chris Burke died. Our policy, again at all levels, was to offer part-timers a full-time job if there was a vacancy. Aldermann was the only one who could do Burke's job, obvious. So he got it.'

'And he's not done it very well?'

'He muddles through,' said Elgood. 'But his heart's not in it. But he can be a charmer too, and he's not without friends at court. There's a few on my board think he's the bee's knees.'

The intercom buzzed. He answered it.

Miss Dominic's voice said, 'The meeting's over, Mr Elgood.'

'Right. Thanks.'

To Pascoe's surprise, Elgood started tidying up, rolling down his sleeves, fastening his tie, buttoning his waistcoat, putting on his jacket. He had assumed that the dishevelled look was specially prepared for encounters with the work force.

Elgood seemed to catch his thought and said as he combed his hair, using the photograph glass as a mirror, 'They expect me to look smart, a bit flashy even, full of confidence. Would you chuck that pork pie in the wastebin? Thanks. And hide that bloody Lucozade. They'll be calling me Doris if they spot that. Now, you'd best shoot off, Inspector. Thanks for your bother.'

Pascoe went slowly towards the door.

'So we're just to forget all this, are we, Mr Elgood?' he said.

'I thought I'd said so,' said Elgood impatiently.

'Goodbye then,' said Pascoe.

As he opened the door, Elgood added in a quiet voice, 'And, Inspector, I mean, *forget* it. It embarrasses me even to think about it, and I don't want to find myself on the end of a defamation action. So no more nods and winks, eh? No more ugly buggers from the CID prowling around Aldermann on some trumped-up business that wouldn't fool a child. I just went neurotic for a bit. It won't happen again. I'm sorry you've been bothered.'

'That's all right, Mr Elgood,' said Pascoe. 'Best of luck with your negotiations. Watch how you go.'

In the corridor he was making for the stairs, when he heard lift doors rattling open at the other end. So Miss Dominic *had* deliberately exercised him. Perhaps he hadn't been so far wrong about the whip!

He retraced his steps. Out of the lift stepped four overalled men and Miss Dominic herself. Clearly she did not care to match her strength with the work force. He nodded at her and stepped into the lift. On the way down it stopped at the second floor and a man entered. He was in his thirties with an oval face, watchful brown eyes and neat black hair. He wore a dark blue business suit of conventional cut. His only departure from executive sobriety was a beautifully formed lilac-blue rose in his buttonhole.

Pascoe had never seen him before but he reminded him of someone. When they reached the ground floor, Pascoe motioned the man out ahead of him. He smiled his acknowledgement and strode away, permitting Pascoe to glimpse the initials P. A. monogrammed on his briefcase.

Perhaps this explained the sense of familiarity – not a physical resemblance, but a resemblance to a mental image. This had to be Patrick Aldermann.

Outside, the man got into a Cortina parked almost in front of the door. Pascoe's car was round the side in the works car park. As he walked past the Cortina, the man looked at him through the still open door and said, 'Can I offer you a lift?'

'No, thanks,' said Pascoe. 'I've got my own car. Excuse me, I couldn't help noticing your rose. What a fascinating colour.'

'You like it? It's a *Blue Moon*. Here, please take it.'

To Pascoe's surprise he plucked the flower from his lapel and put it into the inspector's hand.

'But I can't . . .' said Pascoe, taken aback.

'Why not? Blue Moon means improbability. Everyone needs a little improbability in their life, don't you agree? The thing is, having the courage to accept it. Goodbye.'

The door closed, the car started up almost silently and purred away.

Pascoe watched it go, then resumed his walk to the car park thinking that these words of Aldermann's, though perhaps the most enigmatic, were far from the most thought-provoking utterances he'd heard that day.

9

ESCAPADE

(Floribunda. White rosy-flushing blooms, single, hanging together in large bunches, sweet-smelling when open.)

Police Cadet Singh realized with a sinking heart that the situation was beginning to get out of his control.

Passing through the central shopping precinct on his way to the station, he had not been altogether displeased to run into a trio of old school acquaintances, particularly as the girl in the group showed a disposition to be turned on by his uniform, and the boys (both out of work) though more diffident of manner, were equally interested in what he thought of the job.

Unfortunately the precinct was a popular stamping ground for the young unemployed, of whom there was a tragic plenitude. A couple more old acquaintances joined the group, then one or two other youngsters he didn't know, till suddenly he found himself surrounded by at least a dozen.

The atmosphere was still amiable enough, but an element of horse-play was entering into it. There were now four girls, very audience-conscious, and their admiration was becoming exaggerated to the point of parody. One had 'borrowed' his hat and tried it on. Envious of the applause, one of the boys had taken it from her and gone into a heel-rocking 'ello-'ello-'ello comic policeman routine.

Singh preserved a forced smile while his mind raced to work out the best solution to the problem. Any attempt to retrieve the hat could easily result in a game such as was often played in the old school yard, with a cap being hurled from one hand to another as its owner made desperate attempts to grab it. Also, in the middle of the precinct was a very tempting fountain around which the old folk sat exchanging stories and cigarettes. The thought of having to paddle among the floating fag-packets to retrieve his hat made his dark skin burn with shame.

But something would have to be done. The excited little group was already drawing the attention of passers-by.

'Excuse me, Officer,' said a woman's voice, very clear without being over-loud.

Singh turned. Behind him stood a tall, slim woman with a small child in a papoose-basket on her back.

'Yes, madam,' Singh stammered.

'I wonder if you could direct me to the Chantry Coffee House?' said the woman.

'Certainly, madam,' said Singh. 'Now, let's see . . .'

'I know it's somewhere near the Cathedral,' continued the woman, 'but all those little winding lanes are so confusing. Perhaps if you're going that way, you could show me?'

'Yes, of course,' said Singh. He held out his hand, the hat was put into it, he placed it carefully on his head.

'See you around, lads,' he said. 'This way, madam.'

After they had put the youngsters a little distance behind them, Singh heaved a huge sigh of relief and said, 'Thank you very much, Mrs Pascoe.'

Ellie raised her eyebrows at him.

'You remembered me then? A policeman's memory for faces!'

'I hope so.' He hesitated, then went on. 'Them lads back there, they're all right really. There's just nothing to do but muck about all day.'

'Yes, I know,' said Ellie. 'I didn't think I was rescuing you from a lynch mob. Is that why you joined, so you wouldn't have to muck about all day?'

She spoke with real sympathy. Also, while she firmly believed that the same right-wing policies which were creating unemployment were ironically driving young men to join those bastions of the right, the police and the armed forces, as an escape from the dole, she'd found hard statistics difficult to come by. Even one living and personally known example would be helpful.

To her surprise Singh looked somewhat offended.

'Oh no,' he said. 'My dad's got a shop. I could've helped there if I'd wanted. I just thought I'd rather try the police, that's all.'

'Oh,' said Ellie, feeling put in her place. 'And how's it working out?'

'Not so bad. A bit boring sometimes,' said Singh, who was not about to pour his heart out to this DI's wife, no matter how nice she seemed. On the other hand, there was no harm in trying to do yourself a bit of good. 'What I'd really like,' he went on, 'is to get into plain clothes later on. Uniform branch is all right to start with, but it'd be smashing to be working with someone right clever like Mr Pascoe.'

He gave her the full brilliance of his smile, Ellie returned it, genuinely amused.

'I'll not tell him you said that, I promise,' she said. 'I know it'd just embarrass you, and it might go to his head. Well, thanks for showing me the way.'

She halted and Singh was discomfited to see he had been about to walk right past the Chantry Coffee House. It was an elegant bow-fronted establishment, a long way removed in style and price from the Market Caff. No external grime or internal steam masked these velvet-curtained windows, and instead of the pong of frying fat these ventilators exhaled the pungent aroma of roasting coffee. But a glance through the gleaming panes as he went on his way confirmed that one thing was unchanged. Mrs Pascoe's rendezvous here was with the same woman she'd been sitting with in the Market Caff, the woman whose name he now knew to be Mrs Daphne Aldermann.

That the two women should be friendly didn't strike him as odd. Ellie would perhaps have been irritated, though not necessarily surprised, to learn that in Police Cadet Singh's eyes, she and Daphne Aldermann were two of a kind – confident, articulate, middle-class women who'd never have to worry about things like money and manners. He'd thought a lot about Mrs Aldermann since he and Sergeant Wield had visited Rosemont. There'd been more in that interview than met the eye. There was no real epidemic of car-vandalizing such as Wield had described, certainly nothing to justify spending CID time on. Yet Wield had sat there and asked daft questions, and later he'd choked Singh off when he'd suggested obliquely that the sergeant was more interested in the woman than the car.

That Wield might have been more interested in the man than the woman had not occurred to Singh. In his mind, the vandalizing of the car still had to be the starting-point of CID interest and, aggrieved by Wield's attitude, he had read and re-read the initial report by the uniformed officer who'd first gone to the car park, but its straightforward account of the events had been short, clear and unhelpful.

Arriving at the station, he was making his way through the car park to the rear entrance when he saw PC David Bradley leaning against the bonnet of his car, yawning widely. It was PC Bradley and his partner, PC John Grainger, who'd been sent to the multi-storey when the first complaint came in.

'Hello, Dave,' said Singh cheerfully.

'Hello, young Shady,' said Bradley, using the popular corruption of Shaheed.

'Got a moment?' asked Singh.

'I've got till yon idle bugger, Grainger, gets himself out of the locker-room and into this car. What's up?'

'It's about that car vandalizing in the multi-storey on Monday,' said Singh. 'I was reading your report.'

'Oh aye? Something wrong with my English is there, you cocky young wog?'

Singh forced a tired smile. The fact that much of the racialism he had encountered in the Force was amiably or at least humorously intended did not make it any easier to accept. At school it had been simpler. Long familiarity had bred integration and on odd occasions speed of punch had supported it. In the police force he had quickly realized that references to his background from superior officers had to be borne if he was to survive. Complaint within the Force, and even more so outside it, would make his position intolerable. Racial cracks from fellow cadets and lowly constables did not have to be accepted quite as stoically, however. He had a ready wit and a sharp tongue of his own.

He said, 'No, it'll be grand when you start joining up your letters. Listen, though, it was that Mrs Aldermann I wanted to ask them. The one Sergeant Wield's interested in.'

If Singh had hoped to get some hint of the nature of Wield's interest, he was disappointed, though the form the negative took was interesting in its own way.

'Sergeant Wield? What's he got to do with it?'

'Hasn't he been asking questions about her?'

'No. Why should he? What's CID sticking its nose in for? It's all in my report anyway, if you can read, that is.'

'It's a bit hard when you start using all them long words like *car*,' said Singh. 'What did she say, anyway?'

'Nowt much,' said Bradley. 'We got called in by some old boy who'd found his paintwork scratched. Mrs Aldermann arrived while we were there. She got in her car without noticing the damage. In fact she didn't seem all that bothered when we pointed it out to her.'

'Not bothered?' said Singh. 'Wasn't she annoyed?'

'Aye, but more like with us for stopping her. She was in a hurry, I recall. Something about being late to pick up her kiddie from school. We'd almost missed her, she was so quick. Straight in and off, no seat-belt fastened or anything.'

'She didn't put her shopping in the back then, anything like that?'

'No, she weren't carrying anything but a little handbag. Hey, what's all this questioning, anyway, young Shady? You after Mr Dalziel's job or what?'

'No. It's just part of a training study I'm doing,' lied Singh. 'You didn't say anything about her not being bothered in your report.'

'Relevant facts, that's what reports are about, haven't they taught you that yet?' said Bradley. 'Get a move on, you great clodhopper, afore someone sees us! We should have been on our way five minutes back.'

He was addressing his partner, PC Grainger, whose portly sixteen-stone frame had appeared in the entrance to the station. Grainger mouthed a kiss and began to approach at an easy rolling pace.

'But she did co-operate?' said Singh.

'You still going on?' asked Bradley, opening the driver's door. 'She rattled on a bit, said it wasn't much damage and she'd really rather not get involved. But I told her she'd got no choice. So she gave us details and took off like Stirling Moss.'

He started the engine and revved it up as Grainger reached the passenger door.

'And you said all the cars had been parked there by nine o'clock or shortly after?' persisted Singh.

'That's right, Sherlock.'

106

'What's up with him?' enquired Grainger, getting in with difficulty.

'He's being conscientious,' said Bradley. 'He's trying to find out how real policemen work.'

'He's come to the right shop then,' said Grainger, settling his bulk into the seat and closing his eyes. 'Try to go steady and miss the bumps. That's the secret of getting on the cars, Shady. Going steady and missing the bumps. I doubt a daft sprog like you will ever make it.'

'The cars are on their way out,' said Singh seriously. 'Haven't you heard? The Chief Constable says it's all about community policing nowadays. Eighty per cent of the uniformed branch on the beat, that's what he wants. Starting next month.'

Grainger opened an eye and said, 'Piss off. Where'd you hear that rubbish?'

'It's on the notice-board, haven't you seen it?' said Singh in apparent surprise.

Grainger opened the other eye.

'You're joking,' he said. 'Aren't you?'

'No,' said Singh. 'It's up on the board, right enough. And details of how they're going to pick them as'll be walking.'

'How's that then?'

Singh leaned to the window and said confidentially, 'They're doing it by weight. Fattest first.'

Bradley roared with laughter. Grainger said, 'You cheeky young bugger!' and then his partner set the car in motion and they accelerated out of the car park.

Singh looked after them, grinning at the success of his joke for a while. Then his expression became serious once more. So Sergeant Wield had neglected to talk to Bradley about his report? Well, likely it didn't matter. But there was enough there to be interesting. And he had another idea to follow up. Wield's offhand manner had really stung him, all the more so because he hadn't been able to detect any general racial prejudice in it. It was as if on the level of simple personal judgement Wield didn't reckon he amounted to much as a copper, and that's what hurt. But he'd show him yet. He'd show 'em all!

'If he said drop it, drop it,' said Dalziel. 'You seemed keen enough to get shut of the whole business the other day.'

'I'm sorry, sir,' said Pascoe. 'I know it's all a bit vague, but I just get the feeling that there's something here. All right, forget the alleged killings which are no longer alleged and which in any case seem to have been perfectly straightforward cases of accidental and of natural death. Curiously, in the one case where a bit of skulduggery could have been possible, that was the death of a man called Christopher Burke which opened up the way for Aldermann's full-time employment, Mr Elgood was emphatic it was accidental.'

'Burke? Oh aye, I recall. Fell off a ladder, didn't he? Broke his neck.'

'That's the one. Easier to arrange, I should've

thought, than a heart attack or a car skidding on an empty road. But no, not that one, says Elgood.'

'And no, not the others either,' reminded Dalziel, sticking a pen down the side of his shoe to scratch his foot.

'But there has to be a reason why he came here in the first place. You did take him seriously yourself, sir,' said Pascoe accusingly.

'No,' answered Dalziel, who had now worked back up to his ankle. 'I asked *you* to take him seriously. He's dropped a few useful hints in the past and you shouldn't forget a man's record, good or bad, should you?'

'You mean he's one of your narks?' exclaimed Pascoe in amazement.

'Don't be daft, lad! Can you imagine meeting Dandy Dick on a park bench and slipping him a couple of quid for information received? No, it's just that once or twice, especially in the old days, he's settled a business dispute by dropping a hint about some shady deal the opposition was into. All's fair in love and business, Dick'd say. He'd screw anyone, any way!'

Dalziel spoke admiringly. His pen had now emerged from his sock and he'd pulled his trouser leg up so that he could continue the scratch up to his knee. He didn't seem to have noticed that the pen-top had remained in the sock and the felt tip was now adding a new royal blue line to the scrawl of varicose veins on his calf.

Pascoe said, 'You mean he used us to put the skids under his business rivals? The cunning sod!'

'Aye, he's that, right enough,' said Dalziel. 'Mebbe he's still playing that game, stirring things up to help himself. I'll have him if he is, though he's been quiet for a good bit now. I reckon when they got took over, the game became that much bigger and also he lost a bit of interest. You don't look after someone else's mansion the way you do your own house, do you?'

'He seemed to be looking after it fairly well when I saw him, and single-handed. The place didn't exactly look packed with senior management waiting for the union meeting to finish. Though I did see Aldermann, of course. Mind you, he looked to be packing it in for the day! I told you he gave me a rose, didn't I?'

'He wanted to give me a bunch,' said a voice from the doorway. It was Wield who had entered with his usual quietness.

'God, it's creeping Jesus,' said Dalziel, looking round. 'You want to get some hobnails in them boots of yours, Sergeant. But now you're here, just tell me again what you thought of Mr Aldermann when you called on him the other night.'

'Like I said in my report, sir, he was difficult to get to. Very self-contained, watchful almost, but not in a suspicious way. He came to life when he started showing me his roses, though.'

'You felt he could be more interested in his roses than his wife and family?' said Pascoe.

'There's men more interested in golf and grey-hounds than their wives and families!' interjected Dalziel. 'That doesn't make them killers!'

Wield said, 'Not more *interested in*, perhaps, sir, but more *passionate about*, if that makes sense. He handles them with love. And when he deadheaded them, it was like watching a surgeon at work.'

'Aye, there's some of them buggers'd be better off using a pair of garden secateurs!' observed Dalziel, who tended to regard doctors as causes rather than curers of ill health.

'No, he uses a pruning knife,' said Wield, justi-fying his simile. 'It's a beauty, lovely shape, sharp as a scalpel.'

'I hope you're not suggesting that just because he's got a nice, sharp, shiny pruning knife, he's likely to go around slitting people's throats, Ser-geant?' said Dalziel with heavy sarcasm.

'No, sir,' agreed Wield. 'That doesn't follow.'

'It's what you might call a non-secateur,' mur-mured Pascoe, adding hastily as he saw the look on Dalziel's face, 'and there was the cupboard full of poison, wasn't there?'

'What a way you've got with language!' said Dalziel sarcastically. 'Garden weedkillers, that's what he's got. Which there's no evidence he's used to kill owt but weeds. And what did he do with Burke? Blow the stuff up his trouser leg while he was climbing that ladder?'

He'd finished scratching his leg and now he pulled his trouser down again without noticing the decoration on his calf. Wield met Pascoe's gaze. Pascoe had a sudden desire to giggle, but Wield's rocky impassivity stemmed the impulse.

'One reason,' said Dalziel. 'Give me one reason to waste any more time on this business.'

'Curiosity,' said Pascoe promptly.

'Curiosity? About what?'

'About how a man, who, as far as I can ascertain, has never shown much real aptitude for his chosen profession, should be at the edge of becoming financial director of a subsidiary of a large international company.'

'Christ, by that yardstick we should be curious about fifty per cent of directors, seventy per cent of politicians and ninety-five per cent of Chief Constables!' said Dalziel in disgust. 'Listen, this Aldermann sounds to me like Mr Average. Dull; ordinary; wife and two kids; nice house; loves to get home to his family and his rose-garden. He'll likely go to Corfu for his holidays and have his white-haired old mother to stay at Christmas. He has got a white-haired old mother, has he?'

'Mrs Penelope Highsmith,' said Pascoe promptly, glancing at his file. 'Flat 31, Woodfall House, Denbigh Square, London SW1. Age and colour of hair unknown.'

'Very good,' complimented Dalziel. 'Your information, I mean. Highsmith? Why not Aldermann? Did she marry again?'

'She wasn't married in the first place. Highsmith was her maiden name. Evidently she never let on who Patrick's father was and it was his own idea to take his great-uncle's name when he came of age.'

But Dalziel didn't seem to be much interested in this bit of family history.

'Highsmith?' he said. 'Penelope Highsmith? Used to live up here fifteen, twenty years back?'

'I presume so. At least, he went to school here.'

'Penny Highsmith! By God. Penny Highsmith!' Dalziel's face suddenly lit up, like sunshine breaking through at Elsinore.

'You knew Mrs Highsmith, sir?' enquired Pascoe.

'We met, if it's the same one. She used to come down to the Club odd Saturday nights when there was a dance on. I never knew she had a son, though. She was a real lively lass. Full of fun and bonny with it. A real live spark.'

Whose memory brought a lustful gleam to Dalziel's weary, cynical eyes as well as Elgood's twinkling, questing ones, thought Pascoe. She must have had something! 'The Club' of course, meant the local rugby football club. Pascoe's only connection with it had been a professional one some years before while he was still a sergeant. It was not a game nor an ambience that he much cared for, but the Superintendent had evidently played the game with some skill and (Pascoe guessed) a great deal of physicality in his younger days.

'It doesn't sound as if Patrick takes after her much,' said Pascoe. 'Perhaps he's more like his mysterious father.'

113

'Perhaps,' said Dalziel thoughtfully. 'I'll tell you what, you two. I'm off to this bloody conference tomorrow. And because like as not you'll do what you bloody well want in any case, soon as my back's turned, I'll give you the week I'm away to rummage round in. It doesn't mean you neglect owt else, but if you've a couple of spare moments here and there, well, it's up to you. All right? Now bugger off. I've got things to do before I go home and get packed. Oh, you might leave me that file to glance at.'

It was either a small concession or a great volte-face, depending how you looked at it. Pascoe was not inclined to quibble.

'Have a nice time, sir,' he said, dropping the file on the desk.

Dalziel grunted, looking down at the untidy surface on his desk on which his spade-like hands were arranging and rearranging articles impatiently.

It was not until he was out in the corridor that it occurred to Pascoe that he was probably looking for the top of his felt-tip pen.

10
MOONLIGHT

*(Hybrid Musk. Cascades of white blossom,
full of old-world charm.)*

Daphne Aldermann had been openly amused to note that Ellie Pascoe and baby Rose were clearly as well known in the Chantry Coffee House as they were in the Market Caff. Ellie was unabashed.

'I like it here,' she said. 'The coffee's better for one thing.'

'That compensates for the people, does it?' Daphne attacked, glancing round at the clientele which was largely middle-aged and middle-class females with hats and voices to match.

'I didn't say I liked *them*,' said Ellie. 'People en masse generally get up my nose. But with this lot I can feel irritated without feeling guilty.'

'Whereas getting annoyed at the disgusting habits and awful taste of hoi-polloi brings on an attack of conscience? I see.'

'I wouldn't have put it quite like that,' said Ellie. 'But clearly you understand the principle.'

'It's one you become familiar with when you're brought up in a parsonage,' said Daphne. 'Local ladies squabbling about who did the flowers was infuriating, but no worse than the deserving poor banging on the door just as Daddy was sitting down to his evening meal.'

'Was your sympathy with your father for being disturbed or your mother for having her cooking spoilt?' asked Ellie casually.

Daphne smiled and said, 'Catch question. You want me to say how male-centred our house was! I'm afraid I can't help you. You see, my mother died when I was thirteen and thereafter I was very much in charge of the house. We had a woman-who-did, but her cuisine was based mainly on chips and brown sauce, so more often than not it was *my* cooking that was being spoilt. I used to get furious.'

'And feel guilty?'

'Only when the disturber turned out to be really deserving.'

'Or really poor,' said Ellie. 'It shows up the inadequacies of State care when people can still be forced to beg for handouts from the Church.'

To her surprise Daphne laughed out loud.

'Oh, come on,' she said. 'It wouldn't matter what the State did, there's always going to be people beating a path to the door of a rich parson well known to be a soft touch. It's called human nature, dear.'

Ellie decided to ignore the ideological challenge and said, 'A *rich* parson? I thought the virtue of poverty was one the Church forced its employees to embrace?'

'So it does. Fortunately it doesn't force them to embrace poor wives also. The money was Mummy's, you see.'

Her voice had a wistful note as at some remembered sadness. Ellie said brightly, 'At least it would mean your father could afford a decent housekeeper when you got yourself married.'

Her effort at cheerfulness failed miserably.

'No. Daddy was dead by then too,' said Daphne, tears starting to her eyes. 'It was awful. He was doing so well, he'd become Archdeacon, you see, and he was responsible among other things for checking on church structures in the diocese when there was any question of restoration work and appeals, that sort of thing. He'd gone out to St Mark's at Little Leven. It was in a really bad state, it seems. And a stone fell from the belfry while he was examining it and killed him.'

'How awful,' said Ellie, genuinely moved. 'I'm so sorry. That must have been a terrible thing to bear.'

Her hand hovered over Daphne's. She wasn't sure if physical contact would comfort the woman or merely precipitate a flood of tears and she hated herself for her uncertainty. Fortunately Rose, far removed from adult inadequacies, was ready with a diversion. A passing waitress stooping over the high chair to goo-goo her admiration brought a plateful of cakes within reach of the little girl and she plunged her tiny fist into the mouth of a cream horn with great accuracy and equal enthusiasm.

Daphne's distress disappeared in the ensuing confusion and Ellie happily sat back and let her take control, only interfering when she started to wipe Rose's hand with a napkin.

'Let her lick it off,' she said. 'It'll save on her next feed.'

It was nearly midday when the two women left the coffee house.

'Which way are you going?' asked Ellie.

'Back to the car. I'm on top of the precinct.'

'Me too. Forty p and vertigo just for parking your car. It's a mad world,' said Ellie.

They made their way back to the main shopping precinct. The youths were still lounging around outside the Job Centre and the old people sitting on the benches round the fountain. Ellie had an unpleasant fantasy that what the youngsters were really doing was forming a queue, forty years long, for a place on one of those benches.

They travelled up on the lift together. The shoppers' car park was on the roof of the covered section of the precinct. It was joined by a bridge over the inner ring road to the multi-storey by the bus station. They found that their cars were parked quite close together.

'At least there doesn't seem to be any damage

this time,' said Daphne after a cursory inspection of her gleaming paintwork.

'They'd need to wash mine before they could scratch it,' said Ellie. 'Was this where you were when you got vandalized?'

'No, I was over the bridge in the multi-storey,' said Daphne.

'I suppose it's much quieter over there,' observed Ellie. 'On this side you've got shoppers coming and going all the time.'

'I suppose so,' said Daphne, unlocking her car. 'You need to be a policeman's wife to think of things like that, though.'

'Do you? How disappointing. I thought I'd worked it out all by myself with my little woman's mind,' said Ellie rather more acidly than she'd intended. 'Next Monday then?'

'I'll look forward to it,' said Daphne, getting into her car. She closed the door and wound down the window.

'Look,' she said, 'it *is* your turn and I really don't mind the Market Caff.'

But Ellie laughed and said, 'No, the Chantry's fine. And if the brat's going to make a habit of smashing her way into other people's food, it's as well to keep her out of range of hot meat pies. Ciao!'

She watched as the Polo moved away. Daphne was a neat, confident driver.

And then she set about the complicated business of persuading Rose, who now that she was deprived of her audience of admirers was showing signs of recalcitrance, to let herself be fastened into the baby seat in the rear of the Mini.

She was still, or rather again, recalcitrant at eleven o'clock that night. Her distant protests were making Pascoe uneasy but Ellie whose ear was now finely tuned to Rose's various wavelengths diagnosed prima donna bloodymindedness and made him sit still and enjoy his coffee.

They'd eaten late. Pascoe had been delayed by the news of another robbery. A local family returning from holiday to their small country house had discovered that despite police-approved locks and burglar alarms, they had been burgled. There had been much indignation. Fortunately there was none waiting for him at home. Cold beef, an Italian salad and a bottle of Soave had not been spoilt by his lateness. Indeed it was the kind of meal which gained something from being consumed with the mild summer evening darkening outside the open french window. Ellie described her day in the kind of detail she tended to despise in other at-home mothers. But stories about her Rosie really *were* amusing, she assured herself only half ironically

'And did they charge you for the cream horn?' enquired Pascoe.

'I've no idea. Daphne picked up the tab.'

'Good. You stick to paying in the Market Caff. Let the idle rich cough up in the Chantry!'

'I don't think she's all that rich,' protested Ellie.

'Oh?' said Pascoe. 'Didn't you say her pa was loaded down with ecclesiastical gold, or something?'

Ellie poured more coffee and said, 'It was marital rather than ecclesiastical gold, I gather. Presumably Daphne got what was left over from the deserving poor after Pa's accident, but élitist expenses like school fees, not to mention the upkeep of that mansion, must all eat away at capital, I suppose. Though I presume Aldermann gets a pretty hefty wage packet.'

'Probably. On the other hand he seems to have had a pretty chequered career. There must have been times when he was living largely off capital.'

'Daphne didn't say much about his career,' said Ellie. 'But once the tearful moment was passed, courtesy of the brat, we swapped courtship stories quite happily.'

'Swapped?' said Pascoe, raising his eyebrows.

'Oh yes. In full frontal detail, naturally. Our Patrick was articled to a firm of accountants in Harrogate who looked after a couple of her father's church accounts. She'd popped in during her lunch-hour to pick up something for her pa and Patrick was the only person there. They chatted, lunched together, and it went on from there.'

'Her lunch-hour, you said? What was her job?'

'No job,' grinned Ellie. 'She was still at school. Sweet seventeen. Swish private school, of course, none of your common or garden comprehensives for Archdeacon Somerton's only daughter. All went fairly smoothly for a while. Why shouldn't it? She'd had other boyfriends. But things turned sour six months later on her eighteenth birthday when she announced she and Patrick were engaged to be married. There was opposition from Pa, more to the idea of an early marriage than to Patrick himself, I gather. But various elderly female relatives seem to have got in on the act. Of course, being eighteen, she was theoretically entitled to make her own decisions but you know how nasty things can be made for a kid that age. Then her father died. She obviously still feels guilty that they were at odds when he died. I think she always will.'

'But it didn't stop her marrying Patrick,' said Pascoe. 'This archdeacon – Somerton, did you say? – what did he die of?'

'The church killed him,' said Ellie dramatically.

'Overwork, you mean?'

'No. A coping stone fell off the belfry of St Mark's at Little Leven while he was inspecting it. It cracked his skull.'

Pascoe let out a long whistle.

'That's what I thought. Awful, but ironic,' said Ellie.

'I was thinking, fortuitous.'

'For Daphne, you mean? Come on!' protested Ellie.

'I meant for Patrick. People do seem to have a habit of shuffling off at his convenience, don't they? Come to think of it, this is the second one you've drawn my attention to. You're working well!'

'Now look!' protested Ellie. 'I just thought I was having a nice gossip about a friend, which as everyone knows is what friends are for, and no harm done. You said you thought all this business was a lot of nonsense, didn't you?'

'I did, and I do,' assured Pascoe. 'But you mean if you thought that anything you told me might help prove that someone – Aldermann, say – was a murderer, you wouldn't tell me?'

Ellie considered this.

'No,' she said doubtfully. 'But . . . well, it makes me feel like a grass. What's worse, I don't even get paid!'

Suddenly Rose, whose protest had diminished to a somnolent mumbling, let out a high C followed by a cascade of sobs.

'Oh dear,' said Ellie. 'Now she really is unhappy.'

'Shall I go?' said Pascoe.

'No. Pour us a drink. I'll see to her. She's probably just mucked up another nappy.'

She left the room. Pascoe rose and poured two glasses of brandy. He took his to the open french window and looked out into his garden. No Rosemont, this, but a plot of well-clovered lawn, bordered with thripped and black-spotted roses and bounded by a sturdy beech hedge beyond which rolled open fields. When they bought the house, its situation had been nicely democratic, mid-way between the town and Ellie's college.

Now the college's pleasant rural site was closing and when (or if) Ellie returned in September, it would be to a hideous midtown building which she asserted made the police station look like the Yorkshire Hilton. Recently Pascoe had been wondering if it might not be sensible to look for a house in town too. It would save the time and expense of travel and be better for all the services necessary to a young man with a growing family.

But on evenings like this, with the air balmy and a broad-faced moon peering down from a still pale sky, he could imagine nowhere better. No, he didn't really want to live closer to his work. It was bad enough not being able to get it out of his mind without being within dropinnable distance of the station. Even here and now, brandy in hand and beauty in view, he found his mind idly playing with the circumstances of the Reverend Somerton's tragic death. A stone from a tower. Like the hammer of God! It would all be fully documented in the coroner's records, of course. And there couldn't have been anything suspicious . . .

Ellie returned, nursing a still sobbing baby.

'There, there,' she said. 'She's not wet. She seemed a bit frightened. Perhaps she had a bad dream.'

'A bad dream! What on earth can she have to dream about at her age?' laughed Pascoe. 'Here, give her to me.'

He took the child and rocked her in his arms. The sobs continued.

'Perhaps you really have been dreaming,' he said. 'Here, I feel a quote coming on. "A" level English, selections from Coleridge. He was always going on about his son. *And once, when he awoke in most distressed mood* – that doesn't scan, does it? Then something about *an inner pain having made up that strange thing, an infant's dream*. He was right, wasn't he? What a strange thing an infant's dream must be. If only you could tell us about it, Rosie.'

'More to the point, what did Coleridge do about it?'

Pascoe grinned and stepped out of the french window and raised his daughter skywards.

'Peter! What on earth are you doing?' cried Ellie in alarm.

'What Coleridge did. Showing her the moon.'

'He should have been locked up! And you too. She'll catch her death. Give her here.'

'No. Wait,' said Pascoe. 'Listen.'

And as they listened the baby's sobs began to change in key from minor to major till they were unmistakably gurgles of delight and she waved her small fists high towards the hanging moon.

'Eat your heart out, Dr Spock,' said Pascoe. 'Me and Coleridge, we've got it made.'

And Ellie, standing at the open window watching and listening to her daughter's and husband's delight, suddenly found herself wondering why she should feel it as pain.

11

DESPERADO

*(Bush. Vigorous, yellow flower shading to pink,
ample foliage, scent faint.)*

From the top floor of the car park, Shaheed Singh
had a splendid view over the city. The morning
sun etched in every detail and he amused himself
by picking out familiar landmarks from this unfamiliar viewpoint.

Not in fact that it was totally unfamiliar. The
city's main bus station lay at the foot of the multi-
storey. From it a pedestrian underpass ran beneath
the busy ring road to the town centre, on the fringe
of which stood the comprehensive where Singh
had been educated. Sometimes for a change he and
his mates had eschewed the underpass and ridden
the elevators to this top level, walked thence across
the bridge to the shopping precinct roof-top car
park and descended into one of the big stores.
There had of course been delays for skylarking,
rarely anything more serious than leaning over

the bridge parapet and gobbing spit balls on to the cars far below, though occasionally a breakaway group had headed for Woolworths for a spot of shoplifting. Usually Singh had opted out of this, not so much on moral grounds as because, in a city which didn't have a huge Asian community, he always felt he was the one likely to be spotted and remembered.

When he'd joined the police cadets he'd felt at first that this quality of easy distinction might work to his advantage, but he'd soon changed his mind. The instinctive prejudice and the sheer bloody ignorance he'd encountered had shaken him deeply. On several occasions only his deep-rooted stubbornness had kept him going, the same stubbornness which had resisted all his father's attempts to persuade him to work in the family business. Now it had become focused on Sergeant Wield. The CID were an enviable elite. The unspeakable Dalziel and the high-flying Pascoe were probably hardly aware of his existence. But Wield was, and Wield obviously rated him as useless. His coldly scornful attitude when he took him along to Rosemont, and indeed on every occasion that they met, made this quite clear. To make Wield admit he was wrong had become the boy's main ambition.

And this was why he was here now when he should have been with PC Wedderburn learning the arts of traffic control. The good-natured Wedderburn had readily let him beg off for fifteen

127

minutes on personal grounds, but the fifteen minutes were already up and his clever idea had come to nothing. There'd been a couple of kids who'd got out of the lift five minutes before, but they hadn't dallied as they made their way across the bridge to the precinct roof-top car park which already looked half full. The multi-storey on the other hand filled from the bottom up and on the top floor there were still only about ten cars parked.

Singh glanced at his watch. He was late already. He was going to have to salve PC Wedderburn's ire with gallons of tea and acres of bacon butties. So much for self-promotion to the CID.

At this moment the lift doors clanged open and debouched five youths in a cacophony of laughter and football supporters' cries. Singh had plenty of time to recognize two of them as old schoolmates of his, now on the dole, before they spotted him. One of them was a slight thin-faced lad called Mick Feaver, whose uncertainty of demeanour always gave him a not altogether false look of slyness. He had been something of a butt at school and tended to tag along with Jonty Marsh for protection. Marsh was even smaller than Mick Feaver but he had all the swagger of a banty-cock. He was a bold and lively extrovert, always the leader in any chosen activity and with a considerable contempt for the law. So far, he had narrowly avoided serious trouble himself, but took pleasure in boasting how others of his family, notably his elder brother, Arthur, had done time. Typically it was Marsh who spotted Singh first and, equally typically, his reaction was direct and uncomplicated.

'Hey, there's old Shady!' he cried.

He walked up to Singh, with Mick Feaver in his usual pet-dog position a couple of feet behind. The other three, whom Singh only knew by sight, hung a little further back, regarding him suspiciously.

'What're you doing here, Shady?' said Marsh. 'What's going off?'

Singh nodded a greeting and said tersely. 'Stake out.'

Marsh let out a huge bellow of laughter.

'What're you staking out then, Shady?' he demanded.

Singh mixed truth with fiction and replied. 'There's been some mucking about with cars up here, so CID have put a watch on every morning.'

'But you're not CID,' protested Marsh, who was no fool. 'And it's a daft spot to be standing if you're supposed to be out of sight!'

Shaheed Singh smiled, he hoped inscrutably, and improvised wildly.

'Of course I'm not CID, you daft bugger!' he said in a friendlier voice. 'I'm just along with them as part of my training. When we saw you lot in the lift, I said I knew you and Mick, so they told me to have a word with you. Saves them breaking cover.'

Marsh looked doubtful but Mick Feaver clearly swallowed this farrago of nonsense completely and stared around in anxious search of the hidden watchers while the other three, now within ear-shot, shifted uneasily and muttered among themselves.

Singh, all too familiar with the symptoms of teenage guilt, exulted behind his superior smile. He'd guessed right! It had been this lot, or some of them at least. The seeds of the idea had been sown when he'd had that embarrassing encounter with his old schoolmates outside the Job Centre. And it had paid off!

Then suddenly his triumph faded and he felt properly like a policeman for the very first time, as for the very first time he experienced the tension between the private man and the public servant, between the past and the present. It would be great to make his first nick, but it would be an agony he wasn't yet prepared for to make it at the expense of Jonty and Mick.

Why was he doing this anyway? It wasn't as if the vandalization had been the crime of the century! The truth was he just wanted to impress Sergeant Wield. And Sergeant Wield, he'd worked out, wasn't interested in kids scratching cars, but in Mrs Aldermann herself.

He thought he saw a way of side-stepping his problem without too much conscience-bending.

'Do you come this way every morning?' he asked.

'Nah,' said Marsh vigorously. 'We don't go into the centre every morning. Anyway usually we use the underpass, isn't that right, lads?'

The others, now hunched up close, chorused their agreement.

'Thing is,' said Singh, becoming confidential, 'CID's not really interested in whoever scratched them cars last Monday. In fact, whoever scratched them might've done us a favour. It's a car-stealing ring they're after. One of the cars they're interested in got its paintwork done over that morning. It was a VW Polo, light green. Likely there was a woman driving. Now, you didn't happen to notice that car up here last Monday, did you?'

If they'd simply denied being up on the top storey any time the previous week, Singh would have been happy to let it rest there, and to hell with his certainty that they were responsible. But they hesitated, and looked at each other, and Singh, now well worked into his role, said in a bored voice, 'Look, if you did see owt, lads, it could be helpful. Like, what time the car was here? Did you see the driver? What was she wearing? Was she carrying anything? Which way did she go? You scratch our backs, we'll scratch yours.'

He felt at the same time proud and ashamed of his performance. When it won a prize, he was amazed.

Mick Feaver said, 'Yeah, we did see her. I mean, I think I saw her.'

He looked around at the others apologetically, offering them the path of non-involvement by his correction. But the bait of police favours and the natural human instinct to seek star-witness status combined to make his friends resent rather than be grateful for his attempt to exclude them. Rapidly progressing from a trickle to a torrent, the information came.

'Yeah, a green Polo. Nice little car.'

'About ten past nine. We were just going by when it parked.'

'Tall blonde bit. Middle-aged. Big teeth.'

'No, she was better than that. Quite tasty really.'

'You like 'em old, don't you? I've seen you looking at his mam!'

'My mam's not old. Not *that* old.'

'She was about thirty, this tart. She was smart. Not *with it* smart, but smart like the nobs are smart.'

'That's right. She looked a right stuck-up cow.'

'She had a little handbag. Nothing else.'

'We thought there was something funny when she got in the other car.'

'Not *funny*. We thought she was going for a bit of umpty.'

'Yeah, wham! bang! on the back seat. She didn't look like a crook.'

'What do you think a crook looks like, you silly bugger!'

Here the torrent was interrupted by an energetic scuffle.

Singh said, 'You mean she got into another car?'

'That's right,' said Jonty, as eager as any of the

others to be a star-witness. 'She parked next to it and got out of hers and straight into his.'

'His? You saw the driver?'

'Not really. There was tinted windows. I hadn't even noticed him sitting at the wheel till she got in and he drove off right away.'

'Right away?'

'That's right. He must have started the engine soon as he saw her.'

'What kind of car was it?'

'Audi.'

'Volvo.'

'No, it wasn't a Volvo, they have their lights on all the time.'

'It was a BMW 528i.'

The speaker was Mick Feaver, and he spoke with a note of authority so authentic that no one challenged him with further alternatives.

'You didn't get the number, did you?' said Singh hopefully.

They shook their heads, except Mick Feaver who tentatively suggested an X registration with a 9 before it.

Now Singh really did feel triumphant. This was something to toss casually before Sergeant Wield. He racked his brains in search of any other information he might possibly squeeze out of these eager witnesses. It struck him that this gang were not likely to have been inconspicuous, yet Mrs Aldermann had denied seeing anyone suspicious. That could be very significant.

'Did *she* see *you*?' he asked.

'Probably. She drove right by us,' said Jonty.

'Yeah. And you were playing the fool,' guffawed one of the others.

'What did you do?' asked Singh.

For answer, Marsh made an obscene gesture with his right forearm and clenched fist.

'Well, I thought she was off on the job,' he explained. 'Randy old cow!'

And that was how it had started, thought Singh with a sudden flash of insight. Perhaps the first intention had been to write something rude on the dust on the Polo, but its shining bright paintwork hadn't provided the looked-for slate. So the knife had come out and, once started, the enthusiasm had spread. But he didn't want to know about that.

'Thanks a lot, lads,' he said, glancing at his watch and working out that PC Wedderburn would now be in the Market Caff, probably starting on his second cup of tea and growing steadily more furious. 'I'll pass this on. It could be very helpful. See you around.'

'Yeah. Right. Sure. Great. See you.'

Dismissed, the youngsters walked out away towards the bridge leading to the shoppers' car park. They had emerged from the lift as criminal suspects. They were now moving on as police witnesses. Singh dimly apprehended that it was an evolutionary process he might become very familiar with in his police career.

But his mind was more concerned with the immediate future, balancing Wedderburn's certain wrath against Wield's notional admiration, as he entered the lift and stabbed at the button to take him down.

12
EVENSONG

*(Bush. Vigorous, upright, deep salmon-pink blooms,
little fading, profuse in summer and autumn,
straight firm stems, strong sweet scent.)*

Peter Pascoe was finding himself becoming fascinated by the Aldermann case. Not that there was a case, and not that he intended letting the fascination develop into an obsession. But somehow the personality of this quiet self-contained man, whom he had only met in passing and who had given him a rose, teased his imagination like a half-remembered melody.

The whole business was of course just plain daft. Sex, booze and the strain of executive decision-making had curdled Dandy Dick's mind. It was an occupational hazard of working under pressure. He should know. As well as this increasingly irritating rash of burglaries, the CID case-load at the moment included three alleged rapes, two suspected arsons, and any number of undisputed robberies, assaults, muggings, frauds and minor offences. Yes, indeed, he should know all about the mind-curdling properties of overwork. He could even recognize the symptoms. They included picking up the telephone half way through the morning, with the self-justification that this was his coffee break, and dialling his opposite number at Harrogate.

Relationships with Harrogate CID had been a little strained for a while after a Mid-Yorkshire Investigation into a blue films racket had led to the trial and imprisonment of a Harrogate detective. But things had settled down now, due largely to Pascoe's assiduity in mending fences and despite Dalziel's slightly less conciliatory attitude of *Sod 'em They're likely all as bent as lavatory brushes*!

'Ivan? Hi! It's Peter Pascoe. How's it going?'

'All the better for the old man being away at this Modern Policing Conference!' replied Detective-Inspector Ivan Skelwith. 'I dare say you're missing Fat Andy too. It's funny, I was just thinking of giving you a ring. Those housebreakers of yours seem to have strayed on to my patch. Some people got back from holiday yesterday evening and found they'd been done. From what the computer chucks up, it sounds like the same lot.'

'Does it now?' said Pascoe, suddenly scenting a self-justifying opening. 'Why don't I drive over and have a look?'

'Time hanging heavy on your hands, is it? All right. When?'

'This afternoon?'

'Christ, you don't hang about! All right. Come before three. That OK? By the way, what was it *you* were ringing about?'

Pascoe said hesitantly, 'Nothing really. There's a firm of accountants on your patch called Bailey and Capstick. They had a man called Aldermann working for them up until seven or eight years ago. He may have left under some kind of cloud. I just wondered if anything was known.'

'I'll sniff around for you,' said Skelwith. 'Anything I should know about?'

'The faintest smell and you'll be the first to know,' promised Pascoe.

'Fair enough. Till three then.'

Ivan Skelwith was a dark and dapper Lancastrian who claimed to have joined a Yorkshire force because their mean measuring tapes enabled him to scrape in at the minimum height requirement. He greeted Pascoe with pleasure and a cup of tea and some biscuits, which helped make up for the lunch Pascoe had skipped to propitiate his conscience in wasting more time on Aldermann.

They spent the next hour at the burgled house where the m.o. and attendant circumstances seemed exactly the same as Pascoe's burglaries, right down to the angry householders who as usual were threatening to sue the company who'd sold them their alarm system. The thieves had neutralized this with an expertise which spoke of careful planning. The only unusual feature was that some virginia creeper which covered the wall on which the external alarm bell was set had been torn away and some plants in the flowerbed immediately below were badly crushed, as if someone or something had fallen on them. There were no helpful footprints or anything of that kind but at least it narrowed the limits within which the break-in must have occurred, for though the damage was not apparent to the casual glance, the owner's one-morning-a-week gardener was able to confirm that the border was untouched when he last called the previous Friday.

'So. A weekend job. Does that help?'

'Not bloody much,' said Skelwith.

Back in his office, they had another cup of tea accompanied this time by jam doughnuts.

Skelwith watched Pascoe devour his enthusiastically and said, 'That's the trouble with marriage. It's all instant sex and gourmet cooking till the kids start coming, then it's do-it-yourself or do without.'

'You look well enough on it,' said Pascoe. 'Four, isn't it? How's that long-suffering wife of yours?'

'Five next January, and she's fine. Now, about that firm of accountants, it's Bailey, Capstick, Lewis and Grey, by the way, only Bailey's been dead twenty years and Capstick retired the year before last. It might have been Lewis and Aldermann, I gather. Their Mr Grey was taken on to replace your Mr Aldermann six years ago and has already attained to a partnership. Mr Aldermann, however, blotted his copybook in some undisclosed way and was lucky merely to lose his job, at least so my informant assures me.'

'Your informant being . . . ?' enquired Pascoe.

'Our Sergeant Derby. You might've noticed him on the desk. Rumour has it he was here before they found the spa. He certainly knows something about everything in this town.'

'Very useful,' said Pascoe. 'He didn't give any details, I suppose?'

'I'm afraid not. They tend to keep a well-buttoned lip, these accountants, especially when there's been a bit of naughtiness in the double entry. But Derby reckons your best bet is to steer clear of the active part of the firm and go for old Capstick. First, he was absolute master of the business when Aldermann got the push. Secondly, he himself was eased out last year, having reached seventy and suffering badly from gout. He did not take kindly to being "cut off in his prime by striplings." The quotation is, according to Sergeant Derby, from the speech Capstick made at his farewell dinner. Derby does funny voices too.'

'What a splendid man he sounds,' said Pascoe. 'I'm certain he'll have got me an address too.'

'Naturally,' smiled Skelwith. 'Capstick's got this old house out in the sticks where he's kept in his place by a ferocious old housekeeper, it seems.

Those who rescue him either by visiting, or better still by removing him, are rewarded with long and often scandalous reminiscences of Harrogate social life over the past half-century. And your luck's holding, as usual, Peter. It's on your way home. The address is Church House, Little Leven.'

Herbert Capstick had been rendered symmetrical by age. The shock of white hair which crowned his head was exactly matched in shade by the swirl of white bandage which swathed his foot. In between, a thin but not emaciated body, clad only in a cotton singlet and a pair of old-fashioned, pocketed rugby shorts, reclined in a huge, deep, upholstered wheelchair at the open door of a jungle-like conservatory.

The old woman who had escorted Pascoe through the house frowned disapprovingly at Capstick and withdrew. She hadn't spoken more than two words, listening to Pascoe's request for an interview in silence, then leaving him standing on the doorstep while she vanished inside. On her return she had beckoned to him and led him through a gloomy drawing-room into the miasmic conservatory.

The ferocious housekeeper, guessed Pascoe.

Capstick said in a high, precise voice, 'Mrs Unger has all the merits of her class and situation. She distrusts equally sunshine and strangers. You would probably be more comfortable, Mr Pascoe, if you moved that chair outside and sat in the sun. I

141

should dearly love to join you but this is as far as I dare go without putting myself in the way of punitive reprisals such as lumpy custard and stewed greens. I hope you don't mind talking through the doorway. It should give something of the quality of the confessional to our exchanges, which in view of your profession may be not inappropriate. Which of my many embezzlements over the past sixty years do you wish to discuss, Inspector?'

Beneath the apparently uncombed or perhaps simply uncombable white hair, grey eyes rounded interrogatively in a wrinkled, leonine face, and full lips smiled.

Pascoe returned the smile, took a deep breath, and said. 'Not *your* embezzlements, Mr Capstick, but Patrick Aldermann's.'

'Ah,' said Capstick. 'Patrick. You have, of course, spoken with him about this matter?'

'No. I haven't as a matter of fact,' said Pascoe uncomfortably. 'I've only met him once, very briefly.'

'Yet to me, whom you have not met at all, you are quite willing to broach the subject openly, without preamble? Strange. Perhaps you have been preadvised of my frank, disingenuous nature, my upright character?'

'Perhaps,' said Pascoe.

'Or is it, perhaps, that you have been told that old Capstick is so tired of his own company out here in God's heart-land all day, not to mention a

142

touch of senile dementia, that he has started talking to the sparrows and may be easily persuaded to almost any verbal indiscretion?'

Pascoe took a chance and laughed.

'I see I have been misinformed,' he said. 'I'm sorry. I'm here quite unofficially, Mr Capstick. I can't even hint a threat that I may have to return some day officially. At the moment, though I can never be entirely off-duty, I am merely trying to satisfy my own curiosity. Shall I go on? Or shall I just go?'

Before Capstick could reply, Mrs Unger returned bearing a large tea-tray with folding legs. She stood in front of Pascoe and waited till, catching on belatedly, he unfolded the legs. She set the tray before him and left. It held, besides the teapot, milk jug, sugar bowl and two cups, a plateful of buttered scones.

'Mrs Unger has decided to approve you,' murmured Capstick. 'The buttered scones are the sign. Tea she would bring were my visitor Adolf Hitler. But buttered scones are a sign of special grace. She will be sorely distressed if you do not eat the buttered scones. On the other hand, I should warn you that you will be sorely distressed if you do. This is a dilemma. Such dilemmas cannot be unknown to you in your profession; moments when loyalty to those you work for clashes with loyalty to those you work with. You follow me, Pascoe?'

'I think so,' said Pascoe.

'I had one such moment some years ago with

Patrick Aldermann. I am not sure I may not be having just such another one now. Can you reassure me?'

Pascoe poured tea for both of them and said, 'I'm not sure I can. But what I *can* say is that the only reason on earth I would see for doing anything to harm Mr Aldermann would be if so doing might prevent harm to someone less able to defend himself. I'm sorry if that's not enough.'

He looked uneasily at the ill-omened scones. Then, seizing one boldly, he took a bite.

'Yes, I think that's quite enough, Mr Pascoe,' said Capstick. 'One bite will not harm you. If you care to take the rest and put them on the bird table in the middle of the lawn, we shall be entertained as we talk. The birds appear to be immune, I hasten to add.'

Pascoe took the scones to the bird table, not without an uneasy glance back to see if any curtains were twitching indignantly in the old house. But all seemed still. The well-tended lawn ran down to a thicket of flowering shrubs, including many richly-bloomed bush roses, bounded by a tall cypress hedge beyond which Pascoe could see the tower of the church which gave the house its name. Presumably it was St Mark's church and presumably that was the very tower from which the stone had fallen to crack open the Reverend Somerton's skull.

He returned to his chair by the open door. Without further preamble, the old man began to talk.

'Patrick Aldermann was articled with my firm in 1968 or it might have been 1969. He was not outstanding in accountancy terms, but he was quiet, respectful, attentive and once you got beneath the rather bland shell, interesting and likeable. At least I found him so. Also I had known his uncle, or rather his great-uncle, Edward Aldermann. He had also been an accountant and a very successful one. He made the money which reconstructed Rosemont where young Patrick now lives. He was a quiet man too, but very pleasant when you got to know him. His wife drove him, of course. She drove him to make more money and she drove him to buy that rambling place which was far too large for the two of them. Well, he had her there, of course. He rebuilt the house for her but he rebuilt the garden for himself, and it was big enough for him to hide in. Still, she got him in the end, they usually do. But when his heart gave out, he was in his garden, thank God, pruning his roses. So, by one of life's curious ironies, was she. Interesting, that. Perhaps his ghost appeared to her and frightened her to death! I've often speculated!

'Patrick, now, he loved to talk, and listen to me talking, about old Eddie. It was funny. I don't suppose he'd met him more than a dozen times and then only on short visits. But he loved the old boy as if he'd been his own father. You know he changed his name, of course? He was articled with us when he attained his majority and it was almost

145

the first thing he did. I am no longer Highsmith, he announced. The name is Aldermann. It was all legally done, deed-poll, the lot. Some people thought it odd, I found it rather touching. There are relationships of the spirit, don't you think, as real as those of the blood. Certainly, however you explain it, young Patrick had inherited Eddie's love of gardens and his way with them, especially with roses. You know, I've got roses here planted by both the gardening Aldermanns. You see that *Mrs Sam McGredy* over there?'

Pascoe followed the pointing finger. It seemed to be aimed at a rather angular and emaciated bush which nevertheless had several rich coppery pink blooms glowing on it like gemstones on a dowager's neck.

'Eddie planted that there more than thirty years ago, and another half-dozen too, brought on from cuttings in his own garden. It's old now, far too old. Roses age too, Mr Pascoe, just like humans. It was old and weak a dozen years ago. I doubt if I ever tended them properly, I'm a looking gardener rather than a working one. Also I'm a sentimentalist. I don't much like pulling up things that have given me pleasure over such a long time. But when I showed them to young Patrick, he had no such inhibitions. A lot of these ought to go, he said. And go they did. He dug them out, then prepared the earth. I would have just bunged the new ones in the hole left when I dug out the old ones, but he dug and raked and added God knows what and left it to settle. The old must give way to the new, he said, but the new has to deserve it. And it did, wouldn't you agree? Look at those *Pascalis* and *Peer Gynts*, those *Ernest Morses* and *King's Ransoms*. There's consolation there for all life's failures, wouldn't you say?'

Again Pascoe looked. The names meant little to him but the rainbow of blooms round the margin of the garden certainly thrilled the eye. And behind it at the bottom, the dark, sharp-cut shape of the cypress hedge with the churchyard beyond. Suddenly he had a moment of strange empathy with the old man, sitting here gazing out on this last blaze of colour with the knowledge that it would fade, but the cypress would always be there, unchanging and waiting.

'But you kept one of the old roses?' he said 'Whose idea was that?'

'What? Oh, the Mrs Sam. Both of us, I think. There was no argument. My sentimentality and Patrick's . . . I don't know what. Reverence, perhaps? Eddie would have been amused, perhaps even embarrassed, by the status Patrick accorded him. I believe that's why the boy went in for accountancy, you know. He had no gift for it, no real talent. But he wanted to do what his great-uncle had done.'

Pascoe who had been glancing surreptitiously at his watch saw the opening and moved swiftly in.

'Was that the reason that he had to leave the firm? Inefficiency?'

Capstick smiled and shook his head.

'Oh no. He was never inefficient. He'd have done very well, been a partner now. No, Mr Pascoe. I will not, of course, repeat this before witnesses, but he proved to be dishonest.'

He pursed his full lips as though the word had a sour taste.

'It was totally unexpected,' he went on. 'He was doing well. He had married a charming young girl, they had a child, he gave the impression of being perfectly happy. My only slight concern for him was the upkeep of that huge house. The rates alone must have been crippling to a young man still on a modest salary. And he kept it and the gardens immaculately. I'd talked to him about it when he was living there alone, but he just smiled and changed the subject. At least now, with a wife and child, and perhaps more to come, the place would begin to fill up and serve its function. Also, of course, it seemed likely the girl would have a bit of money of her own and that would help keep them going till he reached his own full earning capacity. Look, there goes your tea!'

Startled, Pascoe looked round to see an undulation of birds, ranging from sparrows and tits to starlings and blackbirds, feeding off the buttered scones.

'Patrick made a good impression on clients too,' resumed the old man. 'That quiet, undemonstrative manner of his inspired confidence. He was managing various minor accounts more or less by

148

himself and a couple of our customers had asked specifically if he could deal with their business, which is always rather flattering. One of these was an old lady, Mrs McNeil, a widow who lived on a substantial pension and made a hobby out of worrying about the investment of her capital, and very tedious it was dealing with her constant demands to take her money out of *this* and put it into *that*, with none of it ever staying anywhere long enough for it to do much good. I pushed her off on to Patrick as often as I felt able and I was quite delighted when she asked if young Mr Aldermann could take over the account altogether.

'Well, I suppose I glanced over his shoulder a couple of times in the first eighteen months, then I glanced no more. Whenever I bumped into old Mrs McNeil, she sang his praises. Nothing was too much trouble for him, she said. Her investments had never been in such a healthy state. She bought Patrick birthday and Christmas presents, I recall, the kind of presents old ladies buy for young men, thick sweaters to protect him against the draughts in our chambers, and rubber galoshes to keep out the damp. It was quite an office joke. Then one day, ironically, because despite Mrs McNeil's best efforts he had caught the 'flu, he was not in the office when the old lady called. She was full of concern for Patrick and wondered whether she ought to call to see him. I shuddered at the thought of the poor boy lying defenceless in bed with Mrs McNeil trying to minister to him, and put her off mainly by the argument that she seemed to be full of cold herself and really ought not to risk aggravating young Mr Aldermann's condition. And to divert her further, I obtained her file from Patrick's office and began to discuss her investments with her, giving her the chance to sing Patrick's praises.

'Now as she talked and I looked, I began to sense there was something not quite right. Nothing specific, and nothing, I believed at that moment, very serious; the result probably of inexperience and being constantly badgered by Mrs McNeil. I had on occasion myself blinded her with science to give the impression I was doing the stupid thing she wanted me to do while in fact doing something else, or nothing at all. So after she'd gone, I went through the whole file very carefully with a view to doing Patrick a favour, nothing more.

'What I discovered devastated me. The whole thing was a charade. As he'd moved her monies hither and thither, he'd dropped off various amounts in the process, never very large individually, but over the three or four years he'd been managing the account amounting to about two-thirds of the whole. It was ingenious, but it was insane. Discovery was inevitable sooner or later. His only hope would have been if he'd had expectations of acquiring the money elsewhere and replacing it.'

Capstick paused and shook his old lion's head

gloomily. As if she had been waiting near by for such a hiatus in his speech, Mrs Unger appeared, nodded approvingly at the empty plate, and removed the tea-tray.

After she'd gone, Pascoe said to the old man, 'And what did you do when you realized what had been going on?'

Capstick sighed and said, 'For a couple of days, nothing. I wanted to think, and Patrick was on his sick bed, remember. But on the third day, having ascertained by telephone that he was out of bed, I went to see him. I put it to him bluntly that I knew he'd been embezzling Mrs McNeil's money. He offered neither denial nor excuse, but sat regarding me with that air of quiet, controlled interest I knew so well. I told him that the first step I proposed was to inform the client, Mrs McNeil, of what had taken place. I would also assure her that the firm would indemnify her against however much of the loss proved unrecoverable. And I would offer her my full co-operation in the event of a police investigation.'

'In the event of,' echoed Pascoe. 'So you had hopes it wouldn't come to that and you'd be able to protect the firm's name? Aldermann must have been relieved.'

'I doubt it, Mr Pascoe. I had no intention that my offer to indemnify Mrs McNeil should be seen as an inducement for her not to prosecute. I told Patrick that this interview with Mrs McNeil would take place, at my request, in the presence of her solicitor

151

and he alone would be responsible for advising her legally. Does that satisfy your doubts?'

'I'm sorry,' said Pascoe. 'I meant no disrespect. I just wanted things to be clear in my mind. So the solicitor's advice was not to prosecute?'

'I'm not certain what it would have been,' said Capstick. 'You see, it was never given. When I contacted Mrs McNeil, I discovered that her cold had matured into 'flu and she too was in bed. Again I waited at the convenience of a virus. This time the waiting was in vain.'

'What do you mean?'

'Patrick, in his mid-twenties, quickly recovered. But Mrs McNeil, who was almost eighty, didn't. She died, Mr Pascoe, she died.'

Pascoe sat back and composed his face into a blank screen across the thoughts running madly round his mind.

'Of 'flu, you mean? Did she go into hospital?'

'No. She died at home. It was quite unexpected, though not, I gather, very unusual in people of that age. Which is one of the reasons Mrs Unger is so solicitous to keep me out of these summer zephyrs which she interprets as Siberian draughts.'

'But Patrick Aldermann still wasn't prosecuted?' pursued Pascoe. 'I mean, I should have thought that whatever chance he had of Mrs McNeil letting him off the hook for old times' sake vanished when she died. The howl of defrauded legatees must have been audible throughout the country!'

'It proved not,' said Capstick. 'Yes, there were

several specific legacies, to old friends, servants, a couple of charities. There were no close relations, you see. There was plenty of money to pay all these. And the residue of the estate was willed wholly and without condition to Mr Patrick Aldermann of Rosemont. The only defrauded legatee was himself!'

'Well, well, well,' said Pascoe.

'Well, indeed,' said Capstick. 'I spoke to her solicitor, of course. He was a man I knew well and I wanted to put him in the picture before he noticed anything for himself, though whether he would have done or not, I have never been sure. We thought long and hard. In the end, there seemed to be no point in instigating an official investigation.'

No, there wouldn't, thought Pascoe, but this time kept his mouth shut.

'I had been over the rest of Patrick's work with a fine-tooth comb and everything was in order. I had one last interview with him. I told him I expected his resignation on my desk the following day. It was. I also told him that it was my hope and intention that I should never see him again. I haven't. But often as I sit here in the summer and look at those exquisite colours out there in the garden, I regret it. It was the right decision, but I regret it. Those of my contemporaries I haven't outlived are as immobile as I am, Mr Pascoe. Acquaintances of younger generations pay the occasional duty visit and begin to glance at their watches while the sun is still high. But Patrick, I think, would have visited me and complained about my neglect of his roses, and taken tea and sat quietly here till the sun went down.'

He stopped talking and his head dropped slowly on to his chest as if he slept. But when Pascoe shifted his chair cautiously, preparatory to rising from it, Capstick looked up immediately and smiled.

'Off now, are you?' he said.

'Yes. I'm sorry, but I've really got to go.'

'Of course you have. Crime waits for no man, I dare say. Did I help you at all?'

'A great deal, I think,' said Pascoe cautiously.

'And did I hurt Patrick?' he asked sadly.

'I can't say, Mr Capstick,' said Pascoe. 'It's a complicated business.'

He stood up and took a last look down the garden. In the still air it seemed that he heard young voices singing.

'Evensong and choir practice,' said Capstick, catching the cock of his ear. 'I did not realize it was so late. Old people never do, Mr Pascoe. I hope I have not spoiled your dinner.'

'Of course not. And likewise,' said Pascoe. 'Is that the church where Mr Aldermann's father-in-law was killed?'

'Patrick's? Yes, it was. Tragic accident.'

'Were you here when it happened?'

'No, I wasn't, as a matter of fact. It was a Saturday. I was away for the weekend. But I recall the whole village was a-buzz with it when I got back.'

'Ah,' said Pascoe, not knowing if he were disappointed or not.

'He was a decent chap, Somerton,' said Capstick. 'A bit serious, perhaps, but decent.'

'You knew him? Of course, your firm looked after some church accounts.'

'You're well informed,' said Capstick. 'But not just the church accounts. We looked after Somerton's own money. A tidy sum, fifty thousand or thereabouts. That's why I thought Daphne would have been able to bolster young Patrick's finances, but clearly I was wrong.'

'You mean the Reverend Somerton's personal account was dealt with by your firm?' said Pascoe, wanting to get this clear.

'Yes. What of it?'

'Nothing,' he said, smiling. 'Just constabulary curiosity.'

But as he shook hands and took his leave, he thought of Patrick Aldermann lunching with the pretty young schoolgirl who'd come into the office on church business, and then later in the day finding an excuse to open her father's file and seeing to his delight and speculation how much he was worth.

With such dark thoughts in his mind he drove back to the station, where he was mildly surprised to find Sergeant Wield waiting for him in the company of Police Cadet Shaheed Singh.

They came together into his office, Wield as implacably and impassively ugly as ever, and Singh with his dark, handsome face uncertain whether his presence was required for praise or for punishment.

'I think you should hear what Cadet Singh's been up to, sir,' said Wield.

Pascoe heard.

'Well, well, well,' he said.

13
MASQUERADE

(Floribunda. Very vigorous, free flowering, rather raggedy blooms changing from yellow to pink to red.)

Andrew Dalziel was bored. His personal opinion was that if God had wanted policemen to attend conferences, he'd have fitted chairs on their backsides, and probably tongues as well.

Saturday, the opening day of the Conference, had been all right. There'd been old friends to greet, stories to exchange, drinks to be drunk. But after a Sabbath full of lectures and seminars, Dalziel was ready to join the Lord's Day Observance Society.

On Monday morning he had set out early from his hotel with a tattered old A-Z street map and found his way to Denbigh Square. He'd noted down Penelope Highsmith's address from Pascoe's file, not with any firm intention of doing anything about it, but more intuitively, in case he should feel like doing anything about it. Woodfall House proved to be a tall old building within hearing distance of Victoria Station. He studied the names under the glass panel on the portico, then turned away and headed for the Yard.

He was late, winning a couple of reproving glances. Lunch-time saw him back in Denbigh Square, but the entrance to Woodfall House only opened once and that was to admit an old man with a dog.

The reproving glances were black looks when he returned late for the afternoon session.

An address on policing racially mixed communities given by a black Captain from Miami was followed by an open discussion. Dalziel joined in vigorously, doubting whether the American experience had much relevance in the UK.

'Over here,' he said, 'we're told that what we need is more blacks in the police force. Now, mebbe that's right for us, I don't know. But if it is, we'll have to use 'em differently from you lot, won't we? I mean, your police forces seem to be jammed full of blacks from what I see on the telly, but you still leave us standing for racial violence!'

There were chuckles from the groundlings, glowers from the brass. The American said, 'Excuse me, sir, but do you have much experience of racial tension in your particular area?'

'Only when there's a London team visiting,' said Dalziel. The chucklers laughed and the glowerers mouthed his name to each other and made notes.

As soon as the session finished, Dalziel was off before he could be caught. This time he was in luck. As he arrived in Denbigh Square, a taxi pulled up outside Woodfall House and a woman got out. Dalziel recognized her instantly. Mentally he'd been adding a decade and a half to his remembered image, but this tall elegant woman in clinging cords and a light cotton jacket seemed hardly to have changed at all. Even her irrepressibly curly hair was as richly black as ever. She chatted pleasantly with the taxi-driver as she paid him, then ran lightly up the steps.

Dalziel strolled slowly by, paused as though his attention had been caught by something and looked uncertainly at the woman unlocking the street door. She, attracted by his still presence, returned his gaze queryingly.

'Penny?' said Dalziel. 'It's never Penny Highsmith is it?'

'That's right,' said the woman. 'Who the hell are you?'

'Andy Dalziel,' he said. 'You probably don't recall. When you were living up in Yorkshire, you used to come down to the rugby club some Saturday nights. Andy Dalziel. We met at the rugby club.'

'Andy Dalziel? Oh God, I remember! You were a copper, weren't you? Andy Dalziel! Crikey, you've put on a bit of weight.'

'Just a bit,' said Dalziel advancing up the steps, smiling. 'You've hardly changed a bit, though.

Soon as I saw you I thought, that's Penny Highsmith or her double. How're you doing?'

He extended his hand. She took it uncertainly and he shook hers energetically.

'Well, well,' he said. 'It's a small world. A small world.'

'Yes,' she said. 'I suppose it is.'

She stood with the key in the door, but she showed no inclination to invite him in. He remembered her as a generous, easy-going woman, but life in London was enough to rub the fine edge off anyone's sense of hospitality.

'I'm down here for a conference at the Yard,' he explained.

'The Yard?'

'Scotland Yard.'

'Oh, you're still a copper then. I thought they all retired at forty.'

'Not quite,' he said. 'And you. What're you doing?'

'Oh, this and that,' she said vaguely.

'Grand,' he beamed. 'Well, I'll tell 'em all at the club I saw you. I'd best be off. I'm just on my way back to my hotel. Usually there's a pot of tea going about now. Cheerioh then.'

He shook her hand again and turned away. If she didn't call him back by the third step, he'd have to think again.

It was on the fourth step that she said, 'Look, if you've got a moment, why not come up and have a cuppa with me?'

'Now that's nice of you,' he said, turning. 'As long as it's no bother. That would be really nice.'

The flat was comfortable without being luxurious, the flat of an active woman who expected to spend more time out of it than in.

Dalziel relaxed in a deep armchair and watched Penny Highsmith bustling around making the tea. Minus her jacket, her generous figure showed to even greater advantage beneath a translucent silk blouse with a high collar which concealed any giveaway wrinkling of the neck. Certainly there was precious little else which put her in her mid-fifties rather than early forties. It wasn't fair, thought Dalziel. Men were supposed to age gracefully, but the same years which had merely rounded Penny's bust had positively billowed his belly.

Still, he wasn't here to seduce her, though once upon a time, once upon a time . . .

There'd been a dance in the clubhouse. It had been the usual thrash with the beer as important as the dancing. He'd hardly moved away from the bar except to go to the Gents. It was as he returned from such a visit that he ran into Penny Highsmith coming out of the Ladies. Distantly a smoochy slow waltz had begun to play. He had danced her along the corridor, then through the door which led to the changing-rooms. There in the darkness in an atmosphere laced with the perfume of liniment and sweat they had embraced passionately and there had been little resistance to his investigating fumbles, till all at once a cry went up outside, 'Andy! Andy Dalziel. Where the hell is he? Andy! They want you back at the cop-shop, chop-chop!' He'd been willing to go on, but Penny had whispered, 'No, they'll be coming in here next. Later. There'll be another time.'

There never had been. The demands of his job had not only destroyed his marriage, he thought bitterly; they had destroyed a lot of his chances of a bit on the side too.

'Here. You once nearly screwed me in the changing-room, didn't you?'

Her voice, intersecting so neatly with his thoughts, made him start guiltily as though he'd been thinking aloud.

She put a tray down before him and sat on a low pouffé beside his chair.

'Sorry. Did I shock you?' she said. 'I didn't know you could shock cops.'

She grinned at him. The grin brought her back completely as she'd been then. Lively, easy-going but with a mind of her own, capable, independent, pleasure-loving, undemanding herself and refusing to be tied down by others. And very, very attractive.

'Not shocked,' he said. 'Just regretful. By God, you've weathered well, Penny Highsmith!'

'You've filled out,' she said. 'And the booze and the late nights have left a few high-tide marks I can see. But you still look basically the same, Andy Dalziel. Hard, fast, and brutish!'

She laughed to take the sting out of her comment. Dalziel laughed too. He felt it as a compliment.

'You went away,' he said. 'One moment there, next gone.'

'It wasn't quite as quick as that,' she said. 'I was always going to go. Yorkshire was all right, but I missed being down here. I only went up for a few weeks to look after my Aunt Florence in the first place. Then she died and I got the house and the money. Well, I got it eventually. And by the time all that was settled, my boy was at school. He liked it there. I suppose we'd led a rather unsettling life before that. Anyway it seemed a shame to disturb him, so I settled down to it for a few years. But a few years was more than enough, begging your pardon. Help yourself to tea. I'm not very domesticated, I'm afraid.'

Dalziel obeyed, restricting himself to his dietary two heaped spoonfuls of sugar.

'You never married then?' he said.

'No. Why should I?'

'Good-looking lass like you, you must've had offers,' he said.

'Oh, yes.' She grinned. 'When you stop getting offers you know the auction's ended. Then it's going, going, gone! No, I always liked my independence. Most people do, you know, only they're not certain they can manage it. I was lucky that way. I had Patrick young and I brought him up by myself, so I learned all about being independent. It was hard at times, but it was a lesson worth learning.'

'Patrick. That's your boy?' said Dalziel, sipping his tea.

'Boy! He's been fully grown longer than I care to think.'

'Still living up our way, is he? Or did he move too?'

'No, he's still in the old house,' said Penny. 'He's really crazy about that place, always has been. I think it'd take dynamite to shift him.'

'Do you get up there to see him at all?'

'Not much,' said Penny. She eyed him shrewdly and added, 'Why so interested?'

Dalziel usually preferred frontal attack to creeping about the bushes but he sensed that he was going to do more good by stealth here than by confrontation.

He winked lecherously and said, 'Just wondering if you'd fancy a sentimental rendezvous in yon changing-room, that's all.'

She let out a good honest laugh. That was another thing he'd liked about her. She wasn't one of your parakeet screechers.

'No,' she resumed. 'I'm never up long enough for that. Just the odd weekend, see the kids. He's married now, Patrick. He married a vicar's daughter, ultra-respectable you see, to make up for his wicked old mama! She's a nice girl. I'm made very welcome, but a couple of nights is enough. I don't know how I stuck it in that great barn of a place for so long.'

'Is it that big?'

She considered.

'Not really, I suppose. Half a dozen bedrooms. Absurd for just two people, and it'd need quite a family to fill it. But there's nothing outside. Just that huge bloody garden. Garden! More like a park. And when you get out of that you're in fields and woods and things. It must be a good mile to the next house.'

'I'm surprised you didn't sell it,' said Dalziel, pouring himself more tea.

'Oh, I did. Well, nearly. I did the right thing, timed it nicely so that Patrick would have finished his "O" levels. That seemed a good time to make the break. He was talking about going into accountancy and it seemed to me he could carry on his studies as easily down here as up there. But it didn't work out.'

She glanced at her watch. Dalziel, untypically sensitive, weighed up the merits of carrying on now or trying to resume later. The latter was a gamble. If she turned him down, it'd be difficult to resume this oblique interrogation here and now without looking very suspicious. On the other hand, the easing effect of a few drinks might work wonders. And he discovered in himself a genuine desire to see Penny Highsmith again at a personal level.

'I'm holding you back,' he said, levering himself

out of the chair. 'I was wondering if I could see you again. It'd be grand to have a proper crack, and besides, us country bumpkins need someone to show us round the bright lights and make sure we don't get ripped off.'

'Ripped off? *You*?' she mocked. 'It'd be like ripping off concrete paving!'

'I'm all soft underneath,' he grinned. 'Well?'

She hesitated.

'Look, I'm tied up tonight,' she said. 'In fact, I'm pretty busy all this week.'

Shit, he thought. I should've sat tight.

'But I can manage Friday if that's any good?'

He thought rapidly. This was the last night of the conference. There was a farewell banquet which meant lots of tedious speeches. The guest of honour was some superannuated judge talking about modern interpretations of the law. God, he'd wasted more time in his job listening to them boring old farts rambling on than he'd had hot dinners, and a combination of both didn't appeal.

'That'll be grand,' he said. 'Eight o'clock suit? Right. And why don't you book us in somewhere nice and cosy to eat to start with? If you leave it to me, you'll likely end up in a chippy!'

At the door he paused. One more question, perhaps his last. It'd be easy enough for her to change her mind on mature reflection and leave a message for him at the Yard, cancelling the date.

'You never said why you didn't sell that house,' he said. 'Couldn't you find a buyer?'

'No, it wasn't that. I found a buyer all right. It was all settled bar the exchange of contracts.'

'And?' prompted Dalziel.

'He died,' said Penelope Highsmith.

14
NEMESIS

(Dwarf pompom. Small flowers, purply-crimson with coppery shadings, clustered on strong young shoots.)

'We have to know their names,' said Wield.

Singh's face twisted into a dark mask of distress.

'But why?' he said. 'When I spoke to you yesterday, you didn't ask. And I told 'em it had nowt to do with scratching them cars.'

'It's an offence,' insisted Wield.

'I know it's an offence, but I thought you were just interested in her in the Polo, Mrs Aldermann.'

'It's not up to you to decide who we're interested in,' snapped Wield. 'You just administer the law, obey orders and keep your nose clean, that's what's up to you.'

Why does he hate me so much? wondered Singh unhappily. When he had confessed his bit of detection work the previous day, he thought there had been a flicker of approval or at least interest in the sergeant's eyes. But now there was nothing, just that intimidating indifference which could only be a cover for dislike.

Wield stared blankly at the youth and wished to hell that the interview were over. From the moment he first laid eyes on the boy, he'd resolved to have as little to do with him as possible. Normally it would have been a resolution easy to keep as cadets usually only made a superficial contact with CID work. But fate and Dalziel and Pascoe had decided otherwise. And the more he saw of Singh, the more his first response was confirmed. He loved him. No! His mind balked at the word. He was attracted, infatuated . . . he didn't know what he was. He only knew it was dangerous.

It was almost a year since the long affair which he'd begun to believe was permanent had come to an end. Separation had killed it, not for him but for his friend whose job had taken him a hundred miles away. Wield on his motor-bike had made light of the distance and his irregular and uncertain hours had seemed to justify that he was usually the one who made the journey. Later he had analysed that perhaps he had preferred to make the journey, perhaps even preferred that there was a journey to make, because it kept his job and life in such very distinct compartments. But the other man had needed proximity. The affair had withered and died.

There had been a period of reappraisal. Bitterness and self-disgust had brought him close to the point of throwing discretion to the winds and coming out into the open. But he had pulled up short, as always. The price of openness was his job. He knew all about his legal rights and all about modern liberated attitudes, but he also knew that as far as Mid-Yorkshire CID went, his career would be at an end. What else did he have at the moment? Nothing. He did his job, pursued his conventional social life such as it was, worked for his next police examination, watched television and sought imaginative release in his one literary passion, the novels of H. Rider Haggard, particularly those featuring the ugly little hunter, Alan Quartermain, who always seemed to be surrounded by strikingly handsome young men. He didn't think of it as sublimation for he didn't think in such terms. Ultimately he felt in perfect control of his life; in an emotional limbo, yes – but in control.

One day there would be someone else. Wield was certain of that. But he was not a man for rapid or temporary attachments. One day there would be someone; someone his equal in age and maturity; someone his equal in discretion.

And now the horror of finding his emotions assaulted by the simple sight of a mere boy! And for it to happen at the very centre of that area of his life he kept most separate from his deepest emotions signalled the gravest danger.

So now here he was once again playing the hard-nosed cop, and not even certain why. Pascoe had spoken to Dalziel on the telephone the previous evening and this morning had announced that the youths had to be brought in.

'Come on, lad,' said Wield. 'Don't muck about. These lads need to be questioned by someone who knows what he's at.'

'But that's all?' said Singh, looking for a crumb of comfort. 'Just more questioning about what they saw? You're not going to do them for damaging the car?'

It would have been easy for Wield to say no. But he was far from sure it was true, not if they copped an admission. And in any case the boy had to learn to face up to that shift in the centre of balance of loyalties that took place when you joined the Force.

And finally it might teach him to duck out of sight when he saw Wield coming, which would cool things down all round.

'There's no saying what Mr Pascoe'll decide,' he said heavily. But touched beyond bearing by the boy's unconcealable worry, he heard himself adding, 'But it'd need an admission before there was any chance of a case, and they'll likely know better than that if they watch a lot of telly, won't they?'

Singh's face cleared slightly.

'I only know two of them by name,' he said. 'They were mates of mine at school. Mick Feaver and Jonty, that's John, Marsh.'

'Feaver and Marsh,' said Pascoe. 'Anything known.'

'Nothing on Feaver. A bit of juvenile stuff on Marsh, nothing serious. But his family's always been a bit on the wild side, and you'll likely know one of his older brothers, Arthur.'

'Arthur Marsh. Rings a bell. Fill me in.'

Wield, anticipating the questions, produced a file.

'Lots of juvenile stuff again. Then got done for nicking things from houses where he'd been called in as a TV repair man. Sacked from his job, suspended sentence, started breaking in and nicking the TV sets themselves. Sent down for eighteen months. Out, another repair job, firm went bust, redundant, dole, six months ago he got done for an unemployment fiddle, claiming full benefit when he was doing a bit of work on the side.'

Wield ran his eye down the sheet and grinned.

'He had a bit of bad luck there,' he said. 'He was doing a bit of labouring work, helping lay a lawn for a fellow who turned out to be someone important at the Social Security office. He sees Arthur and his mates getting down to work that morning, then later the same day he spots him in a queue for benefit!'

'Tough,' said Pascoe. 'What did he get?'

'Fined,' said Wield. 'Likely he'll claim supplementary benefit to pay for it.'

'This confirms what young Singh thought,' Pascoe said. 'Marsh'll be the harder nut. Let's see him first, leave Feaver to stew a bit.'

'Right,' said Wield. 'Interview room?'

172

'No,' said Pascoe. 'Bring him up here. And don't mention his brother or anything like that. Let's follow the road Cadet Singh opened up and get him believing he's got us believing he's just a good citizen, right?'

A few minutes later, Jonty Marsh strutted in, cocky but watchful.

'Sit down, Mr Marsh,' said Pascoe. 'Thank you for coming.'

Over the next couple of minutes, Pascoe carefully fed the youth's cockiness by playing up the important witness angle till eventually the watchfulness had almost faded away.

Wield sat quietly by, admiring Pascoe's technique, while the Inspector took the youth through the events in the car park up to the moment when Daphne Aldermann got out of her car. Then by the flicker of an eye, he invited Wield to take over. Wield wasn't quite sure why, but he continued along the obvious lines, pressing Marsh about the car that Mrs Aldermann had got into. Marsh affirmed it was a BMW, but under Wield's probing rather sulkily admitted that he wasn't sure and was merely echoing Mick Feaver's certainty. But he now did recall that it was a dark blue car and confirmed what he had told Singh, that it had tinted glass windows.

When he had taken the questioning as far as the disappearance of the dark blue BMW, he paused and Pascoe produced a packet of cigarettes, and offered the youth one.

'That's good, Jonty,' he said approvingly. 'All right if I call you Jonty? First rate. I wish all our witnesses were as clear. So, to get it straight, you can positively identify the green VW Polo that the woman got out of as the same Polo that got scratched?'

'Oh, yeah,' said Marsh puffing at his cigarette. 'Definitely.'

'You'd swear to it?' said Pascoe.

'I told you!' protested Marsh. 'I'm dead certain.'

And now Pascoe didn't say anything but sat and regarded the young man quizzically. Puzzlement, doubt, and then dismay trailed each other across his face.

'No, what I mean is . . .' he began.

'That'll do, Marsh. For now,' said Pascoe.

The youth was removed. Wield nodded his congratulations.

'Nice admission,' he said. 'But . . .'

'Let's have the other,' said Pascoe.

With Feaver the approach was quite different.

'We know you and your mates damaged those cars, so you're not going to waste our time on that, are you?' snapped Pascoe.

'No, sir,' stammered the boy.

'What's that. Are you denying it?'

'No, I was meaning, no, I wasn't going to waste time, I mean . . .'

'You mean, yes, we did damage the cars? Say it!'

'Yes, we did damage the cars,' echoed the boy.

174

'That's better. Now I want you to help us. It'll all be taken into account.'

The pattern was then repeated, Pascoe going so far as the change from one to the other and Wield coming in on the second car. Feaver was emphatic that it was a BMW 528i. The colour was dark blue with silver trim. There'd been twin aerials and to the X and the 9 he'd given Singh he now added a possible 2. Finally Pascoe gave him a piece of paper and told him to write down the names and addresses of the other three youths involved.

When he'd gone, Pascoe said to the sergeant, 'Anything we missed?'

Wield said, 'If we're going to do them for damaging those cars, shouldn't we have got statements while they were in the mood? Not that I get the impression statements are what you want.'

He let a slight note of reproof come into his voice.

'No,' said Pascoe. 'Fetch 'em both in together.'

This time there were no seats for the young men. They stood at one side of the table while Pascoe regarded them grimly from the other.

'You've both admitted to unlawfully damaging property, to wit, four motor-cars parked in the bus station multi-storey car park. I said you've *both* admitted it,' he stressed, intercepting an accusing glance from Marsh to Feaver. 'I've checked with Criminal Records and there's nothing against you in the past, which is in your favour. And also I have an officer in this station who is willing to speak up for your known good characters. Now, because of these considerations, I'm going to take a risk. I'm going to recommend that we proceed no further at this time. This does not mean that the case is closed. The file will remain open for as long as I want it to remain open. You're on the record now, understand that. And this is the last favour you'll ever get from me or any other police officer, do you understand *that*?'

They nodded. Pascoe waited.

'Yes, sir,' stuttered Feaver.

Pascoe waited again.

'Yes,' said Marsh. 'Understood.'

'Right. Now push off. For ever!'

But Jonty Marsh was not so easily cowed. At the door he paused and said, 'What about all that other business, the cars and all that?'

'What other business?' said Pascoe stonily. 'There was no other business.'

After the door had closed behind the youths, he relaxed and pushed the list of names Feaver had provided towards Wield.

'See someone from uniformed has a word with these three, will you?'

'Yes, sir,' said Wield. 'And thanks, on behalf of young Singh, that is.'

'Thanks for what? What did I do?' said Pascoe in a surprised tone.

'Well, for a start you –' began Wield, then he paused and smiled faintly. 'Why, nothing. You did nothing at all, sir.'

'Good. I'm glad that's settled,' said Pascoe.

'Yes, sir. What exactly was it that *I* was doing, if you don't mind me asking?'

'Sorry about that. But I wanted you to ask all the questions about the other car. I didn't want to risk directing them.'

'Towards what?' asked Wield.

'Towards details of the car that Daphne Aldermann transferred to. You see it occurred to me that I know somebody who drives an X-registered BMW 528i in dark blue with silver trim and tinted windows. I had a look at it recently. A garage door had fallen on it.'

'Elgood, you mean?' said Wield in open surprise.

'Yes. Dandy Dick himself. And I recalled something else. When I talked to him in his office, I told him about your visit to Rosemont allegedly about Mrs Aldermann's car. And I got the impression then that he might have heard about it from some other source. Who could that be but one of the Aldermanns?'

'What did he say exactly?' asked Wield.

Pascoe hesitated. Dalziel would have just replied that it was Elgood's reference to 'ugly buggers from the CID' which put him in mind of the sergeant, but Pascoe was made of flimsier fibre.

'Oh, just a turn of phrase, something in his tone,' he said vaguely. 'Anyway, I've checked Elgood's car number and sure enough it ends with 29.'

'Which means?'

'Which means,' said Pascoe slowly, 'that we can be as sure as dammit that the day before Dandy Dick came round here to complain that he was in line to be murdered by Patrick Aldermann, he'd been shacked up in his seaside cottage with Aldermann's wife!'

PART THREE

'It's my opinion you never think at all,' the
Rose said in a rather severe tone.

LEWIS CARROLL:
Through the Looking-Glass

1
NEWS

(Floribunda. Semi-double flowers, purple-claret, free-flowering through the season.)

Dick Elgood lay on his back, buoyed up by the gently rocking sea and caressed by the hot-fingered sun, and felt at one with the world.

If he raised his head slightly and looked between his feet he could see across fifteen yards of shimmering water and as many more of light buff sand to a green-flecked sandstone cliff on top which stood an ochre-roofed white-walled cottage. It might almost have been Tuscany, but you could stuff Tuscany, and indeed most points east of where he was now, for Elgood. This bit of the Yorkshire coast, barely an hour from his office, was as far as he ever wanted to go.

Twenty years ago when he had bought the cottage, only the chimney stack would have been visible from where he was presently floating. Winter after winter the North Sea darted out cold

181

hands and ripped great fistfuls out of the soft cliff face, undermining it until more of its grassy head came sliding down of its own weight. 'How long?' Elgood had asked. 'Could be there another fifty years,' opined the estate agent. 'Could be down in ten,' warned the surveyor. Elgood had halved the difference and signed the contract. He had no concern for succession and he liked the idea of a building whose lifespan was as doubtful and as limited as a man's.

Besides, the price was rock-bottom, if that was the right term.

He'd never regretted buying it. Here he came to relax, sometimes in company, sometimes alone. It was the perfect setting for romance; it was the perfect atmosphere for unwinding. Today he had just wanted the delights of solitude. After several days of non-stop negotiations and continuous availability he had finally hammered out an agreement with his work force on the redundancies. It had been hard work, harder than he'd ever known. The turning-point had been yesterday when in a quiet moment with the leader of the works committee he had said, with sincerity as well as with conscious guile, 'If this doesn't get settled without a strike, at least your lads'll have the consolation of seeing me ahead of them in the dole queue.'

The hint had been enough. They had the sense to know that any successor to Elgood was likely to be a much more unpleasant proposition.

So it was settled. And this Tuesday was his own. His therapy. His reward.

Or perhaps not. Dimly through half-closed eyes he saw the roof of a car flashing in the sun as it parked alongside the cottage.

'Shit!' he said, and thought of slipping beneath the surface and swimming out of sight round the corner of the little bay.

But he couldn't hide for long, and in any case he didn't care to hide except occasionally from boring colleagues and angry husbands. This car brought trouble or it brought pleasure. He wasn't used to running from either.

He turned over and with a long easy stroke pulled towards the shore.

As he reached his towel on the sand, he heard a noise and, looking up, he saw his visitor scrambling down the cliff face, a passage made both dangerous and easy by the erosion. Identification didn't help him decide whether this meant pleasure or trouble. It was Daphne Aldermann.

He saw a tall, rangy woman with long blonde hair casually tied back from a face which sunlight and slight exertion coloured with a simple beauty beyond cosmetic art. Beneath her slacks and checked shirt moved long muscular legs and deep heavy breasts, the memory of which excited Elgood as he towelled himself down.

She saw a small man with thick greying hair, usually elegantly groomed but now spiky with damp, topping a slightly lopsided face whose

183

characteristically cheerful expression was quali-fied but not belied by a pair of shrewd, watchful eyes. When she'd first met him she'd regarded him as rather old and faintly comic, but that had soon passed. There had been a moment when she had feared being confronted with an old, pasty-white and scrawny body, but he stripped well, sunshine and exercise keeping him brown and wiry. As for what moved beneath his swimming trunks, she had found nothing to complain of in its sensitivity and vigour, but no memory of it touched her mind as she approached him now.

'Hello, love,' he said. 'This is a nice surprise. How'd you know I was here?'

'Patrick was talking to Eric Quayle on the phone last night. He said you'd reached an agreement with the unions and that you'd be relaxing down here today.'

'Talking to Quayle, was he?'

With himself out of the office, it would be a good opportunity for them to arrange a meeting and plan tactics. Elgood felt he could afford to smile at the thought. Each of them imagining he was using the other! And both doomed to get nowhere! The board meeting at which the question of the new financial director would be resolved was only a week away. Elgood was pretty certain that, with his authority confirmed by the successful cutback negotiations, he could now face down Quayle, but he was taking no chances. Yesterday he had made a phone call to London and put into action another little scheme which with a bit of luck would give him enough ammunition to shoot down Aldermann's nomination once and for all.

'And you decided that a touch of sunshine and old Dick was just what the doctor ordered?' he went on. 'Grand. I'm glad you've come.'

He took her hand, ready to draw her towards him if the moment felt ripe. But those powers of empathy which were the basis of his amorous success, and which functioned even when he was physically most aroused, told him she wasn't ready, so holding her hand lightly in his, he set off for the cottage, saying, 'Let's have a coffee and plan our day. How long can you stay?'

She didn't answer and Elgood chattered on amiably as they clambered up over the chunks of eroded rock and earth which formed a rough flight of steps to the cliff top. Once there he paused by the white-painted stake which he drove into the ground every spring to measure the winter's deprivation. Sometimes he had had to move it a couple of yards or more, sometimes only a couple of feet. Only once in twenty years had it remained still.

Daphne said, 'Doesn't it bother you, that stick? Watching it tap-tap-tapping towards you like a blind man's cane year after year?'

Elgood laughed and said, 'That's a bit fanciful, isn't it, love? Not to say morbid!'

'I'm sorry,' said Daphne. 'It was just the thought of the sea burrowing away underneath. It suddenly seemed so sinister.'

'Sinister? Well, mebbe it's different for me, being a miner's son brought up in a mining village where at any hour, day or night you knew there was someone down there, burrowing away beneath your feet; not the sea, mark you, but your dad mebbe, or your brother, or your best mate; someone, any road, you knew by name. So it doesn't bother me. In fact, it pleases me being able to sit in the cottage odd times in the winter, listening to the burrowing and sometimes hearing a great rending and a crashing as the earth falls, and knowing it's only the old sea down there, not me dad, or me brother, or me best mate, nor any poor devil I know by name.'

'Yes, I can see that,' said Daphne earnestly. 'It's just that it's so pretty here, but so impermanent.'

'Not like your husband's precious Rosemont, you mean? Not even Rosemont will last for ever! There's worms down there, and moles; mice and rats too, I shouldn't wonder; all manner of burrowing creatures. And where they burrow was once level ground too, do you ever think of that? Miners know that. Shapes of leaves they find, and shells, and bones, and footsteps too, printed in the very rock half a mile under the earth. Slow change like that makes a man feel like nowt, his existence like the width of an eyelash. Now, if the old sea gets to the cottage before Old Nick gets to me, that'll make me feel I can live forever!'

Daphne smiled and said, 'And you accuse me of being fanciful!'

Elgood, his verbal tonic having done the hoped-for trick of relaxing his visitor, said, 'Let's go in and get that coffee.'

Once inside, he dispatched Daphne to the small kitchen while he got dressed. For his age, he knew he was well preserved. In athletic motion such as swimming, or in the sultry build-up to – or the torpid wind-down from – the act of love he was happy to stand examination. But however well preserved his body, at sixty, he was not prepared to let it be a still target for the cool appraisal of an uncommitted woman's eyes.

And Daphne, he guessed, was now uncommitted. In fact, he doubted if she'd ever been anything else.

Her first words as she brought the tray of coffee into the simply but comfortably furnished living-room confirmed this without ambiguity.

'Dick, I wanted to tell you that it's over between us.'

'Oh yes,' said Elgood. A postcard would have done as well, he thought. One of his rules was never to resist a woman who said she wanted to finish. Either she meant it, in which case resistance would be foolish. Or she didn't mean it, in which case resistance would be what she wanted and therefore insane.

So he said easily, 'Well, drink your coffee, love, and here's a toast. To friendship. We had a good day and hurt no one. So no need for guilt or recriminations.'

He smiled at her over his coffee cup, and wished her long gone. Hard experience in the past had taught him that the most unexpected successes often turned out to be the most troublesome. His success with Daphne Aldermann had been one of the most unexpected he had ever known.

He had met her shortly after Aldermann had joined the firm as part-time assistant to that awkward bugger, Chris Burke. It had been an act of charitable patronage for old time's sake. And chatting up the wife had been an act of instinct for the sake of keeping his hand in. His instinct also marked her down as a non-starter, but he didn't know how not to try.

It had been second nature to him to hint in a manner so subtle as to be easily deniable that Daphne's beauty as much as Aldermann's deserts had won him Burke's job. And again as he stood in a corner with her at the bunfight after Timothy Eagles's funeral, even though by now the battle of the Board was well under way, he had not been able to resist hinting that Aldermann's permanent elevation to the Chief Accountant's job might well depend on Daphne's bonny blue eyes. This was the mere rhetoric of flirtation, artificial and hollow. But to his surprise there was a response, or rather a reaction, for later he doubted if she really paid much heed to his amorous hints at that time. But she certainly reacted to the mention of jobs and salaries. She had something on her mind. Suddenly businesslike, he had suggested that perhaps here at a funeral feast was not the place to talk. They had met for a lunch-time drink a couple of days later, and again the following week. The atmosphere remained businesslike with an undertone of honest friendship. Elgood had been uneasy because uncertain. Part of him saw the meetings as a means of getting inside information on Aldermann's unsteady finances which might be useful in the forthcoming battle. Part of him saw these meetings as erotic foreplay. And another part, whose location he had not been able to discover, had taken to waking him in the night and telling him his behaviour was indecent, immoral and squalid.

So he had tried to tell her at their last lunch-time meeting that her husband had the Chief Account-ant's job simply because he was *there*, not because Elgood wanted him to have it, and that he person-ally was doing all he could to stop him getting on the Board. And later that same Friday afternoon he had the same kind of clarification session with Aldermann, ending with those suggestive words, *Over my dead body*!

That had to be that, he thought. It had come as a complete surprise when, on the Sunday afternoon, Daphne had rung him in a state of some agitation, wanting to talk. He'd been planning to go down to the cottage the following morning to compensate for a weekend largely given over to company matters. He had suggested they meet in the car park and drive down together. She had hesitated, then finally agreed. He hadn't really been certain she would turn up until the moment she climbed into his car with the look of an apprentice spy.

They talked generally on the drive down. She was no longer certain why she had come, and he could see that. He didn't push, just let her talk. He showed her round the cottage, then they walked on the beach. The sky was overcast, the water a still grey. A straightforward seduction scenario would have had Elgood suggesting a nude swim, but today the script was still unwritten. He heard with puzzlement that Aldermann still seemed completely optimistic about his future. In a strange way, his presence was with them; his certainties, his placidity, his contentment moved with the gigantic understrength of the quiet sea against which their own doubts and worries and dismays, no matter how large and solid they seemed, stood with only the delusory resistance of the soft-stoned cliff.

Before midday, Elgood suggested they ate. Talk had sputtered out, they needed something to do. There was cold chicken and salad and white wine. They ate little, drank a lot. He didn't set out to get her drunk, he prided himself he had never needed that, and he stopped topping up her glass while she was still well this side of inebriety. But she was more relaxed than she had been since arriving. There was still tension there, he felt as he took her in his arms, but it was the tension of resolve, the nervous novice knowing she can do her duty.

They made love. It hadn't been great but it had been promising. There was a deep sensuality there waiting to be tapped, and afterwards they drank brandy together, she chattering away in the reaction of release, he content to wait quietly for his strength to return so that he could really sample the goods he had just begun to unwrap.

Outside a wind had blown up off the sea. A rambling rose, sadly neglected and full of insect life, grew up the side wall of the cottage and the strong gusts set it tapping against the window. Daphne stopped talking and let out a startled little cry.

'What's up?' asked Elgood.

'Nothing. Just the noise,' she said tremulously. 'For a moment I thought it might be Patrick!'

'Disguised as a rose-bush? Aye, that'd be just about what I'd expect,' mocked Elgood.

'Why do you say that?'

'Well, he's a bit obsessed, isn't he? He's got more rose catalogues than company records in his filing cabinet, so they say.'

He hadn't meant to start talking about Patrick again. Absent husbands held a very low place in his list of postcoital topics.

'*Obsessed*? No, I don't think that's the word,' said Daphne, frowning. 'He loves his garden and he loves the house, but I don't think he'd ever put them before the children, or before me either.'

Elgood didn't like the way the conversation was turning.

191

He said, 'But surely the way he's poured all the money you've ever had into Rosemont . . .'

'And us, too,' corrected Daphne. 'Neither the children nor I have ever wanted for anything. So it's not obsessive, it's just rather *uncanny*, this certainty of his that everything will be all right, that nothing will ever be allowed to threaten Rosemont . . .'

'Uncanny, then,' said Elgood, feeling himself almost ready for the second course, and wanting to be shot of this unseemly topic. 'All right, he's got magical powers protecting his fairy castle. Another drop of brandy, love?'

'No, thanks. Yes, it does sometimes seem like that, doesn't it? I mean, he's always said "don't worry," and I've always worried, and yet he's always turned out to be right. Obstacles just seem to get out of his way. I mean, four years ago he hadn't even got a job after he finished with Capstick's and look where he is now without hardly any effort. It's hardly surprising he can still be so sure of getting on the Board, even though you say not, is it?'

There was no guile in her tone, nothing but an honest desire to understand her husband, yet Elgood felt it not only as an atmospheric intrusion, but as a threat. For some reason the memory of the desk lamp came into his mind. He caressed Daphne's breast, massaging the nipple between finger and thumb, but the gesture did as little for him as it seemed to be doing for her and when a little while later she said she ought to be getting ready to leave now if she were to be in time to pick up her daughter from school, he made no protest.

He had dropped her back at the car-park entrance, driven back to the office, sat and looked at the desk lamp, finally laughed at his foolishness and got down to some work. Later he had driven to his flat and put the car in the garage without any difficulty. He had passed a rather restless night, full of menacing dreams in which Bulmer and Eagles figured large. But a good breakfast had seemed to put him right.

Then he had descended to his garage, tugged at the up-and-over door which could normally be moved by a little finger's pressure, jerked at it when it appeared to be stuck, and next moment was flinging himself backwards as the whole heavy structure came crashing down.

Well, perhaps he had overreacted. But it was understandable. And all was well that ended well. He was back in charge now. Indeed things were so normal that he found himself inwardly assessing the chances of persuading Daphne to have one for the road.

Down boy! he warned himself. That was the way to trouble. And in any case, he doubted if she were the type. Her next words confirmed this.

'I'm not really cut out for this kind of thing,' she said. 'I had to see you face to face to make sure you understood. It's just not my cup of tea. I was in real agony when the police came round to ask questions about my car. I kept on remembering those boys hanging around the car park and wondering if they'd remember seeing me there.'

'Like I told you when you rang,' said Elgood easily, 'they likely didn't even notice. And if they were the ones as did the scratching, they're not going to volunteer to chat with the cops, are they? In any case, it was just a bit of vandalization, hardly the crime of the century!'

'But they did send that ugly CID man round to see me,' objected Daphne.

Elgood couldn't contradict this except by telling her what he imagined the real reason for this visit had been. That was an embarrassment he was glad to be able to avoid.

'That's true. Time on their hands, these bobbies,' he said. 'Have you time for another coffee? Or a drink, mebbe?'

As hoped, this provoked her to shake her head and rise.

'No, really. I must be getting back.'

'Right,' he said. 'Still friends?'

'Of course.'

He kissed her lightly on the cheek.

She smiled and said, 'It's silly, but I feel so happy I've seen you and made things clear. It's like coming out of the dentist's.'

'I've been called a lot of things,' he said, 'but rarely a dentist.'

'I'm sorry. I didn't mean . . . it's just that I let

things get inside my mind sometimes and rattle round in there and worry myself into the most absurd ideas! You know, just recently I met this woman, purely by chance, and it turned out she was a policeman's wife. I like her a lot, she's bright and straightforward, and completely independent, of her husband I mean. And yet the other night I woke up at four A.M. suddenly completely convinced she'd been set on me to spy for the police force! I hate those four o'clock horrors, don't you? That's another thing about Patrick, he never has them. Of course, came the dawn, and I could see what a fool I'd been. But that's the way I've been going on lately, like some neurotic!'

This burst of relieved chatter had got them out of the cottage.

'Have you mentioned your new friend to Patrick?' asked Elgood casually as he opened the car door.

'Oh yes. The other night. I didn't know how he'd react, especially as when I met her she was protesting against the school that Diana goes to. But you know Patrick. Nothing bothers him. He just suggested I should invite her and her husband round for dinner one night.'

'I'd be careful about inviting the fuzz into my house,' said Elgood only half jokingly. 'What did you say her name was?'

Daphne told him.

To her horror, Elgood put his hands to his face and leaned against the car with a long, low groan.

'What's the matter?' she cried in alarm. Most

of her alarm was for Elgood who she feared was having a heart-attack. But there was a little bit left over for herself as her mind raced ahead to the possible consequences.

She put her arm round his shoulders. He moved his hands away from his face, revealing to her relief and also her puzzlement the pains not of disease but of simple dismay.

'What's the matter, Dick?' she demanded. 'Are you all right?'

'I wish I knew,' he said.

He looked at her for a couple of seconds, sighed, took her hand in his and said, 'You'd best come back into the cottage. I've got something to tell you. But first of all, you'd better tell me everything you know about this Mrs Ellie Pascoe.'

2
MEMORIAM

(Hybrid Tea. Dates from 1960, – white bedding rose,
sad in the rain.)

Wednesday for Pascoe started with the dead.

Tuesday had finished with Dalziel. Pascoe wasn't sure which he preferred.

The fat man had rung shortly after five o'clock. He had listened in silence to Pascoe's description of his interrogation of the two boys. His reaction to the news about Elgood and Daphne Aldermann was almost dismissive.

'It doesn't surprise me,' he said. 'If they put him into intensive care, he'd likely ask for a double-bed. Gives Aldermann a good motive, though. And it begins to make it a bit clearer why Dick got so bloody neurotic about Aldermann.'

'Well, it surprised me,' said Pascoe. 'Ellie's got to know Daphne Aldermann quite well and she doesn't sound the type for a quick hump. You don't think it could be serious between her

197

and Elgood, could it? That might explain a few things.'

'If it is, then Dick doesn't know about it,' said Dalziel emphatically. 'Elgood's only serious about himself. He got frightened for some reason and he wanted reassurance, about the desk-lamp, and about the garage door, and about them two fellows that died. He couldn't go through the coroners' reports himself, could he? Is your missus seeing the Aldermann woman again? She's a sharp lass, your Ellie, even if she does get some daft notions sometimes. Ask her to see what she can winkle out.'

'I believe they'll be having coffee together in the morning,' said Pascoe. 'But I don't think Ellie would take kindly to being asked to winkle things out.'

'Why not?' asked Dalziel with audible bewilderment.

'I'm sure if you asked her, she'd be happy to explain the moral position to you, sir,' said Pascoe firmly.

'The moral position? I thought that was when a lass did it on her back, in the dark, with her eyes closed,' said Dalziel. 'You'll be seeing Elgood again, I suppose?'

'Yes. I rang his office today but he's down at the seaside again, God knows who with this time. His secretary said he has a very busy schedule tomorrow, and would Thursday do. I didn't want to sound too urgent so I said OK.'

'Aye, you're right to watch how you go with Dick. Fornication's no crime, remember that.'

'Wasting police time is,' said Pascoe.

'You still think it's a waste of time?' said Dalziel. 'Well, you may be right. Here's something else to waste your time on then. Another corpse in Aldermann's track. Penny Highsmith mentioned him. Someone who nearly bought Rosemont. Mid-sixties it'd be, after Patrick had done his "O" levels. Edgar Masson was the old lady's solicitor so likely he'd still have been acting for the family, so he should have all the details. Even if he hasn't, that old bugger knows more about other people's business than most other people.'

Pascoe said, 'Is there anything more?' scribbling wildly.

'Aye. Ask him about the will. I went round to Somerset House today. There was some Kraut here talking about fighting the subversive war. What do them buggers know about fighting wars? They can't remember the last time they won one! So I ducked out. At Somerset House I found out that she died intestate, Auntie Flo.'

'Then there wasn't a will,' said Pascoe smartly.

'I know what intestate means,' said Dalziel heavily. 'I also know that Edgar Masson's not in the habit of letting rich clients get away without paying him for drawing up a will. At some stage, there'd have been one. And talking of wills, after what you told me that accountant fellow, Capstick, said about the Reverend Somerton's accounts being in his office, I thought I might as well take a look at the Rev's will while I was at Somerset House. He had £60,000 to leave, right enough, but he only left £20,000 of it to his daughter. The rest was spread around various good causes, so if Aldermann was expecting riches, he was disappointed!'

'Twenty thou was still a lot of money in 1971,' said Pascoe.

'Sixty thou was near on a fortune,' said Dalziel. 'I'd best be on my way now. There's a seminar going off on the policewoman's role in multi-racial contra-social interaction or something.'

'And you don't want to miss it?' said Pascoe with cautious incredulity.

'Don't be bloody daft!' sneered Dalziel. 'It'll be over soon and I'm using the bugger's phone who's chairing it. Suspicious bastard even keeps his whisky locked!'

Pascoe may have only imagined he heard the splintering of wood before he replaced the phone, but such imaginings in Dalziel's regard were as likely to be hypotheses as fantasies.

He shared the conversation with Wield over a cup of coffee the following morning.

'It was probably the Commissioner's office,' he concluded. 'He's getting worse as he gets older. And it's getting hard to know where you are with him. Before he went, he told us he didn't want us wasting time on this Aldermann business. Now he seems full of it. Why?'

'He's renewed his acquaintance with Mrs High-smith,' said Wield significantly, dipping a chocolate-coated digestive into his cup.

'I can't imagine what you mean,' said Pascoe primly. 'That chocolate's melting.'

'It's the heat. It does that sometimes,' explained Wield. 'He'll be seeing her again?'

'He implied it,' said Pascoe. 'You know, you could achieve the same effect by eating plain biscuits and drinking mocha coffee.'

'It's a different kind of multi-racial contra-social interaction,' said Wield solemnly. 'Does this mean Mr Dalziel now reckons there's something in all this for us officially?'

Pascoe gestured at his desk which was covered with the stationery of death. Police reports, medical reports, coroners' reports.

'The thing about our modern society,' he mused, 'is that no one passes without leaving a mark any more. If there is anything for us in all this, it ought to be somewhere in all these. Let's try to put things in some kind of order, shall we?'

'Chronological, you mean?'

'There are other kinds of order,' said Pascoe kindly. 'But that'll do for starters. Here we go. 1960. Mrs Florence Aldermann dies of a coronary thrombosis. Medical report is unambiguous. She was still convalescent from an earlier attack. And there are no suspicious circumstances unless we count the intestacy which meant that Penny Highsmith got the entire estate. Now we jump on a decade to the Reverend Oliver Somerton. Skull fractured by a piece of masonry fallen from the belfry of St Mark's Church, Little Leven.'

'Hold on,' said Wield. 'There'll be at least one other in between. This fellow Mr Dalziel mentioned, the one who wanted to buy the house but died.'

'Oh yes. I sincerely hope he'll turn out to have died of old age a hundred miles away,' said Pascoe. 'I'm seeing the solicitor, Masson, later this morning.'

'I'll pencil in a query,' said Wield.

'Right. Back to the Rev. Suspicious circumstances? All unwitnessed accidents are, ipso facto, suspicious. But there were no pointers to anything definite, and the coroner seemed quite satisfied.'

'Act of God,' said Wield.

'Watch it,' said Pascoe. 'We need all the help we can get. Anyway, that was 'seventy-one. On to 'seventy-six. Mrs Catherine McNeil. Died of bronchial pneumonia which developed after a burst of some particularly virulent influenza. Was that one of the years when there was a lot of it about, Chinese, Siamese, Patagonian or something?'

'I'll try to check,' said Wield. 'How old was she?'

'Seventy-eight.'

'At seventy-eight there's always a lot of it about,' said the sergeant. 'She's the one Aldermann had been robbing and who left him the money?'

'That's her. Aldermann had 'flu himself, I gather.

It was during his absence from the office that his little games with Mrs McNeil's money came to light.'

'So he sneezed at her till she got a fatal dose of germs?' said Wield.

Pascoe glared at him.

'Let's leave the debunking jokes to Mr Dalziel, shall we?' he said.

'Just rehearsing, sir,' murmured Wield and the two men grinned at each other.

'That was at the beginning of 'seventy-six. Three and a half years later in September 'seventy-nine, Christopher Burke dies, the first of three casualties at Perfecta where Aldermann had started working on a part-time basis some six months earlier.'

'Burke was the one who fell off a ladder while he was painting his house?'

'That's what I thought,' said Pascoe. 'But the coroner's report says that in fact he'd got a firm in to do the work. That morning they'd been replacing a section of guttering prior to painting the eaves. Burke, it is surmised, ran up the ladder when he came home from work to inspect the repair, it slipped and he broke his neck.'

'Witnesses?'

'None,' said Pascoe, looking at the report. 'He died between two-thirty and three-thirty. His wife went out at two-thirty and he wasn't home then. She came back an hour later and there he was, spread out across the patio at the back of the house.'

'What about the decorators?' wondered Wield.

'After they'd got the new bit of guttering in, it started raining, so they waited a while and when the weather showed no sign of improving, they went off to an inside job they were doing as well. You know what painters are like.'

'Strange,' said Wield.

'Painters?'

'No. That a man would go up a ladder in the wet. Straight from the office.'

'I thought so too. But it was showery, it seems. Theory is that he arrived home in a dry patch, was surprised not to see the decorators at work, ran up the ladder just to check how much – or how little – they'd done, and that was that.'

'It's the kind of daft thing you might do,' agreed Wield. 'Especially if you'd had a good liquid lunch down at the Conservative Club, moaning with your mates about what an idle sod the British working man had become.'

Pascoe laughed and said, 'You haven't been talking to my wife by any chance? But it could be worth checking. This and the vicar's are the ones which come closest to being "suspicious" deaths and the more we can disperse the suspicion, the sooner we can forget the whole business.'

'How can you check something like that at this distance?' queried Wield. 'There's no mention of booze in the inquest report, is there?'

'No,' said Pascoe. 'But in the circumstances –

accident at home, wife greatly distressed, etcetera – the coroner might be inclined to muffle any hint that the deceased was stoned. It was Mr Wellington presiding, I see. You know him?'

This was in response to a small earth-tremor of Wield's features.

'He once bollocked me for being cheeky under his examination,' said Wield.

'Good. Then as you're old friends, you can chat to him,' said Pascoe.

He made a note on his desk pad.

'Finally, the first two I looked at. Brian Bulmer who crashed his car after the office party last Christmas. Definitely booze there, I'm afraid. No one else involved, no witnesses. He seems to have lost control on black ice and hit a bollard. He was Perfecta's financial director, remember? And at the beginning of May, Timothy Eagles, the chief accountant and Aldermann's chief rival for elevation to the board, had a heart attack. He was found in a washroom by the night security guard doing his first rounds at eight P.M. He was dressed for going home. He'd said goodnight to his secretary who'd left dead on time, leaving him to sign a couple of letters. Presumably he then got ready, felt ill, either in the washroom or perhaps made his way there for a drink of water, collapsed and was unfortunately not discovered till too late for medical help.'

'Aldermann was his assistant, wasn't he?' said Wield. 'Using the same washroom?'

'I believe so. Spell it out, Sergeant.'

Wield said, 'Aldermann on his way home finds Eagles having his attack. Instead of calling for help, he closes the door and goes on his way.'

Pascoe whistled and quoted, 'Thou shalt not kill but needst not strive officiously to keep alive. A bit cold-blooded! You've met him, what do you think? Could he do it?'

'It's easier than murder,' said Wield.

'Is it? I'm not sure. The strong human instinct is to help.'

'You try telling that to old ladies who see people peeking out of their windows as they get mugged,' said the sergeant. 'They'd tell you about human instincts!'

Pascoe said, 'I suppose so,' and stared in irritation at the papers strewn across his desk. All this, as Dalziel would say, was neither owt nor nowt and it was beginning to get on his nerves. All he could do was keep digging till either something positive came up or the weight of negatives gave him the excuse to leave off. But all the time he dug he was aware of the danger of causing distress and creating talk without the justification of a result to show for it.

But there was no choice, really. Either you did the job or you didn't. He began ticking off the next stages in his mind – talk to Masson, visit Capstick again, interview Christopher Burke's widow, see Elgood – and let out a long deep sigh.

'You all right, sir?' asked Wield.

'Bloody marvellous,' said Pascoe. 'It's just that sometimes I get this awful feeling that if I'm not careful, I may turn into a policeman.'

3

BLACK BOY

*(Shrub. Modern variety with an Old Rose Fragrance.
Purple shading, double flowers, high growing.)*

Police Cadet Shaheed Singh too was beginning to
have serious doubts about the wisdom of his choice
of career.

His superiors were far from encouraging. He had
not been surprised to find in his course-instructors
that combination of hectoring sarcasm and patron-
izing familiarity which he remembered from his
not too distant schooldays, but he'd looked for
something different from the working cops he
met on his four weeks' attachment.

Well, he'd found it. Inspectors and sergeants of
the uniform branch were not unhelpful but seemed
to take it as axiomatic that he was thick and idle.
As for the CID, Mr Dalziel terrified him, Sergeant
Wield clearly hated him and even the amiable Mr
Pascoe seemed to have developed some of Dalziel's
brusqueness in his superior's absence.

At the constable level, while he had a friendly, jokey relationship with most of the PCs, he found their instinctive if unmalicious racism very trying. Even George Wedderburn, with whom he spent most mornings sorting out the traffic at the market roundabout, had taken to using him as a kind of personal servant.

'Here, young Shady,' he'd said this morning, glancing at his watch, 'it's slackening off. You cut along, get me twenty Park Drive and a Mirror, and get the teas set up in the Caff, OK? And no sloping off for a bit of how's-your-father!'

This jocular injunction dated from his lateness the morning he had visited the car park. After Wedderburn had got over his annoyance, he had affected to believe that Singh's halting explanation was a cover-up for an amorous rendezvous. Constable Grainger, still smarting from Singh's jokes about his weight, had knowledgeably opined, 'Aye, they can't do without it, these darkies. They're at it all the time where they come from. It's the heat, tha' knows, and them loin-cloths.'

A sociologist would have seen this as a classic manifestation of the white man's feeling of cultural superiority and sexual inferiority, but Singh had just grinned and gone on his way, secretly wishing that these allegations about his active sex life were even partially true.

As he came out of the tobacconist's with Wedderburn's paper and cigarettes and began to cross the market place, he encountered two more reasons for self doubt.

The first was a young man with very long hair, wearing faded jeans and a grubby T-shirt printed with a clenched fist and pinned with CND and Stuff-The-Tories badges. He was handing out pamphlets headlined Police Brutality – The Facts. He looked at Singh's uniform and bared his teeth in a defiant sneer as the boy passed.

On the other side of the market place, Singh met another young man. This one had very short hair and was wearing faded jeans and a grubby T-shirt on which was printed a large Union Jack. He was handing out pamphlets headlined Immigration – The Facts. He looked at Singh's face and bared his teeth in a contemptuous sneer as he passed.

The Market Caff with its steamed-up windows and inadequate fan, which seemed to act on the bacon fat odours and loud Yorkshire breath which filled the air as an electric whisk acts on cream, thickening the mixture rather than dispersing it, loomed ahead like a sanctuary this morning. But before he could pass through the door and inhale its turgid incense, he felt his arm seized.

'Hello, Shady. You all right?'

Singh turned and found himself facing Mick Feaver. He viewed him with grave suspicion.

'I'm all right. What do you want, Mick?' he asked brusquely.

'Just a word.'

It dawned on Singh that far from being menacing, Feaver looked as if he could do with some comfort himself. His usual uncertain expression was exaggerated to the point of extra anxiety, though perhaps this was partly due to the physical underlining given by a bruised cheek and a split lip.

Someone came out of the Caff, and through the open door, Singh ascertained that PC Wedderburn had not yet arrived.

'I'm just going to have a mug of tea,' he said. 'Fancy one?'

He didn't wait for an answer but went into the Caff. At the counter, he found Feaver close behind. He ordered three mugs of tea and Wedderburn's usual chocolate wafer bar.

'Fetch them two,' he instructed, and picking up one mug and the wafer bar he went in search of a seat.

Mrs Pascoe was here again, he noted, with her baby. He wondered if Mrs Aldermann was coming too and whether she would recognize Mick Feaver as one of the youths in the car park. But it was too late, or too soon, to worry. Mrs Pascoe spotted him and gave him a friendly smile. The only two empty chairs in the place seemed to be at her table, but fortunately a group of market workers began to extract themselves grumbling from a distant corner and he was able to divert to the vacant seats.

Mick Feaver didn't seem disposed to open the

conversation and though Singh's natural inclination was to outlast his silence, he guessed that anything the lad was likely to say would have to be said before Wedderburn arrived.

He indicated the third mug and the chocolate wafer and said, 'He'll be along just now.'

'Yes,' said Feaver. 'Look, Shady, thanks for saying what you did at the nick yesterday.'

'Saying what I did?' said Singh in puzzlement.

'Yeah. That copper, not the ugly one, the other, he said someone had put in a good word for us and I knew it could only be you.'

'Oh aye,' said Singh. 'Well, that's all right.'

'Nothing's going to happen, is it?' pursued Feaver.

'What about?'

'About scratching them cars.'

'Oh no,' said Singh who had received his assurance, albeit in what he regarded as a typically grudging fashion, from Sergeant Wield.

'We both admitted it. That Pascoe fellow said we *both* admitted it. He stressed it, like. *Both* of us, not just one.'

Singh listened to the protesting tone and began to get some feel of what this was about.

'That's right,' he agreed again.

'That wanker, Marsh, he told the others it were just me. He said it were me as blew the whistle on all of them.'

'Aye, that's Jonty,' said Singh philosophically. 'Always liked to look big.'

His philosophy was not infectious and Feaver said angrily, 'Big *mouth*, that's what's big about him. He's been saying things about you as well. He says you're dead friendly when you're chatting to your old mates but then you go straight down the nick and tell 'em everything you've heard.'

'Is that what he says?' said Singh.

Feaver was obviously disappointed in the reaction and said viciously, 'The black pig, that's what he calls you. The black pig.'

Singh sipped his tea. It was strong and rather tannic, nothing like the delicate infusions which his mother would be serving up at regular intervals during the day to his father in the shop. His father was a gentle but strong-minded man who took family obedience as his natural right and Singh had no quarrel with that. But something in him, or perhaps something outside of him in his Western environment, had resisted the idea of being a lifelong underling, which was what helping in the shop would entail, so he had joined the police cadets. To turn back now would be difficult, almost impossible. But as he sat here in this miasmic atmosphere and learned how short a step it had been from 'old Shady Singh' to 'the black pig', he yearned to be in his father's shop, receiving meticulous instructions on the best method of stacking tins on the long shelves.

'You put 'em right, though, Mick?' he said. 'About what really happened.'

'That's a laugh,' said Feaver, fingering his cut

lip. 'This is what I got when I saw them wankers last night. You're all right, but. They daren't touch you.'

His tone was envious, accusing, scornful. It left Singh no route back to their old, casual, uncomplicated school-days friendship.

'Do you want to make a complaint,' he said formally.

'No, what good'd that do?' said Feaver surlily.

What good indeed? wondered Singh. Over Feaver's shoulder he saw Mrs Pascoe who had been glancing impatiently at her watch rise suddenly and organize the baby into her papoose basket. She caught his eye, smiled a farewell, and made for the door. As she passed through it, Singh glimpsed the solid frame of George Wedderburn talking to some old acquaintance on one of the open vegetable stalls facing the Caff.

'My mate's on his way,' he said. 'He'll be here in half a minute.'

'It's Jonty Marsh,' said Feaver in a sudden rush. 'You know how he's always going on about his brother, Arthur, what a hard case he is and all that?'

'Yeah, I remember.'

'Well, a week back, while I was still knocking around with that lot, Jimmy Bright said something about Arthur, like, what's he doing now? something like that. And Jonty said, keeping busy, but like, he meant more. And Jimmy said, you mean he's nicking stuff like before? And Jonty said no, that lark's for kids like you; you know, sounding big again. And it got up Jimmy's nose and he said, well, he got nicked doing kid's stuff, didn't he? So how's he managing to do something really clever all by himself? And Jonty got narked and said there was a few of them in it and it was big operations they did, not just breaking kitchen windows and nicking a few transistors, but big houses with good stuff they needed a van to cart away.'

He paused and Singh looked into his tea mug because he couldn't look at Mick Feaver, this weak, uncertain but basically good-humoured lad whom they'd all tended to protect a bit, and who was now his first grass. His silence worked where words might not have done, for after one deep breath, Feaver took the final large step, from the general to the particular.

'He said that Arthur had invited him on the next job. He said they were short-handed because there'd been a bit of an accident. Jimmy said it was all a load of crap, anyone could say that, and next time there was a big job say they'd been on it. So Jonty said all right, it was the first weekend in July and if Jimmy could read the papers, he'd read all about it. The first weekend in July and the house was called Rosemont.'

He was finished. The door opened and Wedderburn came in. Mick Feaver stood up and Singh raised his eyes till they met the boy's gaze.

'See you,' he said abruptly and turned and left,

pushing by George Wedderburn violently enough to make the big policeman glare after him.

'Mate of yours?' he said, sitting himself in the chair vacated by Feaver.

'That's right,' said Singh, looking at the closed door. 'Just an old mate, that's all.'

4
BLUSH RAMBLER

(Climber. Very vigorous, flowers profuse in summer but little thereafter, blush pink, large-headed, resistant to weather but not to mildew.)

Pascoe approached the offices of Masson, Masson, Grey and Coatbridge, Solicitors and Commissioners for Oaths, with no great expectation of success. It was a sad fact that the Law's guardians and the Law's practitioners generally regarded each other with a great deal of mutual suspicion. Only the readiness with which Mr Edgar Masson had agreed to see him gave him any hope at all.

The reason for this readiness became apparent in the course of a chat with a very friendly Irish receptionist. Old Mr Edgar, she revealed, was the senior partner, and officially retired, but still retaining his office which he occupied most mornings, constantly devising new schemes to defeat the evasive tactics of his younger partners.

'He's just lonely, the poor old soul,' said Irish.

'You'd think they could have left him a bit of business to occupy himself with, but it's not like it used to be, is it? When you're old now, you just get pushed aside to make way for the young men. I like the old man myself. Many an hour we talk together, but that's no credit to me. The poor old devil would talk to anyone who'd listen, anyone at all. He's not at all particular. Why don't you just go straight on up?'

So Pascoe went on up, hoping to be treated as *anyone at all*. He was not disappointed, the only trouble being that Mr Masson, who turned out to be a completely bald, completely round and completely rubicund seventy-five-year-old, seemed inclined to talk about *anything at all*. He was a living proof of the seductive power of verbal association, shooting off tangentially along new lines of thought suggested to him in mid-paragraph, even mid-sentence, as if terrified that his life might end with things yet unspoken. The way to deal with this, Pascoe learned by trial and error, was to ignore all irrelevancies and use key phrases like *Florence Aldermann* and Penelope Highsmith as verbal sheepdogs to drive him back in the required direction.

After twenty minutes Pascoe had learned that there had been a will leaving the majority of Mrs Aldermann's estate to be divided equally between the RSPCA and the Church Missionary Society, with small legacies for various individuals including her niece, Penelope Highsmith. A few days before her death, she had summoned Mr Masson to Rosemont to discuss with him a radical revision of the will which would increase her niece's portion to some forty per cent, mainly at the expense of the RSPCA. This alteration was to be dependent upon the satisfactory conclusion of negotiations with Penny Highsmith for her to stay on at Rosemont as a sort of companion-cum-housekeeper. Nothing definite had been decided on, Mr Masson had left after what were (Pascoe did not doubt) lengthy discussions, with the understanding that Mrs Aldermann would be in touch in a few days. The old lady had retained the will.

Before she could make the promised contact, she had died.

'In her rose-garden, it appears,' said Mr Masson. 'They say that gardening is a soothing and healthy pastime for old and young alike. I have not found it so. There was a case I recall in which a man sued the manufacturers of a patent garden fork which obviated, so it claimed, the risk of lumber strain . . .'

'Mrs Aldermann,' interposed Pascoe hastily. 'Her will. Her niece.'

'The will was not to be found,' said Masson, who always returned to the path as if he'd never strayed off it. 'Her niece, Mrs Highsmith (*Miss* Highsmith in truth, but such a nice woman, such a nice woman), said she'd never seen it. She also said she was still thinking over her aunt's offer, but I knew Mrs Aldermann, I knew her well. It wouldn't cross *her* mind that her invitation could be rejected. No, that had not been a possibility seriously considered when she spoke to me about the will. So it seemed quite clear to me that, certain of her niece's agreement, she had destroyed the old will in anticipation of drafting a new one when we met again in a couple of days' time. Yes, that's what must have happened.'

Pascoe looked at him doubtfully. This seemed an extraordinarily naïve assumption for someone deep-versed in so cynical a profession.

'You never suspected that the will's disappearance was, perhaps, a trifle . . . convenient?' he ventured.

'Convenient? For whom?'

Perhaps age had softened his brain, thought Pascoe.

'For those who benefited from the intestacy,' he spelt out. 'That is, for Mrs Highsmith and, eventually, her son.'

'Good Lord no, why should I think such a thing?'

'Well, it's just that it seems a little . . . convenient,' Pascoe repeated.

'If I thought *that* every time a client died intestate, I'd be suspicious enough to be . . . a . . . *policeman*!' cried Masson. 'Why, didn't Mrs Aldermann's own husband, dear old Eddie, himself die intestate? And no one went around suggesting it was *convenient* for Mrs Aldermann!'

Pascoe gave up. 'You continued to act as Mrs Highsmith's solicitor?' he said.

'Of course. She asked me to. Why shouldn't I?'

Why not indeed? thought Pascoe. The missing will had benefited Masson's law firm too. They merely exchanged one rich client for another.

'I believe Mrs Highsmith attempted to sell Rosemont later,' he said.

'Oh yes, but several years later. I managed the sale for her, of course. A fine property, Rosemont. Not everyone's cup of tea, of course, and a lot of people demurred at the asking price. But I advised her to hang on and in the end we found a buyer. Every house has a buyer, of course, if only you can find him. I recall . . .'

'Rosemont,' said Pascoe.

'It was a great shame. Contracts were on the point of being exchanged, then he died. Had he died *after* exchange of contracts but *before* completion the situation would have been most interesting, as in the case of . . .'

'So Rosemont was not sold?' said Pascoe.

'How could it be? To whom? On the basis of what contract? The situation here was quite unambiguous. Even his deposit had to be returned to his estate. It was disappointing for Mrs Highsmith. It was, of course, tragic for Mr Neville.'

'Mr Neville? The purchaser? What exactly did he die of, Mr Masson?' asked Pascoe, crossing his fingers and hoping for a car accident on another continent.

Masson's answer was worse than he would have believed possible.

'Poisoned,' said the old solicitor with relish.

'Poisoned?'

'Yes. Don't you recall? Quite a *cause célèbre* mainly because the Grandison and the Old Brew House were so determined to be clear of blame that they started washing each other's dirty linen in public.'

The Grandison Hotel and the Old Brew House Restaurant were two of the most expensive establishments in the area.

'He stayed at the Grandison? And ate at the Old Brew House? and he was poisoned at one of them?'

'Probably not. But *qui s'excuse, s'accuse*, as they say,' said Masson gleefully. 'Poor Mr Neville ate something with parathion on it. It's used as an insecticide, highly toxic they tell me. Probably helped himself to some recently treated fruit as he was tramping round the countryside. But there was fruit in his room at the Grandison and he dipped generously into the fruit bowl at the end of his meal at the Brew House. There were rumours of crate-loads of peaches and grapes being dumped before the public health people got round there. Knocked their trade back a bit, I tell you.'

Masson spoke with the satisfaction one overcharging profession must feel when another gets its come-uppance, thought Pascoe.

He said, 'Why was this chap tramping around the countryside anyway?'

'Inspecting his acres, I should think,' said Masson.

'He was just back from Rhodesia as it still was. His family were staying in London while he looked around up here. He was from these parts originally and fancied ending his days doing a bit of farming up here. End his days he certainly did, poor chap. There was a nice parcel of land he fancied, but the farmhouse wasn't up to much. Then the agent drew his attention to Rosemont which abutted on the farm land in question. He fell in love. Fancied a bit of squiring, I suspect. And all those gardens gave him oodles of space to put up stock buildings, with electricity and water close at hand. He'd already settled to buy the land when he died, but contracts hadn't been exchanged on the house. The family wanted neither, but they were stuck with the land. Sold it back to the previous owner at a loss! There's no one sharper than a Yorkshire farmer.'

'And this is where he'd been tramping that day?'

'I expect so. Called in at Rosemont to discuss some points with Mrs Highsmith, but he seemed well enough there and only took a cup of tea. Terrible business all round. A great disappointment for Mrs Highsmith, of course.'

Pascoe said, 'Didn't Rosemont attract any other buyers?'

'No, I mean, there was no chance. Mrs Highsmith seemed quite knocked back by the experience. She took the house off the market. Of course, it wasn't the money she wanted, though the upkeep must have been considerable. Her inheritance had been

223

substantial and Mrs Aldermann's investments, or rather her husband's investments, had been wise and showed a steady appreciation. It was London she missed. She began virtually to live there when her son started his accountancy course and not long after he reached his majority, she contacted me about making the new arrangements.'

'Which were?'

'Simply, a transfer of assets. A common enough transaction to avoid or at least minimize the punitive taxes which accompany straightforward inheritance.'

There was a tap at the door which opened without a pause for an invitation. A man in his early thirties came in, nodded pleasantly at Pascoe, and said to Masson, 'Sorry to interrupt, Edgar, but I wanted a word with you before I went off to court. There are a couple of points you might be able to help me with. Will you be long? I must be off in twenty minutes.'

'No, no,' said Masson enthusiastically. 'I'll be with you instantly. The Inspector and I are just about finished, I think.'

'Inspector?' said the newcomer.

'Yes. Inspector Pascoe, this is Ian Coatbridge, our junior partner.'

'How do you do?' said Coatbridge. 'Anything I can do to help.'

Pascoe grinned amiably at him. He suspected that Coatbridge had just learned from the Irish girl that old Masson was entertaining the fuzz and had come rushing up post-haste to stem the flow of confidential information he suspected the old man was pouring out.

'I don't think so,' he said. 'I think we've just about finished. Mr Masson has been most helpful.'

The other man's surface of friendly interest shimmered into pained exasperation for a moment. Pascoe smiled and stirred the waters a little more.

'And Patrick got the house as a result of this transfer of assets?' he said to Masson.

'That's it. That was the only odd thing. She split the inheritance straight down the middle, you know, which meant he got the house and a bit of cash. What would a young fellow want with a rattling great place like that? I wondered. I thought he'd sell, but he didn't. No, the following week he was back here, enquiring about changing his name to Aldermann and of course he's lived in the damn place ever since. Odd, that. What do you think, Ian?'

Coatbridge gave a wan smile and said, 'Our clients must be permitted their little quirks, Edgar.'

He was clearly acutely embarrassed, but as Pascoe took his leave, he doubted whether the junior partner had as much cause for concern as he imagined. There was little doubt in his own mind that Masson's rambling reminiscences had concealed as much as they had revealed.

5

ICEBERG

(Floribunda. Very vigorous, upright and shapely,
graceful poise, well-formed, pure white blooms,
useful for large beds, excellent hedger.)

Ellie Pascoe was not in the best of tempers when the phone rang.

The previous evening she had been unpleasantly reminded that she was now theoretically back in full-time academic employment by the arrival on her doorstep of a cardboard box chock-full of examination scripts.

The middle-aged colleague who delivered them had wanted to do nothing but talk at great circular length about his future in the new institution that was being created. His name was Rothmann and he was a self-banished Johannesburg Jew of unimpeachable liberal credentials who embarrassed Ellie sorely by constantly cracking jokes whose racist content from another source would have made her scream with rage.

'The Principal says we will all be well looked after in the new Institute,' he now said anxiously. 'But, Ellie, I keep on hearing this voice saying *you will now all der shower be taking; please to form der orderly line and into der shower be moving.*'

Finally he left. At the door Ellie asked when the department would like the scripts returned.

'Oh, a couple of days,' he said vaguely. 'With all this time on your hands, it shouldn't take you long.'

She had closed the door with great force and made a rude gesture at the trembling woodwork.

But the scripts had to be read and the sooner the better. The only firm commitment she had the following day was coffee with Daphne Aldermann again. They had met in the Chantry on Monday as arranged and she'd enjoyed it so much that she'd offered no resistance when Daphne, obviously thirsty for friendship, suggested Wednesday and insisted they should return to the Market Caff. It had been this gesture towards democracy which had persuaded Ellie that, scripts or no scripts, she shouldn't put the meeting off, and to find herself stood up had not pleased her, though she had no doubt there was a perfectly adequate explanation.

And when after an hour of yawning her way through the scripts as though her jaw were seeking a physical dislocation to match the logical and linguistic ones which abounded therein, she snatched up the phone and heard Daphne's voice, it was this perfectly adequate explanation she expected to receive.

Instead Daphne said abruptly, 'I want to see you.'

'You do? Now, if you'd been in the Market Caff at nine-thirty as arranged, you might just have managed it,' replied Ellie with spirit.

'I'll come round,' said Daphne. 'I just wanted to check you were home.'

'Yes, I'm at home. And I'm also extremely busy marking exam scripts,' said Ellie, feeling all her irritation welling up. 'Daphne, what is it . . .'

The phone went dead.

Puzzled, Ellie replaced the receiver. Trouble was imminent, she felt sure of that. Daphne had sounded cold and hostile as only the well-brought-up English girl can sound cold and hostile. Ellie had read enough Marxist interpretation of history to know that the wrath of the bourgeoisie was not to be taken lightly.

She returned uneasily to her marking.

Half an hour later the doorbell rang.

'You found it then,' said Ellie inanely.

'It wasn't easy,' said Daphne accusingly.

Ellie guessed that the taut fury which she had sensed behind the telephone call had slackened off to some extent during the drive, and now Daphne was seeking new devices to renew the tension. Ellie resolved to make things difficult for her.

'I'm so glad to see you,' she smiled. 'You've no

idea what a hundred exam scripts with half an idea between them can do to the brain.'

'No, I wouldn't have, would I? Middle-class reactionaries with kids at private schools aren't intellectual enough to recognize even half an idea, are they?'

There was a fine high colour in her cheeks, the divided emblem of anger and embarrassment. It made her look extraordinarily attractive. If I caught a man thinking that, I'd call him a sexual fascist, Ellie thought.

She said, 'Daphne, something's upset you . . .'

'Sharp!' mocked the other, now fast re-approaching the pole of her cold biting anger. 'Really keen! What I wouldn't give for such sensitivity! Well, I may be just a plain little pawn in the class war, but at least I'm not the kind of two-faced bitch who goes around spying on her friends!'

Ellie had retreated into the lounge where she was working, with Rose in her carrycot lying at the open french window and gurgling at the sparrows quarrelling over scraps on the bird table. She now subsided into an armchair so that Daphne towered over her.

'You don't look much like a plain little pawn from here,' she observed, still determined not to react. 'Daphne, please, forget the forensic fire and just tell me in plain words what you're talking about.'

'Oh, don't pretend you don't know,' said Daphne,

attempting a sneer which came close to being a sob.

'I may have my suspicions, but I won't know till you tell me,' said Ellie. 'And if you could sit down first, I'd appreciate it.'

Daphne hesitated, then sat on the edge of a high, wing-chair. Rosie, momentarily attracted by the prospect of quarrelling adults, decided that size was no substitute for savagery and returned her attention to the sparrows.

'Just answer me one thing,' said Daphne. 'Yes or no. Did you know when you decided to take me under your little left wing that *your* husband was in charge of an investigation into *mine*?'

'Oh dear,' said Ellie, her worst fears confirmed.

'Yes or no!' insisted Daphne, latching on instantly to this hint of assent.

'It's not as simple as that,' protested Ellie. 'Any simple answer to that question accepts all the implications of the question, which I don't.'

'Oh come on!' said Daphne. 'Don't play the nit-picking academic with me. It's a simple question.'

'And don't you play the WI plate-cake and flower-arrangement dummy with me!' retorted Ellie, happy to let go now she knew what she was into. 'It's not a simple question and you know it. Let's get my reasons for making your acquaintance quite clear for a start. First, I gave you a lift because it was raining. Nothing more. I'd no idea who you were. All right, I did work out you were a St Helena parent and it did amuse me to see your reaction when you spotted the placard in the car, but my motive was simple humanity. Second, I didn't decide to take you under my little left wing, though I must say I quite admire the phrase. It was just that as I talked to you, well, I found I *liked* you.'

'Rather to your surprise, you mean?' said Daphne. 'What did you do? Watch three Party Political Broadcasts as a penance?'

'There, that's one of the reasons,' said Ellie, risking a grin. 'You're sharp! And, all right, if there was a touch of political condescension in it to start with – you know: *Fancy little activist me liking someone like her*! can you deny that there wasn't a bit of social condescension in your reaction? *Hey, look at good old moderate tolerant me passing the time of day with an anarchist*! Right?'

Daphne said sourly, 'You say I'm sharp. I'm sharp enough to see you're avoiding the main point of the question.'

But she had relaxed perceptibly in her chair.

'Clearing the decks, merely,' said Ellie. 'All right. When you told me your name and mentioned where your husband worked, yes, I realized that Peter had a professional interest. I didn't do anything about it because all I could have done was nip our acquaintance in the bud and I wasn't about to do that. Why not? You want yesses and noes and all I give you is a multiplicity of reasons! I'm sorry, but here's three more. One, because I don't let my husband's concerns affect my own freedom of choice; two, because what he'd told me about his interest in your husband made it all sound like a bit of a joke anyway; and three, because I'd taken a fancy to you. Liberty, equality and human rights you can fight for, but friends are much harder to come by and you've got to grab them fast when they come along.'

'Now, that's very moving,' said Daphne in a hard clear tone, then she paused and when she resumed her voice had softened and become more hesitant. 'I'm sorry, I meant that to be sarcastic, but really it's not, I don't think. It *is* very moving what you've said, about friends and everything. You know, I haven't sat and talked about being *friends* with anyone since I was a schoolgirl and all those awful childish loyalties and loves and feuds meant such a lot! What I don't understand is how, if you're my friend, you could sit and listen to your husband talking about Patrick and . . . and . . .'

'And what?' said Ellie.

'I don't know what, do I?' burst out Daphne. 'You tell me. Just precisely what did you do when Patrick's name came up again? His name did come up again, didn't it?'

'Yes, it was mentioned,' said Ellie. 'Perhaps it shouldn't have been, but look, Peter trusts me. He talks about his work, I want him to. Sometimes I think it's a pretty shitty and disgusting trade but he's not a shitty and disgusting person and I know that a police force with Peter and a few more like him in it is going to be a damn sight better than one without him. So yes, he has mentioned your husband, and yes, I have mentioned you. I can't really tell you what was said about your husband, can I? Except that nothing's been said to me which has seemed to put *our* relationship in any difficulty, please believe me. As for what I said about you, I talked about you as a new friend and one I hoped would grow into an old friend.'

'And nothing more?' persisted Daphne, undiverted by this sentimental flourish. 'You mean nothing of what I told you about myself has been passed on in detail?'

Ellie recalled uneasily her late-night vinous discussion of Daphne's background, courtship, character and finances, crossed her fingers mentally, and said 'Nothing I wouldn't have said about any close friend.'

It was a Jesuitically vague response but it seemed to have substance enough to blunt the keen sceptical edge of Daphne's questioning. Or perhaps the frowning introspective silence she now fell into was merely a mustering of resources for a second assault.

Ellie decided a quick counter was the best tactic.

'Daphne, I'm sorry. I've let myself get into a situation where I'm bound to be wrong, and I admit it, and I'm sorry. But what's brought all this on? Something must have happened to bring you round here breathing fire. How did you find out about Peter's interest in your husband for a start?'

'Can't you guess?' said Daphne bitterly. 'After all, my private life must be an open book to you.'

'I've no idea,' said Ellie. 'Honestly. I'll cross my heart if you like. I can't think of any other way of convincing you I'm honest!'

Daphne looked at her doubtfully, then said, 'I wonder if I could have a drink? I know it's a bit early, but I feel rather shaky. I'm not very good at quarrels. I wasn't brought up to it.'

'Sure. Scotch OK?'

Ellie took her time preparing the drinks, going to the kitchen in search of ice and polishing the glasses on a clean towel before pouring the Scotch. Her intuition was proved right when she heard Daphne begin to talk even though her back was still to her.

'I heard from Dick Elgood. I mentioned your name to him, making a joke about your being a policeman's wife. And that's when he told me.'

'About what?' said Ellie, pouring the whisky drop by drop as though adding olive oil to a mayonnaise.

'About that stupid complaint he made to the police. And about your husband being in charge of the investigation. He also said that after I told him about that odd-looking CID sergeant coming round to the house to ask questions about my car, he'd let your husband know he'd made a silly mistake and didn't want things to go any further. But they have gone further, haven't they? *Haven't they?*'

Now Ellie turned.

'Yes,' she said, 'I believe they have. But why or how far I've no idea, believe me.'

She handed over the drink. She'd poured one for herself, well-diluted, to be companionable. She didn't want it – once this trying scene was over, the rest of those scripts would still require a clear head and a sharp eye to glean the wheat out of the chaff.

'You keep on asking me to believe you,' said Daphne, sipping at her Scotch.

'I realize I'm not very credit-worthy at the moment,' said Ellie. 'But I'm puzzled. Why did Dick Elgood tell you this? Or, going further back, why should you have told Dick Elgood the police had visited you about your car?'

'You don't know? You really don't know?' said Daphne.

'No!' said Ellie with sufficient emphasis to turn the baby's head again. 'I've said so!'

'Well, I'll tell you. Because after I parked my car that day, the day it was vandalized, I got into Dick's car and we spent the day together at his cottage, that's why!'

'Oh, I see,' said Ellie blankly.

'So I told him about the car being vandalized, and I told him about that sergeant visiting the house. I recall he seemed very interested in what he'd said, but I didn't know why.'

'No, no, of course not,' said Ellie, now feeling herself completely at sea. 'Daphne, you went to Elgood's cottage to . . .'

Untypically she found the sentence difficult to finish.

Daphne said in her loud, clear, confident, privately educated voice, '*Screw* is, I think, the word you're looking for. So you didn't know? That's interesting. Which means either that your husband hasn't told you. Which is also interesting. Or that *he* doesn't know either, and you've got to make up your mind whether your deep friendship for me permits you to tell him. Which is perhaps the most interesting thing of all.'

She rose, set down her glass and made for the door.

'Daphne!' cried Ellie. 'Please, let's talk some more.'

'All right, if that's what you want, but not now,' said Daphne, very cool and Noel Cowardish. 'Let's meet tomorrow morning. In the Chantry. I was going to come along to the Market Caff this morning and tell you what I thought of you, but I funked it. But I'll feel more confident in the Chantry, won't I? And you can let me know what you decided, can't you?'

It was too good an exit to spoil by pursuit and expostulation. Ellie remained fast in her seat, like a spellbound princess, hearing the front door close and the Polo start up and draw away.

She imagined she sat quite still during this time but when she finally stirred and looked down at her glass of unwanted Scotch, she discovered it had somehow become completely empty and she felt more than ready for another.

6

CLYTEMNESTRA

*(Hybrid musk. Crinkled pinky-yellow blooms, leathery
leaves, of a spreading bushy habit, excellent in Autumn.)*

'Mr Capstick's not at home,' said Mrs Unger in the
severe tone of a governess finding it necessary to
repeat what should not have needed to be said in
the first place.

Pascoe wondered if the old woman was using
the phrase literally or conventionally.

'I see,' he said. 'I'm Inspector Pascoe. I was here
a few days ago, you may recall.'

The unblinking blue eyes in the old apple-
wrinkled face fixed themselves on his forehead
as though in search of some authenticating mark.
It struck Pascoe that perhaps their peculiarly
unnerving quality derived from myopic first sight
rather than keen second.

'I talked to Mr Capstick in the conservatory,' he
went on. 'You brought me some delicious buttered
scones.'

The features relaxed. He had been approved once, and she was not, he guessed, a woman to change her mind very often.

'He's gone to Harrogate,' she pronounced with the intonation of one who might be saying Xanadu. 'One of his cronies came to fetch him.'

So he really wasn't at home. In fact, it suited Pascoe very well. He said, 'Perhaps I could have a word with you, Mrs Unger. It won't take long, I promise you.'

Her lips puckered fractionally at his presumption. He got the message. It would take precisely the amount of time she condescended to allow. His promises didn't come into it.

But she opened the door wide and stood aside to let him enter. Then, closing the door and bolting it (an instinctive rather than a significant action, he assured himself uneasily) she pushed by him and walked down the hallway to a handsome inner door where the process was repeated save for the ramming home of the bolt.

'Sit down,' she ordered.

Pascoe sat. To his surprise, Mrs Unger immediately withdrew.

Musing on her intentions, he looked around. It was a fair room, a little too square perhaps, and rather too high for its width. An oak sideboard and a large glass-fronted oak bookcase, both solidly mid-Victorian in style, filled the wall to the left of his wing chair which was placed square to an ornate marble fireplace. Daringly, he rose and went to look at the bookcase. Through the diamonds of glass he read some of the titles engraved and gilded on the leather-bound volumes. A taste for Trollope was perhaps forecastable, but Colette came as a surprise.

Behind him there was a rattle and he turned to see that Mrs Unger had entered the room with a wooden tea-trolley which she was now manoeuvring into position alongside the wing chair.

'You'll have some tea,' she said.

It wasn't a question. He guessed that, like Dalziel, she knew what was best for most people. He nodded and said, 'Thank you,' and sank deep into the chair, but not so deep as his heart when his glance lit upon the plateful of buttered scones on the lower tray of the trolley.

Direct attack seemed the best defence.

'I wanted to talk to you about the day the Reverend Somerton was killed, the gentleman who got hit by the stone falling from the tower of St Mark's. Now I know this happened more than ten years ago but I wonder if you remember the day.'

Mrs Unger did not reply. As he spoke, she had poured him a cup of tea. He stirred it and sipped it. The silence continued. With a wan smile he took a plate, helped himself to a scone and bit into it.

'Delicious,' he said.

'It was a Saturday in March. Second Saturday in

239

the month, I seem to recall. It was a real March day, cloudy one minute, clear the next, and blowing a gale all the time.'

This accorded precisely in both date and meteorology with what Pascoe had read in the coroner's report. The windy conditions, it was theorized, had been in part responsible for the falling masonry.

'Mr Capstick wasn't at home that day, I gather?'

'No.'

'But you were?'

'Yes.'

'Was there anyone else here?'

Silence. He took another bite. And another.

'Yes. That young fellow who did the roses was here, I recall,' said Mrs Unger.

In his excitement Pascoe finished the scone and did not hesitate to take another when the old woman flickered her eyes at his empty plate.

'Did the roses, you say? That would be Mr . . . ?'

He bit.

'Aldermann, his name was. He had a way with flowers, I'll give him that.'

But not with Mrs Unger. Pascoe guessed that Patrick had not been fed with buttered scones.

'What precisely was he doing?' he asked.

'Pruning and planting. March is the time for it, so they say. I told him Mr Capstick was away and he said never mind, he'd do a bit of pruning and planting. I let him into the garden and left him to it.'

'What time did he leave, can you recall?'

'About four o'clock. It started raining cats and dogs; it came sideways in that wind. He shouted that he was off and off he went.'

The Reverend's corpse had been discovered by the local vicar at four forty-five on his return from the reception of a wedding he'd officiated at earlier in the afternoon. He had arranged to rendezvous with Oliver Somerton at four P.M., but had been delayed.

Reading between the lines, Pascoe guessed that the reception had been a lively and well-liquored affair.

Finishing his second scone, he said, 'Could I take a look around the garden?'

Silently she led him out of the room, through the conservatory in which Capstick had been placed like some delicate Eastern plant, and into the garden.

'Thank you,' he said.

He walked swiftly across the lawn towards the thicket of boundary-marking shrubs over which rose the tower of St Mark's. There were rhododendrons here in full bloom, their colours vying with the richness of two or three lilac trees, but their scent unable to compete with the heaviness of half a dozen clumps of lavender which had been allowed to spread widely. Indeed, the whole of the shrubbery looked as if it had been left untended for several seasons now and the little path which wound its way through the bushes was overhung by their branches. Pascoe shouldered his way through till he arrived at a small gate in the cypress hedge. It was hinged to a rotting post by a circlet of wire which rain and dew had rusted to an autumnal brown. Beyond stretched the rough untended grass of an old graveyard, broken by stones whose inscriptions were eroded and obscured by time and weather and the tiny scrabbling fingers of innumerable lichens.

He forced the gate open with difficulty. Clearly the Capstick household used other routes to heaven. Treading with apologetic lightness across the graves of Little Leven's ancient dead, he made his way to the church and, after a small effort of recall, found himself at the spot where the Reverend Oliver Somerton had been struck down by a piece of consecrated stone. Uneasily he peered up at the tower, but all looked secure enough now. He presumed the Archdeacon's death had given a boost to the restoration fund if nothing else.

Here at this side of the church he was quite out of sight of the main gate and the tiny village beyond. The only sign of habitation was the roof of Capstick's house and those of his immediate neighbours, unless of course one counted the tombstones. Looking at them rising from the gentle ripple of the long grass, Pascoe realized he had no sense of neglect. The old gave way to the new always, and death did not stop the process. Men died and life went on in the space they vacated. For a while their remains were marked by clean, smooth obelisks with sharp-edged lettering, and it was right that the grass around these should be razed and flowers laid at their feet. But as the new became old and the survivors in their turn came to rest, it was also right that the old stones should be absorbed into the landscape as surely as the remains they marked were absorbed into the deep, dark strata of the earth.

Something whizzed past his head and hit the flagged path beside him. Startled, he stepped back and looked up. High above, a beaked head cocked itself to one side as though resetting its aim.

'Thanks for the thought anyway,' said Pascoe, looking at the white splash on the flagstone and recalling that it was supposed to be lucky to be hit by a bird-dropping. He glanced at his watch. It was time to go. There were other scenes of death to be visited, other metaphysical meditations to be meditated, miles to go before he could sleep. Miles to go.

By the time he reached No. 12, The High Grove, the home of Mrs Mandy Burke, widow of Christopher Burke, one-time assistant to the Chief Accountant of Perfecta Ltd, Pascoe was no longer in the meditative mood. For a start Mrs Unger's scones, impervious even to a lunch-time pint of best Yorkshire bitter, lay heavy on his stomach. Next, the pink and white lozenges of ornamental stone which formed the patio on which Mr Burke had met his end were in no wise as atmospheric as the worn grey flags where the Archdeacon had been struck down, nor did the pebble-dashed rear wall of No. 12 with its puce-painted window-frames soar into the imagination in quite the same way as the dark tower of St Mark's Church.

And finally, instead of the quiet company of the ancient dead, Pascoe was entertained by the presence of the Widow Burke whose antiquity was unassessable beneath the cosmetic art of mid-Yorkshire's best beauticians, but whose quickness was never in doubt.

'This is where he fell, Inspector, or Peter, may I call you Peter?' she said. 'This is the very spot.'

She pointed with all the dramatic style of those stately-home guides who point to the very spot, often marked by ineradicable bloodstains, where some unfortunate scion of the noble family now living off the entrance fees met his end. There was no bloodstain here, only a tray on which stood a glass and a jug of what looked like iced lemon squash.

At least, thought Pascoe, she had had the good taste not to cover 'the very spot' with the sun-bed from which his insistent finger on the front doorbell had at last summoned her.

Strangely, the news that he was a police officer had seemed to eradicate rather than exacerbate her annoyance at being disturbed. Modern middle-class attitudes to the police usually stimulated an instant expression of grave distrust followed by a demand for warrants to be flashed and business clearly stated before the threshold was crossed.

Instead she'd flung open the door to him, invited him to walk through and had evinced neither surprise nor reluctance to talk when he had diffidently referred to her late husband.

'Shall we stay out here to chat?' she said. 'One can hardly afford to miss such divine weather, can one? There's a deckchair in the garage if you can find it. I'll get you a glass. I'm sure you're dying of thirst. Won't be a moment!'

With a promissory smile, she went back into the house. Pascoe took the chance of being alone to get his bearings. He recalled the High Grove estate vaguely from his own house-hunting days. It had just been completed and he and Ellie had taken a quick look, which was all they'd needed. Not that it was bad as such up-market development went. There were three types of detached property, arranged in groups of five as though the builder believed in the mysterious properties of the quincunx. The Burke house was a Chatsworth second only in size and luxury to the Blenheim. This particular group of Chatsworths backed on to a bunch of Hardwicks which were two-bed, two-recep (or three-bed, one-recep) bungalows. It had been a Hardwick that the Pascoes had been persuaded to examine, a pleasure denied the owners of the Chatsworths by a seven-foot-high length of pastel green composition screening (based, Pascoe recollected the agent's blurb, on an Italian cloister design), plus whatever vegetation had matured at the foot of the Chatsworths' longish lawns.

Presumably, however, a man up a ladder would be visible from the bungalows.

He entered the garage through a side door. It held a Volvo estate, the back of which was packed with what he took to be wares intended for her market stall – straw mats, cane baskets, bead curtains, silk flowers, that kind of thing. Cardboard boxes containing similar items were piled up in the small area of space left by the Volvo's length. Among all this colonial cane, he found a good old English deckchair.

He was still wrestling it into submission when the Widow Burke returned with a tall glass which she proceeded to fill with the inviting-looking iced squash.

The chair suddenly fell into shape.

'Sit,' she commanded, handing him the glass.

He sat, and she removed the wrap-around robe she must have wrapped around when summoned to the door, and subsided not ungracefully into her sunbed.

Without the robe, the question of her age became more accessible of inductive reasoning. This sun-tanned skin certainly did not cover the firm muscular flesh of youth, but neither had age scored and puckered the smooth veneer with its excoriating frosts. Beneath the narrow bikini-top, her breasts arched as much as they spread and the contour of her stomach was Cotswoldian rather than Pennine.

Mid-forties, Pascoe assessed. And well worth a second look.

She spotted the second look and smiled her understanding.

'Cheers,' she said.

'Cheers,' said Pascoe, taking a long pull at his lemon squash. It hit the back of his unprepared throat like lava and he spluttered eruptively. The basic dilutant was not water, but vodka. At least this provided some explanation of her manner.

'I'm sorry,' she said. 'I should have warned you. Is it true you're not allowed to drink on the job?'

'Only in moderation,' said Pascoe, placing the glass firmly on 'the very spot'.

'Me too,' she said, drinking, and eyeing him over the rim of the glass in what should have been an embarrassingly ludicrous parody of a 'twenties Hollywood vamp, but wasn't.

Pascoe said firmly, 'About Mr Burke.'

She said, 'Is it the insurance company or has someone been making naughty phone calls?'

'Pardon?' said Pascoe.

'You must have some reason for wanting to talk about poor old Chris after all this time. I was just wondering if there was any way I could get it out of you.'

She laughed as she spoke, vodka-moist lips drawing back from good white teeth.

'It's really just routine, Mrs Burke,' said Pascoe lamely.

'Mandy,' she said. 'If you're not going to be frank, you can at least be friendly. Don't think me callous, Peter, but I'm well over it now, you

247

see. Life goes on. I'm all for life. Not everyone is, you know. It's a great jostling race, but all the fun's in keeping on running. They'll have to knock me off the track before I let anyone get past, but Chris now, he was just my age yet he acted like my father sometimes. Forty did it for him, he got to forty and somewhere in his mind a little clock went *ping*! like a kitchen timer, telling him he was now into middle age, and in six months that's what he became – middle-aged!'

'Yet he went running up a high ladder in the middle of the afternoon,' observed Pascoe, glancing up at the eaves. 'I shouldn't have fancied it.'

'That's because you're a mere youngster,' she said firmly. 'Checking up on workmen's part of the middle-age syndrome. Value for money. He had a good head for figures, Chris, but not much for heights.'

'Yes, he was an accountant, wasn't he?' said Pascoe, spotting the opening.

'That's right. Perfecta. They make bathroom fittings and such like,' she said. 'You should take a look in my bathroom, Peter, I have everything.'

'Yes,' said Pascoe. 'In your evidence at the inquest, you mentioned the bathroom, I believe. You said you had a shower before you went out.'

'Oh yes,' she answered. 'So I did. I recall thinking later that perhaps it happened while I was actually in the shower. You can't hear a thing in there – telephone, doorbell, *nothing*. And I wouldn't look out on to the patio before I left. Perhaps he was lying there already. Somehow that made it all seem so much worse.'

The coroner had recorded laconically 'break' at this point. Presumably Mrs Burke had been overcome. Even now her handsome face was shadowed.

'It wouldn't have made any difference,' said Pascoe gently. 'He died instantly, I gather.'

'Yes, that was a comfort,' she replied, dabbing at her eyes, smiling bravely, and taking a long drink. 'Isn't it warm today? Why don't you take your jacket off?'

'No. I must be going shortly,' said Pascoe. 'When you found him, was there any sign that anyone else had been with him?'

'What on earth do you mean?'

'Well, a couple of glasses, for instance,' said Pascoe holding up his own. She tried to refill it, but he moved it back hastily and she topped up her own instead.

'No. Nothing like that. I recall I put the car in the garage, came out of the door straight on to the patio, and there he was. No sign that there'd been anyone else here. Why should there have been? I mean, if there had been, they would have said, surely?'

'Yes, of course,' said Pascoe. 'Tell me, as a matter of interest, did Mr Burke socialize much with his colleagues at Perfecta? Mr Elgood? Or Mr Eagles? Or Mr Aldermann, say?'

'My, you do know a lot, don't you?' she said

admiringly. 'I thought, the moment I saw you, *there*'s a man who knows a lot. Let me see. Elgood, no. He was friendly enough but only in a boss-ish sort of way. Tim Eagles and his wife we swapped dinners with a couple of times a year. As for the other, Aldermann, the one who got his job, Chris reckoned nothing of him. There'd been talk of some trouble when he was in private practice, I believe, but it wasn't that. Chris wasn't a man for gossip. Very strict moralist, Chris. Old Testament judgements, but he had to see for himself, he wouldn't condemn without he had the firm evidence before his very eyes. But he didn't care for Mr Patrick Aldermann. He said he was superfluous to requirement, even as a part-timer. It was a fix, he said, and Chris didn't care for fixes.'

'Did he complain about Mr Aldermann?'

'You mean officially? Oh, I expect so. He would hold his peace till he was certain about something, but then there was no holding him. He would make his view known even if it meant half the country knowing his business. Oh bother. The jug's empty. It just evaporates in this heat, you know. I'm going to make myself some more. Why don't you unbutton and have a swallow or two with me?'

She stood up, swayed, placed a hand on Pascoe's shoulder to steady herself and let gravity direct the heavy bombs of her breasts towards his upturned face. Alarmed, he slipped sideways out of the deckchair, going down on one knee in the process.

'Careful!' she said anxiously. 'You haven't torn your trousers, have you? Never mind if you have. I'm a demon with a needle. I can stitch you up and send you home so your wife wouldn't notice you'd been mended.'

'No, no, it's fine,' Pascoe assured her. 'I'll have to be on my way. Many thanks, Mrs Burke.'

'Mandy,' she said. 'Call again. Or drop by my little boutique in the market. Mandy's Knick-Knacks. I can always find something interesting for a friend.'

'Perhaps I will,' he said. 'Isn't the market open today?'

'Oh yes,' she said. 'But I roasted there all morning and decided my assistant could manage by herself this afternoon. It's all right when you're young and skinny, but when there's a bit more upholstering, the sweat just *runs* off you.'

She shook herself gently as if to demonstrate the phenomenon.

Pascoe smiled and retreated, not without relief. But as he drove away he was surprised by an uneasy feeling that, drunk and gamesome though she had been, and though he had resisted all her offers, even of running repairs with needle and thread, yet she had somehow managed to stitch him up in some not yet definable way.

7

EMOTION

*(Hybrid perpetual. Beautifully formed flowers,
opening from tight buds, pale foliage.)*

Sergeant Wield was privately convinced that the whole Aldermann business was a load of time-wasting crap, and a morning spent catching up on CID paperwork followed by a hasty lunch in an overcrowded, overheated pub, had sent him to his interview with Mr Wellington, the coroner on the Burke inquest, in a far from happy mood.

Wellington was now retired, a dried-up stick of a man with a strong belief in all those virtues, such as temperance, chastity and respect for authority, which time recommends to the old. But if the years had blunted his appetite, they had done little for his temper.

'Wield? Wield? I remember you. You were saucy with me once, young man. In my own court! I reprimanded you. Severely.'

'That's right, sir,' said Wield and pressed on to the matter of Burke. There was no joy here either. Wellington was indecisive only about whether to be more offended by the suggestion that Burke, a man of notorious sobriety, might have been drinking, or that he himself, a man of notorious probity, might have played down such a fact. A lecture followed on the inadequacies of modern policemen, the immorality of modern youth, and the immaturity of modern coroners.

Musing on the delights of giving evidence at an inquest on Mr Wellington himself, Wield was almost past the station desk when the duty sergeant's call brought him to a halt.

'Young Singh was asking after you,' he said. 'Seemed to think it was urgent.'

'Did he?' said Wield sourly. 'Where's he at?'

'I think he's down in the canteen,' said the sergeant. 'Said he was hot. You wouldn't think these darkies would feel it like us, would you?'

Wield grunted, and thought that perhaps a cup of tea would cool his own fevered brow, not to mention his simmering temper. He went down to the canteen. It was almost empty, with no sign of Singh. A DC on his way out said he thought the cadet had gone further down the corridor to the locker-room.

His irritation resurfacing, Wield walked the extra twenty yards and pushed open the door. But he didn't go in.

At the far end of the room, naked to the waist,

Singh was bent over a washbasin, splashing the running water on to his chest and arms and gently crooning the latest sentimental hit.

The muscles of his slight, flawless torso moved like light on a pool under a wintry sky. Wield caught his breath, holding perfectly still against the door-frame, but the boy sensed there was someone there and turned.

'Hey, Sarge,' he said cheerily. 'I was looking for you.'

'Were you? What the hell are you doing?' demanded Wield roughly.

'Just having a wash down. Who decides when you can go in shirt-sleeves? These tunics are not what you'd call lightweight, are they?'

His attempt to sound friendly touched Wield's heart, but when the boy started moving towards him, drying himself off with a handful of paper towels, Wield said, 'I'll be in the canteen for two minutes. No more,' and left.

He bought himself a cup of tea, then added a glass of orange squash. There was no need to take brusqueness to the point of boorishness, he felt. And Singh's attachment was almost up.

But how long will my attachment continue? he asked himself ironically.

The cadet appeared half a minute later. His apprehensive expression relaxed slightly when Wield pushed the squash towards him.

'That'll cool you down,' he said. 'Now, what's so urgent?'

'Well, I saw Mick Feaver this morning,' began Singh. 'You know, him that we had in because of vandalizing them cars.'

As he unfolded his story, Wield's professional instincts became involved above the personal.

'You're sure he said Rosemont?' he demanded.

'Certain,' protested Singh. 'And *he* was sure that's what Jonty had said because that's how he could prove he wasn't lying, wasn't it?'

'Sorry?' said Wield, unsure of the pronouns.

'Anyone could say he was going to do a house next week, couldn't they?' explained Singh. 'There's always plenty of houses get done. Then he could just pick one and say that was it! Anyway, I thought I'd best tell somebody.'

'You took your time, didn't you?' said Wield. 'You talked to this lad this morning, you say, and now it's the middle of the afternoon.'

'I couldn't find anyone, and I was kept pretty busy,' said Singh defensively.

'Oh aye. I forgot how busy they keep you,' said Wield gently, realizing that the probable truth was the boy had agonized for hours before taking this further and decisive step in his relationship with Jonty Marsh and Mick Feaver. From old mates to villain and 'grass' in three days, it was a turn-around rapid enough to bring on a nasty bout of nausea.

Fortunately, or unfortunately, youth is resilient even in its betrayals, and now Singh proceeded, 'This Rosemont, Sarge, could it be that place we went out to, with the woman whose Polo got damaged, and the little girl?'

'Could be,' said Wield. 'But likely there's other houses called Rosemont, so don't be putting in for the police medal yet.'

'But if it is,' insisted Singh, excitement glowing in his dark, handsome face, 'will there be a stake-out? Will I be able to come on it?'

'I shouldn't be so keen,' said Wield. 'Even if this lad is talking about the same house, there's still a lot can happen. Most stake-outs I've been on, you just sit around all night, and it's cold, and it's dark, and it's uncomfortable, and nothing ever happens. Come the dawn, you're red-eyed and stiff and knackered and all you've got the energy to do is strangle the silly bugger who put you there in the first place, if you can get your hands on him. So I wouldn't be so keen to get on the job!'

He finished his tea and pushed back his chair.

'But we'd better let Mr Pascoe know when he gets back,' he said. 'He's got more artistic hands than me, so the strangulation process shouldn't be so nasty. On the other hand, *he'll* probably pass it on to Mr Dalziel when he comes back from London at the weekend. Have you ever had a good look at Mr Dalziel's hands?'

Shaking his head, he stood up and slowly made for the door.

Peter Pascoe didn't know whether to be delighted or not with Shaheed Singh's news. He distrusted simple coincidence. By the time he'd finished questioning the young cadet, Singh felt glad that he wasn't a criminal and not all that pleased to be a policeman.

'What do you think?' Pascoe asked Wield after the door had closed behind the relieved youth.

'Rosemont fits the picture,' said Wield. 'Big, but not big enough to have a living-in staff. Nicely isolated without being buried in the countryside. And probably with enough good stuff lying around to be worth nicking without being so good that it's all carefully catalogued and put in a bank vault when the house is empty.'

'That's the first thing to check, whether the house is going to be empty in the next couple of weeks,' said Pascoe. 'It's a bastard. If the Aldermanns *are* going away for a week, say, we can't afford to stake the place out for seven nights.'

'Might be a fortnight,' said Wield helpfully.

'Thanks! And I don't see much percentage in young Singh chatting to his mate again. He's probably terrified already at what he's done! Still, we can't ignore it. You check with the Aldermanns – no, on second thoughts, I'll do that. It's about time we met formally, I think. You get hold of Arthur Marsh's file again and see if there's anything useful there. And let all ears start flapping for any sound of a link-up between Marsh and these jobs. Mr Dalziel said he'd ring late this afternoon, so I'll fill him in then. He'll be thinking that, one way and another, Aldermann's really managing to hog the limelight! Which reminds me, how'd you get on with Mr Wellington?'

'He didn't take kindly to the suggestion that an eminent, worthy and respected churchgoer like Burke might have been pissed out of his mind,' said Wield. 'He was even less happy at the hint that he might have played down such information.'

'So Burke is stone cold sober,' said Pascoe. 'Which was more than you could say for his widow.'

'How did you find her?'

'Available,' said Pascoe. 'But evasive too. I had the feeling that I could put my finger on anything but the complete truth.'

At half past five the phone rang and next moment Dalziel's stentorian voice was sounding in Pascoe's ear. After listening to a succinct, pungent, and actionably obscene analysis of the conference so far, Pascoe gave his equally succinct but metaphorically more restrained account of his interviews with Masson and Mrs Burke.

Dalziel asked several questions, then said, 'Right, so you think Masson was up to something and Burke's widow was hiding something?'

'I suppose I do,' said Pascoe cautiously.

'I'll think on it,' said Dalziel heavily. 'You carry on talking while I'm thinking.'

Pascoe now told him about Singh's tip.

'Grand,' said Dalziel. 'The lad's done well. Tell him I'm pleased.'

'But it may be nothing,' said Pascoe, surprised by the fat man's enthusiasm. 'It's so vague.'

'Vague or not, next time the Aldermanns are out of that house, you've got the perfect excuse to be in. You'll be able to go over the place with a fine-tooth comb. Never know what you'll pick up!'

'I thought the idea would be to *prevent* illegal access,' said Pascoe, faintly scandalized.

'You're not taking a high moral tone with me, are you, lad?' said Dalziel threateningly. 'Listen, we've got that mad Welsh bugger here, the one who's always shooting his mouth off on television. What *he* wants, apart from hanging, flogging, and machine-guns, is for cops to have right of access without warrant, day or night, to any premises anywhere, and all householders to deposit duplicate keys at their local station! He thinks I'm a wet pinko, so you just count your lucky stars.'

'Sorry, sir,' said Pascoe. 'I'm counting. It's all right. Now I've finished.'

'You're a telephone hero,' said Dalziel with scorn. 'Listen, getting back to Masson, do you think he mebbe reckoned Penny Highsmith destroyed Aunt Flo's will herself?'

'I wondered about that,' admitted Pascoe. 'There was certainly something there, I felt.'

'I'm seeing her on Friday night, I'll put out some feelers,' said Dalziel. It was an image which set Pascoe's mouth twisting in a silent rictus.

'Talking of wills, this Burke woman looked comfortable, did she?'

'Very,' said Pascoe. 'And financially too.'

'You dirty young sod,' said Dalziel. 'Does she make money out of her market stall, do you think?'

'Maybe. But I get the impression she probably just likes the hustle and bustle and the company, preferably male. She's pretty flamboyant.'

'That's a new name for it,' said Dalziel. 'It's probably worth checking on her money, what Burke left her, what her income is now. She's in the covered market, isn't she? How did she get a pitch there? They're not easy to come by, inside or out. One comes vacant, the market traders usually have it sewn up in advance. It's notorious, any councillor on the market committee is kept in King Edwards for life.'

Pascoe made a note and said, 'Any special reason you're so suspicious, sir?'

'Who's suspicious? Just curious. Another thing. You say she drove down to the shops at two-thirty, came back at three-thirty, walked out of the garage straight on to the patio, and there he was, dead?'

'That's right,' said Pascoe. 'I've got all the reports here. Inquest, police, medical. It all tallies.'

'Have a look at the list of possessions,' said Dalziel.

'Sorry?'

'When they took Burke in for cutting up, they'd empty his pockets and itemize the contents,' explained Dalziel with violent patience. 'Find the list and read it out.'

Hastily Pascoe sorted through the papers.

'*Well*?' demanded Dalziel.

'I have it. I have it. Wallet containing . . .'

'Stuff the wallet. Get on to the loose stuff.'

'Handkerchief. Small change. Car keys . . .'

'Stop there,' said Dalziel. 'All right, where was the car?'

'Whose car?' asked Pascoe blankly.

'Burke's car! I take it them houses just have single garages and driveways? Right, then. If Mrs Burke could back her car out at two-thirty, there wasn't any other car in the drive was there? And if she could drive back into the garage at three-thirty, there still wasn't, was there? So where was it?'

'Somewhere else?' offered Pascoe brightly.

'Right! And why?'

'Well, he was just popping in to collect something he'd forgotten, and didn't think it was worth taking the car up the drive.'

'Something he'd forgotten up a ladder?' asked Dalziel.

'Or he knew his wife might be going out later, so he parked on the road in order not to block her.'

'He was a well-known considerate fellow, was he?'

'Not from the sound of him,' admitted Pascoe. 'What do you suggest we do, sir? I mean, do you think it's important?'

'I can't do your thinking for you, lad,' said Dalziel heavily. 'You talked to Dandy Dick yet?'

'Tomorrow,' said Pascoe patiently. 'I did tell you.'

'Oh aye. You lose track in this bloody place. It's like a bloody ant-hill down here. I like streets where I know half the buggers I meet and I can understand most of what the rest of 'em say. I'll be glad to get back even if it does mean putting up with you lot again. Keep in touch!'

'I will,' said Pascoe. 'Enjoy your conference.'

The phone went down with a crash.

'You know, he sounded quite homesick,' said Pascoe to Wield.

'It's nice to know we're missed,' said Wield. 'What do we do now?'

Pascoe glanced at his watch.

'There's only a couple of dozen things we could do,' he said. 'None of which should take more than a few hours by the time they got spread out. But on the other hand, I'm feeling a bit homesick too. I think I'll just go home.'

Ellie seemed slightly distracted that evening, but he put it down to the spiritual shock of coming to grips with the stack of exam scripts which still littered the lounge, though it was harder to explain in the same terms her perceptible start when he observed casually, 'I'm going to be getting a look at your mate, Daphne, at last.'

'Why? What do you mean?'

'Just that I'll have to call round and have a word with them. We've had a tip that Rosemont is going to be done, that's all. Probably nothing in it.'

'It's not just another excuse to get into the house and have a poke around, is it?' she asked earnestly.

He regarded her with puzzled amusement.

'You think like fat Andy, do you know that?' he said. 'No, it isn't. It's a genuine tip, come to us courtesy of young Sherlock Singh. How's the marking going?'

'Rosie got hold of a couple of the scripts, and chewed them,' said Ellie gloomily. 'God knows what the external examiner will think.'

'He'll put it down to rage,' said Pascoe.

'He could be right. How was your day? Anything new on the Elgood front?' she said casually.

'Not much. I'm seeing him tomorrow.'

'Are you? Why?' she asked sharply.

'Just a couple of points to clear up. Is there some beer in the fridge? I just fancy one. What about you?'

'No, thanks,' she said. 'Peter, you will remember that Daphne's my friend.'

'When I visit Rosemont, you mean?' he said evasively. 'I'll be awfully polite, I promise.'

He went out of the lounge to the kitchen, leaving Ellie staring sightlessly at the pot of ferns in the fire grate.

'Oh shit,' she said.

8

INNOCENCE

*(Bush. Vigorous, upright, flowers creamy white
with a few pink flecks – sweetly perfumed.)*

Pascoe was five minutes early for his appointment
with Elgood. As he approached the office door,
it opened and a man in a creased grey suit was
ushered out by Miss Dominic who regarded Pascoe
coldly, though whether on account of his earliness
or because he'd used the lift he could not tell. The
departing man headed virtuously for the stairs.

Creep, thought Pascoe and went in.

'You're early,' said Dick Elgood. 'I hope this
means you're in a hurry. I know I am. I'm up
to my eyes.'

'I'll try not to keep you long,' said Pascoe. 'Just
a couple of questions.'

'Haven't you asked enough questions, for God's
sake? Last time we spoke, I told you to drop the
matter. But since then from all sides I hear you're
still snooping around!'

Elgood sounded angry, but Pascoe thought he detected a note of anxiety as well.

'I've got a job to do, Mr Elgood,' he said solemnly. Ellie had once remarked that the main perk of being a cop was that you could talk entirely in clichés and no one dared throw rotten eggs. 'It's not an easy job,' he continued, warming to his banalities, 'and it has this peculiarity. Once you start on something, you take it as far as you can until you're convinced that no crime's been committed. It doesn't matter who says yea or nay. You carry on regardless.'

'Is that right?' sneered Elgood. 'Even when it means setting your own wife on to spy on people?'

Pascoe sat upright, jerked out of his role-playing.

'You'd better explain that, Mr Elgood,' he said quietly.

'What's to explain?' said Elgood. 'Except if you're going to say it was coincidence that the day after I spoke to you at the station, your wife struck up an acquaintance with Mrs Aldermann.'

'I'm not sure I need say anything about that,' said Pascoe, 'except to wonder how you're so familiar with Mrs Aldermann's affairs.'

'It's not only the police who hear things in a town this size,' answered Elgood challengingly.

He wants me to say what I know, thought Pascoe, still slightly off-balance as a result of the crack about Ellie. It could only mean Daphne Aldermann had mentioned her new acquaintance to Elgood. Damn. It must look suspicious, to say the least. Not that that bothered him, but the thought of the embarrassment to Ellie if the Aldermann woman took it wrong . . . perhaps it had happened already; there'd been something in Ellie's manner last night . . . a restraint . . . on the other hand, she had said she was having coffee with Daphne this morning, so . . .

He shook the wisps of thought out of his head. Wisps. A good word for most of his thoughts on this case. Everything vague, nothing to grasp at.

Perhaps it was time to hit Elgood with a few facts.

'Let me tell you what we know to remove any temptation you may feel to lie,' he said. 'We know that the day before you spoke to me at the police station you met Mrs Daphne Aldermann in the top floor of the multi-storey car park. We know that she transferred from her car to yours and you drove away together. We know that she did not return to her car until approximately five hours later.'

'Your wife told you all this, did she?' said Elgood.

'No,' said Pascoe wearily. 'My wife has told me nothing about you. As far as I'm aware, she *knows* nothing about you. I may be wrong, of course. To get back on track, Mr Elgood, we have independent witnesses to your rendezvous with Mrs Aldermann in the car park. Are you denying it?'

Elgood shook his head, stood up and began to walk round the room with his graceful dancing step. He didn't look at all like Fred Astaire, yet there was in his simplest movement that same quality of rightness. He was immaculately suited in Oxford blue mohair with a striped claret and gold waistcoat with mother of pearl buttons.

'I'm not denying I met her. Why should I? My private life's my own affair, isn't it?'

'It seems to me you made it mine when you complained that the husband of the woman you had this private rendezvous with was trying to kill you,' said Pascoe in exasperation. 'For God's sake, in simple terms of motive alone, it alters everything.'

'Because he's jealous?'

Elgood began to laugh. It sounded fifty per cent genuine.

'What's so funny?'

'You are, Pascoe,' said the little man. 'You keep on getting it wrong! Aldermann's not the jealous type, believe me. Any road, there was nowt to be jealous of. It was the first time me and Daphne had met, apart from a couple of lunch-time drinks where anyone could see us. Come between him and his precious roses, that might be a different matter!'

'Isn't that what you are doing, by blocking his advancement?' answered Pascoe, trying a different tack.

'Mebbe,' said Elgood, serious again. 'But that's for him to decide. Me, I'm just doing what's best for the firm. It'll all be sorted next Wednesday, by the time he gets back.'

'Back? From where?' asked Pascoe.

267

'He's going off on Monday to that fancy school near Gloucester that his lad goes to. No wonder he's short of a bob or two, paying out on them places! I've brought the next board meeting forward till Wednesday, so he should be safely out of the way.'

He spoke with the satisfaction of absolute authority, but Pascoe was much struck by the disproportionate influence this (by all accounts) quiet, unassuming man Patrick Aldermann seemed to have over the lives and decisions of others.

'Out of the way? Yet you say you don't feel threatened?' he mused aloud.

'No. I want that forgotten,' said Elgood. 'How many times do I have to tell you? My private life's my private life. Keep out of it! I've seen you today, Mr Pascoe, to give you a last warning. Any more prying by you, or your men, or your missus for that matter, I'll treat as police harassment. And I'll go a long way over your head, aye, and over Andy Dalziel's too, to get it stopped. I've got friends in most high places, Mr Pascoe. So think on.'

Pascoe rose slowly.

'Friends,' he said. 'High places. Threats. Nasty sneers about my wife. I quite liked you when first we met, Mr Elgood. I thought you were . . . natural. Unspoilt. An original. But suddenly the mould is beginning to look very familiar.'

To his credit, Elgood looked uncomfortable.

'Listen, Pascoe. About your wife, I meant no

offence. The rest stands, but a man's wife's a different matter.'

'And you are something of an expert on the difference,' murmured Pascoe making for the door.

The telephone rang. Elgood snatched it up as though relieved at this reunion with the outside world.

'Yes?' he snapped, turning his back on Pascoe who opened the door. He felt his exit if not ignominious was at least undistinguished.

'Pascoe!' said Elgood. 'It's for you. Try to keep it short.'

It was Wield.

'Hoped I'd catch you, sir,' he said. 'I had a moment this morning, so I thought I'd knock off one or two of these little jobs from your list. First up was Mrs Burke's finances. Her husband left her comfortable, but not really comfortable enough for a motive. But I checked on that market stall of hers. The word is it's a little goldmine. More interesting though is how she got the lease in the first place. There was a bit of queue-jumping there, I gather. A bit of calling in of old favours.'

'I'm listening,' said Pascoe.

He listened for another three or four minutes, ignoring Elgood's terpsichorean expressions of impatience.

'Thanks, Sergeant,' he said finally and replaced the receiver.

'Finished, Inspector?' said Elgood. 'Perhaps I can have my office back, eh?'

For answer, Pascoe sank slowly on to the hard chair once more.

'Just one more question, Mr Elgood, if you don't mind,' he said.

'I do bloody mind!' exploded Elgood. 'Can't you take a bloody hint?'

'I'm quite good at hints,' said Pascoe. 'I've just had a couple. Mr Elgood, before I go, I'd like to discuss with you for a little while the precise nature of your relationship with Mrs Mandy Burke.'

While her husband was not being offered coffee by Dick Elgood, Ellie Pascoe was sitting drinking her second cup in the Chantry with only Rose for company.

Not by nature a nervous woman, she had approached this meeting with the trepidation of one who feels herself in the wrong with little clear idea of how she got in it and less of how she can get out of it. She would dearly have loved to talk things over with Peter, but that had been impossible without revealing the cause of her concern, which would have made her undeniably guilty of the treachery she stood accused of. Yet she had sensed something evasive in her husband's manner also which suggested to her that he already knew of the liaison between Daphne and Elgood.

Nervously she lit a cigarette. It was a silly and expensive habit but the body had its needs which were often as dangerous to deny as to satisfy.

She found herself beginning to hope Daphne

would stand her up again. Not that it would put her any more in the right, but it would place Daphne just a little in the wrong. Rose, peevish at having only her introspective mother for company, was beginning to turn and twitter in search of a wider audience. Any moment now she would advertise her neglected state by a bellow which would set the tinted coiffures of the Chantry clientele a-bobbing their disapproval.

Time to go. Ellie stubbed out her cigarette and finished her coffee. The door opened. Daphne came in.

She looked untypically flustered and sank into her tweed-upholstered chair with a sigh of relief. Rose let out a gurgle of welcome.

'Sorry I'm late,' she said. 'Hello, Rosie. Yes, please, two coffees, I think. No, no scones.'

The waitress who, like all of her kind, leapt forward eagerly the instant Daphne appeared, went off to the kitchen.

'Nothing the matter, I hope?' said Ellie.

'Not really. It's just that I was coming straight into town after dropping Diana at St Helena's, but I realized I'd forgotten my purse, so I had to drive home for it. Not that that would have made me so late, but when I got back to the house, there was a car in the drive and a man wandering round the side of the house. I asked him what he wanted and he said he was from the Water Board and he was just trying to locate the house's main stop-cock. When I asked him why, he said that our water-rate bill hadn't been paid and he'd called round to say that if it wasn't paid instantly, proceedings for recovery would be taken, and not finding anyone at home, he thought he would locate the stop-cock in case it became necessary to cut the water off!'

'Good Lord!' said Ellie. 'What did you say?'

'I sent him away with a flea in his ear, of course. I would have rung Patrick, but he's gone off to London today, won't be back till Saturday morning. I poked around in his desk and found the water bill. Sure enough, it wasn't paid, but that can't give them the right to wander round at will, can it?'

'Depends on how many threatening letters you've had,' said Ellie. 'This man, did he show you any authority?'

'A badge or something, you mean? No. He didn't get the chance.'

'And he was driving a car, you say, not one of those blue and white vans?'

'No. An old Ford Escort. What's the point of all these police-type questions, Ellie?' demanded Daphne.

'Something Peter said last night,' answered Ellie. 'Look, I really shouldn't be saying this, but in the circumstances . . . And he's going to be coming round to see you in any case. There's been quite a lot of break-in's recently at medium to big houses, a bit isolated, and they've had a tip that Rosemont's on the list.'

'What!'

'Yes, but Peter thinks there's a good chance there'll be nothing in it. Only it struck me, this chap you saw this morning might have been casing the place.'

Daphne looked so alarmed that Ellie was sorry she'd spoken.

'It's probably nothing,' she said hastily. 'I'll get Peter to check, if you like.'

'Yes, yes, I would like,' said Daphne.

After a moment's silence, she added, 'I suppose all this came up when you were giving your husband a blow-by-blow account of my visit yesterday?'

'No, I didn't tell him you'd been, nor anything of what you said,' said Ellie evenly.

'Cross your heart?' said Daphne, faintly mocking.

'And Guide's Honour. But he did say he was going to see Mr Elgood this morning. I don't know why, but if it turns out to have anything to do with you, please believe me, Daphne, I haven't told him.'

Their gazes met and locked for a moment.

Then Daphne smiled wanly and said, 'I believe you. I thought a lot about things last night and it struck me that the picture of you as a police spy was almost as ridiculous as you wearing a funny hat at the Tory Conference.'

'Thanks,' said Ellie.

'I'm usually pretty good at first impressions,'

continued Daphne, 'and my first impression was that you were likely to be honest to the point of embarrassment, perhaps even tedium.'

'Thanks, again,' said Ellie. 'I'm not sure that my gratitude is going to last out if you continue on those lines, though. And don't get carried away. Remember, I confessed to having chatted about you with Peter. I may not be your dyed-in-the-wool agent provocateur, but I'm not your sea-green incorruptible either.'

'You're the best I've got,' said Daphne, finishing her coffee. 'Look, if you've got the time, I'd like to talk with you about Dick and me, and Patrick too. What happened, and everything.'

'Are you sure you want to?' asked Ellie, troubled.

'Can't I trust you?'

'Not unless you can trust me,' said Ellie. 'All right. Shoot.'

'Not here,' said Daphne, 'If Special Branch haven't bugged this place for your sake, the WI certainly have for mine. Let's stroll around, if that's all right.'

A slight head movement brought the eager waitress.

'My turn, I think,' said Daphne, opening her handbag. Then her composure vanished.

'Oh damn!' she said. 'With all that fuss, I forgot to pick up my purse anyway. Ellie, would you mind?'

'You can always tell the very rich,' said Ellie opening her bag. 'They never carry money.'

Daphne laughed, but the waitress on her behalf was clearly not amused.

Elgood caved in quite suddenly. Pascoe was surprised. Even by using the old trick of implying much greater knowledge than he had, he hadn't been able to sound very knowledgeable. If Elgood had simply stuck to his first story that his intercession on Mandy Burke's part in the matter of the market lease had been a simple act of charity to ensure that the widow of a former employee didn't fall on hard times, Pascoe might well have ended up believing him.

All that he had besides was the business of the car not being parked in the drive and his own recollection of Elgood's defensively aggressive response when he had tried to associate Burke's death with those of Eagles and Bulmer.

Plus, of course, Elgood's reputation as a Lothario, Mrs Burke's lively manner, and above all her easy reception of his questioning as though perhaps she had been forewarned.

But the strongest suspicions are straw to the fire of a respectable citizen's indignation, and Pascoe was ready to retreat at the first digit of the Chief Constable's number.

He pressed his insinuations. The receiver was lifted, the finger poised.

Then Elgood said wearily, 'To hell with it. What am I doing? I'm acting like a bloody criminal and I've done nowt. I'll be calling for my lawyer next.'

He sat down behind his desk and pressed a button on his intercom.

'Miss Dominic,' he said. 'Let's have some coffee, love. Aye, for two.'

He looked his age suddenly. Sixty and tired. But he managed a wan smile as he spoke.

'You, Pascoe,' he said, 'I've got you worked out. You'll not leave this alone, will you? Christ, I started something when I talked to you, didn't I. Andy Dalziel's not daft. I could chuck you out of here and you'd be right off round to talk to Mandy Burke again. Right? Of course it's bloody right. Well, listen. I don't want that. Not that I've done anything criminal, you understand, but I don't want any aggro, not just at the moment. So what I'm going to tell you now is to get things straight and get you out of my hair. And it's off the record. Right?'

The efficient Miss Dominic entered with two cups of coffee on a tray. She set it on the desk, glanced assessingly at Pascoe, and left.

Pascoe said, 'It's not in my power to give you that assurance, sir. Not in advance.'

Elgood opened a drawer, produced a bottle of almost colourless liquid and poured a shot into each of the coffee cups.

'Plum brandy,' he said. 'You can hardly smell it. All right. You decide when you like. Me, I'll just deny everything! But this is what happened. Yes, you're dead right. I was having a thing with Mandy Burke. She'd been down to my cottage a couple of times. She was keen, you follow me? Too much for poor old Chris Burke.

'Well, we met by accident that lunch-time. I'd been having a business lunch in the White Rose, I recall. There was me, and our sales director, and Patrick Aldermann was there as well for some reason, and a couple of chaps from the Council. It wasn't a big deal, fitments for a new old folk's home or something, but these Council lads like their pound of flesh in the form of best fillet steak. Afterwards the others all went off, but I slipped into the bar to wash the talk out of my throat. And who should be there but Mandy. We had a quick one together and I think we both began to feel our oats, you know how it is. We'd both drunk enough to be a bit reckless, so when she said *How about a little ride*? I said, *Why not*? and we went out to the car park and got in her car. I thought she'd be heading for some nice quiet country lane, but no, she just pointed the car homewards. I sobered up pretty quick when I realized where we were going, I tell you! But there was no stopping her, so all I could do was crouch low in the car and hope I wasn't spotted!

'I had another fit when I came out of her garage round the back of the house and saw the decorators' stuff, but she said they'd buggered off for the day and we'd be all right. So I went in. Since I was there anyway, there didn't seem any point in arguing the toss any more!

'To cut a long story short, we enjoyed ourselves

for about an hour and I was just saying I ought to be getting back when we heard a noise outside. Well, we thought the decorators had come back. Before I could stop her, Mandy jumped off the bed and ran to the window. She's like that, never thinks, just acts on the spot. She pulled back the curtain and let out a huge shriek. No wonder. It were like a French farce, there was Chris, like a monkey on a stick, perched on a ladder and peering in!

'I can only guess what'd happened. Perhaps he saw us in town. Perhaps he'd been on to us for a while. Any road, he'd come home, parked his car up the street and walked to his house. He likely checked that Mandy's car was in the garage, then tried to get into the house, quiet like. But Mandy's a bit of an old hand at this game, I always reckoned, and she'd slipped the bolts home in the front and back doors, just to be on the safe side. Then, seeing her bedroom curtains drawn and the ladder standing there handy, he decides to climb up it! Jealousy's a funny thing, Mr Pascoe. These poetic fellows write about men climbing mountains for love. It took jealousy to get old Chris Burke up a ladder! He'd no head for heights and he wasn't a very nifty mover. Two left feet at the office dance, I'd noticed. Now the shock of seeing Mandy all of a sudden, like, standing there shrieking, stark naked, with me behind her, must have made him jump. The ladder toppled sideways and he went out of sight. I'll never forget that moment, Pascoe. Never.'

He shook his head at the memory, finished his coffee, diluted the lees with another shot of plum brandy and downed that also.

'We got down there straight away. He was stone dead. Mandy was hysterical and I wasn't much better myself. But finally I got her calmed down and we got dressed. Whatever we did, it wasn't going to help matters if we were discovered running around in the nude, was it? By now it was beginning to dawn on us just how awkward things were. Don't get me wrong, Pascoe. The man was dead and we were shocked and sorry. He was my colleague, her husband. But he wasn't a very likeable man, old Chris, not the kind of man you'd mourn for longer than was decent. Neither of us wanted him dead, but now it had happened, neither of us wanted to see ourselves all over the Sundays. The head of I.C.E.'s a Dutchman, a very good-living, religious sort of man. He'd not take kindly to having the Chairman of one of his subsidiaries featured in anything as titillating as this was likely to be. As for Mandy, already she was seeing headlines: DID HE FALL OR WAS HE PUSHED? That sort of thing.

'So when I suggested I should get out of the way, it wasn't just self-interest, you follow me? It was for both our sakes. No one had come round to the house or tried to ring, so presumably none of the neighbours had spotted anything. I got down in the back of the car, Mandy drove me back into town and then went home and discovered the body. Simple! We didn't attempt to alter the immediate circumstances of his death at all. He climbed a ladder, he fell off. We just altered the reasons a bit, that's all. No crime committed, no crime intended. Just a bit of diplomatic rearrangement.'

He looked at Pascoe as though in search of an acquiescent nod.

Pascoe said evenly, 'Everything you did from the moment you failed to call the police was criminal in fact, Mr Elgood. And Mrs Burke, of course, perjured herself at the inquest.'

'Does that count? Legally, I mean?' asked Elgood naïvely.

'It's a court of law like any other,' said Pascoe. 'And the law doesn't like being lied to. And it tends to regard the suborners of witnesses just as seriously.'

'Suborner?' said Elgood.

'I presume your assistance to Mrs Burke in setting up her business was an inducement to, or reward for, silence?'

'Bollocks!' exploded Elgood. 'No such thing. The bloody woman started talking marriage a couple of months later, so I dropped her pretty bloody quick! The market stall was just something that came up, a sort of farewell present, that was all, something to keep her busy. I've had practically nowt to do with her since.'

'But you did ring her and warn her in case I came round, didn't you?'

'Aye. And I was bloody right to, wasn't I?'

grumbled Elgood. 'All right, Inspector, now you've got the story. So what happens next?'

'You wouldn't like to put it all in a written statement, would you?' asked Pascoe hopefully.

'Do I look bloody daft!' said Elgood. 'Listen, I've told you this so you can stop sniffing around, stirring things up. It's not a good time for trouble.'

'You mean your Dutch boss wouldn't like it?'

'A bit of scandal just now could seriously weaken my position,' said Elgood. 'Particularly when it's both juicy and comic.'

'Not to mention criminal,' said Pascoe. 'And this is why you choked me off when I came round to see you about the Aldermann business?'

'Partly,' said Elgood. 'But also, like I've said, because I realized I was just being stupid about that. Why do you keep niggling away at it, for God's sake, Pascoe? You haven't really come across anything to make you suspicious, have you?'

'Your own behaviour has been enough for that, wouldn't you say, Mr Elgood?' said Pascoe, rising and proffering his hand. 'I'll have to talk over what you've just told me with my superiors, I'm afraid.'

'As long as you remember I've told you nowt,' said Elgood, shaking his hand. 'And Mandy Burke won't talk to you with a witness present either.'

'We'll see,' said Pascoe. 'Oh. One last thing before I go. What was it that Mrs Aldermann said to you that made you suspicious of her husband in the first place?'

Elgood shook his head sadly.

'Nothing. I've told you. Nothing. Just leave it, Pascoe. Please.'

'He was attentive. Interested. Amusing. All in a rather old-fashioned way. Old too, yes, but old-fashioned is how it struck me. Not fuddy-duddy. Certainly not that! But playing to rules that pre-dated this modern permissive make-your-choice-you're-a-free-agent stuff. Very sexy with it? Six inches shorter and thirty years older than me – I would never have believed it possible! I suppose, perhaps, I wanted a father-figure, but that's no excuse. And I did drink a lot of wine that lunch-time. But even that usually makes me sleepy rather than randy!'

Daphne laughed, then put her hand over her mouth, half in embarrassment as though she'd started laughing in church.

In fact, she almost had. She and Ellie were sitting on a bench set on a small green formed where a crescent of red-and-cream bricked almshouses reached its arms out possessively as if to embrace a little age-blackened tall-steepled church, built in 1669 to replace one destroyed three years earlier when a local lunatic, jealous of Yorkshire's good name, had decided to start a fire which would be to London's as a pitch-link to a taper. The fire had gone no further than the medieval church. God had sent his rain to put it out, the City Fathers had rebuilt in a more Protestant mould in thanksgiving, and two hundred years later their Victorian successors had added charity to piety in the form of the almshouses.

It formed a pleasant quiet backwater within a hundred yards of the city's main shopping streams, too quiet for some of the old people who lived in the crescent (now an official civic sheltered-housing project), who complained, half-jocularly, that it was a bit too convenient for the boneyard most of them could see from their sitting-room windows.

'Are things bad with you and Patrick?' asked Ellie.

'No. Or rather I don't know. I never thought about it until recently. We seemed to move along in such a tranquil state. Patrick's so *unworried* about things. You know that feeling, when you're sitting in the sun at a table in some Italian square and you've had a couple of glasses of wine, and you feel perfectly at one with the world? Well, Patrick seems to be like that permanently!'

'That doesn't sound a bad way to be,' said Ellie.

'To be, perhaps. To live with is different. It's all right when you're in the moment too. But moments like that pass. A breeze comes up, you get a little chilly, there's the dishes to wash, you're woken up in the night by your daughter's bad cough, your period comes, you're reminded in a hundred different ways that life is movement. And yet there he is, your helpmeet, your husband, back there somewhere, quite content, quite *still*!

After a while it stops being an irritant, it becomes a worry.'

'And you ease your worry by jumping into bed with a sixty-year-old Don Juan?' said Ellie.

'I thought you'd be more help than this,' said Daphne accusingly.

'Sorry, sorry, sorry.'

'And perhaps we should get it straight. I didn't *jump*. I moved hesitantly, uncertainly. It was stupid, but you know what put me in Dick's way to start with? My desire to talk about Patrick! I wanted to know how things were at work. I'd detected signs of a change in recent weeks, a sort of suppressed excitement, or unease, I couldn't tell which, he never shared it with me. I'd begun to wonder if his contentment mightn't all be a front and perhaps things were seriously wrong somewhere in his life. I see now it must have looked like manna from heaven to Dick. I didn't know to start with, of course, that he'd already decided to block Patrick's promotion to the board! We met for drinks a couple of times, usually at lunch-time. He never put a foot wrong. A hand occasionally, just brushing me half accidentally, or a sympathetic squeeze of the arm, or the knee. I knew there was desire there too, don't mistake me. I didn't mind it. I suppose I even responded to it. But it was still innocent.'

Ellie's ears pricked at the choice of word, but she had sense enough not to make it an issue.

'To do Dick justice,' Daphne continued, 'he

never made a direct proposition, though perhaps he was clearing the decks, so to speak, the Friday before I went to the cottage when we had a lunch-time drink together and he suddenly spelt it out that he was actively opposing Patrick's elevation to the board. He said he was sorry if I'd been relying on this financially, but I had to understand, he didn't think Patrick was the man for the job. I brooded about this all Saturday. I'd never really thought of our having money problems. I vaguely knew how large our expenses were. And I suppose I vaguely wondered how Patrick managed to get by with no apparent trouble on what I assumed couldn't be a huge salary. But that Sunday, when I'd been more than usually irritated by that secret-happy manner of his, I let fly. I still wasn't really worried, you understand. I knew there'd be some investment income, from Patrick's own capital and also from the money I'd inherited from Daddy. Patrick had taken charge of it when we married and tied it up, so I thought, in some long-term high-yield investment. All I wanted was to pierce his shell, to get some kind of response out of him.

'Well, I got more than I bargained for.

'He told me without batting an eyelid that my little inheritance hadn't existed as such for seven or eight years. It had just been eaten away by necessary capital expenditure! I couldn't believe it! I asked about his own money. There'd been some other money left to him by some old client at Capstick's. He told me that had gone too and that in fact as far as capital went, we had precious little to fall back on. And he admitted that even with his salary as Chief Accountant since Mr Eagles died, it was difficult to make ends meet. You have to understand he spoke with no anxiety whatsoever!

'I demanded to know how we could go on living at the rate we did. He said that, yes, it was hard, but he had every confidence in the future. In fact, things should be looking up very soon now. I screamed at him that if he imagined he was just going to walk on to the Perfecta board, he had another think coming. He looked puzzled and said that getting on the board would be nice and he could see no real obstacle, but even if he didn't, it wouldn't be the end of the world. I was furious now, furious and a bit frightened. I asked him how the hell he, an accountant, could justify continuing to live in a house as large as Rosemont with all those gardens to maintain when we could solve our problems of income and capital at a blow by selling up and moving to somewhere more manageable.

'That got to him at last. It must have been the mention of selling Rosemont that did it. Not that he got angry or anything. He just went on very earnestly about how something had always come up in the past to maintain his position at Rosemont and that he had every reason to believe all future obstacles would fade away with similar ease.

'I was sick at heart. All this meant to me was that he'd conned himself into believing the seat on the board was his. I rang Dick. I had to talk to him, I said. He suggested we should spend next day together. We arranged to meet in the car park. I'd heard stories about his seaside cottage, of course, but I didn't see this as a lovers' tryst. I was frightened by what seemed to me to be Patrick's lack of balance. Also, of course, I was bloody furious that he'd spent all my money without a by-your-leave!

'So Monday morning came, I met Dick, we headed for the coast.'

She fell silent. Two old ladies circumambulating the green paused to admire Rose noisily, and to deplore silently this upstart occupation of their personal bench.

'At what stage,' enquired Ellie casually, 'did it seem better for your financial deliberations to be carried on in bed.'

The two old women moved on, one indignantly, one reluctantly.

'I don't know. It just happened. I suppose I drank a lot. I know I talked a lot. It was funny; as I talked, I began to see what Patrick had meant. Things *had* tended to fall his way, if you looked back. He could almost be forgiven for his stupid optimism. I started off by wanting to complain about him, yet I ended up half defending him!'

'But not yourself?'

'Evidently not. I don't recollect much about getting undressed. I remember the actual event all right. Well, he *was*, after all, the only other man I'd ever been with. It was quite pleasant, I suppose, but it felt very different. I mean felt *physically*, that is. He was very bony. Even his muscles felt hard and knotted and bony. And he seemed very big, you know, *there*. I'm no expert, but he did seem to be disproportionately large.'

'Big for his size, you mean?' said Ellie.

Daphne giggled.

'Yes, that's it, exactly. Afterwards he said it had been great, but I'm not sure he really meant it. I don't think his mind was really on it either. I'd worried him, I realize now. I'd no idea! Somehow he got the idea I was warning him that Patrick contrived to dispose of everyone who got in his way! So he went running off to the police like a terrified hamster! It's laughable, really. These men who call us neurotic and fanciful, give them half the chance and they're standing on their executive desks, screaming at imaginary mice!'

'You're learning,' approved Ellie. 'They're a laugh a minute.'

'Not quite so frequent, perhaps, when they're policemen, and they start chasing the mice,' said Daphne.

There followed a long silence in which they studied the blurred and mildewed tombstones visible through the green-painted railings that had been put up when the churchyard wall had been declared dangerous. The tombstones themselves looked well decayed, their ranks crooked, their heights irregular and their stances awry and stooping, like a rabble of aged veterans drawn up on a last parade.

'Well?' said Daphne.

'Well what?' said Ellie. 'I don't particularly want to attack Peter for doing his job. And if I defend him, I might seem to be implying that *your* husband may have a case to answer. You see my dilemma?'

'Not really. Surely Peter can't *really* think Patrick may have a case to answer? I haven't met this husband of yours, but he sounds a pleasant rational man.'

'I haven't met this husband of yours either,' evaded Ellie. 'You'll have a chance to meet mine soon. He'll want to see you and Patrick before you go off next Monday.'

'Well, it'll have to be lunch-time on Saturday at the earliest,' said Daphne.

'I'll tell him. Come on, Rosie, time we were moving. I suspect we're preventing these two old dears from enjoying their daily contemplation of last things.'

She rose, feeling like a coward, but not knowing what else to say or do, and organized the baby into her papoose-basket.

As they moved away, the two old women took over the bench with the speed of legal tenants moving in behind the bailiffs.

'I always thought it was the young who took the place of the old,' said Daphne, not resisting Ellie's flight.

'Never believe it,' said Ellie. 'We're turning into a geriatric society. The old are fighting back. They have the great advantage of an irresistible recruitment programme. It's called living.'

They walked away together, two tall women, one dark, one fair, in a state of friendship which they both knew might well turn out also to be a state of truce.

9
PENELOPE

(Hybrid musk. Tall-growing, prodigal of bloom, pale-pink while young, but fading almost to white in age, good hedger, heavily scented.)

Penny Highsmith was a good drinker but she was no match for Dalziel in whom ancestry, employment and inclination had combined to form a true professional, who never acknowledged a master and rarely a peer. Prolonged bouts of reunion drinking had taken a toll, however, and Dalziel was getting most of his sleep by cat-napping blatantly through the conference sessions. He had borne a distant headache with him, like a thunderstorm in the next valley, to his rendezvous with Penny. But a couple of pints of watery London beer at the simple steak house she suggested they visited had washed his mental heavens clear and he had kept the carafes of red wine coming at a rate which had the Maltese waiters exchanging suggestive grimaces.

They were wrong, of course. Dalziel did not rate wine as a drink in the drinker's sense of the word, and his purpose was simply hospitable rather than amatory or even interrogative. Also he was enjoying himself, just sitting here, eating the biggest steak they had been able to produce and talking to a lively, intelligent and attractive woman.

He said as much to Penny, who had by this time wisely asked for a bottle of mineral water to cut the wine.

'I'm glad you're having a good time, Andy,' she said. 'You know, after you left the other night, I got to thinking how strange it was that you should just be happening to stroll by my place as I came home. And I began to wonder if there might be more in it than mere coincidence.'

'Fate, you mean?' said Dalziel. 'Written in the stars? That sort of stuff?'

'Not exactly,' said Penny. 'More like, ambush. Written in the CID notebook. *That* sort of stuff. But now I see how much you're enjoying yourself, I think, no, he couldn't be putting this on. Could you?'

'Don't be daft,' said Dalziel. 'This is the best time I've had since they banned hanging.'

'I'm pleased,' she said. 'Mind you, I did check on you when I spoke to Patrick yesterday.'

She was watching him carefully over her wine-glass.

'Yesterday? Rang him, did you?' said Dalziel, somewhat taken aback.

'No. He dropped in. Just here on a quick trip. Like you. Made his duty call.'

'Unlike me,' said Dalziel gallantly. 'No duty, just pleasure.'

'Well, I half believe you,' said Penny. 'But only because Patrick says he's never heard of you.'

'You asked him?'

'Oh, just in passing. Checking through old acquaintance. You must be slipping, Andy. There was a time when you made enough noise to be heard all the way to the Scottish border.'

'I've quietened down,' said Dalziel. 'Stay long, did he?'

'Not long. He never does. We've never been terribly close.'

'Funny that, with you bringing him up all by yourself. Did you ever think of marrying his dad? Or was he married already?'

'None of your damned business,' said Penny.

'Sorry,' said Dalziel, emptying the carafe into her glass. Another was delivered almost before he could nod his huge grizzled head at the waiter. 'But it can't have been any joke bringing up a lad by yourself. The money side must have been hard enough. And in them days, they didn't have one-parent families, they had tarts and bastards.'

She gave out her splendid laugh.

'You really know how to talk to a girl, Andy! But it wasn't so bad. There were some nasty sods around, there still are for that matter, but most people weren't much bothered, particularly down here. As for money, I got by with a little help from my friends.'

'Including Aunt Flo?' prompted Dalziel.

'Aunt Flo and Uncle Eddie were very generous,' she said tightly.

'Yes, the old girl left you nice and comfortable,' agreed Dalziel. 'Were you surprised when you heard the will?'

He watched her closely as she replied. Pascoe had reported on his visit to Masson and Dalziel had worked out some conclusions of his own, but whether they would prove helpful or not remained to be seen.

'There wasn't a will,' Penny replied, sipping her wine. 'I inherited because I was the only living relative.'

'And Patrick.'

'Oh yes. And Patrick.'

'He seems to have taken a real shine to Rosemont. Was that just since you started living there after your aunt's death?' asked Dalziel.

She shook her head. Her rich dark curls danced, casting back sparks from the imitation coach-lamps which lit the restaurant.

'No. Patrick always loved Rosemont. We used to visit on odd occasions right from the time he was a baby. I'd been going much longer, of course, with my mother while she was alive. It amused me sometimes to think that Aunt Flo, after doing her duty by her errant sister, found herself having to do the same duty for her errant niece!'

She laughed, but without much humour this time.

'At least she did it,' proclaimed Dalziel.

'With a bit of arm-twisting,' said Penny grimly.

'From your uncle, you mean? What was he like?'

Her expression softened.

'Oh, Uncle Eddie was a lovely man. Kind and thoughtful and gentle. Flo drove him, of course. It must have been the attraction of opposites in the first place, and once she got him, she just kept on driving him. He was first class at his job, I believe, and a shrewd investor, but it was her who kept him at it hard enough to make the money that paid for Rosemont and kept her in luxury. It was marvellous really that he beat her in the end. I mean, she must have thought Rosemont was her own personal status symbol. A small country house to match her snobbish aspirations. But he turned it into a refuge for himself. He loved the house, and even more he loved the gardens, especially the roses.'

'Like Patrick, then?'

'Oh yes,' she said reflectively. 'Very like Patrick. He took to Rosemont in a big way, right from the beginning, even though we only used to get there for odd weekends and Aunt Flo would be telling him to keep quiet and watch his manners all the time. Me, I'm not one for putting down roots. I'm a city girl, too. Always will be. I don't wander as much as I used to nowadays, but I still love it here in London even though it belongs to the Arabs now. This is where the life is. Stay too long with the vegetables and you vegetate. But Patrick was different. He never complained, mind you. But two days at Rosemont obviously meant more to him than two months anywhere else. I suppose it was the only sort of permanent thing he ever came across. Me, I hate permanency, but I'm beginning to feel as if I might be permanently pissed. Listen, can we have some coffee before I fall off my chair?'

Dalziel turned his head towards the waiter who rushed forward with another carafe, a reasonable assumption on past performance and as they were only half way through their main course.

'Coffee,' said Dalziel. 'He must have been upset when your uncle died.'

'He was, I guess, though he kept it all inside, as usual. He loved Eddie, I think, more than me in many ways. I tried to explain to him that I didn't think we'd be going to Rosemont so often now. What I really meant was *ever*. But that didn't seem to bother him. Not, you understand me, because he wasn't bothered by not going back, but more as if he thought I was being stupid for suggesting we wouldn't. As it turned out, he was right. Aunt Flo had a heart attack while she was in London. I was with her. She'd just brought me tea in Harrods. It was a sort of annual treat! I visited her in hospital, helped her around as she recovered, and then she asked us to go up to Rosemont with her till she had thoroughly convalesced. I suppose she knew she was never going to be fully recovered, that's why she suggested I stayed on permanently. But I told you all this the other night, didn't I! Hey, how come we're talking about all this again?'

'Just passing the time. So Aunt Flo dropped dead in the rose-bushes. And fortunately for you, she'd just torn up her old will.'

He hadn't meant it to come out quite so cynically. Or, if he had, he had overestimated the degree of alcoholic intimacy between the two of them. The contented, wine-languorous expression slipped from her face.

'And what the hell does that mean?' she demanded harshly.

'Nothing. Just remarking how lucky things fell out,' said Dalziel. 'They're taking their time with this coffee.'

'Bugger the coffee,' she said dangerously. 'What are you trying to say, Andy Dalziel? That I got rid of Flo's will when I realized she was dead? Is that it?'

Her voice was raised sufficiently for some other diners to glance curiously towards their table. Dalziel wasn't bothered. In Yorkshire it was generally reckoned there was more chance of getting Dalziel pregnant than getting him embarrassed.

He did, however, regret that this discordant note had been sounded in an evening he was genuinely enjoying. But as what Penny was accusing him of meaning was precisely what he did mean, he saw no reason to evade the issue.

'Well, didn't you?' he said. 'No one would blame you if you did.'

Except perhaps the governing body of the RSPCA, not to mention the reverend gents directing the Church Missionary Society. But their hypothetical cavils were as the bleats of a sheep being sheared to Dalziel's mental ear.

His generous reassurance did not produce the desired calming effect.

'You fat bastard,' she said. 'You haven't changed, have you? They all said you were a nasty bit of work then, and you still are now. I'll leave you to finish this muck. Next time you take a lady out, probably in another fifty years, try to buy her a decent bottle of wine instead of five gallons of this sludge, will you? Give my regards to Yorkshire.'

She rose as she spoke, almost knocking her chair over, turned and strode towards the door. She was fairly steady, Dalziel noted approvingly. And he admired her steadiness too in sticking to her story. In ninety per cent of cases, whatever threats, promises or inducements had been offered, the criminal who coughed was a fool.

Not that he could think of Penny Highsmith as a criminal, he thought, as her fetchingly rounded rear elevation vanished through the door.

The waiter arrived with the coffee and whisky.

'Bill,' said Dalziel tersely.

He downed the Scotch in one, studied the bill which the prescient waiter had quickly prepared as the quarrel developed, approved it, paid it and stood up.

Plucking Penny's handbag from the back of the chair where she'd hung it on arrival, he made for the door. The pavement was empty, but he stood with the bag held in the air which a passing taxi took to be a signal.

As it stopped, Penny emerged from a nearby shop doorway.

Dalziel got into the taxi, leaving the door open. After a moment, the woman joined him. He gave her address.

'Can I have my bag, please?' she said.

He handed it over and she opened it and began to look through her purse.

'It's all right. I paid out of my own pocket,' he said.

'Just checking,' she said icily.

'Look,' he said. 'I'm sorry. You got the wrong end of the stick.'

'In your case, I imagine both ends are dirty.'

They finished the journey in silence. At the door of the block of flats, Penny turned her key in the lock and tried to slip inside alone, but Dalziel's shoulder was too quick.

'Where the hell do you think you're going?' she demanded.

'Listen,' he said, his great slab of a face set with earnestness, as if a second-rate Renaissance sculptor, stuck with an angry Ajax, had smoothed down its features a bit in an effort to sell it as a St Peter in prayer. 'I just wanted to say, for me it's been a grand night, one of the best I've had in a long while. Grand. I mean that. Sincerely. Thank you.'

She regarded him with astonishment modulating to simple puzzlement.

'What are you after?' she asked. 'I mean, really?'

'Friendship,' said Dalziel promptly. 'Look, hadn't I better step inside and just check for muggers? These cockneys are all at it.'

She shook her head and laughed. He took this as an invitation, put on an alert, constabulary expression and stepped forward.

'Seems all right here,' he said. 'I'll just check the other rooms.'

With the aggressive confidence of one who has no expectation whatsoever of trouble, he opened the bedroom door. The man standing just inside struck him firmly and accurately on the nose, crashing him back against the wall. Penny screamed as he shoulder-charged her to the ground, then his footsteps were receding down the stairs.

'Jesus Christ!' groaned Dalziel, rubbing his watering eyes. They cleared enough for him to see Penelope who was struggling to her knees. The fall had dislodged her crowning glory of lustrous black curls and beneath the wig appeared a crop of tightly crushed locks, grey almost to whiteness.

'Are you all right,' asked Dalziel.

'No better for having you here,' she answered. 'God, your nose is a mess!'

He helped her up and together they went round the flat. The intruder proved to have been a neat burglar if burglar he was. He had clearly made an attempt to leave things as he found them and Penny had to admit that she might well have never noticed he'd been there.

'What the hell was he after?' she asked, having ascertained there was nothing missing.

'God knows,' said Dalziel from the bathroom where he was bathing his nose.

'What do you think I should do?' asked Penny. 'Call the police?'

'I am the police, remember?' said Dalziel, himself remembering he had sent a message saying he had a bilious attack to excuse his absence from the closing dinner. 'First thing I'd do is get your lock changed. That thing wouldn't stop a backward parrot.'

'You're bloody cool, I must say,' she protested. 'I've been burgled, and is this the best you can do?'

'You've seen nowt yet,' said Dalziel, removing his jacket and tie and sitting down on a sofa.

'What the hell do you think you're doing?' she asked.

He looked at her in surprise.

'You don't think I'd let you stop here by yourself tonight?' he said in a pained voice.

For a second she thought of getting angry again. Then with a sigh she removed her black wig which she had quickly rearranged and ran her fingers through her whitening hair. She aged fifteen years in a second.

'My top teeth come out too,' she said.

'Grand,' he said. 'I was getting worried I might be too old for you. Me, apart from my nose, I've got nowt that's detachable, I'm afraid.'

Now she smiled knowingly.

'We'll have to see about that,' she said.

They had Scotch, then they went to bed, and then they sat up in bed and had some more Scotch.

'Wasn't there some story, one of those old myths, where some god used to come to earth in various forms to have a bit of fun with the girls?' said Penny.

'Seems a sensible sort of thing to do,' observed Dalziel.

'Once he came as a swan, and once he came as a shower of rain, then another time he came as a bull.'

'How'd he manage it as a shower of rain?'

'I don't know. But I've a damn good idea how he managed it as a bull!'

Dalziel smirked modestly as though at a royal accolade.

'You should have had me that time fifteen years back,' he said. 'I've slowed down a lot.'

'Haven't we all?'

'Not you,' he said. 'Must be living down here that's done it. It's all too fast for me.'

'Like Yorkshire was too slow for me,' she said. 'I really missed London, I admit it. And the funny thing was, it didn't get any better as time went by. I paid visits, mind you. I mean, it's only a couple of hours or so on the train. But it wasn't the same. I had to get back.'

'Is that why you decided to sell up?'

'That's right.'

'How did Patrick react?'

'Patrick? He didn't say much. He was never one for big dramatic scenes. But I could see he wasn't too happy. But it was my life too, and there's only one life apiece, isn't there? He'd just finished his "O" levels, it was a good time to move. And another couple of years and he'd be taking off by himself anyway. So I went ahead with the sale.'

'And Patrick!'

'He went ahead with his life as if there wasn't any question of leaving,' said Penny. 'Good, that boy! He could be infuriating, he'd always been like this; anything happening or about to happen that he didn't care for, he just ignored it. I remember he came home about that time and told me he'd been discussing things with his teachers and he was going to take up accountancy. Just like that. I said he could do that just as easily in London as Yorkshire, but he didn't seem to hear me. I couldn't even see why he wanted to do accountancy. I mean, he was all right at

303

maths, but not great. Whereas for biology, and in particular anything to do with plants, he always got top marks. He even won prizes. But no, it had to be accountancy.'

'Perhaps it was because he admired his great-uncle so much,' said Dalziel.

'I don't remember telling you Uncle Eddie was an accountant,' said Penny, frowning.

'I bet you don't remember half of what's been said since we got under these sheets,' laughed Dalziel. 'What stopped you from selling up in the end?'

'I recall telling you *that*,' said Penny. 'You're not only a nosey sod, you're an absent-minded one too.'

'Oh aye. The poor bugger died. Accident, was it?' said Dalziel, whose last telephone conversation with Pascoe had given him full details of the death.

'In a way. He got poisoned, something he ate,' said Penny. 'Some insecticide hadn't got washed off, or something.'

'And didn't you get anyone else interested in buying?' asked Dalziel.

'No. I sort of lost heart, I suppose,' she said. 'I took it off the market. It struck me that perhaps I really ought to consider Patrick's feelings a bit more. I mean, the house was just a white elephant to me, but clearly not to him.'

She spoke almost defiantly.

'So what did you do!' asked Dalziel, though he knew full well.

'I had a talk with him. I told him that we'd stay on at Rosemont for the time being, but as soon as he reached his majority, I was off back to London and he could make his own mind up whether he wanted, or indeed could afford, Rosemont. I was thinking of twenty-one when I said it, but the age of majority was lowered not long after to eighteen, and Patrick seemed determined that should be the decision date. It came. He wanted to stay on by himself, he said. I said, if that's what you want.'

Dalziel whistled and said, 'You must've thought a lot, or very little, of the lad to let him get stuck with a bloody great house like that when he was still only eighteen and not properly earning!'

'Oh yes, I know it seems odd,' said Penny. 'But Patrick Patrick . . . well, you've got to meet him to know what I mean. When he wants something, he just sits quietly there till he gets it. He always did, from a baby. Things weren't quite as bad as they seem, mind. Aunt Flo had left me pretty well heeled. After I'd had Rosemont valued and added that to all the other assets, then divided by two, Patrick got a few thousand on top of the house and I got enough to buy the lease on this place and keep me comfortable, at least until they invented inflation. I'll probably start spending capital in the end. I made it quite clear to Patrick that this deal ended his expectations from me. In fact, whatever little there's left when I go will go to my grandchildren when they're twenty-one. But I can't see it being very much!'

'Well, you can't take it with you,' said Dalziel. 'You said he changed his name, your lad.'

'No I didn't!' said Penny, sitting upright. 'What the hell is this, Andy Dalziel?'

'What's what?' asked Dalziel, looking puzzled. 'You said before that your lad's name was Aldermann now. I can hear you saying it.'

He spoke with such authority that the woman's doubts were momentarily assuaged, but he guessed that he had gone as far as he dared without finally convincing her that his motives for the evening were interrogative rather than romantic.

Besides the sight of those still splendidly firm breasts pendant above his reclining head was enough to blunt even the sharp spur of constabulary duty.

He reached up and drew her down towards him.

'This Greek god fellow,' he said. 'What did he try his hand at after the bull?'

PART FOUR

And in the midst of this wide quietness
A rosy sanctuary I will dress
With the wreath'd trellis of a working brain . . .
KEATS: Ode to Psyche

1
HAPPINESS

(Hybrid tea. Brilliant crimson blooms on long sturdy stems, perfect for developing under cover.)

Daphne Aldermann rose early on Saturday morning with a feeling that this was a day of important decision.

Since her talk with Ellie she had seemed to spend every waking moment analysing the state of her marriage. Oddly, all previous attempts at self-understanding now appeared vague, ineffectual, and delusory, as if her education, her upbringing, and her whole genetic inheritance had been aimed at misting her view of reality. In a way, it was true. The surface was far from all, but a well-ordered surface certainly compensated for a lot. Beneath it she had not felt particularly unhappy, or wildly neglected, or desperately unfulfilled. And the knowledge that she lived a life which must make many people envious had helped to make her believe that most of its suspected inadequacies were to be traced to her own shallowness. Now something had changed, or at least come to fruition. Perhaps Ellie Pascoe's openness, her frank discontents, her admitted sense of ambiguity in relation to her own marital role, and her saving humour when she seemed to be getting too near to that awful earnest greyness which the left wear as proudly as the right do their blacks and browns, had encouraged the reaction, but it hadn't caused it. She had merely been living through a sort of extended adolescence and at last she'd grown up.

Diana was spending the morning with a friend. Daphne was assiduous in making sure that Rosemont's isolation didn't mean her daughter's too, and she'd driven the little girl to the friend's house shortly after nine. Patrick had rung briefly the previous evening to say he'd be home mid-morning. He had sounded strange, highly charged with some emotion unidentifiable at the end of a very crackly line. The police had also rung and she'd arranged for them to come at midday.

Now she sat and drank a coffee and waited for her husband to return.

When he did, there was going to be open speaking. How open, she was not sure. She had not inherited her High Anglican father's love of confession, but she believed herself willing to reveal the truth of her brief relationship with Dick Elgood if that seemed necessary to shock Patrick into a retaliatory openness. The time for mysteries was past. Patrick had to admit her into his mind if they were to have a future together.

With these and similar rock-hard resolutions she sat and passed the time till on the stroke of eleven she heard the front door open. Instantly the rock began to crumble, and suddenly the thin surface of her life seemed quite strong and certainly rigid enough to carry her not unhappily to the grave.

But the knowledge of her weaknesses had given her a knowledge of her strength too, and by the time he entered the lounge she had summoned up her spirit of resolution once more.

Unfortunately the man she was resolved to confront was not quite the man who came through the door. It was Patrick all right, but instead of the small reserved smile and the gentle peck on the cheek she would have expected, he advanced with a positive beam on his face, caught her in a full embrace and kissed her almost passionately.

'Hello,' he said. 'It's good to be back. These are for you. Where's Di?'

'She's at Mary Jennings'. Patrick, thank you . . . but *buying* flowers . . . *you*?'

These were a bunch of roses, carefully wrapped in tissue paper.

Patrick sat down, relaxing into the deep armchair with a positive grin on his face.

'Even Rosemont doesn't have *every* variety,' he said.

Carefully she removed the paper. There were

five of them, rich golden blooms on long stems, a couple of them opening to reveal a scarlet flush and emit a sweet, delicate perfume. Daphne, fairly expert perforce, could not identify them.

'Darling, they're beautiful. What are they?'

'There's a tag, I think,' he said off-handedly.

She looked. Wrapped round the stems was a green plastic nurseryman's tag. She read it, then once more, still not understanding.

Type – hybrid tea. Variety – Daphne Aldermann.

'You mean, this is their name?' she said in bewilderment.

Patrick threw back his head and laughed in pure delight, a sight almost as bewildering as the rose-tag.

'Yes,' he said. 'Yes, yes, yes! You don't remember, do you? I told you years ago that when I bred a rose worth naming, I'd call it after you.'

'Yes, I do remember, but I thought that it was, well, just a compliment, a romantic way of speaking . . .'

'I always mean what I say,' said Patrick seriously. He jumped up and moved to the fireplace. She had never seen him full of such nervous excitement.

'I started on this one five, no, six years ago. I knew it had potential after the first blooming, but I'd been disappointed before. Three years ago, I reckoned it was good enough to send to the Royal Society's trial ground. I was right. It got a First Class trial certificate. And what's more, it just won a Gold Medal at the Society's show.'

'This is marvellous,' she said. 'Marvellous. Patrick, I'm so . . .'

She wasn't sure what she was except that she was no longer ready for the immediate confrontation she had planned. Indeed it was beginning to dawn on her that many of the explanations she had hoped to elicit by confrontation might now be given to her, undemanded.

'And I'm not finished,' Patrick went on. 'I've signed a deal with Bywater Nurseries. It'll be in their next catalogue. They're going to produce it commercially!'

'Patrick! Why didn't you say anything?' she cried, but there was no stopping him.

'And *that's* not all,' he said. 'Not only have I put you on the Garden Centre stalls, I'm putting you into the bookshops too. You know how I keep careful notes of everything I do in the greenhouse? Well, I showed them to a publisher. They said there was a book in it, an account of all the trial and error that's gone into producing *Daphne Aldermann*. They're going to launch the two of them together, the book and the rose. It's a gimmick, of course, but they seem delighted with it. And what's more important, they're commissioning me to do what I've always wanted to do, that is, write a full and detailed history of the rose!'

Daphne shook her head, not in denial but in bewilderment. All this excitement in him, for *months* at least, and yet not a word, not a sharing.

'Darling, are you all right?' asked Patrick, momentarily diverted from his euphoria.

'Yes, of course. It's all so overwhelming. It's marvellous, but it's a shock too.'

'A shock?'

'Yes. I never guessed. I mean, you never said anything. All this, and you never said!'

'No, I never did,' he agreed. 'It was all so uncertain. Or rather, I couldn't believe it myself till it was all settled yesterday. But I never hid anything either. It was all there to be seen, what I was doing. The writing, the roses. It was all there.'

Was it a reproach? She didn't know. And she didn't want to know either. A reproach would have to be answered. Or accepted. But she was in no mood to accept reproaches. At least, five minutes ago she hadn't been in any mood. Now she was not altogether certain what mood she was in. These revelations explained many things perhaps – his preoccupation, his secret excitement, even his apparently ill-founded optimism about the future. Oh God! She suddenly realized the implications of her misinterpretations. They had led to Dandy Dick's bed and to a police investigation. Guilt and resentment were warring in her. It was her fault, it was his fault; she had been uninterested, he had been secretive; nothing had changed, everything had changed.

He came across the room and sat beside her.

'Are you all right?' he asked anxiously.

'Yes. Of course. Just a bit overwhelmed.'

'Yes me too.' He laughed boyishly, looking about

twenty. 'I thought it might all fall through and I wanted to spare you that. But when it didn't, I wished I'd had you with me. I missed you.'

'Did you?'

She turned her face towards him. He kissed her gently.

'Yes. I did.'

He kissed her again. Suddenly there was no doubt about the passion there.

'Patrick!' she said with the instinctive alarm of one not accustomed to such things in such locations at such times.

'Diana's out, isn't she?' he murmured. 'And you're not expecting anyone, are you?'

Oh Christ! The police! she remembered. But she didn't say. Twelve o'clock, they had said they would call. She squinted round Patrick's head at the ormolu clock on the mantelshelf. It was just after eleven. Surely the police wouldn't be early?

But who cared? Some risks were made to be taken. She drew Patrick down towards her and embraced him with arms and mouth and long slender legs.

Their love-making was short and savage as if they had both been simmering just below the boiling point through many hours of foreplay. Drained, they lay on the cool woodblock floor, clinging to each other like spent swimmers.

Time for talk without fear or reproach. Hardly words. More like the murmur of the sea.

'You should have told me.'

'Yes. But you always seemed so calm, so self-sufficient, I didn't feel able to involve you in my hopes and perhaps disappointments.'

'That's how *I* seemed? Calm and self-contained?'

'Yes. Or perhaps I feared, which would be worse, that my hopes wouldn't involve you. It was a project so dear to me, I couldn't have borne for it not to be dear to you also.'

'Oh Patrick.'

She drew him even closer. Above their naked bodies the clock ticked on.

'Not that it matters,' she said, after a while, 'but will there be much money in all this?'

He drew back a little and smiled at her and said, 'Some. Not a fortune. But more to come, perhaps. At least it means I'll be able to make my peace with Dick Elgood.'

'Elgood?' she sounded more alarmed than she intended, less than she felt.

'Yes. It's been bothering me, all this unpleasantness about the financial directorship. Dick clearly doesn't want me. And I've never been all that keen, but it seemed silly to miss a chance. But now, well, at least I know where I am at the moment. I can do the job I've got now standing on my head. There'll be minimum interference with the books and the roses.'

'You mean you'll withdraw?'

'That's what I mean.'

'Oh, I'm so glad.'

And in her gladness and her relief that it was all

over she found herself launched on a description of Elgood's allegations and the police investigations. But she had not gone far before a slight tension in the naked body in her arms triggered off an awareness of her own foolishness. Nothing good lay at the end of this road. Desperately she looked for an escape route. Ingeniously she found one, chattering on like the idle female gossip she hoped to be taken for.

'I got all this from Ellie Pascoe, you know, the policeman's wife I've been telling you about. We almost fell out about it, it was so absurd, well, I think she thought so too, that's why she told me.'

'Mrs Pascoe told you about her husband's work? Not very discreet. Or loyal. And you didn't tell me.'

He sounded not suspicious but surprised. And speculative.

'I didn't know what to say. Oh Patrick, we've both been stupidly reticent, haven't we?'

She kissed him passionately and caressed him intimately. It was the right response. She felt the tension in his mind relax as the stiffness between his legs returned.

And then as he rolled her over on her back once more her eyes caught the clock face. It was ten to twelve.

'Oh hurry, hurry, hurry!' she cried.

He hurried. As they got dressed she breathlessly explained about the police visit and its reasons.

'You mean all that haste wasn't passion?' he said.

'Yes, of course, most of it, I mean, I'm sorry,' she began. But when she looked at him, he was smiling.

In the event the police were ten minutes late, and though Daphne still felt certain that the evidence of the recent activity in the lounge was clearly there for the professional eye to see, she found she did not give a damn.

'Hello,' she said to Peter Pascoe. 'I've been looking forward to seeing you in the flesh.'

Did he grin faintly and look at the three buttons she had left undone on her blouse as he said, 'Me too.'

Pascoe didn't know how he looked to her, but to him she looked exactly as Ellie had described, a classical English beauty, tall, long-limbed, fair, and sexy with it.

But Aldermann himself, standing alongside her, came as a slight surprise. 'Reserved and watchful' were the words most commonly used of him, and on their one previous meeting he had instantly been aware of the man's privacy, even in giving a stranger a rose.

Aldermann too recalled the meeting.

'Mr Pascoe, how are you? We've met already, haven't we? At Perfecta. I hope there's no plot to burgle my office also?'

He smiled as he spoke, but Pascoe noticed a sudden stiffening in his wife's posture at the mention of the encounter.

'No. I was there on another matter,' said Pascoe

equably. 'Sergeant Wield I think you've met also.'

Wield nodded a greeting.

'Of course. How's the window-box, Sergeant?'

'Haven't really had time to think about it, sir.'

'You must make time. Plant ye roses while ye may,' said Aldermann in mock reproach. 'Let me know and I'll pass on a few potted cuttings to you. *Baby Faurax* I think took your fancy. Now some *Pigmy Gold's* and *Scarlett O'Hara's* would provide a really bright setting.'

The man was positively ebullient, thought Pascoe. Outward-going, full of chat. He sensed that something had happened.

He said, 'To get down to business, sir. Mrs Aldermann's probably given you the gist. We've had a tip that your house is next in line to be done by a gang that have been active in this area for a couple of months now. She also probably mentioned the man she found looking around the house who said he was from the Water Board.'

Aldermann glanced interrogatively at his wife and said, 'No, she hasn't mentioned him. But of course I've just got back and we haven't had all that much time for talking.'

This occasioned a kind of splutter from Daphne Aldermann as though she was choking back something. Pascoe felt himself in the presence of secret signals which he did not too much care for. He put on his best official voice.

'Our enquiries have revealed that no such man was sent round by the Water Board. It may well be that this man is connected with the gang I mentioned. And as I gather that you will be leaving the house empty for a couple of nights next week, it is a matter we are taking seriously.'

'Of course,' said Aldermann. 'How can we help?'

'Well, we'll need a list of all the people you would normally inform that you intend being away.'

'That can't amount to many,' said Daphne.

'You'll be surprised, madam,' said Pascoe. 'Especially if you count those who'll find out by association, as it were. I presume you've informed St Helena's that your little girl will be off for a couple of days?'

'Why yes, of course.'

'Then we can assume the teaching staff and the secretarial staff at the school all know. Plus, of course all your daughter's friends and presumably many of their parents.'

'Well, yes, I suppose so. But not even Ellie has suggested that St Helena's is the centre of a crime ring,' said Daphne a touch acidly.

'You amaze me,' Pascoe said, grinning. 'But you see what I mean. Also I'd like to look around and check the layout of the house, look at your alarm system, that kind of thing.'

'Then why don't we divide and rule?' said Aldermann. 'I'll give Mr Wield what information I can down here, and Daphne, why don't you give Mr Pascoe the guided tour?'

Was there something in his voice, a suggestion

320

perhaps? Daphne nodded and said, 'Of course. If that's all right with you, Peter. Oh, I'm sorry, I've got so used to thinking of you as Peter through talking with Ellie.'

'I'm glad she doesn't refer to me as Mr Pascoe,' said Pascoe. 'And Peter's fine. Shall we go?'

For the first fifteen minutes of the tour, their conversation was practical and professional. The alarm system was old but adequate. Pressure mats under all possible entry windows; magnetic switch sensors, flush fitted, on the downstairs doors; and an automatic telephone dialling system. This last was the important item. The house was sufficiently isolated for the alarm bell to disturb nothing except perhaps the odd ploughman on his weary way home who would probably take it for the curfew anyway.

In addition Pascoe made a note of the stealable contents of each room, particularly silverware, ornaments and paintings, the focus of the gang's previous hauls. Not that they showed any particular expertise, taking copies and junk as readily as the genuine stuff. Presumably they had a fence they trusted to sort out the wheat from the chaff without cheating them too much.

In the bathroom, Pascoe noted that the suite bore the name Elgoodware, presumably dating from Eddie Aldermann's connection with the firm, but it would have taken a Dalzielesque indelicacy to mention this, he felt.

The tour ended in the master bedroom. Pascoe

finished his notes, then remained at the window admiring the view.

'What are you thinking?' the woman asked behind him.

'I'm just lost in envy,' he answered, turning and smiling at her.

'Envy? But you have a splendid open aspect too.'

'That's right. But I don't *own* quite so much of it. 'Tis *possession* lends enchantment to the view. So, despite my egalitarian principles, I feel envious.'

'I thought perhaps you were merely feeling embarrassed at the prospect of bringing up the topic of my relationship with Dick Elgood,' she said.

'Oh dear,' said Pascoe. 'He's been in touch then?'

'It was the gentlemanly thing to do.'

'As opposed to the policemanly, which is to plot to discuss a wife's infidelity upstairs while her husband sits innocently below? At least you gave me credit for embarrassment.'

'Wrongly, so it seems.'

'Perhaps rightly,' corrected Pascoe. 'But we won't know as, in fact, I didn't have to bring it up, did I? You saved me the bother. But, truly, I didn't intend to bring it up anyway. Why should I? As Mr Elgood was quick to point out, what business is it of mine?'

'None, I hope. But there have been several misunderstandings, I think, and if complete frankness is necessary to clear them up, then I'm willing to be completely frank.'

She sat on the edge of the bed, knees demurely

together, hands clasped on her lap, cheeks gently flushed, long fair hair falling over her shoulders.

'Yes,' murmured Pascoe, mostly to himself, but she caught the word.

'Yes, what?'

He smiled and said, 'I was just remembering something Ellie said about you.'

'Ellie?' she said alertly.

'Yes. I'm sorry, I shouldn't pass things on, should I? But I've gone too far now. She said you were . . . sexy. I see what she meant.'

Daphne rose abruptly, ran her hand through her hair and left it there.

'Clearly she didn't tell me enough about you,' she said.

'No? What's enough, I wonder?' said Pascoe. 'It strikes me, Ellie's rather pig-in-the-middle in all this.'

'Poor Ellie.'

'You mentioned the open view from our house. I didn't know you'd been there.'

'Once,' said Daphne, still holding her pose which unselfconsciously echoed a position favoured by Hollywood starlet publicity photographers. 'I went to have a row with her.'

'And you can still walk. She must be slipping,' said Pascoe.

'Yes. I didn't really get going. I suppose basically I like her too much.'

'Me too,' said Pascoe ruefully. 'It can be a disadvantage, can't it?'

'Look,' said Daphne. 'There's something I want to put right. In a way I started all this silly business by . . . well, let's just say I misinterpreted certain things. I know better now. I was going to tell Ellie all about it, and tell her to tell you, but it makes more sense to do it the other way round now you're here.'

Rapidly she told Pascoe most of what had passed between her and Patrick that morning. His cool, appraising gaze half convinced her he guessed the rest and she found herself blushing at the thought.

When she had finished, he said, 'So he is no longer a candidate for this place on the board?'

'He's going to contact Dick Elgood and withdraw.'

'I see. Well, to be honest, it never seemed a particularly good motive for murder!' said Pascoe. 'And Mr Aldermann hasn't struck me as a particularly ambitious man either.'

'Nor, I hope, as a potential killer,' she said sternly.

He gave her a smile which she took as assent but which saved him from the honest answer that in his time he'd seen far more unlikely candidates than Aldermann admit to committing the vilest acts.

'Let's go down,' he said. 'I'm pleased. I really am. Ellie will be too.'

'Yes she will,' said Daphne thoughtfully. 'It's rare to find a radical so *ungrudging*, isn't it?'

Ellie knows how to pick 'em, thought Pascoe smugly as they descended. This is no stupid woman.

He felt genuinely pleased for Aldermann. During the past few days he'd been doing some gentle probing into the man's financial position and discovered that it was to say the least delicate. The pseudo water-official could have claimed to be representing the gas, electricity or telephone companies with equal authenticity. There were large outstanding bills in each case.

At the lounge door he paused.

'Does your husband know you were going to tell me about his success?' he enquired.

'Oh yes. I'm sure he does,' smiled Daphne.

They went in.

Aldermann and Wield had obviously passed the official stage and were now standing at the window talking gardens.

'Well, Mr Pascoe,' said Aldermann. 'You'll have seen that we've really got very little worth stealing.'

'If you think that, sir, I'd have a word with your insurance company,' said Pascoe. 'It'd be easy enough to pack a couple of thousand pounds' worth at least into a few suitcases. And it could be a great deal more. Those little Dutch flower paintings in your study: I'm no expert, but if they're genuine, they must be worth a bomb.'

'Good Lord. I'd forgotten about them. They were Uncle Eddie's. In fact, a lot of the stuff in the house was his. You can take things in your life so much for granted that you lose sight of their value, can't you?'

'Very true, sir,' said Pascoe. Briefly he explained that they would like to put some men on watch in the house on the two nights the Aldermann family would be away.

'Of course,' said Aldermann. 'You must do what is necessary. I do hope there won't be any mad dashes across the garden, though?'

'We'll try not to damage anything, sir.'

Somewhere a telephone rang. Daphne went to answer it.

'I believe congratulations are in order,' said Pascoe.

Typically Aldermann did not make any pretence of not understanding.

'Thank you. Yes, it's splendid. I feel I've achieved something worthwhile,' he said. 'And started something worthwhile too. A new beginning.'

Daphne returned.

'It's Dick Elgood,' she said. 'He wants to talk to you.'

'And I to him. Goodbye, Mr Wield, Mr Pascoe. Happy hunting next week!'

He went out. Pascoe and Wield exchanged glances which said they were both finished, and allowed Daphne to usher them to the door.

As they passed the open study, Pascoe glimpsed Aldermann at his desk with the phone in his hand. He was listening intently.

At the front door Daphne offered her hand.

'I hope we'll see more of you and Ellie,' she said.

'I'd like that,' said Pascoe.

2

SOUVENIR D'UN AMI

(Tea-rose. Delicate, requires protection in winter, a sheltered wall, and good soil, coppery-pink blooms with yellow stamens, beautifully fragrant.)

Shaheed Singh felt his left wrist seized and his forearm forced upwards behind his body which was rammed sideways against the wall, pinning his right arm uselessly against the rough brick.

'I've been looking for you,' growled a hoarse voice in his ear.

Twisting his head round, Singh found himself looking into the deep-set and vein-crazed eyes of Superintendent Dalziel whose normal ferocity of expression was not improved by a bruised and swollen nose.

'Come on, lad,' said the Superintendent, releasing him. 'You've got some answering to do.'

Feeling more like a prisoner than a colleague, Singh trailed along behind Dalziel's huge hulk, out of the car park where he'd been intercepted and into the station and up the stairs to the Super's room.

Dalziel settled comfortably into the extra-large executive-type office chair, all black leather and chrome, which baffled the annual inventory-takers, and said, 'Sit yourself down, son, make yourself at home,' with a geniality Singh found even more frightening than the initial assault.

'You might as well enjoy the facilities,' continued Dalziel, 'as I gather you've been kind enough to lend CID a hand while I've been away. Sort of filling the gap, so to speak.'

Some gap, thought Singh, and the comic response, though naturally internalized beyond identification without truth drugs, relaxed him a little.

'Mr Pascoe has left me a full report of *everything*,' said Dalziel. '*Everything*. He's out just now, acting on information you've supplied him with. That must make you proud, lad. To have a Detective-Inspector, not to mention a Detective-Sergeant, occupying a Saturday morning at your behest. And now you've got me. So tell me all about it.'

Singh told. Dalziel questioned. After twenty minutes they both fell silent. Singh sat anxiously, waiting for blame, praise or just simple dismissal. Dalziel stared gloomily at his desk surface, shoulders hunched as though under a burden, and right index finger gently patrolling the fold of flesh which hung over his shirt collar.

'Want to be a copper, do you?' Dalziel said suddenly.

'Yes, sir,' said Singh in a positive tone.

'Why?'

Singh thought of the tangle of reasons which had led, if such a tangle could be said to lead, him to his decision. He settled for simplicity.

'Because I think it's an interesting job, sir. And I think I'll like it. And I think I'll be good at it, sir.'

'Strikes me you think too bloody much, lad,' growled Dalziel. 'Mebbe you should try *knowing* and *doing* instead of all this thinking.'

'I'm sorry, sir,' said Singh. 'I just thought . . .' He tailed off miserably.

'There's only two places in a bobby's life, son,' said Dalziel, 'and you've got to be able to live in 'em both. One's out there.'

The index finger emerged from the carnal crease at his collar and poked a hole (metaphorically, though to Singh's eyes the violent digit looked as if it could have managed it figuratively) in the station wall to reveal the outside world.

'Out there it's dark and dangerous and dirty,' said Dalziel. 'Out there, there's men with clubs and knives and sawn-off shotguns who don't much care who gets in their way when they're at their work. Worse; out there, there's men with paving stones and petrol bombs whose work is to provoke us to get in *their* way. Oh, it's an interesting job all right.

'And then there's the other place and that's in here.'

The finger stabbed down. Singh grasped that

what was being indicated was not the interior of Dalziel's desk, but the police station, indeed perhaps the whole of the police force.

'*Out there* is bad. But sometimes,' said Dalziel, 'sometimes *in here* makes you long to be back *out there*, like you long for a pint of ale when you've had a hot, hard day and you're drier than a Wee Free Sunday. Do you follow me, lad?'

Curiously, Singh did. There was no way that he could know that Dalziel was still smouldering at the memory of his last encounter at Scotland Yard. Summoned to the office of the Deputy Commissioner co-ordinating the conference, he had been told in no uncertain terms that his behaviour had caused so much complaint that an adverse report was being sent to his Chief Constable. *Insubordinate, disruptive, inattentive and absent* were the principal epithets used, not all of them compatible with each other, Dalziel had pointed out, which had provoked the final outburst. Last words are a privilege of rank, and Dalziel was still smarting.

None of this was he about to tell Singh, of course, but the cadet was already beginning to realize that *in here* was peopled with monsters, or monstered with people, who could cause as much terror and pain as any robber or rioter. So he nodded his head in genuine not just sycophantic agreement.

'Good. You've nearly finished your attachment here, haven't you?'

'Yes, sir. Just another four days.'

'You've done well,' said Dalziel unexpectedly.

'Not much chance usually for a cadet to do well as far as CID's concerned. But you've shown a bit of initiative. I'll see it gets mentioned on your report.'

'Thank you, sir,' said Singh, his stomach turning with pleasure. 'Thank you very much.'

'Right. Push off now. Tell one of them idle buggers down below I'd appreciate a mug of tea. I'm only away a few days and they're sliding into idle habits!'

'Yes, sir,' said Singh standing to attention. 'Sir . . .'

'Don't hang about, lad,' said Dalziel.

But Singh, emboldened by praise, said, 'Sir, if there's going to be a stake-out, at Rosemont, I mean, sir, because of my information, like, I wonder if mebbe I could . . .'

Dalziel's basilisk gaze froze the trickle of words.

'Fancy a bit of action, do you, lad? Bloody a couple of noses, get a police medal?'

'No, sir. I just thought mebbe the experience . . .'

'Let me tell you about the experience,' said Dalziel. 'Either you'll sit on your arse, bloody uncomfortable, all night, and you'll end up in the morning, cold and tired, with bugger-all to show for it, and the officers you're with will all know it's been on your say-so they've wasted their time. Or the villains'll come and there'll be a bit of aggro and mebbe a bit of blood. Any road, when the lights go on, there'll be you, standing there feeling all pleased; and looking right at you will be your old mate, what's his name? oh yes, Jonty

Marsh. Are you ready for that, lad? Whichever way it goes?'

Singh hesitated, recalling Wield had warned him along similar lines.

There was a tap on the door behind him.

'Come in!' bellowed Dalziel.

The door opened and Pascoe appeared with Wield behind him.

'Here they are, the heavenly twins, Castor and Bollocks,' said Dalziel. 'Run along, son, and don't forget about that tea.'

Singh left, passing under the craggy indifference of Wield's expression like a nervous pinnace beneath a fortified cliff.

'Welcome back, sir,' said Pascoe, observing the swollen nose with keen interest. 'We weren't expecting you till this afternoon.'

'I skipped the fond farewells,' said Dalziel. 'I've been going through all this stuff on Aldermann, then I had a word with young Abdul.'

'Singh, you mean, sir? Shaheed is his first name, I think,' said Pascoe.

'Aye, Abdul. He's not daft, that lad. Has someone been giving him a hard time? I just got an impression he might be feeling he's being shoved around a bit.'

He glared accusingly at the two men.

'I won't have officers throwing their weight around,' he said. 'Consideration for subordinates, that's what it takes to knit a good team together. Understood?'

Pascoe glanced at Wield, then said, 'I entirely agree, sir.'

'Good. Now what have you two idle sods been at these past few days? This joker Aldermann, are we arresting him or protecting him?'

'Protecting him,' said Pascoe promptly. 'I've found nothing concrete to suggest he's ever stepped over the line except in the case of the old lady's money when he was working for Capstick in Harrogate.'

'One step's often enough,' said Dalziel.

'We're all permitted one bit of stupidity, sir,' said Pascoe. 'Anyway, there's something else.'

Briefly he recounted what Daphne had told him at Rosemont.

Dalziel sniffed, rubbed his nose and winced.

'That's something,' he said grudgingly. 'That explains a few things.'

'A lot,' said Pascoe firmly.

'You're recommending we wrap it up, are you?'

'We have no complainant, no evidence of crime, nothing!' said Pascoe.

The internal telephone rang. Wield picked it up and listened.

'Sir,' he said to Dalziel, 'there's a Mr Masson to see you.'

'Masson! The solicitor? What's he want?' asked Pascoe.

Dalziel made a face. It wasn't pretty.

'Acting on information received,' he intoned, 'mainly from you, Inspector, indicating you believed

334

Masson wasn't coming clean with us, I rang the old sod at his golfclub and told him he'd better get his arse down here if he didn't want to be retrospectively struck off. Or words to that effect.'

'Oh dear,' said Pascoe.

'Now you tell me that the case is closed,' said Dalziel. 'Perhaps you'd like to talk to him?'

'No, thanks,' said Pascoe.

'Tell 'em to wheel him in,' Dalziel said to Wield. 'Christ, is there nothing we can charge anyone with? Have you been right through the index in the big book?'

'We might try Elgood and Mandy Burke with perjury?' suggested Pascoe. 'Or perhaps she actually gave the ladder a push . . .'

'Do you really believe that? No? Nor do I. Accident. Perjury now, they'd have to cough in front of witnesses, and they're not going to do that, are they? No, the lines I was thinking on were that Aldermann spotted Burke and Elgood making off after lunch at the White Rose and gave the husband a ring in the hope he'd catch them in the stirrups. Good as a killing, that. He'd not be likely to stay on at Perfecta, would he? Still, now you've washed him whiter than snow, that's buggered that, hasn't it?'

There was a tap at the door. Wield opened it and Masson stepped in. He was wearing a red sports shirt and checked trousers.

'Right, Inspector Pascoe, that'll do for now, but

I'll want to talk to you later,' said Dalziel sternly. 'Mr Masson, good of you to come!'

Pascoe and Wield left. As Pascoe closed the door he heard the beginning of Dalziel's conversation.

'Promising lad, that Pascoe, but a bit overkeen sometimes. I'm sorry if he's been bothering you about the Mrs Highsmith business.'

'What business is that?' said Masson sharply.

'You're not still her solicitor, are you?' said Dalziel. 'You'll understand then, I really can't say. Of course, if she herself wanted to see you . . .'

He nodded significantly at the wall, as if suggesting Penelope were chained to the other side of it. It was simply his intention to get rid of Masson with minimum aggro, but it was already striking him as curious that the man hadn't come in with all guns blazing indignation. He decided to try the all-boys-together line. Besides, he felt in need of sustenance.

'What about a drink?' he said. 'And a little chat off the record.'

He took a huge key from his pocket, opened the cupboard in his desk and produced a bottle of Glen Grant and two glasses which he filled to the brim.

'Here's health,' he said.

They drank.

'Of course,' he went on, but not sure where he was going, 'you *were* Mrs Highsmith's solicitor after she inherited the house, weren't you? There was all that business about the disappeared will . . .'

For a moment he thought he was going to get the expected explosion from Masson but then the old man relaxed and drank deeply from his glass.

'Look,' he said. 'I'm not absolutely sure what this is all about, but there are some things it might help you to know, only . . .'

'Only . . . ?'

'Between these four walls?'

'Of course. You have my word,' said Dalziel solemnly.

'All right then,' said Masson, taking a deep breath.

What came was an anti-climax.

'I've no idea what happened to the will,' said Mr Masson.

'None?' said Dalziel disbelievingly.

'Nothing that I could offer in evidence,' said the solicitor firmly.

'But suspicions?'

'Ah, *suspicions*! Suspicions are only malicious guesses, aren't they? There had been a will. I had left it with Mrs Aldermann after she had called me in to discuss the possibility of changing it substantially in favour of her niece. She died. There was no will to be found. Why should I be *suspicious* rather than accept that in all likelihood the old lady had torn it up prior to getting me to draft a new one?'

'Because,' said Dalziel gently, 'because you buggers are like us buggers, you're bred up to be suspicious. Instead of which you're sitting there all

sweetness and light and Christian understanding!
You weren't having a bit on the side with Mrs
Highsmith, by any chance, were you?'

'Mr Dalziel! How dare you?' cried Masson, scandalized.

'It's not impossible,' protested Dalziel. 'She's a
very attractive woman. You were a vigorous young
man, well, in the prime of life, twenty years ago.'

'I was, I was,' said Masson, suddenly smiling. 'I
could tell you a tale . . . but I won't. And I certainly
wouldn't have dreamt of bending my sense of duty
in the interests of a mere personal relationship!'

'But you did suspect that it wasn't Mrs Aldermann
who'd got rid of the will, didn't you?' pressed
Dalziel. 'So why did you sit on your arse and say
nowt? *Why*?'

'All right, I'll tell you why,' said Masson with
sudden passion. 'Because justice was best served
by doing nothing. Because I was absolutely certain
that three years earlier, Florence Aldermann had
deliberately and maliciously destroyed her husband's will, that's why!'

Dalziel finished his whisky in his surprise and
had to pour himself another.

'But why should she?' he wondered. 'This chap,
Eddie Aldermann, wasn't the kind to disinherit his
wife from what I've heard of him.'

'Of course he wasn't. He was the fairest, the
kindest, of men. I drew up his will, of course. In
it he left the bulk of his estate to his wife. But he
also left a substantial legacy to Mrs Highsmith to

be held in trust for her son, Patrick, till he came of age. It was this that so offended Mrs Aldermann, I suspect. Oh yes, there was no doubt in my mind but that she destroyed the will. Unfortunately I had just suffered a bereavement myself, my wife. And I had gone to Australia on a six-month visit to my daughter there. I didn't know anything of all this till I came back. No will! I was furious. But I was uncertain what to do. There were constraints upon me, you see. After all, I might have been wrong. It wasn't until she herself was struck down two years later and Mrs Highsmith came to Rosemont to take care of her that I learned that the allowance Eddie had always made her had been discontinued. Then I was sure! But it began to look as if things might be regularized without my intervention. There was all this talk of Mrs Highsmith staying on permanently, and of a new will. I was determined that justice would be done in this one, and to Mrs Aldermann's credit it must be said that she'd come to a much truer estimate of her niece's worth. It takes a brush with death to put things in perspective sometimes, Mr Dalziel.'

Dalziel rubbed his huge hand across his huge face.

'Look,' he said in his kindliest tones, 'I still can't see why you let it pass. I mean, I can see why someone else might do it, but I know you, Mr Masson, I know how you've always gone on about the letter of the law being as important as the spirit, and I can't see how, on what you've told me, you could convince yourself you were right to say nothing if you thought Penny Highsmith had removed that will. Why not take it to the law and try to sort out things there?'

Masson laughed. It was an unexpected sound, high and clear and girlish.

'It was because I could have done that and won very easily that I did what I did, Mr Dalziel,' he cried. 'That was the whole point! But I'd promised Eddie, you see. And also there'd have been a very great scandal. Things in those days weren't quite so free as now. This way achieved the same, the right, the proper result, without any of that.'

'You've lost me,' said Dalziel. 'What result? What did you promise Eddie Aldermann?'

Masson shook his head. 'A promise is a promise.'

'To a dead man. Listen, you've bent your principles a good way, just bend them a little more. If you don't, I'll just have to go on probing. People will start talking, I don't know what about yet, but they will. And I'll probe till I find out. You've given me a direction, Masson. I'll keep going till I get there.'

No one could view the menacing thrust of Dalziel's huge head and the determined clamp of the jaws without believing him.

'All right. But no further!'

'Than necessary,' said Dalziel, uncompromising now he knew he'd won.

'Patrick's father,' said Masson.

'Yes?'

'Patrick Highsmith's father.'

'*Yes*?' said Dalziel, there already, but determined to make Masson say it.

'Patrick Highsmith's father was Eddie Aldermann.'

3

WILL SCARLET

(Modern shrub. Wide-spreading, bright red blooms,
long-lasting, with a musky scent.)

Saturday had started well for Dick Elgood. At
eleven o'clock he had been sitting in his office
in the otherwise empty Perfecta building waiting
for a visitor.

The man, who arrived dead on time, wore dark
glasses and a light grey hat. These were simple
measures to cut down the possibility of recognition, matters of habit rather than fear though
there were certainly people in this town whose
recognition was to be avoided.

Pascoe for instance might have recognized him
as the man he'd glimpsed last time he had visited Elgood, but that was unimportant. Daphne
Aldermann, however, might have recognized him
as the man who'd masqueraded as a Water Board
official, and that could have been embarrassing.
And Andy Dalziel would certainly have recognized

him as the man who'd punched his nose the previous night, and that would probably have been fatal.

'Come in, Mr Easey,' said Elgood. 'What have you got for me?'

Raymond Easey was a private enquiry agent, based in London, and recommended to Elgood by a business friend as having those qualities of speed, discretion, and scant respect for the law as long as the money was right, which Dandy Dick had specified.

His main brief had been to procure an accurate representation of Patrick Aldermann's financial position. His work here had been satisfactory to the extent that Elgood could now prove to the board that Aldermann was in some financial embarrassment. But that in itself might not be enough to discredit him.

Easey's secondary instructions had been that any evidence of unlawful activity on Aldermann's part would bring a large bonus. The man had seemed clean, however, and the agent's efforts to penetrate Rosemont in search of evidence to the contrary had been thwarted by Daphne's unexpected return. Fortunately his intimate knowledge of the household debts had enabled him to talk his way out of that.

He had returned to London where one of his employees had been checking on Aldermann during his brief visit there. It had all been boring stuff, flower shows and publishers, except for one unexplained visit to a flat in Victoria. Easey took over. He did all his illegal work himself on the grounds that employing others to do it cost too much, laid himself open to blackmail, and you couldn't trust the bastards anyway.

Getting in was simple. He'd waited till he saw the woman leave with a fat, balding man. Always ultra-careful in such matters, he had tracked them to a restaurant and seen them safely launched on their meal before returning to the flat and getting in with a pick-lock.

A systematic search had elicited the disappointing information that Mrs Highsmith was the subject's mother. Still, mums were notorious for keeping letters and other memorabilia, and loving sons often poured their hearts out into the maternal ear in search of a totally uncritical sympathy. But there had been nothing until he had noticed that the lining of the old leather writing-case he'd just been through with no joy was torn. He stuck his fingers in. There was something in there. He had just pulled it out and read the words in an almost Gothic script *Last Will and Testament of Florence Aldermann* when the outer door of the flat had opened.

Carefully he'd put the will in his pocket, replaced the case in the drawer, and waited. His escape from the flat, the bruises on his knuckles, and the pounding in his heart as he fled along the street, had almost convinced him that the game wasn't worth a candle. But now Elgood's face as he looked at the will told him different. There was pleasure there, and a man had to pay for his pleasure.

'Will she miss it?' wondered Elgood.

'Hard to say. It was well hidden to the point of being lost. You know how it is. People put things away *somewhere safe* and a week later they've forgotten where the hell they put 'em. Eventually they forget they even had 'em!'

He was perfectly right. Penny Highsmith had had two decades to lose track of the will and with her happy-go-lucky nature, she needed far less than that. After Aunt Flo's death, the will had been genuinely mislaid, and when Penny came across it a couple of days later she'd stuck it in the lining of her writing-case, not with any real criminal intent but as a simple device for gaining pause to think. After all, hadn't that nice, amiable lawyer said with something approaching a wink that, in his view, the absence of a will would mean justice was done the way Eddie Aldermann would have liked it? Not that she'd ever felt she had any rights as far as Eddie was concerned. A dear, kind man, sadly hag-ridden by old Aunt Flo, it had seemed perfectly natural when he came across her sunbathing in the garden one balmy afternoon, well away from her aunt's disapproving eye, to draw him down beside her and give him what the old bat had clearly denied him for years. He'd been extremely concerned and generous when Patrick came along, but she'd never made any demands and it hadn't surprised her when, after Eddie's death, Flo had stopped the allowance.

But now as the lawyer steered her towards this large inheritance, it had begun to seem foolish to worry about a will which gave everything away to some daft charities, and by the end of a year it had gone quite out of her mind.

'You've done well,' said Elgood. 'I'll see you're rewarded.'

Easey smiled. He saw to his own rewards.

He put another piece of paper on the desk.

'My bill,' he said. 'Terms are cash.'

Elgood looked, whistled, but paid. He was, after all, in some ways paying for his future.

And then had come the happy moment when he phoned Aldermann.

Daphne had answered. She'd sounded surprisingly pleased to hear his voice, but he'd cut her off sharply and asked for her husband.

Aldermann he'd offered even less chance to talk. There was, he was discovering in himself, a distaste for what he was doing. It was close to blackmail. In fact, what else was it but blackmail? But Elgood had a lifetime of ruthless business dealing behind him and he was not about to go soft now.

'Aldermann?' he said. 'Listen to me. I've got something you might like to see. No, don't interrupt. It's a will. Aye, that's what I said. And it seems to me to make it pretty clear that that big house of yours and them gardens and all that cash you've got through, shouldn't by right have ever come to you in the first place!'

There was a long pause.

Finally Patrick said mildly, 'I should be interested to see this document.'

'Bloody right you'd be interested,' said Elgood harshly.

'Yes? Are you at the office now? Shall I come round?' asked Aldermann reasonably.

Elgood sitting alone at his desk was suddenly aware of the vast silence all around him. There would be a security man somewhere in the building, but he could hardly ask him to lurk outside the door while he spoke to his own accountant! What he feared he was not quite sure. But even if, as he now believed, all his previous suspicions of Aldermann had been simply and embarrassingly hysterical, it would be foolish to be alone with him when he threatened the thing the man most loved. A restaurant, perhaps? A bar?

Suddenly a better idea occurred.

'No. I'm just leaving,' he said. 'I'll be down at my cottage tomorrow, though. There's a few people coming round for drinks and a snack on the shore at lunch-time. Why don't you join them? Bring the wife and your little girl. They'll enjoy it. Oh, you might like to bring a letter too, withdrawing your candidacy for the board. Twelve to half past. Right?'

'I shall look forward to it,' said Aldermann courteously. 'Could you give me directions?'

'Oh, ask Daphne. She'll know where it is,' said Elgood.

He regretted what he'd said even as he replaced the phone. It had been silly and unnecessary. Still, it could be taken in all kinds of ways, most of them innocent, he assured himself. He put it out of his mind. Carefully he placed the will and the rest of Easey's papers in a large envelope which he put in his briefcase. Then, after a moment's thought, he took out the will once more and went next door into Miss Dominic's office, where he ran off a copy on the Xerox machine. It had struck him that permanent retention of the original might be no bad thing. Putting it in a plain envelope, he opened the wallsafe in his room and placed it inside. Returning to his desk, he took out his diary and examined the list of telephone numbers which filled a couple of pages at the back. Then he began to ring.

It was late notice and after forty-five minutes he had only gathered half a dozen adults and three children for his lunch-time picnic.

It'd have been a bloody sight easier and probably cheaper to hire two coppers and a hungry Alsatian, he told himself. Then something in the thought made him smile and finally laugh out loud. He picked up the phone and dialled once more.

4

SUMMER SUNSHINE

*(Hybrid tea. Rich yellow, smallish blooms, often a late
starter, some black spot, sweetly scented.)*

'There's one thing you've got to give these jumped-
up South Yorkshire miners,' declared Andy Dalziel.
'They never forget how to push the boat out.'

In proof of his assertion, he brandished a half-
pint tumbler in one hand and in the other a bottle
of malt whisky over which he had clearly established proprietorial rights. Not that there were any
serious challengers. The sun was high and hot and
it was the beer, soft drinks and chilled white wine
that were attracting the greatest trade. Everyone
was dressed for the weather. The children were
naked; a few of the ladies, including Ellie and
Daphne, might just as well have been, for all
the protection their skimpy bikinis afforded; those
who weren't in swimming gear were in summer
dresses, or slacks and sportshirts; and even Dalziel
had made the double concession of removing the

jacket of his shiny grey suit and covering his head with a huge khaki handkerchief, knotted at the corners.

'He looks grotesque,' murmured Ellie to Pascoe. 'And that nose! I bet what really happened was that Patrick's mother punched him! You don't really believe he had it away with her, do you?'

'I hope you don't use such phrases in the Chantry Coffee House,' answered Pascoe primly. 'And yes, that's what I believe. Erotic bragadoccio is not among Andy's many vices, but certain nods and winks and a general impression of remembered pleasure whenever the lady is mentioned convince me I'm right.'

'Yes, I know what you mean,' admitted Ellie. 'I've noticed it with Daphne. I don't know what Patrick's doing to her but a kind of blissful glaze comes over her eyes every time I mention him. Get me another glass of wine, love. I'm too hot to move. Isn't this glorious! I bet you wish you'd brought your swimming trunks.'

She arched her back with cat-like complacency at her own forethought. Pascoe looked down at her and shuddered and was glad that he wasn't wearing his tight-fitting trunks. Not that Ellie would have been anything but amused and flattered to see the evidence of his desire, but she might not have been so happy to observe the reaction maintained when he turned his attention to Daphne.

She came out of the sea now and flopped down

alongside Ellie, water still trickling down the curves and promontories of her body.

'Isn't this lovely?' she said. 'Diana, you are taking care of Rose, aren't you?'

The little girl had elected herself guardian of the baby at first sight and was now digging a protective moat in the sand around her. Rose clearly regarded this as a first step towards the castle which was her proper due.

'She's fine,' said Ellie. 'It's role-stereotyping, of course, and in principle I object. But I'll hire her by the hour if you like! Daphne, I'm so glad everything's turned out so well.'

'Yes. I like a happy ending too.'

'You didn't tell Patrick about your little adventure, did you?' asked Ellie casually.

'Oh no. I got a bit too close for comfort, but I steered myself safely away. I suppose you think I should have done the perfect frankness bit, do you?'

'Not I,' said Ellie. 'Confession may be good for the soul but it's pretty lousy for marriages. Ah, here comes our genial host now.'

She had found Dandy Dick's charm at their introduction a little too carpet-salesmannish for her taste and the sight of him now stepping swiftly through the shallows didn't change her impression.

'He's not exactly Johnny Weissmuller, is he?' she said, looking at the small body whose well-developed muscles and heavy tan couldn't conceal its age.

'Go on. Make me feel good,' said Daphne drily. 'I hope one day you get seduced by that fat cop with the swollen nose.'

'Please, no!' said Ellie. 'I take back everything I've said!'

Elgood walked along the beach, enquiring after everyone's well-being but not stopping till he reached Patrick Aldermann who was talking to a couple by the huge food-hamper which a catering firm had supplied. He put his arm round Aldermann's shoulders and said, 'Patrick, there you are. I wanted to ask you; I've been trying to establish a few plants round the cottage, but nowt seems to take properly. All I'm doing is providing salad suppers for a swarm of bloody insects. It struck me, if anyone knows how to sort this lot out, it'll be our Patrick. Would you take a look? Come up with me now. I've got to pop up to make myself decent. It's all right for the ladies to flash the flesh, but when you get to my age, you don't want to put folk off their food!'

'Of course,' said Aldermann. 'It'll be a pleasure.'

The two men made their way across the beach and up the broken cliff face.

'All sweetness and light,' said Dalziel in Pascoe's ear. 'Does you good to see it. That stuff'll rot your nightstick.'

'It's a rather pleasant Orvieto,' said Pascoe, replacing the bottle in the cool-box. 'And I'm pouring it for Ellie.'

'Oh aye? And that's another thing,' said Dalziel.

'I wouldn't have let my wife lie around a beach like that. She'd have frightened the bloody seagulls!'

He roared with laughter, and Pascoe thought with surprise, he's a bit tiddly. It was hardly surprising. The whisky bottle was two-thirds empty. Also, it was quite clear that the fat man was suffering from the sun. He squinted upwards now with a malevolent eye and said, 'No wonder most foreigners are half daft. All that bloody heat boiling their brains. Well, I'm off to find somewhere cool inside. I'll see you later.'

Pascoe watched him stride determinedly towards the cliff, stumbling occasionally as the sand caved in beneath his bulk. He returned to Ellie and handed over the drink.

'Back in a moment,' he said.

He caught up with Dalziel as he began the ascent.

'You following me or something?'

'No, I just felt like a leak,' said Pascoe.

They laboured up a little further.

'Too bloody rustic for me,' growled Dalziel. 'This lot'll come down some day, all of it. Including that bloody cottage.'

'Must keep him on his toes,' agreed Pascoe.

Dalziel got to the top with only one stop for another couple of ounces of Scotch. Patrick was alone in front of the cottage.

'Where's Dick?' asked Dalziel.

'Having a shower and getting changed,' said Aldermann.

'What's he want with a shower? Just been in the bloody sea, hasn't he?' said Dalziel, passing into the dark of the interior.

Pascoe caught Aldermann's eye and the two men smiled.

'By the way, you might as well have these,' said Aldermann. He handed over a key ring with some small labels attached. 'It'll save you calling at Rosemont later. I've marked them all.'

'That's kind of you,' said Pascoe. 'We'll take great care. Especially in the garden. You're leaving in the morning, you said?'

'That's right. Shall I leave the alarm on?'

'Everything as normal, sir,' said Pascoe. 'We'll see to it.'

'Sir,' echoed the man musingly. 'Perhaps we could be less formal, if professional etiquette permits? With our ladies so friendly . . .'

'And our lords too,' smiled Pascoe, nodding at the interior where Dalziel could be heard raucously demanding where Dandy Dick hid his ice. 'Peter.'

'Patrick.'

They shared a moment, then Elgood came through the door, dapper in black Italian sports shirt and immaculate grey slacks.

'Hello, there,' he said, nodding at Pascoe. 'Now, Patrick, what do you think? What ought I to do?'

He gestured at the small patch of 'garden' which surrounded the cottage, distinguished from what lay beyond only by a few straggly roses long since reverted to briar.

'Salt air. Sandy soil. You've got problems,' said Aldermann. 'You've also got wasps, I see, and a lot of other insect life which needs to be controlled.'

'Yes, it's a bloody nuisance, isn't it?' said Elgood, swiping at a passing fly. 'It's OK by the sea, fortunately, but up here, it's getting a bit much. I've brought down a boxful of stuff that ought to sort out the buggers, though.'

He kicked a cardboard box standing just inside the door. Aldermann stooped and opened it. He frowned as he studied its contents. Elgood obviously bought insecticide as he bought picnic food, indiscriminately by the hamper.

'You've got enough here to kill off most of the insect life of Yorkshire,' he said reprovingly. 'Also some of this is extremely dangerous to humans. You shouldn't use it without protective clothing. And you certainly shouldn't leave it lying around especially with children in the vicinity.'

Elgood looked rather put out at being reproached in this fashion but he said, 'All right, all right. I'll find somewhere safe.'

He picked up the box and led the way into the cottage, the other two following. Dalziel looked up from an armchair, his eyes opening wide as he saw the box.

'Reinforcements!' he said, holding up the now empty bottle. 'Grand!'

Elgood ignored him and looked around for somewhere to store the box. Finally he put it down in the small passage between the living-room and the kitchen, reached up to the ceiling and drew on a cord which pulled open a trap with a foldaway ladder.

'I had the attic properly boarded when I put the tank for the shower in,' he said. 'It's good for storage and insulation too.'

He went up the ladder with the box and returned a few moments later, closing the trap after him.

'Satisfied?' he said rather sarcastically to Aldermann, who didn't reply.

'Nice spot you've got here, Dick,' said Dalziel with a leer. 'Just the right size for a loving couple. Cosy.'

'Remind me to ask you some time, Andy,' said Elgood.

'That'd make the buggers talk!' laughed Dalziel. 'You staying on tonight?'

'No. I've got to get back. I'll be busy first thing in the morning. I'll probably come down on Tuesday, though. I like to relax the night before an important board meeting.'

He glanced at Aldermann as he spoke with a hint of gloating triumph which seemed to Pascoe unnecessary in view of the peaceful solution of their problems.

'Relaxation you call it!' said Dalziel. 'Things must have changed!'

'A quiet swim, a quiet night all by myself, that's what I call relaxing, Andy. Don't you find quiet nights all by yourself relaxing? You must have had a few.'

Elgood was not a man to mess with, thought Pascoe. But nor was Dalziel.

'Aye, that's right, I have. And they are relaxing. But then I've got a clear conscience and most of my enemies are locked up, so what's to trouble my sleep, Dick? What's to trouble my sleep?'

On the beach below, the only thing troubling Ellie Pascoe's sleep was Daphne's voice, low and confidential in her ear. Her euphoria at the revitalizing of her relationship with her husband was beginning to be just a little tedious. Perhaps, thought Ellie with a sudden rather painful flash of self-awareness, I prefer my friends to be at odds with themselves so that I can be witty and wise.

'You know,' said Daphne, 'for the first time I think I'm really getting close to an understanding of what things mean to Patrick; in fact, you might say, of what it really means to *be* Patrick.'

It occurred to Ellie to suggest that it might be better if Daphne concentrated her attention on understanding what it really meant to be Daphne, but, perhaps fortunately, suddenly sun, sea and Orvieto exerted their authority and Daphne's voice, and the ripple of the waves, and the crying of the gulls, became one lulling note. Here, it seemed to say, was a place where storms, nor strife, nor pain, nor evil, could ever come.

Ellie slept.

5

DAYBREAK

(Hybrid musk. Rich yellow buds opening to light yellow flowers, golden stamens, deep musky fragrance.)

Sergeant Wield sat on the edge of the bed, acutely conscious of Police-Cadet Shaheed Singh's presence only a few feet away in the scented darkness.

They were in one of the bedrooms of Rosemont. A potpourri of rose petals stood on the window-sill and the draughts of air which penetrated from the stormy night outside carried the sweet perfume on their breath.

There were only another four men on the operation. Pascoe and a large DC called Seymour were in a bedroom on the other side of the house and two uniformed constables were seated in a car parked up a track about a hundred yards from the main gates. These were all the men that could be spared, Dalziel had explained. The Minister for Employment was touring the area the following day; demonstrations had been arranged

(Pascoe had avoided discovering the depths of Ellie's involvement), threats had been received, and the Chief Constable wanted every available man on the job for the duration of the visit.

'And he doesn't want the buggers half asleep,' said Dalziel. 'Not that he'd notice. He hasn't been fully awake for forty years or more. And young Singh had better not go either. With so few of you, if there is any bother, he might be tempted to start mixing it, and the last thing I need at the moment is to have to explain how I came to let a cadet get thumped.'

It had been Wield who'd argued the other way, knowing how disappointed the boy would be.

'He'll be useful to keep someone awake, otherwise we'd have to have one man by himself,' he said.

Finally Dalziel was persuaded.

'But he stays upstairs. Even if he thinks they're massacring you lot down below with a chain-saw, he stays out of sight. Right?'

And when Wield had departed, the Superintendent said to Pascoe, 'And you can put young Abdul in with that bugger to keep *him* awake. Wield must be shorter of beauty sleep than any other man in the county!'

So here they were, waiting. It was nearly midnight. Sunday's glorious weather had spilled over into Monday morning, but storm clouds had begun to simmer in mid-afternoon and the long midsummer evening had sunk into premature darkness shortly after nine, and into almost total blackness a couple of hours later. Wield had waited for his night vision to develop, but even now the room only existed as a wash of black over some heavier concentrations which marked the furniture. The narrow slit in the curtained window let in no light worth mentioning. It overlooked the east side of the house, which meant that the horizon was smudged with the tangerine glow of city lights, but this only served to accentuate the nearer darkness. In the last hour a strong wind had blown up which so far had failed to clear the sky and had merely served to fill the old house with creaks and groans and eerie flutings, while at the same time whipping the dark mere of the garden into such a frenzy of formless movement that Wield had ceased to peer out, finding his straining eyes were filling the night with advancing shapes.

'Sarge,' whispered Singh.

'Yes?'

'Do you reckon they'll come?'

'What's up? Getting bored?' asked Wield.

'No!'

'Then you must be either drunk or unconscious,' said Wield. 'Mebbe they'll come, mebbe they'll not. Just think yourself lucky it's the middle of summer.'

'Why's that?'

'You could be freezing your bollocks off and sitting around here till six or seven in the morning. As it is, it'll start getting light around four. You might even get an hour's sleep before you go back on duty. So count your blessings.'

There was a long silence from the patch of blacker black which was Singh.

'Sarge,' he said finally, emboldened by the lack of visibility and the feeling of intimacy such conditions can engender between even the most antagonistic of couples. 'Do you think I'm doing the right thing, training to be a cop, and all?'

'What do you mean?' asked Wield. 'Why do you ask?'

'It's just that, well, you've never been very encouraging. I've talked to some of the others, you know, some of the DCs and the uniformed lads I've got to know, and, well, they all say you're fair, and very sharp too. There's a lot of 'em reckon you ought to have got on a lot further by now . . .'

'Are you building up to a retirement presentation, or what?' wondered Wield.

'No, well, all I was wondering was, if you're as fair and sharp as everyone says, and you don't rate me . . .'

The boy's voice faded from a whisper to an uneasy, embarrassed silence and the wind's endless moaning took control again.

'What makes you think I don't rate you?' asked Wield.

'You've always been a bit, like, sharp,' said Singh. 'I'm sorry, look, I'm not complaining, but I just wondered . . .'

'What'd you do if you didn't become a copper?' asked Wield.

'I'd help in my father's shop, I expect,' said Singh.

'You don't want to do that? Don't you get on with your dad?'

'Oh yes, we get on fine . . . only . . . well, if I worked in the business, I'd have to sort of do things his way. I mean, his way's the right way, I think, because he's done very well, and I don't mean he's strict about religion and that; he wants the family to belong here, he says, not to just be passing by; but if I stayed at home, I think I'd always be, well, like, a lad, a boy, I know I *am* still, everyone calls me "lad", but at home in my father's shop, I think I'd stay as a boy until . . . until . . .'

'Until he died,' said Wield softly.

'Yes, I think so. And I don't want to ever be wishing that my father would die.'

The darkness between them was now vibrant with the electricity of confession, binding them in a circuit of intimacy Wield had not wished for but now could not deny.

'My dad died,' he said softly. 'I was thirteen. He was very strict, very stern. He kept pigeons. I had to keep the loft clean. And when there got to be too many and some had to have their necks pulled, he made me help him. I think I wanted most of all in the world to be like my dad, to be big and strong and certain and able to pull pigeon's necks and not care. I never could, though. Perhaps, if he'd lived, I might have come to it, but I doubt it. They're such soft birds, trusting . . .'

He yearned to reach out and touch the boy's shoulder. A simple, uncomplicated, encouraging gesture.

But he reminded himself bitterly that just as in his professional world there were no free lunches, in his private world there were no simple gestures.

'You carry on and be a cop, lad,' he said harshly. 'As long as you can pull the pigeons' neck and not start enjoying it, you'll be all right.'

They both fell silent and remained silent while outside the wind at last blew itself out and dawn's green light began to move across the badly ruffled gardens.

When it was full light, Pascoe came yawning into the bedroom.

'All right,' he said. 'That'll do.'

Singh regarded him miserably, expecting reproach, but Pascoe just grinned and, ruffling the boy's hair in the gesture Wield had not dared, said, 'What're you doing tonight, Shady? Hope you haven't got anything heavy planned.'

'Are we coming back, sir?'

'Why not? Mr and Mrs Aldermann won't be home till tomorrow.' He yawned again and added, 'Seymour's switched off the alarm. I've told him to go back with the lads in the Panda and send a car out for us. Meanwhile I'm sure Mrs Aldermann wouldn't grudge us a cup of coffee.'

They went downstairs, Wield and the boy turned towards the kitchen, Pascoe said, 'I'll get a breath of air, I think,' and made for the front door.

But as he passed the door of Aldermann's study, he saw it was ajar and heard a noise inside.

Carefully he pushed it open till he could see one end of the handsome hard oak partner's desk which he guessed had belonged to Eddie Aldermann. There was a figure stooping over an opened drawer. He pushed the door open a little further.

'Come in, Peter, come on in. Had a good night, have you?'

It was Dalziel, looking wide-awake and healthy, except where a nicked undulation of flesh over his left jaw, repaired with pink toilet paper, showed the dangers of early morning shaving.

'What are you doing here? Sir?' demanded Pascoe

'Pastoral care, Peter,' said Dalziel genially. 'I woke up and got to thinking about you, stuck out here all night with nothing happening. Nothing did happen, did it? No, I didn't think it would. In fact, I didn't think it would last evening, but it seemed silly to be a kill-joy when you'd gone to all that bother to set things up.'

What the hell did he want? wondered Pascoe.

'Looking for anything in particular, sir?' he asked, nodding at the desk.

'No, not really. Aldermann's in the clear, isn't he? I've got your word on it, and that's good enough for me. Just my natural curiosity, lad. Unpaid bills, mainly, but he'll soon have that sorted. And a lot of stuff about roses. He corresponds with the best people, doesn't he? Even I've heard of some of their names. Let's bung this stuff back and take a stroll around, shall we, Peter? Best time of day, this. You ought to try getting up early more often. Taste the dawn.'

He watched like a benevolent Nature spirit as Pascoe tidied up the papers he'd disturbed and closed the drawers.

'It's all right, lad,' he said, observing the Inspector's hesitation. 'They weren't locked. Trusting soul, Aldermann. And it helps your tender conscience, I've no doubt. Where's Beauty and the Beast, by the way?'

Pascoe led the way to the kitchen. Wield and Singh were deep in conversation which stopped as he entered, and when Dalziel came in behind him, they both stood up, Singh's chair practically falling over in his eagerness.

'Take it easy, lad,' said Dalziel in his kindly voice. 'Not quite got the hang of chairs yet? Don't worry. It'll come, it'll come. You know, I could just fancy a cup of tea. Think you can manage that, son?'

Singh nodded.

'Good. And have a bit of a poke around in the larder. I don't expect you'll find any beef dripping here. That's what I'd really like, a beef dripping sarnie. Failing that, a bit of toast with Marmite. I'm sure they'll have Marmite. Lay it on thick so there's a bit of flavour. Will you do that for me?'

'Yes, sir,' said Singh.

'Good lad. Come on, Inspector. We'll take a turn round the garden.'

'I'll have a coffee,' said Pascoe to Wield. 'But no Marmite.'

As he walked towards the front door with Dalziel, the fat man boomed, 'A good lad, that darkie. He'll go far. Wouldn't surprise me if he went all the way. I'd like to see that. Make a change from some of these pasty-faced buggers I saw last week. You'd think they lived under stones down there!'

Outside Pascoe was puzzled to see no sign of Dalziel's car. He couldn't have walked here, surely! The turbulence of the night was long past and a fine summer's day was unfolding like a flower. But the storm had left its mark. Dalziel tutted as he walked across the once smooth lawn now strewn with twigs and leaves and petals.

'Bit of tidying up for our Patrick here,' he observed.

'I think he pays someone to do the basic stuff,' said Pascoe.

'Aye, he would. No expense spared with this lad. Mind you, he'll need help. There's a lot of land here, a lot of land.'

They strolled round the formal gardens till they arrived at the small complex of greenhouses.

'This is where it all happens, this hybridization is it?' said Dalziel, peering through the glass like a voyeur hoping to glimpse flesh. 'Clever fellow, our Patrick. Very clever.'

'Sir,' said Pascoe determinedly. 'Do you still suspect him of something?'

'Me? No. Why should I? A lot of people died, it's true. But there's always people dying, isn't there? And we've no bodies, have we? That's what we're short of Peter. Bodies.'

He sounded almost regretful. Pascoe was reminded of the police pathologist who demanded flesh.

'Plenty of nothing, that's all we have,' continued Dalziel. 'And all we're likely to have from the look of it. Let's get back to the house. All this morning air's making me hungry.'

'You really fancy him for at least one of these deaths, do you, sir?' persisted Pascoe as they walked back through the rose-garden.

Dalziel paused to pluck a crimson bloom which the wind had half snapped off its stem and put it in his button-hole.

'*Milord*,' he said, displaying that expertise in unexpected areas with which he sometimes surprised his subordinates.

'Very fitting,' said Pascoe drily. 'About Aldermann . . .'

'He frightened his mam,' said Dalziel. 'No, that's too strong. He had a lot of influence over her, and she's not an easy woman to dominate, I tell you. But you think he's all right?'

'I quite like him,' admitted Pascoe. 'And you?'

'Only met him once, haven't I?' said Dalziel,

adding thoughtfully, 'But I must say I quite like his mam!'

Back in the house, they found a pot of tea and a plateful of Marmited toast waiting for Dalziel. He tucked in with a good appetite, telling a long rambling anecdote about his army experiences as a military policeman. Pascoe drank his mug of coffee and responded to Wield's interrogative glance with a minute shrug.

'Right,' said Dalziel, glancing at the kitchen clock which said seven A.M., 'let's get washed up. Always leave a place as you'd hope to find it, you shouldn't forget that, son.'

Singh nodded as if this were the most helpful piece of advice he'd ever heard.

Carefully, they washed up with Dalziel doing the drying. When he'd finished, he folded the tea-towel carefully and draped it over the draining-rack.

'Now, Peter,' he said, 'if you'd set the alarm again.'

'We're going?' asked Pascoe.

'Oh no. We're staying,' said Dalziel.

He led the way upstairs. Silently, the other three followed.

Dalziel opened the master bedroom, looked with approval at the large, deep, double bed, removed his shoes, and spread himself out across the silk coverlet.

'Wake me when they come,' he said closing his eyes.

'When who come?'

One red-shot eye opened.

'The burglars,' said Dalziel. 'That's what we're here for, isn't it? To catch some burglars.'

The eye closed. The fat man appeared to sleep.

Just after eight o'clock, they all started, except Dalziel, as they heard a distant noise. It was the grind of an approaching vehicle. Pascoe joined Wield at the window. An old green van was coming up the drive. It turned and disappeared along the side of the house, momentarily revealing the legend *Caldicott and Son, Landscape Gardeners*.

'Are they here then?' said Dalziel, sitting up. 'Let's take a shufti out the back.'

He rolled off the bed and went out on to the landing and walked round till he reached one of the bedrooms overlooking the rear.

'The gardeners?' said Pascoe, following him. 'You mean, it's *them*?'

'It's in Arthur Marsh's file,' said Dalziel. 'That unemployment benefit fiddle he got done for – he was working for a gardening firm. I'm surprised that didn't strike you as odd, Peter! Trained electrician. If he'd wanted to do a bit of moonlighting, why start humping wheelbarrows and garden forks about?'

'He's there. Jonty's there!' said Singh, excitedly peering between the drawn curtains. 'And Artie too. I can see them!'

'Can you? Good lad. Watch you don't move them curtains though,' said Dalziel.

'But if you spotted this yesterday, why didn't you say anything,' said Pascoe indignantly.

'It was just a theory, lad,' said Dalziel soothingly. 'Besides, I weren't sure whether Arthur Marsh was using the gardening job just to case places which he then turned over independently, or whether the whole firm was in it. He might have dropped in last night, in which case, the nick was all yours. But when I checked this morning and nothing had happened, then theory two seemed to be on.'

'They don't much look as if they're planning to break in,' said Wield, who'd joined Singh.

'What do you want? Masks and bags marked "Swag"?' demanded Dalziel. 'They've got work to do in the garden, haven't they? They're paid to be here. They're entitled to be here! That's the beauty of it.'

Pascoe produced Aldermann's list of tradesmen and others who would know the house was going to be empty and quickly scanned it.

'He doesn't mention the gardeners,' he complained.

'Why should he? Likely he just mentioned the people he's cancelled, like milk and newspapers,' said Dalziel. 'He wouldn't cancel the gardeners. Gardens keep on growing even while you're away. I checked one of the other places that'd been done. Yes, they had Caldicott's one morning a week. Yes, they remembered Artie, he was the friendly one, always popping in to fill his teapot, always ready to help in the house with a bit of lifting or moving. It's a good set-up, isn't it? Lots of opportunity to case the target. And no crawling around in the middle of the night. You just drive up at your usual time and some time during the day, when observation's taught you you're least likely to be interrupted, you get inside, lift what you want, dump it in the van in a couple of old sacks, and drive off with it!'

'Eventually they'd have run out of houses,' said Pascoe in an aggrieved tone.

'Yes, likely they would. That would certainly have been another way of stopping them,' said Dalziel judiciously.

'Why'd they bring in Jonty Marsh, sir?' wondered Wield.

'There was another lad, Caldicott junior, I think you'll find. Only he broke his arm the other week.'

'Harrogate,' said Pascoe, remembering the torn ivy that Ivan Skelwith had pointed out. 'I bet that was at Harrogate.'

'Aye, and likely they needed another nippy little sod to do any clambering about that was needed, so Arthur recommended his kid brother.'

'They still don't look as if they're up to anything,' said Wield doubtfully.

'O ye of little faith,' said Dalziel. 'Come back to the front bedroom.'

Obediently they followed. Wield and Singh resumed their watch at the front window, stupidly in both their opinions as the gardeners were all round the back. Then ten minutes later, Singh said, 'Here's somebody. It's the postman!'

He cycled up to the front door, sorted out his mail, thrust it through. On his way back he diverted to the side of the house and addressed himself to somebody, then passed from sight.

'He'll be having a cup of tea,' said Dalziel. 'It'll be a habit every Tuesday morning. They're not going to let him see owt suspicious, are they?'

Reproved, the watchers resumed their watching and Dalziel his position on the bed.

'He's gone,' said Wield at last.

'Right. Shouldn't be long now,' said Dalziel, eyes still closed.

'Where should we be watching, sir, back or front?' asked Wield.

'No matter. You'll not really see much. They'll fix the alarm bell first. That'll likely be a job for young Jonty. Jam it, or muffle it, or even cut it, depends on the type. Arthur will have sussed it out. Next, the nipper will be sent up aloft again, this time to cut the telephone wire. Normally of course this'd set the alarm ringing, but as they've fixed that already, all it means is that the alarm dialling system is knackered too. Then one of them will come in, through a window mebbe, or a door if Arthur's managed to get a key. The others will carry on with their business so that any passing peasant wouldn't notice anything out of the ordinary. Only from time to time as one of 'em passes by the house with a barrow, he'll pick up an old sack and later chuck it into the van.

'I'm just guessing, of course,' concluded Dalziel. 'But that's the way I'd do it.'

He's right, of course, thought Pascoe, full of bitter self-reproach. For the past few months he'd begun to wonder arrogantly if Dalziel might not be past it. A creature from another age, that's how he thought of him, a dinosaur about ready for extinction. Well, what came after the dinosaurs? The apes. Almost unconsciously he dropped his jaw and did a little simian shuffle. Dalziel's eyes, which had appeared firmly shut, opened wide.

'You all right?' he asked.

'Yes, sir. Touch of cramp.'

It was another ten minutes before they heard a noise downstairs.

'Sir!' said Wield urgently.

Dalziel slowly rose, yawning.

'Give 'em a moment to start loading up,' he said.

He looked at his watch like a commander about to send his troops over the top.

'Right,' he said. 'Off we go. No, not you, young Abdul. You stay up here, son. Sorry, but I made promises about you. Don't worry, you'll get mentioned in dispatches, I'll see to that. You've done all right.'

Singh looked disappointed, but clearly Dalziel's praise was some consolation.

Dalziel led the way with no apparent attempt at concealment, but moving down the stairs with incredible lightness for a man of his bulk.

As they reached the hallway, a man clutching a sack appeared at the study door. It was Arthur Marsh. He stared at them in complete amazement for a moment, then dropped the sack with a hoarse cry of alarm and turned and fled. The policemen followed in order of seniority, though this was accidental rather than hierarchical. At the study door Wield glimpsed Arthur trying to get out of the window with Dalziel clinging on to his left foot with all the proprietary strength of a hungry bear. A noise behind him attracted Wield's attention. He turned and saw that in one thing Dalziel had been wrong. There was not just one man in the house. Coming out of the dining-room with a silver candlestick in his hand was Jonty Marsh.

'All right, lad,' growled the sergeant, advancing.

Jonty feinted to retreat, then suddenly sprinted forward, ducking under Wield's outstretched arms and nearly falling. Wield grabbed and the boy swung the heavy candlestick against his knee-cap.

'Jesus Christ!' cried Wield as Jonty recovered his balance and went dashing up the stairs. On the landing he paused uncertainly. In some little pain, Wield was hobbling after him. The fleeing boy turned once more and rushed into the master bedroom.

Wield heard a babble of voices, then one voice – Jonty's – screamed, 'You fucking black wanker!' Then there was a crash and a cry and a thud, then silence.

Pain forgotten, Wield ran up the last flight of stairs and flung himself into the bedroom.

The window was open. On the floor beneath it lay the crumpled body of Police Cadet Singh. By his head was the silver candlestick and from his head coiled a line of blood like an undone ribbon.

There was a cry from the window. Wield peered out. Distantly he saw the green van careening down the drive, doors still open and banging against the sides like some discordant cymbals. But it was going nowhere. A police car was gently nosing forward between the avenue of holly bushes, blocking the way.

The cry was closer at hand. Jonty Marsh had swung himself over the sill and was trying to reach a drainpipe some five feet to his left. He clearly wasn't able to make it. The one hand by which he still clung to the sill was white with the strain, but not as white as the terrified face that looked up towards Wield.

The sergeant instinctively grabbed the boy's wrist just as the fingers began to slide off the smooth stone. Despite his slight build, he was heavy enough to make Wield gasp as he felt the full weight pulling at his arm. He was leaning too far out for his strong back and leg muscles to contribute much to the effort, but the greatest weakness was in his will. His mind was full of the boy at his feet with his eyes closed and his head bleeding, rather than the boy at the end of his arm with his eyes wide with terror and his mouth piping piteous bird-like cries. The sweat of effort and the sweat of fear lubricated their gripping hands and he could feel Jonty Marsh slipping away and he was not sure that he cared.

Then Pascoe was by his side, leaning out to grab the boy by the arm, saying 'Come up, you young bastard!' and suddenly he was a feather weight and came plunging back through the window like a hooked trout.

Pascoe dumped the boy on the floor with a force which knocked the remaining breath out of him and said, 'Lie still, sonny, or I'll chuck you back.'

Now he turned to help Wield with the injured cadet. To his surprise the sergeant was kneeling by the boy's head, his hands fluttering nervously over but not touching him, his craggy face, in whose rocks and hollows emotion usually lay deeply hid, cracked wide in an earthquake of violent grief.

'Sergeant!' said Pascoe.

The stricken eyes turned up to meet his.

'He's dead,' said Wield in a hoarsely vibrant tone. 'He's dead!'

Below the moving hands, Cadet Singh's eyelids twitched, then opened.

'You'd better not tell him that,' said Pascoe. 'Now for God's sake, go and rustle up an ambulance!'

6

FÉLICITÉ ET PERPÉTUE

(Climber. Vigorous, healthy, abundant foliage,
profuse white flowers with faint blush, high climbing,
sweet-scented.)

Dick Elgood had not been lying when he said that he liked to relax alone on the night before an important meeting.

He left the offices of Perfecta at six o'clock, pausing to glance at the old Elgoodware artefacts on display in the vestibule. This is how it had all started. Here were the beginnings of the road which had led him to where he was now. Which was where? He felt uneasy at the thought. It was daft! How could the condition, the achievement, which only a few weeks ago had seemed such a cause for congratulation, for complacency even, now appear hollow, empty, meaningless? Perhaps a man needed more than work. An interest, an obsession. Like Aldermann's garden and his bloody roses! What did he have? Women, a lot of 'em, more than he could recall. That was *something*, surely. Pleasure; ecstasy; and more to come. His strength was less than it had been, but far from failing. Perhaps he should have arranged for a bit of company tonight. He thought of telephoning around, but decided it was too late. And surely it was best to stick to his plan.

Nevertheless, the desire for company remained, and he didn't go straight to the cottage but drove first to a favourite restaurant some ten miles up the coast where he had a steak. There was a new waitress, a smiling lass, who caught his fancy and he lingered longer than he intended over his coffee and brandy. But when he judged the moment ripe to ask what time she finished, she replied promptly, as though the question had been anticipated, that her father collected her shortly after eleven. Dick finished his brandy philosophically, guessing that one of her colleagues had played bitch in the manger and warned her off. He had certainly used the place often enough for his reputation to be known, and like most dedicated followers of the fancy, his sexual vanity did not permit him to consider that perhaps the girl simply didn't like the look of him.

It was after ten-thirty when he arrived at the cottage, much later than he had intended. He felt vaguely dissatisfied as he stood by the white post which marked the furthest encroachment of the sea and gazed down at the darkling shore where a thin white line and a rhythmic susurration signalled the retreating tide. He should have stuck to his original intention and come straight down. Now he would have to forgo his anticipated swim. Food, alcohol and an ebb tide were ingredients which mixed to disaster. And in any case, though usually he regarded the water as simply an alternative element, tonight the moving darkness stretching away to an imperceptible horizon filled him with a sense of menace and being alone. Shivering, he turned and went inside.

His customary pre-bed cup of cocoa with a shot of rum soothed his slightly ruffled nerves and he soon fell asleep. But he passed a broken night, waking frequently out of ancient dreams of flying and falling to listen to the strange patterns of noise that sea and wind and darkness were weaving all around. He was glad to get up on Wednesday morning, gladder to see that even so early the sun was already beaming promises of great warmth from an untroubled sky. The sea was its old self, dancing invitingly in the little bay below the cliff. He was tempted to go straight down, but at his age such suddenness was to be avoided. He did some stretching and warming exercises, then took his usual little breakfast of pure apple juice and a dry crispbread and black coffee. Then he relaxed and smoked a couple of cigarettes. Finally he was ready.

He put on his towelling robe and clambered down the broken cliff face to the beach. He removed the robe, looked around, and removed his trunks also. He liked to swim naked but was very careful to do so only when he could be almost completely certain of being uninterrupted. He had no desire to be dragged into court on an indecency charge.

As always, his swim invigorated him mentally and physically, reminding him of both his fitness and his self-sufficiency. He was hardly puffing as he clambered back up the cliff and re-entered the cottage.

He went straight into the shower cubicle to wash off the salt water. Carefully adjusting the jet till he got the perfect temperature, he stepped inside. First he soaped himself all over, then he poured shampoo on to his still thick and vigorous hair and began to massage it to a lather. The water ran steadily, caressing his body. It wasn't for some time that he felt the first prickles of discomfort. It wasn't bad, just as if he were showering after too long an exposure to a burning sun. He raised his head to the streaming water, letting it run over his face. His eyes prickled as if he'd got soap in them. He opened them to wash it out. And screamed as they seemed to burst into flame.

He staggered sideways out of the shower, but the pain came with him. His mouth tasted acrid, he couldn't see out of one eye and vision from the other was blurred and distorted. He crashed across the living-room, making for the front door. He was twitching convulsively and his mind was hardly able to function beyond his desperate desire to get down to the sea. The sea would cleanse him, soothe him, save him. He was in the little garden now. He hit the white post, reached the edge of the cliff and fell rather than descended down its broken face. Now he could hear the water though sight was almost gone. Even the bold red sun was only a match-head to his unblinking gaze. He staggered on, his feet dragging through the shingle and the sand till he felt the waves lapping at his feet. He kept going a step or two further, then fell forward and let the water take him. After a while he rolled on his back and tried to float. Above him seagulls mewed, but the sound barely touched his ears, like the cry of children playing on a distant shore.

Shaheed Singh awoke first to the dawn chorus of hospital life and didn't manage to get back to sleep till after nine A.M. When he opened his eyes an hour later, Dalziel, Pascoe, and Sergeant Wield were standing by his bed.

''Morning, lad,' said Dalziel. 'We've finished your grapes. How're you feeling? Always thought you needed a turban to finish you off.'

Singh put his hand to the swathe of bandage which crowned his head and smiled, not at the comment but at Inspector Pascoe's undisguised pained reaction to it.

'They wouldn't let us see you till last night and by then you were asleep,' said Dalziel accusingly. 'You sleep a lot for a young copper.'

'The doctors say that there's no fracture, just a heavy concussion,' said Pascoe. 'You'll be out in a day or two. Your dad's outside, but he insisted we came in first.'

'What about Jonty and them others?' said Singh. 'Did we get 'em?'

'Oh yes. And don't worry, we'll see you get mentioned in all the right places,' smiled Pascoe.

Wield said, 'I brought you some books. And some chocolate.'

'Thanks, Sarge,' said Shaheed.

'Right. We'd best be off. Can't have all the best brains in CID stuck in hospital at the same time, can we?' said Dalziel. 'Thanks for your help, lad. We'll send your dad in now.'

He and Pascoe turned away.

Wield said, 'I'll drop in again.'

Singh said, 'Oh, no need to bother, Sarge. My dad'll be coming. And my mam. And then there's all my brothers. I'll have plenty of visitors.'

'All right then,' said Wield. 'Cheerio.'

'Cheers, Sarge.'

On their way back to the station, Wield was in such a deeply introspective mood that it drew the attention of the others, used though they were to his blank impassivity.

'You all right, Sergeant?' enquired Dalziel.

'Yes, sir.'

'Gut rot, is it? The takeaway trots?'

'No, I'm all right.'

'You don't look it. You ought to get yourself married and start eating properly.'

But the news which reached them shortly after

their return to the station put all thoughts of Wield's health out of their minds.

It was Dalziel who was told first and he burst into Pascoe's office without preamble.

'He's dead! Dandy Dick's dead!'

'What?'

'Aye. Found drowned. He should've been at a meeting at ten, didn't appear, they got the local bobby to check down at his cottage, and there he was, bobbing around in the sea.'

'What caused it? Cramp? Heart-attack?'

'I don't know. Get on to it, will you, Peter? Check what the quack says.'

It was early afternoon when Pascoe got back to Dalziel. The inspector was grave-faced.

'It's not nice,' he said.

'What ever is it? Get a move on, lad!'

'The first doctor that got called thought there was something odd about the body and our man's confirmed it as far as he can without pathological tests.'

'Confirmed what?'

Pascoe said, 'Dick Elgood had been in contact with a large concentration of some chemical reagent shortly before he died.'

'What chemical, for Christ's sake?'

'Oh, I'd say at a guess something like parathion or dieldrin.'

'*You'd* say! What's the quack say?'

'Still checking, but he agrees. You see, I had a good go at our local lad. He was a bit upset he'd noticed nothing queer about the body. The eyes were a bit funny, he thought, but he put that down to immersion in the sea. Well, we went over everything and he recalled that when he first went into the cottage he'd found the shower on. Now that struck me as odd. Why shower, *then* go into the sea? So I took a look in the attic. You recall that box that Elgood put up there last Sunday?'

'The garden stuff? Jesus Christ!'

'That's right. It had somehow found its way into the water tank.'

'Found its way?' echoed Dalziel incredulously.

'That's where it was anyway. I got a pair of rubber gloves and lifted it out. There was a real mixture of stuff, some powder, some liquid, all highly concentrated from what I could read on the labels, and a lot of loose tops. I showed the box to the doctor and he said it fitted. Parathion compounds can easily be absorbed through the skin without much local irritation, and it's easy to take a bit of water through the mouth when you're showering. The effects of a cocktail like this could be quick and devastating. Disorientation, lack of muscular control, spasms, respiratory problems – the poor bastard probably staggered down to the sea with some notion of rinsing himself clean and simply drowned.'

'You've organized the tech lads down there?'

'Of course,' said Pascoe, adding hesitantly, 'not that I think there's much for them to find. Look, sir, it looked to me as if Elgood must have simply rested the box on the edge of the tank. There were some pretty violent winds in that storm the other night and they'd go funnelling through that roof space at a hell of a lick. Over goes the box . . .'

'Do you really believe that, Inspector?' asked Dalziel harshly.

'What else? You can't still be thinking of Aldermann? Where's the motive? That's all been settled! And opportunity? He's been away since Monday! And don't say Sunday night. They left Elgood's picnic at the same time as us and we asked them to drop in at our place as they passed. One thing led to another, we had a drink and a snack, and it was after ten when they left.'

'Very cosy,' growled Dalziel. 'All right. What's to stop him driving his wife and girl home, then taking off back to the coast?'

'Nothing, I suppose,' admitted Pascoe. 'But his wife would know. I mean, it'd take at least two hours, there and back.'

'You're going out there today to tie up the burglary business, aren't you?' said Dalziel. 'Ask her.'

Pascoe hesitated, then said, 'If I must, sir.'

'Oh yes,' said Dalziel intensely. 'You know you bloody well must.'

It was three o'clock when Pascoe arrived at Rosemont and its gardens were still awash with the high tide of the sun. All along the road from town he had driven with his windows down, letting the fresh air cleanse his mind, confounding his worries in the green and gold beauties of an English midsummer day. Turning into the gates of Rosemont had meant plunging for a brief moment into a dark tunnel of overshading holly trees. But when he emerged once more into the bright air, it seemed as if he must have stumbled upon the very source of all this richness and warmth. The brick of the house, the green of the lawns, the rainbow spectrum of bloom curving around the borders – all seemed part of a single design with the great arch of blue sky in which the sun shimmered like a bonfire reflected in a deep lake

In front of the house a Mini was parked. As he halted behind it he recognized it as Ellie's.

'Oh shit,' he said aloud.

He rang the bell. A few moments later Daphne opened the door.

'Peter!' she cried. 'How nice. Come in. Ellie's here, we're out on the terrace.'

'Daphne,' he said, 'have you heard about Dick Elgood?'

Her face shed its smiling welcome and darkened to pain.

'Yes. The office rang soon after we got back just before lunch. Patrick went in, but there was nothing he could do. It's dreadful, isn't it? No one seemed quite sure what had happened. Was it a heart-attack while he was swimming?'

She wasn't acting. Pascoe was certain. He steeled himself for the next question whose purpose must seem obvious, but before he could speak, she said, 'Look, you go through. I was just getting some more lemon squash. Will that do for you, or would you prefer a beer?'

'No, squash will be fine.'

He walked through the house and out on to the terrace.

'Hi,' said Ellie. 'So this is what you really do when you ought to be beating up prisoners with a rubber truncheon.'

'So this is what *you* do when you should be chaining yourself to the Minister of Employment's left leg,' he said, stooping to kiss her. 'I'm here on business. What about you?'

'Oh, I rang to say welcome back and chat about the burglary attempt, and Daphne was in a bit of a tizz about Dick Elgood, so when she said come round, I came. It's awful, isn't it?'

'Awful,' agreed Pascoe. 'Where's Patrick?'

'In his rose-garden, where else?' said Daphne from behind. She set down a jugful of squash on the table. 'He's rather cut up about Dick, I think, and he always flies to his flowers in time of distress. David, stop bothering your sister!'

Baby Rose was once more in the care of little Diana. With them was a good-looking young boy with his father's brown eyes and stillness of expression.

'We brought him back because he got rather upset when he overheard us talking about the burglary,' explained Daphne. 'He had to see for himself that his precious room and all its contents hadn't been disturbed. I think he rather resents not being the centre of Diana's attention. David, stop it, or you'll go back to school this very evening!'

'Boys take much longer to mature than girls,' said Ellie comfortably. 'Peter, what *did* happen to Dick Elgood? Have you heard anything?'

'There'll have to be an inquest,' said Pascoe vaguely.

'He always seemed likely to go quickly,' said Daphne. 'All that exercise at his age.'

Ellie choked into her squash and Daphne glanced reprovingly at her.

'It's funny,' she continued, 'but I felt as if I were seeing him for the last time on Sunday. There seemed to be something very final when we said goodbye.'

'Come on,' said Ellie deflatingly. 'We all have these premonitions after the event.'

'No, that night, after we got back from your place, I couldn't sleep. I went to bed, but in the end I had to get up. I was sitting out here half the night drinking whisky. It was a strange feeling to have after such a lovely day. A sense of some horrible happening being quite close. You can believe me or not,' she said defiantly.

'And Patrick? Did he have this premonition too?' asked Pascoe with sudden interest.

'No.' Daphne laughed. 'He slept solidly, till I woke him getting back into bed about four. Then we had to get up again so *he* could have a drink.

Then we sat out here and drank and talked for another hour or so.'

She blushed faintly as she spoke and Ellie guessed that conversation wasn't all that had passed between them on the terrace.

'I slept all the way to Gloucester,' concluded Daphne. 'I was still yawning when I met the headmaster and the staff, I'm afraid.'

'That's all right,' said Ellie. 'In those places the teachers are used to that reaction to their presence.'

'Tut-tut,' said Pascoe, filled with relief at what he'd just heard. Surely even Dalziel would admit this unsolicited alibi? 'I think I'll go and have a word with Patrick, if you'll excuse me.'

He found Aldermann hard at work in his rose-garden.

'Hello, Peter,' he said. 'I didn't know you'd arrived. I'm sorry to have been so unhostly.'

'That's OK. No, don't stop. It's nice down here.'

'There's really such a lot to do,' said Aldermann, still apologizing. 'That storm the other night – it must have been the night you were in the house – such damage!'

All the time he talked the silver blade of the pruning knife was moving with swift economy around the rose branches, severing broken twigs and damaged blooms which were then popped into the canvas bag slung around his neck.

'And now, of course, you're minus your gardeners,' said Pascoe.

'Yes, that's almost the worst thing,' said Alder-mann. 'I was flabbergasted. Caldicott! Why, he's been coming to Rosemont ever since he was a boy. And his father before him was with Uncle Eddie from the beginning.'

'It was Brent, the son, who was the trouble, it seems,' said Pascoe. 'He had a bit of a record, nothing serious, but that's how he met Arthur Marsh when they were in the nick together. Later Arthur had this bright idea. It *was* quite bright, I suppose.'

'But how did they get old Caldicott to go along with it?'

'Feeling the pinch, I suppose. Everyone's been cutting back lately, wanting Caldicott to come half a day a week instead of a full day, but expecting much the same work. It's easy to start resenting their big, comfortable houses and all the goodies you glimpse through doors and windows. Marsh saw other things – alarm systems, sensor locations, bypass switches, wiring circuits – he's a trained electrician and there's plenty of written material about these systems nowadays. They were able to do such neat jobs, not being hurried and working in daylight, that often it wasn't till the owners got home, sometimes days later, that the break-in was discovered.'

'I still find it hard to believe, or forgive. I certainly never cut back on their time here.'

No, you wouldn't thought Pascoe.

He said, 'Caldicott senior did say as much. He's

the one who's cracked and coughed the lot. He hadn't wanted to do Rosemont. That's where the business had really started, he said, and you were that rare thing among employers, a *real* gardener rather than just a flash Harry wanting to put on a show.'

'He said that?' Aldermann looked pleased. 'Well, I'll have to find someone else now, of course. It was quite a shock. But then this other business of Dick Elgood – that was really devastating. You've heard, of course?'

'Yes,' said Pascoe. 'I've heard.'

'Poor Dick. It's such a tragic waste. But then, so much of his life was, wasn't it?'

'He looked very successful to me,' said Pascoe.

'Did he? Yes, I suppose he would. And I dare say that's how he thought of himself too. But I doubt if he was really a *happy* man. I honestly believe that in Nature there's only one true course of development for each of us, and the trick is finding it. At some point Dick took a wrong road. Like a rose-tree. You can cut and trim it away from its true growth and be quite successful with it for a long time. But in the end, the misdirection shows.'

'What will happen at Perfecta now?' asked Pascoe.

'I don't know. It's all in the melting-pot. There'll be changes, I expect, but nothing ever really changes.'

Patrick Aldermann spoke with the confident disinterest of one who knows where the real centre of things lies. And why should he not? Had not life confirmed his judgement at every turn? Some might have called him an opportunist, but opportunity so invariably offered must assume the dimension of fate. There had been no doubt in his mind this lunch-time, for instance, that when he went to Perfecta he would find that Quayle had already assumed the mantle of acting chairman and managing director, and in that capacity had installed himself in Elgood's office. It hadn't even been necessary to find a pretext for getting him to open the safe. A stricken Miss Dominic had already opened it at his behest. And just as inevitably, the plain white envelope which Patrick had picked out and pocketed had contained the original of his Great-Aunt Florence's will. This was no opportunism but destiny! With such assurance of maintaining the true order of things, where for instance had been the risk in wandering into Elgood's cottage as the departing guests crowded the little garden outside to make their good-byes, pulling down the attic ladder, ascending and depositing the cardboard box with bottle tops slightly loosened into the open cistern? Three minutes. No one had noticed he'd gone. So it had always been. So, he assumed, it would always be. Beyond choice. Beyond morality. Preordained.

He became aware that Pascoe was observing him curiously. And not only Pascoe. His son was standing close behind the policeman, almost invisible in the camouflage of sun-flecks through the breeze-stirred roses.

'Hello, David,' said Aldermann, resuming his pruning. 'What are you up to.'

'Mummy sent me to say it's rude for you to keep Mr Pascoe standing out here so long.'

'And she's right, of course. Thank you, David. Peter, I'm sorry.'

'It was my idea,' said Pascoe.

'That's no excuse,' said Aldermann, slicing another bloom off its stem with a single economic motion which set the sunlight spilling off the silver blade like alien blood.

'Daddy,' said the boy.

'Yes, David.'

'What is it that you're doing? I mean, I can see what you're doing, but why do you do it?'

'Well,' said Aldermann with his knife poised above another deadhead. 'I'm . . .'

Then he paused and smiled as if at some deep, inner joke.

Carefully he closed the pruning knife and put it in his pocket.

'Later, David,' he said. 'I'll explain to you some other time. We have our guests to look after. Peter, you must be roasted, standing out here in the sun. Let's go and find a cool drink and sit and talk to the ladies. Isn't it a perfect day?'